ACKNOWLEDGEMENT

ACKNOWLEDGEMENTS FOR BOOKS ARE A BIT LIKE THE 1960'S PRANK OF TRYING to cram as many college students into a Volkswagen Beetle as humanly possible. Ultimately there's not enough room for all of the people that participated in the original idea. Books generally take a lot of time and thought to create, craft and complete. Some books, the ones that venture deeper beneath the surface of the people and situations and cultures they speak about and speak to, require their authors to reach back across a lifetime of chance meetings, long standing relationships, pivotal moments and humdrum every day existence to exact the necessary information the writer needs to tell their tale. I, like the kids in the Volkswagen, have too many of these events and people to properly note and thank for their contributions. So to all of you living and dead, close and far, present and past, thank you for helping me to look more closely into the mirror at myself and the world around me. You know who you are. Your presence has helped me to smirk at life's irony and absurdity; their sometimes taunting, sometimes amusing, shadows forever etched into the human looking glass.

Published by:

FriesenPress
Suite 300 – 852 Fort Street
Victoria, BC, Canada V8W 1H8

www.friesenpress.com

Distributed to the trade by The Ingram Book Company

DEDICATION

To Graziella, Lisa, Kaitlin and Jacqueline with love

NOBODY'S LAUGHING

Jeffrey Arnold

PART 1: HOPE

The Devil can cite scripture for his purpose.

—Shakespeare

CHAPTER ONE

"FUCK YOU AND FUCK EVERYTHING THAT YOU STAND FOR. " THESE WERE the damning words my darling daughter said to me just before she turned on her heel and walked out of the door. At the time she was high on "eight-balls." I later learned these are a potent mixture of cocaine and heroin whose sole purpose, though apparently somewhat misguided, was to make you feel better about yourself and your surroundings. This exchange hurt me very deeply, but over time I have come to view these words for what they really were. A wake-up call.

I can see this disintegration of my family happening before my eyes, yet I am struck powerless to act in any meaningful way. The world has become a virtual place — a computer game. Gargoyles, and other demonic monsters in our lives, like my daughter's addiction, rampage toward us in flack jackets, shooting ray guns of fear or throwing imaginary incendiary bombs of despair, that explode with synchronized electronic sounds in our faces. We have sacrificed our own children. They have become lost and disillusioned. We have shat in our own backyard. What other animal does such things? I want to make amends. I want some answers. It's probably true what they say about the world being a funny place, yet from where I'm standing nobody's laughing.

*

My name is Richard Bonhom. My two bawdy gay neighbours teasingly call me, "Mr. Big Stuff." I am a Commodities Trader. In this capacity I make what most would say are scandalous amounts of money watching blips on a computer screen. Blip,blip,blip. These supposedly represent the market value, as opposed to real value, of things in our day-to-day lives. These two values can vary greatly — but not in my world. In my world, everything has a price: lumber, currencies, your morning orange juice and coffee, gold and other precious metals — anything that can be picked, dug up, cut down or packaged. Everything is for sale. Great caches of loot change hands every second of every day on a twenty-four hour clock that never sleeps. People shouting orders, their arms waving spasmodically, hands miming coded signals to the floor traders. Traders are the janitors of this chaos, adrift in an endless sea of paper. If alien beings from another planet witnessed this scene, and were told that it was the foundation for our global financial systems, they would probably say that we were a backward civilization, board their flying saucer leaving us to evolve for another millennium or two. It's a bona fide zoo and, I suppose in a way, I am one of the gatekeepers.

*

I sometimes watch naked people in their candle lit bedrooms or glaring bathrooms or dimly lit sitting rooms. I see them at night from my darkened windows. I suppose that this is one of the unmentioned recreations that city-dwelling condo inhabitants all silently share like a bonding rite or primitive Stone-age ritual brought forward from our ancient cave dwelling forbearers. Something that lets the others in the clan out there watching know that it's all right to get down and real with your furry partner. Over the years, I feel that I have come to know some of these anonymous souls, to the point that I have even given them pet names. There is Jumping Jenny Lee over to the south of my building and down a couple of floors. She is a young Asian girl with flowing black hair that cascades down the curve of her slender scalloped spine falling provocatively between her buttocks when she kneels on the carpet, her head thrust defiantly back. Her lovers, hulking brutes all, straddling her like a gamesome wench from the English countryside out for a playful haystack romp with a local ploughboy. And then there's dutiful and somewhat dour Colonel Klink, two floors above young Jenny and over in a corner unit. He is neither old nor particularly military in any way other than his propensity to stand at rigid attention as his lovers, both men and women, bend before him performing any number of lewd sexual acts. There are many others, slapping and lip smacking their heedless ways across these open window spaces with reckless abandon. Certainly, for the most part, they are all acutely aware that their private embraces and nude cavorting are being noted and even catalogued by their nosy neighbours. These revelers letting the anonymity of the night and the distance between the buildings act as a screen of sorts for their inhibitions. It is as if anything goes so long as one is somewhat certain that they will never be brought to task on any of it. The slightest suspicion that someday someone may publicly expose them at a party or knock on their door and demand some explanation for their wanton behaviour would dampen their enthusiasm and end these shameless free-for-alls. The mask would be pulled aside, suddenly making them as vulnerable as children playing dress-up. My demure wife, Genevieve, has on occasion stood beside me smirking, her cheeks growing crimson, giggling as she whispered, "Are we leaving our curtains open tonight Major? — Will it be the long wig or the riding crop?" And to be certain, on more than one evening after a night of too many glasses of vino it was her that left those very curtains flung open, taunting all, allowing only the luster from a full August moon to light the room. And our passions were indeed more eager, less inhibited, as if this recklessness opened a doorway to another dimension within us both that some puritan rulebook had previously smothered. All of those moments now seem far too distant and disconcertingly irretrievable. Time will tell.

*

Those around me are noting what they perceive to be the tell-tale signs of emotional slippage. I am teetering on the brink of my fiftieth birthday and wondering whether my life has been time well spent. I sometimes fear that I am becoming the hapless relative in whose arms the burbling baby starts shrieking inconsolably, or the one at whom an otherwise docile pooch starts barking non-stop, everyone's accusing stares saying, "the innocent creatures instinctively know one's true character, bless the beasts and the children." So far I don't see myself as the loser next door. The one to whom hesitant neighbours proffer an obligatory Christmas or Thanksgiving invitation, half hoping that it will be declined. Dr. Martha Sitwell is a family psychologist we saw for a little over a year, when the first biting whispers of our parental calamities surfaced. She soon detected hints of this, as well. My emotional withdrawal. At the time our two adolescent daughters were encouraged to call her, "Dr. M." I suppose this informality was geared toward making us all feel better about the fact that we, as a family, needed psychiatric help in the first place. Now the girls are both adults, one with children of her own. Can this be possible? Where has the time gone? The reality drives a shiver down my spine. In hindsight, the good doctor may have been hitting closer to the mark than I would like to admit. It is true that my now increasingly secluded evenings are spent seated before my television screen, its ghostly blue flicker offering little refuge from the irritating reminder of the clock's tick, tick ticking, foretelling that there are urgent things that I should be doing. Perhaps I am one of those lost souls, the kind that topple over in despair when confronted with one of life's debilitating encounters. These can come in many different forms, a wayward child, a marriage on the rocks, or maybe just waking one morning and coming face to face with a scaling pustule or malignant node discovered firmly attached to a once ever-playful private part below the belt. This happens everyday to someone that we know.

If this is indeed happening to me I don't have to look very far to find out why. My apprehension is being fed by four badgering impasses. Three of these would be classified as potential heartbreakers, the family kind that can take a lifetime to recover from, if one really ever does. The fourth has to do with my job, one of those business problems that start out as a relatively easily managed speck on the horizon but all too soon take on a life of their own, looming forward out of the mist like a marauding horseman—the nightmarish, Sleepy Hollow kind, whose steed spits fire from its flared nostrils and pounds a relentless tattoo upon the unforgiving earth with its iron hooves.

*

In any census the government or public opinion pollster might conduct I would be slotted squarely into the middle class. I am part small *c* conservative, and part small *l* liberal. A son of The Middle World. I suppose that I am viewed as someone you can count on when the chips are down. Slap a uniform on my back and a rifle in my hand and point me in the direction of the nearest Hun. I have much to be grateful for, therefore much to fight for. This would be the government of the day's abiding wish. This assessment of me would be determined by many factors, including income, the neighborhood in which I live, my education, and quite possibly something as seemingly superficial as my car — a black BMW sedan. Why the government keeps close tabs, on such a tranquil citizenry, I do not know. However, if they had to guess as to the probability that I will suffer a debilitating illness over the next ten years or even to speculate whether my spouse and I might go past our occasional voyeuristic lovemaking sessions before our moon lit window, and stray into a steamy threesome or foursome with a hesitantly curious neighbour or venturesome associates from the office, as a mid-life jolt to our flagging libidos, then I'm sure—off the record, of course—these same enumerators would muster a few juicy tidbits.

This morning, as I was standing in my kitchen watching television and eating my high-fiber psyllium-charged bran buds a CNN announcer was bringing everyone up to speed on the recent hostage-taking in the city of Soledad in the south-eastern part of Mexico. A band of disgruntled peasant farmers (referred to as a Neo Left-Wing terrorist faction) had stormed the local school and were holding a group of fifteen children between the ages of five and nine for ransom. The news update ended with the guarantee that "the President had personally given his assurances to the parents of these children that everything humanly possible would be done to reach a peaceful conclusion to this violent and unlawful assault, but the people responsible had to take full responsibility for whatever happened because the democratically elected government of Mexico was not about to hand over any control to a lawless bunch of banditos." The world was now watching this small, impoverished village in Mexico and praying for those children's safe release. I have my doubts.

There is a lesson in this, a lesson that my work in the world's financial markets has taught me. Like these markets, life does not always simply piffle away its store of energies—thus giving us umpteen chances to turn over a new leaf and make things right—but instead sometimes crashes, then commences a slow and often agonizing bleed. These "soft landing and hard landing" eventualities visit each of our lives. This is a given. As I have already said, I have them at my door now. Most of us kindle a flinty resolve when handling the slow assimilation of the smaller types of woes—the lack of money, the kid's insolence, the cooling of the marriage bed—and the host of other needling aspects of life's insecurities. A good work ethic teaches us to buck up and soldier on. However, we are little prepared for the larger and often more devastating of life's blows, the ones that change everything we've known from that day forward. When these come calling, it might be best to just dig in and hunker down, while others look on in horror. As good friends or family members they will attempt to mitigate the situation by uttering sometimes vacuous but well-meaning messages of support. Unfortunately these can sound as hollow as droplets of water hitting the bottom of an empty barrel. As always, as in that tiny village in Mexico now thrust onto the world stage, we all just have to wait and see how these hard times play out in the larger scheme of things.

*

A co-worker of mine went bonkers. He stripped all of his clothes off and ran through the offices shouting like a lunatic, only the message that he carried wasn't all that crazy. Merv Hindlich is his name. The last time that I saw Merv he was bending over the desk of the oldest woman in our administration department, Miss Gweneth Frollick. He was trying to give her a goodbye kiss on the cheek, as a heartfelt expression of his gratitude toward her years of dedicated service. This in itself wasn't so damning, if it weren't for the fact that he was dressed in nothing but a strait-jacket, and when he bent forward to plant his smooch on Miss Frollick's face, the entire office could see his shriveled scrotum hanging limp and lifeless between his legs. To everyone's surprise Merv also had a small pink rose tattooed onto his right buttock. To say the least this came as a big surprise to all. He had always seemed like such a conventional fellow. As the dutiful ambulance attendants ushered Merv Hindlich to the elevators his breathless non-stop rant continued.

"We are lost people. We have no compass, true north no longer exists. We have no value. No one gives a fuck anymore. We say a piece of stone is worth a fortune, yet a child's life is worth nothing. We are lawless, rootless, faceless, soulless things that forage among the ruins we create daily. Our laws are not obeyed. Our hospitals are polluted with diseases. Our governments are self-serving. Our families have left us. We are all alone." He was crying like a baby, but his eyes were fixed and dilated, like a soothsayer who has stumbled upon a holy grail he didn't actually believe existed, and now has to tell everyone that what he had always foretold, but did not really believe, was coming true. "Run with me my friends. It's not too late. Let's rout this contagion from us like a cancer so that we can *feel* once again....I have to feel something...I need to feel before it's too late." As the elevator doors closed on old Merv, I must admit to being more than a little disturbed. Not only because a man that I had known for almost fifteen years had suddenly come unglued before my very eyes but because everything he was saying was exactly what I had been feeling. As the doors slammed shut on our past such as it was, I could have shouted back to him that I understood, and was with him in spirit. But I didn't want to take the chance. I was afraid that if I even whispered such fanaticism, it would start an unseen clock in some subliminal tower ticking down to the time when they would be taking me out in the same disappointing fashion.

Who Told You? was a television show that aired briefly in the late 1970s. In today's marketplace it would be called a reality TV program, similar to the instant-celebrity-creating ones we are currently seeing nightly. I worked on this show as a third writer one summer when I had finished university and was trying to find my way in the world. As it turned out, I only wrote eleven words that made it on air. My wife and daughters still refer to this as my Warhol fifteen minutes of fame. People's reluctance to openly greet change or at the very least, to reach out and embrace hope, not surprisingly reminds me what people looked like on *Who Told You?* when they were caught flatfooted and vulnerable. We would arrive uninvited on their doorstep with television cameras intrusively rolling. The dazed expressions on their contorted faces were living testament to their humiliation as the camera crew and announcer chimed, "Who Told You?" in front of a gleeful television audience. Each week, the producers of the show, a very British twit named Dorian Fisher and his asinine transgender assistant Mog, would source out some private, often titillating, tidbit about someone's personal life—usually volunteered by a close relative, coworker or disgruntled spouse. However, it occasionally went amiss, creating gut-wrenching moments of pure anguish, like when the bewildered female contestant emerged from her doctor's office and was greeted with the point-blank question, "What's the baby's name?" She stood frozen in anguish as the crew and television audience shouted, "Who Told You?" She then burst into tears and apologized to her boyfriend, confessing to just having had an abortion; or when we took the cameras into an unsuspecting husband's office with his beloved wife of thirty-seven years in tow. Our aim was to surprise him with two all-expense-paid tickets to Jamaica on this, his last day of work and first day of blissful retirement. Instead, we found him lying dead on the office carpet from a self-inflicted gunshot wound to his temple.

CHAPTER TWO

I SCAN MY EMAIL. THERE ARE SEVENTEEN NEW MESSAGES. THEY ARE THE usual lot, promoters attempting to furnish upbeat reports concerning dour drilling results, or poor first quarter sales figures recently made public on their projects. As if a positive attitude will help make the glum documented realities of the situation go away. Brokers call this, "putting lipstick on a pig." There are a few clients checking in to see what I think about this or that investment. Throw the dart. Take your shot. No less than six notices from our administration department advising us of new regulatory changes or due diligence requirements signaling yet another additional form to be signed by clients prior to making purchases. A couple of updates from our financing partners on a prospective Cuban deal which I'll come back to before the end of the day. I scroll down to my travel itinerary for next week. It is a virtual ticket. Nothing is real anymore. I am in Toronto for a day then on to Cuba for two days, with a return day-stop in Thunder Bay. This is a lost town smack in the middle of Canada. It is where I was born. It was founded as an outpost for fur trappers. A fort on Lake Superior, a gateway to the wild untamed west connecting it to the major markets of the east. These cities, Toronto and Montreal, once old fortresses themselves in this early colonization framework. Places to bundle raw materials and send them out into the world for processing into the Queen's own grenadier's furry hats or shawls for the grand ladies of Europe. Thunder Bay later survived on pulp mills and mining, now moving their goods east via the St Lawrence Seaway. This is a man made canal connecting Thunder Bay to the St Lawrence River and the Atlantic Ocean. But now the earth no longer yields its bounty as generously, so the ships aren't as plentiful as before. Business is slow, people are reluctantly leaving here as they are abandoning so many other small birthplaces throughout the globe, no longer deemed useful to the larger economic interests residing in the larger centers. The town itself is surrounded by scrub boreal forests growing from the muskeg and rock. This geological structure is known as The Pre-Cambrian Shield. It's the oldest rock formation on earth. Some old-timers living in the area find this fact interesting, as if it is a timeless testament to the place's ultimate value. I haven't been back to Thunder Bay in four years. I am going there now to tend my mother's and father's graves, even though technically, my father's actual physical remains are not buried there, or anywhere else remotely accessible. I will do this before coming back to my home base in Vancouver. This is a beautiful happening city on Canada's Pacific Coast. People in the know say that it is a world-class city. This seems to make the locals feel a growing sense of pride as if they have contributed in some tangible way to some worthy accomplishment, not unlike the unfathomable pride assumed by a loyal sports fan or a lottery winner.

With my travel plans confirmed, I look for my personal list of things that need tending before my boarding call tomorrow. In our business lists are like gods. Lists reassure us that we're achieving our ends. There are six notations listed that I have re-read more than once already this morning. The recent onslaught of what bleakly appears to be a never- ending chain of vexing problems has, temporarily I hope, whittled away at my confidence somewhat. This is slowly reducing me, like a wood cutter chipping away with his axe at a towering evergreen, to someone lacking the decisive edge that people in my position need, for a number of fairly straightforward reasons. Traders are gunslingers. We are supposed to be ready to pull the trigger, capable of immediate execution.

I find myself revisiting things again and again, making sure that I have the directions in proper working order. I realize that this is disarmingly similar to a person suffering from early onslaught dementia, which doesn't help. Did I turn off the stove this morning? Is it possible that I left the hot water running in the bathroom sink after shaving? Am I going crazy or did I put the mail in the refrigerator? I have found myself standing in a parking lot vacantly searching for my car only to realize that I walked to work that day. I am aware that this mental lethargy could be an early warning sign, a signal clearly stating that I may be only steps away from being seized in the grip of a shadowy and amorphous bout of depression. And these steps may be all too short. At the moment all I can hope is that I will see this foe coming and deal with it when, and if, it happens. Perhaps Dr. Sitwell can prescribe a synthetic elixir. A calming balm wouldn't be so unwelcome at the moment, providing me a chance to float for a bit, rather than thrash around like a drowning man. I find my list on a rumpled piece of notepaper stuffed into the chest pocket of my shirt. I smooth it on my desk and place my index finger beside each numbered notation, as if I am reviewing a complex formula or memorizing the directions on a secreted map that will take me out of an inhospitable forest and back onto a familiar path leading home.

1. Drop the keys with my neighbors, Randy and Clive.

2. Contact Genevieve, my wife…maybe "ex" wife. Genevieve and I are not actually legally separated, even though we have been living four thousand miles apart for the past six months. I will let her

know I'll be away for four days and that I'm attending a Narcotics Anonymous meeting tonight. It's for our daughter who is a full-blown heroin addict... so much for the Dr. Martha Sitwell sessions at $400 a pop. Who really knows why a child goes off the rails... choosing a life of obscure occult teachings, or wanton physical and spiritual depravity over that of a loving nurturing environment sustained by caring parents and siblings. Perhaps, in the end, it all comes down to a simple case of my being too stern a father. Or too lenient a friend. Or maybe it's as dismal and uncontrollable a thing as teenaged rebellious curiosity gone mojo.

3. Talk to Julio Banasi about the latest work stoppage on the Port Moody jobsite.

4. Pick-up my 1957 Edsel from its springtime tune-up.

5. Call Emily, my other daughter who isn't a heroin addict, and let her know I'm okay and will be out of town for a week. (My sick daughter's name is Tess. I seldom say her name of late. This is not because I do not love her, but rather, may relate to my growing sense of fear. Whether this fear is *of her* or *for her* is unclear to me at the moment.)

6. Write Ethan, my brother, who's a resident in custodial care at a high-security loony bin, a quick salutary note letting him know that he is not alone, which he is, and that I love him and think of him, which is true, and that I will come to visit when I'm back from my business trip to Cuba. I will not mention the other side trip to Thunder Bay because the introduction of our family's sometimes turbulent history, our father's suicide ranking high on this scale, can be upsetting for him. This, even though, if the truth be known, it was his own murderous rampage that ultimately brought the whole feeble house of cards tumbling down about our ears, since we are the only two surviving, such as this may be, sons.

That's about it. Most of us in the broader Middle World spend inordinate amounts of our energy trying to simply hold onto what *is*. This is what we deferentially refer to as "the daily grind." Even after all this time and repetition, some of these little chores and duties leave me momentarily despondent. Buck up. Soldier on.

My phone rings. I push the button on a remote receiver attached to my belt, activating the headset I wear throughout my workday. I am a Senior Partner in our Corporate Financing Department. In this capacity, I help raise interim financing, we call this bridge financing, for some fairly major international projects. The financing is my big picture stuff, while the daytrading is how I keep the loaves and fishes on the table between often far-flung paydays on the other front. At the end of the day, all things being equal, I am a textbook example of our post-war, post-modern definition of "success," the broken marriage, delinquent child, dysfunctional family and pressing financial fiasco, tucked aside.

I have two of these financing deals on the go at the moment. One is a real estate development project in Port Moody, a booming bedroom community on the outskirts of Vancouver, one of Canada's many abiding jewels snuggled against the looming emerald coastal mountains, the Pacific Ocean lapping at its pointy designer toes. The other is a multi-faceted development deal in Cuba. My income consisting of fees, com-missions and trading profits often reaches $500,000 a year. This year, with my profit sharing bonuses all figured in from the Cuban deal, it could well exceed a million…even though at the moment I am flat broke and risk facing regulatory sanctions. All I have to do is start wearing red suspend-ers and slicking my hair back like a Latino disco dancer and I'll be the spitting image of Gordon Gecko. Although I don't see my life as all that dramatic, I must concede that the elements of high dramatic tragedy, and possibly a few dollops of low comedy, are becoming increasingly evident.

"Hey, Richard. It's Frankie. Just confirming everything is ready for today's meeting."

Frankie is a number cruncher. He would dearly love to be a partner but this will probably never happen. He has lots of opinions—some of them valid and even helpful—but he doesn't place a bet, he just talks. I, on the other hand, am known on the street, and in the confines of our corporate offices as a player. This is due in no small measure to a couple of financial home runs I belted over the outfield fence in the past two years. Both of these fetched enormous injections of cash, not only into my jeans but into our partner's shared corporate account as well, these successes catapulting me to an almost heroic stature in their otherwise glacial eyes. But, as I have said, I am currently teetering dangerously close to a chasm, the breadth and depth of which are, for the moment, at least, incalculable.

Frankie has IBS, irritable bowel syndrome, and likes to talk about it. At such times his two hands are clamped stoically onto his knees, as if this structurally reinforced position somehow compensates his now compromised body. His dark mutt eyes invariably travel from the floor, to his hands, and then dramatically upward to lock onto the listener. This further conspires to entrap whatever hapless victim happens to be caught in his snare of wrenching exposition. He also suffers from bouts of fetid flatulence, all too regularly bombing the air around himself with a humid layer of sour gas. Since he was diagnosed with IBS about six months ago, he has turned into a walking, talking Encyclopedia Britannica for any and all bowel, colon or rectal maladies, including but not limited to, Crohn's Disease, diverticulitis, rectal polyps, colostomy procedures, the host of dreaded strangulated bowel disorders and everything associated with a prolapsed sphincter. Since neither a girlfriend, nor friends period, are blossoming in his life, his proctologist is foremost on his list of daily calls. At lunch the other day, he dominated the conversation with a detailed description of the euphoric sensations associated with his latest preventative medical procedure, colon irrigation, during which a dedicated young naturopathic healer in her open toed Birkenstock sandals and green hospital scrubs, gently plunge a warm cleansing solution into his all too receptive anus. He is a man who, for lack of a better description, is scared shitless because he now believes—despite the constant reassurances to the contrary by leading people in the forefront of medical matters concerning those nether regions of the body's cleansing systems—that he is one small poop away from contracting an incurable disease for which IBS was a mute harbinger. All of this dismal and focused trepidation on Frankie's part has only further irritated his previously treatable condition, obliging the normally smooth, rippling muscles of his large anaconda-like intestine to convulse in erratic, painful spasms similar to the gaping mouth of a giant blowfish as it gulps water over its fluttering gills. He may well have a point, as I, too, tend to lean toward conspiratorial supposition when it relates to my body and its many mysterious private functions.

Despite his manic ways, I feel a hesitant brotherly responsibility towards Frankie at times, even though I don't particularly like him. He is a dyed-in-the-wool, right-wing conservative with a fundamentalist bullying bent that is not uncommon to his type. He is not well liked, but this is not uncommon in our business. Relatively successful people that have few, if any, redeeming features. This could be why I feel a somewhat familial sense of duty towards him. No one else does. I have a sneaking suspicion that Frankie Butts runs the risk of doing serious harm to either himself or nameless, faceless others if he wakes up one day and recognizes that he may have, in fact, been wrong about almost everything in his life. We all know that it's the quiet ones, those the neighbours say were friendly but aloof loners, that are the ticking time bombs who sooner or later rain shrapnel or bullets down in all directions. If this happens, I would feel some measure of responsibility because I had seen the first stark signals of this coming and didn't sound an alarm bell or at the very least, reach out however feebly.

Frankie supports Canada's present involvement in the war in Afghanistan—a war we inherited, for the most part, from the Americans. Frankie loves everything about America. This admiration is primarily based on a perception that its sentimental preoccupation with heroism demonstrates strength of character. How fighting in far off places conjures such patriotism I do not know. It may only demonstrate a blatant lack of defined leadership—the kind of leadership that has kept us separate from our southern neighbors, the United States of America, ever since we won the war of 1812. Although, it is true that King George had gone completely squirrelly by then, and the Americans were tired of fighting, wanting to make money instead. Historically, both of these circumstances boded well for our unprecedented victory over a stronger, more dominant foe. If people bothered to read history before committing lives and financial resources to lost causes, they would know this often happens, the seemingly weaker adversary, winning. Alexander the Great died trying to liberate Afghanistan. The Turks, Brits, Russians and Americans have all spent billions of dollars and sacrificed thousands of lives—civilian and military—trying to persuade a bunch of folkloric tribesmen that their particular religious mythology isn't nearly as accurate or honest as ours. But I may be wrong in all of this, as I have possibly been in so many other important things in my life.

With this said, my politics are a little dicey at the moment as well. By natural inclination, I gravitate toward a fiscally conservative central government. However, my rising discomfort with this war leaves me very little wiggle room when it comes to casting my next ballot.

"Yes Frankie, the meetings still on. What else is new and exciting? I can tell you that Pacific Copper is moving up the board faster than your grandmother takes her girdle off after church."

After saying this, I flick the screen to a chart that shows the company's trading history for the past three years. This may give me some insight as to whether this recent skyrocketing price is simply a product of a bullish metals market or if some other less obvious engine is driving it. It's this other possibility that I'm interested in because in the world of professional trading—unlike the world of your average "Wednesday afternoon marvel" who relies on yesterday's news and bullshit luck—this undetected force pushing the stock price is the insurance I want at my back. Luck is always welcome, but you shouldn't rely on it to deliver. It would leave too much *chance* on the table. Vegas casinos offer their players this questionable opportunity in abundance. It is a mug's game. By nature, successful professionals in any field, be it Indy driving or widget making, are risk averse, at least wherever possible.

"Is there anything else I should bring today?" Frankie asks. "Are we prepared?"

He's referring to the Cuban deal that we are joint-financing with a Toronto and New York syndicate of investors. It's a big deal by our standards if for no other reason than it's in Cuba and, thus, carries all of the intrinsic financial and political intrigue that these types of international activities tend to spawn. Also, Frankie, being a number cruncher, is scared skinny. Being skittish is his nature. It's part of the IBS lifestyle, I presume. Frankie has been taught that *study* is the key to successful business decision-making. Preparedness. Frankie lacks animal instinct. He abandoned it to higher education, hoping for a more ordered life that favors intellect over instinct. People who detach themselves from their instinctive nature run a serious risk of becoming lost, uncertainty lurking like an unwelcome mugger, at every darkened corner. This is when their body suddenly turns and bites them with IBS or any number of other diseases requiring horrendous and disfiguring surgeries or countless hours on the couches of people like Dr. Martha Sitwell. We see it in the animal world every time the charging lioness swipes its outstretched paw at the hindquarters of a fleeing gazelle. What separates the completion of a successful hunt from the spectre of starvation is the lioness's instinctive knowledge of which way the gazelle will feint in its final waning effort to survive. If the exhausted and beleaguered prey succumbs to a millisecond of doubt as to what to do next — if it hesitates for that decisive moment, and *thinks* — in that infinitesimal pause, the cat intuitively achieves the higher predatory ground. These hesitant moments are always costly, part of a natural law that transcends the imaginary boundaries between past and present, hunter and hunted, species and species. So go the best laid plans of mice and men, and Frankie.

I must admit to having some experience in the doubt department. Our daughter's drug dependency has raised such issues. However, it has not compelled me to take a fighter's stance, waiting for the opportunity to lash out and beat on whatever unknown aggressor shows its face. Rather it has, for the moment at least, knocked the wind out of my sails and left me feeling vulnerable to whatever else may come my way. Currently, I definitely identify more with the gazelle than the lion on the personal front. I find myself slipping, but where I am not certain. I am not fighting this drifting sensation as hard as I once may have, when I was stronger, or weaker, I'm not sure which. In the end, will this transition make me more alive? Like some gravity-defying mountaineer or sun- spackled Great Barrier Reef surfer, will I see the light or have some other life affirming epiphany? Perhaps. Anyway, I don't think that Frankie fully appreciates this primal stuff... this letting go. He's more from the hold–on–for–dear-life school of thought.

There's a very real chance that the Cuban deal will make us much richer men. I suppose when it's all said and done, Frankie's bean-counting ways are helpful on this one. The legal and accounting tangle is a nightmare. Co-mingling tax laws and legal precedent between Canada, Barbados, the U.S.A. have caused more than enough grief already. None of the above bodes well for a seamless venture.

"I think what I think." I intone, attempting to convey the air of the philosophical indifference of a battlefield general. "Pay the ticket...Take the ride." I've got an important call to make before the market closes, and re-hashing minutiae with Frankie Butts doesn't move the campaign forward. "Bring the most current financial projections. *Ciao bello!*"

Before Frankie can say anything more than a feeble "Okay, gotcha," I cut the line and turn back to my screen where Pacific Copper has just tipped the scales at $4.13. I'm a pro and, not unlike the lion, I take what I feel most likely avails itself to me. My brain says that Pacific Copper has more upside life in it for a number of fundamental market reasons, but my gut tells me to take that which is within my reach today. I pick up my direct line to the trading floor and exhale a long balloon of air into the stillness of my corner office. After quoting the transaction order number, I mouth one word to the clerk on the other end of the line—a word that silences the multitude of doubts inside the head of any trader. "Sell!"

CHAPTER THREE

FROM MY NORTH-EASTERLY FACING WINDOW I LOOK OUT ACROSS Burrard Inlet and the snow- covered majesty of the north shore coastal mountains. Two particularly imposing peaks, named "The Lions" because they are loosely shaped like two lions in repose, have captured a momentary burst of sunlight knifing through the shroud of gloom. However, on wet, early springtime days like this, the northerly winds coming down off these mountains can be as bone-chilling as the cold breath of a cruel story-time stepmother.

Canada is a vast country, its boreal regions a seemingly endless sea of trees. The northern barrens and tundra are a rugged, snowy desert of ancient rocks as old as the earth itself; and in the mid-west its wide, elliptic prairies, a breadbasket for the world. Adventurous peoples, since pre-historic times when North America was a part of the European continent, have crossed its barren arctic wastes and boarded sea going boats with their prows pointed here. They have landed on its Atlantic and Pacific shores, and settled in its valleys. Vancouver is such a place to this day. The world is at its doorstep. The coastal Cascade Mountain Range stands like a dauntless resolute border. It wedges its inhabitants onto the narrow band of ground emerging out of the ocean spray. Whatever is to be made of this place is defined within the reaches of this narrow inhabitable spit. The mountains have imposed this rule of order on mankind since the first native tribes set foot here thousands of years ago. The Haida, the first people of the North Pacific, found this to be true and honoured it as such. Although their heavy carved dug out canoes no longer navigate these rocky shorelines, their totem poles may still be found standing in muted silence, their chiseled images of raven and orca, spirit bear and eagle, watching from long abandoned villages. It is as if their sightless eyes are recording the history of this place. They are timeless, yet they wait — they are patient, but for what, none know.

Having completed my trades, and now looking out over this thrilling scene, I feel for the moment at least, not unlike those two lions after a well-earned kill, and pause to reflect on happier, more contented times.

I have been thinking about something that happened many years ago. Since it's about my daughters and my wife I guess that it is all tied up in the general category of sentimental reflection. I don't think that even a Dr. Sitwell would fault me. After all isn't my family life in danger of permanently slipping away? The remembrance concerns the springtime of our tenth year of marriage. The girls were three and five, their mother thirty and ever so beautiful and I a strapping thirty-four and feeling confident that I was approaching that space of my life that would be later looked back upon as my "winning years". This is not just referring to my personal health or professional well-being, but to every aspect of my broader sphere of influence, including marriage, children, community responsibilities and inner strength. This memory that I have been contemplating captures a particular moment one day when my daughters came running to me with their little hands cupped into pockets as if shielding something of great value and importance. We were working in the garden, planting some early pansies and border groundcover, and the girls had been standing by Genevieve conspiring and giggling about something that I could not quite hear. They both came rushing toward me shouting, "Daddy… Daddy.." their chiming voices full of expectant jubilation while Genevieve stood back watching and suppressing a genuine smile that said for me to mind this moment carefully because it was a validation of who and what we had become as a couple and a family. Anyway, as the two girls got closer they could not contain themselves. They both started stammering and giggling that they had something in their awkwardly cupped hands that was so special and secretive I would be in awe for the rest of the day if I would just peek inside. As I stooped ever lower to peer into their hands they flung them open in mock hilarity and shouted, "Fooled you! Fooled you Daddy!" I feigned indignant outrage, which made them laugh all the harder. Genevieve laughed so openly then. For that moment we were all together and safe. Strange, how something so seemingly transient comes back to me now with all the force of an historical armistice being signed, a world event worthy of timeless record. But it was just us, for that moment, in our garden with each other.

Genevieve and I have two houses. Actually, one house on a half-acre lot by a wooded northern lake, and the other a concrete bunker at the edge of the rocky, wind-blasted shores of English Bay in Vancouver's fabled West End. These places carry fine memories for us both, yet now at times they seem somewhat burdened with the weight of these same memories. Adding to this vexing reality is the ominous personal cloud hovering over my head as "the Big-Five-O" closes in fast on the old calendar. Seven short days away. I dread the all too likely possibility that my goofy endearing neighbours may throw a surprise party for me. I am quite frankly in no way, shape or form up to playing the congenial host, brimming with wistful, nostalgic remembrances of my life's most important milestones, pausing to share insightful perspectives on a bright and fulfilling future.

Such birthdays usually bring with them the additional inclination to put one's ducks in a row. This all leaves me with a sense of abiding apprehension that is not helpful at the moment.

Even though my wife and I are no longer "an item," as they say, unlike so many of my associates who have been completely pillaged like cowering peasants when wifey hits the bricks, I do not fear the skulking apparition of the divorced man's musty basement digs. No, for the present at least, a West End house with hanging gutters and peeling weather worn paint, a crazed bag lady living upstairs with her coven of feral cats, is not in my cards. You see, Genevieve and I are not on the outs in that way. We are living apart because she felt—and I guess I agreed—that living together witnessing each other's hearts slowly breaking would ultimately destroy us both. I know there are many sound arguments against such isolationist thinking, these chaste suburban dramas are often depicted in movies as being the glue that holds everyone together, the fiber that makes them stronger as a unit. But at the time neither of us seemed emotionally capable of rising above the tedium and despair tethered to the fading family portrait of a drug-addicted, drowning daughter. So, although we are no longer in residence, we still love each other. And because of the very bond that has forced us to live under different roofs—the impact upon us of our daughter's tragic folly—we will remain in love, together or separately, until death do us part. The irony of this has not been lost on either of us.

Genevieve is an over-achiever. In school, she was repeatedly a scholarship winner and a formidable athlete. All of this is wrapped in a beautiful package. She is a striking woman whose looks have caught more than one person's attention while seated in a bustling restaurant or while driving past her walking down a busy street. I well remember bringing her late night meals while she slaved over laboratory experiments to complete her graduate degree. More than once during these wee hour humanitarian relief missions, we found ourselves suddenly seized in the grip of youthful passions, joined together on the cool smooth surface of a lab table or thrust against a bank of cages occupied by silent watchful lab rats, whose quizzical black, beady eyes locked on us as if our frenzied movements were a part of some heartfelt plan to liberate them from their unsettling destinies. Then this young medical doctor received the one thing that she could not control in her otherwise unblemished life of achievement: a daughter, a troubled daughter. And the troubles were messy. The kind that made her stop dead and absently look down an empty alleyway while shopping for vegetables on a Sunday morning in Chinatown. The kind of trouble that invaded her thoughts in the middle of an important meeting at work, with concerned colleagues having to summon her back to the topic at hand. Suddenly nothing made any sense anymore. Something had come forward and put up an impossibly high barricade on Genevieve's road to perfection.

Genevieve has moved back to Iceland, where she was raised, to be closer to her aged parents and loving brothers and sisters, all of whom she adores. I presume that this move is temporary, a chance for her to get her bearings. It pains me to think of her so far away from the world we shared for so many years, but I also muster some veneer of bravery and try to mine some feeling of resolve for her. God willing, she is at least coping better in her native climes, perhaps dipping her statuesque nude frame into a vaporous hot spring with her siblings, jabbering away in their singsong tongue as they skit naked and unashamed across the icy snow to join her. Or perhaps she is stoically jostling to and fro while seated in the cramped cab of her father's Isuzu 4x4 heading out upon some hard-packed lake for a day of ice fishing.

I really have no idea what she does during her days and evenings. Although she is an MD, she has never practised family medicine, choosing instead, to work in bio-research. Before all this business with our daughter nobbled her, she was working on studies related to less invasive drug therapies for pain management. A measure of irony once again. A testament to Fate's barbed tail reaching right around from one side of probability's enigmatic lair to stab you through the heart as you curl up, seemingly safe and sound on the most far-flung of distant shores. For all I know, tonight she may be closeted in some bearded, bespectacled fellow research scientist's Quonset hut, both tucked snuggly under his Special Forces-rated, cold-weather sleeping bag, their heavy fishermen's cable knit sweaters cast recklessly in a jumbled heap upon the floor's cold planking as they whomp away in their life-and-death throes not unlike the reclusive endangered Arctic Auk, a creature he has dedicated his life's work to preserving. It's highly unlikely, but nonetheless possible. As painful as that thought may be, I only hope against hope that she is getting stronger and staking a newly won claim on a better tomorrow. I am not unlike those patient lab rats now, caged and waiting for a welcome outcome far beyond my immediate control. Of course, all of this agonizing may not have been in the stars if our beautiful daughter hadn't chosen the crooked path that drew us all into this labyrinth of woe.

CHAPTER FOUR

I have to place a phone call to Julio Banasi, the elder sibling in the Banasi brothers construction company, Cielo Casa Developments. Translated from Italian it means "Sky Home Developments", which is their way of saying that the sky is the limit for you when you buy one of their townhouses. I have known both of the Banasis for over ten years and have helped with the interim financing of two of their numerous residential and commercial development projects around the increasingly populated lower coastal mainland of British Columbia. They are old-country guys through and through, generous to a fault with friends and family, hard as tacks in business.

They arrived in Canada from Naples as bricklayers working their thick, hairy asses off seven days a week to build a business through the boom times of the mid- seventies, when the Baby Boomers were abandoning their hookahs and communal ideologies and entering the first-time home-buyer's market with a vengeance. Julio and Tony didn't understand much about free love and peace. They were probably scared skinny that one of their own dark-haired, buxom daughters or lithe, soccer-ball-bouncing sons might arrive home from university with a Negro boyfriend or girl-friend fresh from a student exchange in Kenya attached to their arm. They imagined the new couple's expectation would be to live in the basement, raising their brood of mulattos and sharing their daily whole-grain experi-ences at the supper table each night before retiring to their quarters for evenings of smoking cannabis, playing bongo drums and contorting their wafer-thin, scantily-clad bodies like pretzels into shamelessly provoca-tive yogic positions. Maybe they didn't know much about everything else going on around them but they sure as hell understood the laws of supply and demand, and that hard work is its own reward.

Genevieve and I and our two daughters have visited the Banasi brothers in their homes, and they ours. This was before heroin addiction took my family from me. We have broken the hard-crusted peasant bread of their homeland and eaten the spicy bowls of spaghetti. I have sat across from the brothers and quaffed the squat glasses brimming with the tannin-loaded red wine identified with their central Italian region until we all felt like breaking out in song. But when it comes to doing business with the Banasi brothers, you proceed at your own peril. Their respect, like that of many immigrants from meaner streets, requires that you keep your eye on the bocce ball and drive a hard bargain, because when the last stanza of *Volare* fades, business is business.

The phone rings twice before Julio picks up and answers gruffly, as if he's talking to his foreman about a concrete truck being late for a substantial pour.

"Yeah. Julio here."

When he's in the office, he forgets that other people doing other things exist out there.

"Hi Julio. It's Richard. Who's beating you up today?"

He instantly shifts to a more congenial tone, as if someone were holding a sign up in front of him with instructions on how and how not to talk to your bankers. Plus, he's begun to favor the conspiratorial nature of such talk with equals, as opposed to the knuckle-cracking, arm-waving diatribes with the hardhats on a site that has made him his millions.

"Ricardo. What's up besides your blood pressure?" Julio laughs at this. He's one of those thick-necked guys that's glad as hell to be considered a businessman on par with the white- collar types downtown like me that make their money doing things that don't require getting their hands dirty. He also thinks he's as funny as someone on TV, which he is in a way that he wouldn't understand.

"Listen, buddy. I got lotsa troubles wit da geotech. Those guys are saying now that I may have something wrong with da whole focken mountain's stability. Can you believe this focken shit ? Now they want to sink a bunch a da test holes all over the focken place."

These are the kind of things that Julio and Tony never thought they'd live to see when they first started building other people's dreams. In the '70s, they found some land owned by an older couple or, rather, their dumb-assed kids who had inherited it after Ma and Pa passed away. They bought it and built on it and that was that. Things are more complex now. Everything is always on your doorstep to deal with, and no one can make a decision without an engineer's stamp or an architect's professional liability guarantee because no one wants anything coming back to haunt them. Zoning. Permitting. Environmental studies. Social and community assessments.

"Hey Julio. You know that's the way it is today. Those mudslides last year in North Vancouver have all the city planners and engineering firms wringing their hands, saying there isn't a solid piece of ground in the entire lower mainland. It's all slipping into the ocean. And, who knows, they may be right."

This is obviously not what Julio is looking for from me this morning, but it's what I think. I try to be forthright with him because I like him and besides I don't have time to arm wrestle with him or anyone else today. These are his problems. I have my own. He also probably just wants to keep me posted on the latest developments, which is a smart thing to do with someone who may finance your project, so I don't get antsy wondering what's taking so long and start thinking about a thousand problems that may be off the mark by a country mile.

"Yeah, I know, I know. Assholes. Everybody's looking for some hole to hide their focken-asses into."

He's right again. This little chat is probably making him feel a bit better—at least not alone, which is more important than most of us think in our day-to-day lives.

"Don't worry, Julio. I know that shit happens, and I know you've got a great big fuckin shit shovel there to scoop it up and throw it over the neighbor's fence. I'll sit tight and wait to hear from you. We need this geotech report before we go to the bankers."

Julio is more relaxed, now that I'm off his list of people to appease today.

"Okey-dokey, Rich. You keep making that easy focken money down there in the markets and I'll get back to you when I've got the geotech report back. Ciao!"

Throughout the tough times in the early '80s and the mid-'90s, the Banasis were up and down more times than a *putana's* panties, which is Julio's favorite English expression. The project they have asked me to look at now is a ten-acre site located on a steep, wooded hillside in Port Moody, a growing town hugging the shores of Indian Arm, a long, two-pronged inlet on the eastern side of greater Vancouver. This area is primarily a blue-collar neighborhood, mostly single-family post-WWII bungalows with fading coral and pastel-blue cedar sided exteriors. Mature, tangled hedges and shade trees dot the otherwise tired streets whose crumbling asphalt and dated road lighting reflect that progress has left this place behind. The Banasis, and others like them, are here for one reason, to bulldoze the houses and reconfigure the landscape envisioning higher densities in which to build their Cielo Casa dreams.

The Banasi brothers are builders of medium-density, multi-family residential townhouses. They build for the young families that are migrating to these bedroom communities around Vancouver, as real estate prices in the city- proper edge them farther and farther out into the Fraser Valley or up the shorelines of jutting rock and pine forested eddies closeted here and there flanked by the coastal mountains. The kind of places where prices have remained sluggish for whatever reason—an unsightly mill still operational despite the neighbours' complaints; a railroad shunting yard uncoupling and re-coupling freight cars, their engines rumbling noisily through the night; a family farm stubbornly holding on with their herd of lowing dairy cows or a rancid sty of nursing sows. But moving the goalposts of home-owning accessibility a mile or two down a once forlorn side road or up a steep switch-backing mountain incline often created a whole new set of problems with zoning, official community plans, and servicing. That's why I suppose I knew what Julio wanted to talk about today. It wasn't the neighbors, even though they're already colluding on street corners during their morning walks, their pampered Cockapoos and Shiatsus wagging their little feathery tails and sniffing each other's asses like foppish puppets masquerading as wild pack animals from a storybook emerald forest. The owners lean in close to each other, voicing exasperated objections to "it all," as if these "outsiders" were trying to ram through approvals for an abattoir on the site, rendering hides and offal in blast furnaces day and night with the fowl stench of seared flesh and entrails discharging out of side vents and rooftop portals into these very neighbors' backyards. Julio understands this kind of trouble and can cajole the old ladies and make a concession or two for the city planners where appropriate. And if that fails, he can bull-moose and strong-arm with the best of them. It's the other new stuff that's got him fuming and sitting in his cavernous yesteryear dark-paneled office, with its musty burgundy shag carpeting and gilt-edged Louis XIV copper toned frosted mirrors. I can hear an uncharacteristic contemplative tone in his voice today. I can almost see his pudgy working man's hand absently massaging his balding globular pate, the corded veins in his temples protruding like knotted lengths of rope beneath his olive skin, wondering if the time may be approaching when all this bullshit isn't worth it anymore. Delays—the Banasi brothers' worst enemy.

After he hangs up, I turn off my screen and remove my headset, unclipping the remote receiver from my belt like some wartime aviator exiting the cockpit after another successful mission over bogie territory. I have to go across the street to the underground mall and wend my way through its neon tunnels and caverns like some myopic mole in a last-minute search for a few travel toiletries. I know there's a London Drugs somewhere underneath, although for all the times I've visited the store I'm vaguely uncertain as to its exact whereabouts. Such glaring urban shrines have an eerie effect on me—possibly over-stimulating my senses—which leaves me perplexed and strangely disoriented. Genevieve was so good at navigating these subterranean corridors. She could find true north instinctively, as if she were marking her route across the frozen reaches of Iceland with a pike pole or whaler's harpoon, a definitive bi-product of her polar traditions. I, on the other hand, will move back and forth along these passageways, retracing my steps like a dazed and possibly doomed laboratory mouse. A test subject searching for its next fix of nicotine or whatever other endorphin mimicking substance the researchers have strategically hidden throughout the deadening, florescent Bristol board maze.

Like Julio and Tony Banasi, I have my own little Armageddon brewing at the office to deal with at present. I hesitate to think about it for the totally irrational reason that too much attention will inexplicably magnify it out of all proportion or somehow make it more intrusive than it may actually become. "What you give attention to you give power to." My grandfather's anthem. I have what is known in the brokerage industry as a "margin account deficit," which basically means that I have over-extended the authorized and legal limits in one of my day-trading accounts at work. This is not an overly uncommon thing to happen from time to time in positions such as mine. Even if discovered, the result is usually nothing more than a rap on the knuckles and an immediate, pointed request to put the subject accounts into proper order. A notation in my personnel file would alert everyone to the fact that certain minor trading irregularities had occurred. This notation would cover everyone's behind in the event that at some future date I chose to commit an act of grand larceny, inciting an unwelcome spate of bad publicity and embarrassing the firm. Taking the offensive, they could then hold these file notations up in righteous indignation, branding me a "bad apple" that repeatedly ignored past warnings and selfishly spurned management's overtures of help. In truth, management's tolerance of these occasional forays across the prescribed lines of acceptable daily conduct may be due in large part to the generous fees they are receiving from the very transactions that are currently holding me at ransom.

None of this by any means suggests that I am insolvent or in real, immediate trouble. However it does carry with it the distressing realization that if it's not addressed in a timely fashion, as in prior to our month-end account audits or commodities exchange commission's registered representative random spot checks, it could suddenly mushroom. If, for any reason, it were to fall into the hands of a bloodthirsty press, it also could blowup into one of those situations that bring good people to their knees in an all-too-public flogging.

This whole debacle is the aftermath of what amounts to two bad trades that went against me like falling dominos. In one account I was "shorting" African coffee contracts. In layman's terms this means that I was selling contracts hoping that the price would go down so that I could buy them back at the lower price. Unfortunately I was caught offside by an unseasonably dry monsoon season. Endless sun instead of torrential rain — too much water, the coffee plant's worst enemy. The much anticipated scrubby and water logged coffee plants now as dry and hearty as desert palms. At last report, they were stretching heaven ward, their sun-kissed leafy branches plump with ripening coffee beans and their thick trunks standing as high as an elephant's eye. At the same time, in another account, I was long in South American zinc, which simply means that I was betting on the price of zinc going ever higher. Unfortunately zinc production from the eastern block of Balkan satellite states escalated, sorely flooding the market. The price of zinc skidded ignominiously into the toilet, where it now continues to reside. I sat passively watching this happen. I had several options readily available. I have no excuse. I came face to face with the looming possibility of calamity and I did the one thing that no one in my position can ever allow himself to do. I blinked.

Looking at the brighter side there are remedies for my situation. The first one that comes to mind is the one least likely to yield much success: collecting the $100,000 that Rickie "Big Snake" Ricco owes me. Rickie is called "Big Snake" because rumour has it that his cock looks like a coiled python. He owes me this money because, against conventional wisdom, I held his accounts open way past the mandatory order for immediate liquidation. Our rules regarding the continued operation of client accounts that are in default are quite clear. I should know. I helped draft them. He was offside and I let it slide. He begged me on bended knees, his pathetic tear-streaked face turned upward like a woeful penitent. At the time, his kid was sick with leukemia and he had other overwhelming problems. These included a pregnant hysterical girlfriend and a demanding, increasingly suspicious, and unsympathetic wife. Yada, yada. He walked on the $100,000 loss and I, the senior broker, had to make good on the debt. I had broken two cardinal rules in the brokerage business: don't listen to any stories, and never assume responsibility for anyone else's problems. My account overages are well in excess of $100,000, but this windfall would certainly help get the train back onto the tracks.

I am currently weighing this with all of my other possible options, like an assayer placing a gold miner's bag of precious nuggets on the scales beside the unwavering opposing mass of leaden truth. As I walk through the office, I pass the scores of desks and cubicles jammed neatly into the common area where numerous administrators toil in a never-ending struggle to keep the paper trail intact for the favored few. I think of the account problem now because I am, in fact, concealing this information from these same administrative people with whom I work every day. This, in itself, is an unsettling gross breach of trust in the eyes of a blind judiciary. Each of these people—mainly women in their early twenties before child-bearing or in their late forties post-child-rearing—works diligently, seldom looking up. They are like plodding manatee. Air breathing mammals that have adapted to spending implausible hours submerged in a familiar, but not altogether natural, sea of paper.

I stride past Desiree's desk and rap my knuckles on its metal surface. This gives her a mild start. I must confess to having had carnal thoughts about Desiree since she came to work in our office. These may be nothing that I ever act upon, but their mere presence somehow helps on the darker days, when I allow myself to accept and even understand that Genevieve and I may never regain our past life together. I must be candid here and confess I do occasionally contemplate stepping out and foraging among the fairer sex, if not like a youthful hound routing for truffles in a sub-alpine forest in the Tuscan countryside, then at the very least like a middle aged man seeking some comforting shelter from life's current forlorn mien. The trouble is that I cannot engage in these hedonistic activities with any pretense of the reckless abandon I enjoyed in my youth, and that other men my own age still manage to cultivate. This is mainly due to the constant image of our daughter wasting away in some squalid hotel room with God knows who and, of late, my lovely wife heartbroken and valiant in her heroic effort to stay afloat. So I, like Charlie Chaplin of old movies, simply gaze with maudlin eyes through the brightly-lit pastry shop front windows. The little hobo that can only look and conjure, rather than acquire and hold.

Maybe soon I can put my accounts in order and snatch our sorry lives from the clutches of despair. I'll then pledge untold dollars into private Swiss rehab retreats harboring countless Austrian psychologists with names like *Glockenspiel*. With destiny's fatalistic nod we can all go forth, if not like the Waltons from *Walton's Mountain* then, at least, like the people that we once were.

Desiree looks up with her best "come hither" wink, her dark gypsy eyes promising delights of the dampest and most musk-laden variety.

"And what's Mr. Bonhom up to these days? I'm beginning to think you don't like me the way you've made yourself so scarce lately." She let's her head fall forward and her mouth drop into a saucy little pout. "Is it something I said? I know it can't be something I've done, since you never let me *do* anything."

She is thirty-two years old. I know this because I happened to be having lunch with our Personnel Director, Russell Balzeep, and he told me.

"You know, she's never been married. Nor has she any cheeldren. Such a bloody pity with so beautiful a vooman."

Desiree's last name is Margolis, which smacks of some Mediterranean heritage. Perhaps she's a fisherman's granddaughter from some seaside village off Portugal's El Garve coastline, or the wayward love child of an Italian peasant girl, exiled to Canada's barren shores, only footsteps ahead of scandal.

Desiree processes my paperwork and would ultimately be the first person to tally up all of my trading slips and reach the basic mathematical conclusion that something was terribly amiss. Whenever I'm around her I reflex slightly looking into her eyes trying to detect any early recognition that she is onto me and may well have to be the one, out of the many seated here, who will reluctantly, but dutifully, blow the whistle. Unlike my wife, who is tall and blond and Nordic as all get out, Desiree is shorter and more compact with the well-molded haunches; perky, upturned champagne-glass breasts, and fresh spanking sensuality of a peasant farm girl. A cheap detective novelist would label her as "comely." I can only conjure what down-to-earth comforts her favors can hold.

I sometimes find myself wanting to will such simplistic and unfettered times to return, my manhood put to a grueling test. "Any port in a storm," as they say. I increasingly wonder if underlying this electrically charged current sometimes running all too close to the surface between us is another, more complex but possibly no less palpable energy — that of pure beguiling danger. Am I becoming one with the nocturnal arsonist and his hidden Freudian desire to be exposed, or the upscale celebrity shoplifter and his latent need to be publicly shamed? I don't think this, but I am continuing to straddle the darker possibilities of her allure and its potentially volatile consequences on my future as a husband and a father. I keep walking so as to avoid the temptation of letting this good-natured veiled banter escalate. For today, at least.

"I'd rather be cast into a midnight storm than miss a moment with you, Desiree, but alas, I'm heading out of town for a while. I'll buy you a coffee when I get back." The truth of it is that women, even my beloved daughters, are often an enigma to me.

"Hasta la vista, you lucky duck," she calls down the hallway as I turn left and stand in front of the elevators sporting an adolescent smirk. I know she knows, as does everyone else in the office, big fish may soon be landed in ol' Rich's net. This fact probably doesn't hurt my chances in the casual liaison department, either. If only I could retrieve my anguished thoughts from the murky alleyways and dingy dayrooms that are the derelict landscape of the heroin addict's refuge, maybe everything else, for better or for worse, could be set free to take its natural course.

While standing at the elevators I glance around the corner to see if the man his-self is in. He isn't. The man is Jefferson Jackson Stump III, known to most as JJ and to a few closer colleagues and friends simply as Stump or The Stump, an address used with the deepest of respect for one of the great ones in our business and certainly in this office. He is very ill at the moment and no longer keeps regular office hours. The sad truth is he has lung cancer and is dying. He will soon join his beloved wife, Betty, who passed several years back. He makes no bones about letting all know that he is ready for this heartfelt reunion. J.J. Stump is a seventy-one-year-old black man of medium build and height that was as close to being a mentor to me as anyone I have met. When I first started here, he watched me galloping past his door on various errands, as keen as a barking hound. He would occasionally come out and stand directly in my path. This was his way of saying that he had something to say that I should pay attention to. The first time that he did this, he said, "Two natural phenomena you have to learn and abide by in this business kid. First. Shit. All kinds of shit, has a natural tendency to trickle down. That's a law of physics. Second. Try to make a point of not standing where you think it might land. That's a law of the jungle."

Stump has told people that his family acquired its name from his great grandfather. He was a stump puller, clearing land on the plantation on which he was enslaved. The tradition in those days was for the Negroes to be arbitrarily named in relation to what types of work they were indentured to do. Field hands often became Fields, house staff became Kitchens or Halls or Brooms...and so it went. When he told these stories, his heavy lidded, watery eyes would remain focused on the person that he was addressing. The whites of his eyes, although yellowing with age and poor health, didn't undermine the intensity of the dark, clear pupils. He usually held an ever- present cigarette in his burnished, mahogany- tinted hand, a polka dot bow tie neatly in place at his throat against a starched white shirt. These same hands, once solid as oak and capable of much good work, tremble slightly now. His resolute stare defiantly penetrated the most taciturn of listeners, like a finger poking at their chests. He was putting them on notice that such indecencies were committed and that if we as a civilization were to ever move forward this fact was never to be forgotten. Or completely forgiven. Stump is a well educated man who first received a degree in civil engineering. He couldn't find a job due to the colour barrier alive and well in Canada in the fifties. Ironically, Stump's forefathers had crossed the border into Canada from the New England states in the 1600s to escape all of this. So he determinedly returned to more schooling, four years later receiving his Masters Degree in Law, but this occupation didn't hold many doors open to him upon graduation. He could have opened a small law shop practising as a defense attorney for the marginalized in society, those who through sheer poverty and need held no uppity notions regarding people of colour. But this wasn't his goal. He had aspirations of beating the system by meeting the dominant players head on. He eventually settled into the world of financial markets. He often said that money has no prejudice against race, colour, religion or sex. People became righteously blind if they were making good money by doing so. I dread the day when I can no longer walk into his office and feel his abiding strength of character and the kindness that accompanies it coming across the space between us. Kindness is a complicated thing. It often emanates with the greatest warmth from those that have walked long distances without its presence to help guide them. It is as if, contrary to love alone, it grows strongest in places where there is no nurturing light or warmth.

*

"Damn…shit…damn…!"

The first time that I heard my drug addicted daughter (Tess, the unmentionable) talking this way she was standing in her room trying on clothes that she felt no longer fit properly. They didn't. She had inexplicably started to lose weight, or more importantly, body mass, as if she were shrinking with age instead of simply getting youthfully fitter. I ventured in to see what was the matter. It was then, or more accurately what she said then, that the first real alarm bells rang loudly enough to warrant a call to action. She looked at me with a vacuous stare as if she either didn't recognize me or I didn't even exist to her and said,

"Whatever you're about to say, don't! Because it's already been said by someone smarter than us both, and it still didn't do any good. If you don't believe me, just take a good look around."

Genevieve and I had been concerned that she was going through some post-adolescent, pre-adult coming of age thing for the past year or so. She was just about to turn eighteen. The usual signals were lighting up. Falling grades at school, lack of social interaction with us or her sister, fewer extracurricular activities and, withdrawal from long standing friends. I stood there at the door to her bedroom without moving or saying anything for several minutes. She turned and continued to fumble with the hasps on a sweater that she was trying to remove.

"Is there anything wrong?" I asked, almost afraid of the response. She let her hands drop to her sides in abject defeat, failing at this simple task of unbuttoning a top and looked up at me as if I were a blind person trying to figure out a Rubic's Cube.

"Don't you see? Don't you even get any of it?" She slumped down onto her bed and stared at the floor. "It's over, Daddy. Over, over, over and out."

"What is, honey?" I whispered, afraid to disturb the thick brittle nature of the air between us as if any sudden movement or loud noise might shatter her into too many pieces to ever be put back together again. "What is it that's over and why is it finished?"

Here, she thought for a long time and then abruptly, yet vacantly, looked up directly into my eyes and said,

"This whole Sicilian thing…OVER!" She then started to laugh hysterically and fell back onto the bed, closing her eyes. We had often quoted lines from The Godfather movies around the house when we were trying to make a point or spoof one another, but the way she said this line sent a shiver down my spine. It was too out of place, fracturing the moment into a schizophrenic interlude that startled me more than I would have previously thought anything emanating from one of my children could have. Anyway, shortly after that, we started the sessions with Dr. Sitwell. Unfortunately it may have already been too late. This precipitated the feelings of guilt and criticism in Genevieve and me concerning why we didn't see it all coming down upon us and react sooner. I mean, we knew that the girls would be having a drink at a party or be in the presence of the occasional joint and we, as responsible parents had talked to them both about where the limits might be and what boundaries they should respect. To be fair, we had no idea how fast she was hurtling through this otherwise common adolescent space and entering another dimension, one that neither Genevieve nor I had any foreknowledge or advice about. In one of the first family counseling sessions, I remember the doctor asking each of us, "And when these sessions come to an end sometime in the future, what is it that you want to have accomplished?" We, in turn, pondered this somewhat awkwardly, conscious of the fact that we didn't want to paint too rosy a picture of our expectations for fear that we would look foolish, but also aware of the fact that this might be our last opportunity to reach out and touch happiness before colliding with whatever unnamed menace was just beyond our door. So, Genevieve and I and our healthy daughter, Emily, all expressed hopeful yet somewhat guarded optimism but when our troubled daughter spoke the storm clouds clearly cast a pall over the otherwise sunny perspectives that the rest of us were sketching.

She looked at the psychologist as if Dr. Sitwell were a recently arrived alien from another planet and although speaking a form of language that seemed familiar was not connecting all of the sounds correctly. Her message was being altered slightly or even coded so that it took some thought to decipher. Then, she said, "What if you are all just saying this stuff like the words were memorized from a play and that if you just sat back and said what you really think it would make this whole thing look ridiculous to the point of absurdity? I mean, don't you see yourselves and how desperate you all are to find something that isn't even there? If it ever was?"

Later, after a number of subsequent meetings with Genevieve and I bouncing between feelings of hopefulness and abject despair the doctor took us aside and confided that she believed our daughter was an addict and that she would need a much more comprehensive regimen of one-on-one therapy sessions to bring her back to us. Shortly after this, the sessions stopped and our dear daughter was gone out of the door and out of our day- to- day lives. Thus began the degeneration of the family unit that not so very long before had felt so secure and insulated against things as foreign to us as that which ultimately came a' calling. Looking back, I can only say to parents out there, "Beware of happiness's abilities when it comes to dispelling the darker elements in your teen's lives. It needs constant reinforcement and nourishment. It isn't that flexible and can snap in a strong wind like a twig or like an assailant snapping his fingers to summon your undivided attention, just before delivering the fatal blow."

CHAPTER FIVE

"THE INQUISITION," A VIETNAMESE STREET RAPPER POSSIBLY CARJACKER, drug dealer, mob enforcer is standing directly in front of me on the street corner, selling newspapers from a plywood kiosk. I'm sure his resumeȼ reads like one of Allen Ginsberg's poems—trapped between a scream and a Buddhist prayer. His real name is Jimmy Gnu, but over the past year and a bit he's morphed into his street persona of rapper and goes by the handle "The Inquisition." Each morning, he wheels his ramshackle vendor's buggy onto the corner of Pender and Howe Streets selling newspapers and sundries, then wheels it back to somewhere else every afternoon around 3:00 p.m. No doubt, it's padlocked to a standpipe or some other immovable buttressed structure, although I question if anyone who knows Jimmy would ever tamper with it or its contents. My feelings in this matter stem from the premise that his street name suits him just fine, and I also get the distinct impression that he can be one handy fuckin' ball-breaker, if the spirit so moves him. I could use his services to squeeze Rickie "Big Snake" Ricco for the $100,000 he owes me, but that would be crossing a line that says, "Once past this point, there is no returning." I could use the money and wouldn't mind seeing Rickie kneecapped, but it won't be me instigating any of it at this moment.

Jimmy Gnu is trying to assimilate into the broader Canadian culture— probably to please his once captive parents who bravely fled the nightmarish rat-tat-tatting of machine gunfire strafing through their otherwise tranquil Mekong Delta village. I, for one, am all for Jimmy and others like him landing on our rugged amethyst-fractured promontories and green-forested shores and would gladly do whatever I can to bolster his chances and give him a leg up.

As I walk past, he intones, without looking my way, "Big B, hold onto that winning spree. Don't take no shit. No one, two, three. Be cool. Don't be nobody's fool. Say what, Rich. Ain't it a bitch."

I smile back over my shoulder. "Mr. Inquisition. Always holding a firm position."

Jimmy now turns toward me, his starched, florescent, razor-cut bangs flashing purple and terra cotta across his forehead. He flexes his sinewy biceps, animating the jailhouse tats escaping from his shirtsleeve and undulating down his arms. Images of skulls, bloodied sabers and coiled serpents with the menacing, flared nostrils of the Asian pit viper. These nightmarish harlequins are his constant bedfellows.

"I am R-E-G-U-L-A-T-I-N-G, bro. Keeping my eye on this thing and that thing. Making sure all of the cogs in the great machine are in sync. So you folks upstairs don't smell no stink. You know what I'm sayin'?"

I keep moving, but swivel slightly so that I'm walking backwards for a moment. "I hear what you're saying, my man. You're saying that we'll all sleep safe tonight."

He bows his head. "No fright, man. No fright tonight" and resumes hawking his wares.

One of the reasons I feel that I understand the likes of "The Inquisition," is that in Jimmy Gnu's world—like mine in the markets—it simply is or it isn't. No shaded areas left for guessing, no unturned rocks or mid-stream changes of mounts to present any further quandary as to the whys and wherefores of our earthly existence. We both live in the here and now.

*

The bank meeting starts on time, Frankie Butts managing to keep his monosyllabic remarks confined to the spreadsheets with no references to the ominous specter of IBS. The bankers' team is comprised of the usual phalanx of crisp paper-pushers of various Eastern and Middle-Eastern heritages. They are flanked by two upper-management international specialists who are actually pretty sharp cookies. This is an "advanced stage" meeting to discuss our progress on the project regarding the tax lawyer's work and to give these moneybags a chance to ask any housekeeping questions. These are, for the most part, directed at Frankie, with some concluding requests for additional site information that I can gather during my meetings in Cuba at the end of the week.

The woman leading the bank's International Investment Advisor's team is Gloria Gladstone, a no-nonsense ball breaker who has worked her way up through the system from the cash cage to what I would guess is a $250,000 dollar-a-year salary, plus some profit-sharing bonuses that would make anyone sit up and take notice, one precious dollar at a time. She knows her stuff well and, despite her seemingly remorseless examination and re-examination of the facts (many of which are still categorized as unknowns at present and won't be quantifiable until other variables become clearer), my all-around appreciation of her continues to grow, and I find myself liking her style and even feeling twinges of admiration for her toughness. Although she gives no quarter, she has the class not to ask for any, either.

Gloria came on board about six months ago. In a previous meeting to the dismay of all of us, she challenged one of her own people regarding the merit of his income projections. The young man was stunned by such public candor from his own boss and stumbled to defend his figures. Gloria made her approach to being a team player abundantly clear to all present that day. She would use the same measuring stick for interpreting all facts and wouldn't assume two (or three) different postures on as many issues so that the bank would appear to be right no matter what way the wind was blowing.

Gloria had been to Cuba on several occasions to look over the sites and assess the sincerity of our Cuban partners—never when I was there, which disappointed me. I would like to have gotten to know her better and maybe even be considered as a friend. Before I'd even heard of the deal we are currently working on, she also had a bit of a coup in Cuba through a joint-venture mining deal spearheaded by the Canadian mining giant Sherwood Hodges. The mine was now in production. In modern-day Cuban business folklore, it has quickly become the darling of the month, the propaganda machinery holding this venture up as proof that economic development works when partnered with some good old-fashioned communist know how. This apparent success story made her bank bosses happy, since their reputations as wise men had been badly tarnished by their holus-bolus leap into the dot-com world and their subsequent ass-kicking when the music stopped and they were all left with billions of dollars worth of DVD discs that wouldn't play.

Life in these upper management echelons and corporate towers is not easy for a woman, even in today's so-called "liberated," socially conscious atmosphere. I remember standing in the stifling humid heat of a typical Louisiana June day looking over a desolate bayou purported to be hosting a new and undiscovered oilfield chock-a-block full of sweet Texas crude. It didn't. I was down there with a petroleum engineer, Tracy Gold, who was smart as a whip, cute as a bug's ear, and full up to here with sass, since she was always stuck out in these hell holes with roughnecks and field crews. She was expert at trying to figure out the long shots of where to set up a drill platform or run a line of seismic charges. On this day, I was standing beside a big, oafish southern cracker who was also a petroleum engineer. We were watching Tracy pace off a quadrant for some surface soil sampling. As soon as she was far enough out of earshot, he turned to me and drawled, "Do ya know why Gawd gave women pussies?"

I didn't say anything, hoping that my silence would dampen the mood so that my sweating, fat-assed companion would let it die a natural death of silent suffocation. It didn't, and he continued to shuffle in a bit too close, so that there was no chance the punch line could be caught on a sudden wisp of wind, float out over the brackish backwater, and reach Tracy's unwelcoming ears.

"Because if he din't, men would hunt 'em with dawgs."

He paused, as if waiting for my laughter to signal that it was okay for him to chime in, as well. When my response was slow and forced—confined to a baffled headshake, as if halfheartedly saying that at the very least the punch line had come out of left field—he burst the floodgates with a deep and open belly laugh. The booming sound sent a brace of mallards, hidden nearby in the swamp grass, into the air in a loud, quacking wing-thudding rush. Spittle swung from his glistening, cotton-filled jowls, like a Mississippi bloodhound on the trail of a reclusive possum. We then stood side by side, his laboured breath rhythmically breaking the silence, both of us now staring vacantly across the flat landscape toward the shimmering silhouette of Tracy Gold as she methodically retraced her quadrants in the sticky, acrid-smelling southern mud.

The bank meeting ended promptly with each side taking a note pad filled with questions and comments away from the table. I am now back outside after bidding adieu to Frankie, who remains standing motionless on the sidewalk. As I turn to leave, I get the impression he is like a kid after receiving his first kiss, uncertain that such life-changing moments should be terminated without sharing a thorough, thoughtful post mortem. Not today.

I now trudge up Howe Street through the beginnings of a thin, wind-swept drizzle.I am on my way to a brief meeting with my personal banker—a meeting that will at best further flesh out the idea of a possible mortgage on our properties, giving me the cash to clean up my situation and, at worst, provide me with enough information to strike this option from my list of possibilities. After this, I will go directly on to the specialty car shop that has completed the work on my Ford Edsel. Then it's back to my apartment to pack for my trip and get ready for the Narcotics Anonymous meeting at six o'clock. I am looking forward to getting home.

*

Our condo in Vancouver is in the older part of the fabled West End. Its benefits include inspired westerly ocean views, with close proximity to cozy little ethnic restaurants that bring a mosaic of cultures to the neighborhood. There is a quiet sense of community replete with the aged and the bohemian and the young and the restless. Vancouver is a gathering place for a large and visible congregation of gay people, two of whom are our neighbors and closest friends. The part of downtown where I live skirts the well-worn path to the trendy new glass and cement high-rises of Yaletown and its environs, these sheer glistening abysses home to the avant-garde, stiletto-booted, always profound looking, sunken-cheeked, uptown youth that will soon be mothers and fathers themselves, pushing baby strollers along the bustling streets with offspring, looking for the world like little black caped troglodytes. We residents of the "old" West End, have the privilege of anonymity, with easy access to the thronging excitement of this other circus with its cheeky wacky ways whenever the spirit so moves us.

Cities are like anything that grows organically—every new shoot more whimsical than the old growth stem that is its host. Each Vancouver neighborhood is like a community unto itself. Our neighbourhood's buildings are monuments to the tasteless sixties. The flat geometric glass and plastic surfaces an arrogant reminder of the ornate art deco buildings of the '40s and '50s that they have replaced. The newer buildings, mine included, are now home to old women who have buried their husbands, young girls who work in the city's restaurants and offices, and the legion of gays. It is the gay men and women who, for the most part, supply the texture and vitality that ultimately defines the area's character. My building is getting a bit long in the tooth. I wince thinking what will happen to it when "the big one" hits. Vancouver rests on one of the Pacific Northwest's largest and most active geological fault lines. After centuries of laying quietly beneath the ocean floor, it now shudders with increasing frequency.

One of the primary reasons Genevieve and I originally liked our place is its size. In terms of West End condos, it's big. We have 1,400 square feet plus an open deck. The space includes a very large living room and dining area, a spacious chef's kitchen, three smallish bedrooms that we gutted to create one super large master and one optional office/guest room, and two bathrooms, one an ensuite with Jacuzzi tub and the other with a toilet, pedestal sink and roomy glass shower stall. Over the past ten years, we have embarked on extensive renovations. Genevieve's keen eye for nuance and comfortable detail has set the tone. People say that our place is truly "us" -— if there even *is* an "us" anymore. It's comfortable with a bit of funk. An abiding sense of understated style dominates throughout, defined by such things as the homey, old-world stained wooden window casings and Japanese screens that she has placed here and there to separate individual spaces—one in front of a small sitting/reading area that has the best natural light in the room, and another designating a more intimate area for simply standing and staring out at the ever-changing harbour and mountain views. We usually keep a set of binoculars and a few books depicting the history of the area on a small wicker stand beside the picture window. People often stand there with a drink and fall into a meditative, comfortable mood when they are visiting for supper or waiting for us to get ready for a morning walk or afternoon outing to browse through the small art galleries and bookshops that line these streets. Genevieve and our daughters and I have known happiness here, and in my stronger moments I have every hope that we will again.

Genevieve and I also have recreational property—a comfortable, lived-in, west coast-styled bungalow on Anderson Lake, which is north of Vancouver, about an hour past the Whistler Ski Resort. Westerners have their foothill ranches with registered quarter horses. People from back east in Ontario have their lakeside cabins nestled conspicuously among the wispy tamarack and tundra spruce, looking for all the world like miniature Tom Thomson paintings. And we Vancouverites have our ski condos in Whistler or vacation homes in Hawaii or golf retreats in British Columbia's arid interior Okanagan Valley or down south in Arizona's reclaimed desert oasis. Our Anderson Lake property is a place to get away, to stop and take refuge from the hectic life in the city. The towering Douglas Fir and Red Cedar of the coastal rainforest envelop us. Both Genevieve and I love it there and have often mused about retiring to this pastoral setting at the end of our working lives.

When I stand back and look at my life, it seems better than it actually is, or at least better than it feels. Why is it heading in this uncomfortable direction? Like most, I think that I am a good person. However, like most my day-to-day life is often a disappointing example of many lapsed opportunities to demonstrate this inherent goodness. I can remember my grandfather often saying that the road to hell was paved with good intentions. This was said, I suppose, to teach me to be accountable and to stand up and do the right thing and act like a man. Wise words, but at times hard to follow. I can quite easily identify what I'm against but find it much harder to pinpoint exactly what I'm *for*. I don't often make clear choices, clean cuts. Although politically I'm a fiscal conservative, I'm quite liberal in many social areas, excluding the weak-kneed performance of our judiciary on certain abominable crimes and our increasingly casual disregard for our citizen's individual rights. Most would probably consider my middle-of-the-road positions to be an admirable trait and a beneficial characteristic. I would have thought this myself at one time. Now, more often than not, I find the opposite to be the case. I'm not talking about helping someone who has fallen down or about cutting the neighbor's lawn when they're on vacation. It's more about my hesitation to make a straight call, to tackle a direct decision. I vacillate of late, considering too many variables, even hesitantly contemplative of what others may think. The Middle World I inhabit likes lionizing the very qualities in itself and society that I think we should be trying to rise above. The Middle World abhors change, seeing it as one enemy, if not the prevailing one, of these values. This excludes all the gadgets and electronic gizmos we have conveniently cited as a reflection of actual change, which may well be proven over time to have been totally unrelated to change at all. We have grown comfortable with lying. We tell lies, and perhaps even more troubling, we accept lies as truths when they are told to us. It all depends on who is doing the telling. The lies have grown so big that we have lost any sense of scale or degrees of damage. For instance when Bill Clinton lied about his sexual relationship with Monica Lewinski the American people indignantly commenced impeachment proceedings. Since then, the Bush years unleashed an apocalypse of death unlike anything since the second Great War. Violence and murder have replaced ill-advised groping under the Executive Office desk. Hindsight being what it is, and lying being generally an accepted fact of modern life, banging the secretary actually doesn't look all that serious. So, people's angst is all consuming right now. It's an epidemic. It is at such vulnerable times as these that we start looking for something to show us the way, someone to hold the light and point it to the path that takes us, like a well trampled elephant walk, to the fertile lush grasses of the wide and welcoming savanna of a better tomorrow. But what history has not seemed to teach us is that this path is not found when staring down the raised bands of rifling in a gun's dark barrel. It cannot be taken by force. It must come to each willingly. Openly. What is it we seek, and that I am presently finding in short supply? It is Hope.

CHAPTER SIX

AS I CROSS BURRARD STREET AT GEORGIA, A BUSY CORNER AT THIS TIME of day, I think about all the headaches invested into the Cuban venture. The thousands of air miles traveled. The countless nights alone in deadening Cuban hotel rooms, their chipped plaster walls and fetid-smelling cornices and lack of fully working amenities whittling away at one's resolve. I have been involved for over a year and a half with absolutely no assurance that it will ultimately gel.

I sprint across Georgia Street's slick wet asphalt skirting around a Yellow cab that has pressed its nose into the pedestrian crosswalk ahead of the changing light, the opal eyed Sudanese driver pushing every light and violating every rule, hoping, along with the rest of us to make ends meet at the end of another punishing shift. I reach the Hongkong and Shanghai Banking Corporation (HSBC) on Georgia Street and for a moment stand in front gazing up at the gigantic metal pendulum sculpture suspended from the ceiling of the massive atrium. It swings silently to and fro, as if signaling to one and all that time is ticking by and the bank may, in some tangible way, alter destiny's winged course on our behalf with a loan consolidation, or possibly an extended line of credit at prime-plus-three, if, of course, you have the underlying collateral supporting such a helpful gesture.

I have an appointment with a senior account representative, Ms. Jodie Beazley, who, for all intents and purposes, doesn't really know me beyond the numbers she sees recorded in my file. We have met twice before, but have exchanged no meaningful confidences beyond those isolated prisms of information casting their fractured light on my once happy home's financial matters. These numbers that comprise my fiscal history were recorded by my last senior account representative, John Duckworth. He was a pretty good guy, all things considered, but decided that having been passed over for an overdue promotion and after having served the bank in all good faith for nearly twenty years — that he didn't need their shit anymore. He now owns a bicycle shop on Vancouver Island and hopefully is doing a bang-up business. Ms Beazley is courteous, in a matter-of-fact sort of way, but in my opinion, a bit too emotionally austere to develop the requisite "relationship bonds" deemed necessary in today's high-touch world. This may be even more evident when dealing with people like me, whom the bank has categorized as being "individuals of wealth", which I suppose that I am, if not for the fact that at the moment I don't have any money.

Gone are the brambling chats that I enjoyed with John Duckworth, the two of us chafing at the vagaries of business, guffawing like Bedouin traders about the perfidious path men like us had chosen to walk. Then, as if we were both alerted by some unseen telepathic flick of a switch, we would segue effortlessly and painlessly into the financial matters at hand. I felt that John Duckworth was actually trying to buck the system and make things happen, which was probably a weighted reason behind his boss's decision barring him from any further movement up the corporate ladder. At some future date, he may have become problematical; okaying loans that did not, under scrutiny, fit squarely into the boxes on a Loan Application Form, or even worse, that did not fit into the general theoretical frame of reference that was the very foundation of sound banking practices. Now it's pretty much brass tacks. A familiar, but not cordial, handshake and smile, the grating sound of the glass door rattling shut, the clearing of throats, and a momentary awkward silence that shouts, "So what's on your mind, asshole? Time is money."

As Jodie Beazley seats herself behind her Spartan, orderly desk, she looks across at me with a distant expression, as though she were searching for some sign that other forms of intelligent life existed there, or just beyond. A newspaper lies neatly folded on her credenza, the headlines declaring, "*THIRTY UNSOLVED DRUG RELATED MURDERS IN VANCOUVER'S ONGOING GANG VIOLENCE—POLICE REMAIN OPTIMISTIC*"

"It's nice to see you again, Richard. It's been a while."

She glances at the file lying open on her desk and checks the date of our last chat to confirm this statement for accuracy, which no doubt is how she approaches everything in her regimented life. I harbor a growing suspicion that she is a lesbian or hermaphrodite keeping this closely guarded secret bottled up inside of her protected from judgmental and unsympathetic eyes. I glance at the lone, pewter-framed photograph on her desk—a fluffy, white cat with piercing blue eyes. It has a large red bow looped and tied around its neck. It is quite possibly a last minute Christmas gift from herself to herself.

I know exactly when I last visited this office. It was six months ago, shortly before Genevieve went back to Iceland. We had both come in to review our retirement savings plans. Although I'm in the investment business, my wife and I had mutually agreed to keep the "safe" money tucked away out of temptation's slippery reach in the dullest of portfolios comprised of dividend-yielding stocks and Treasury Bills — a slow road to retirement, but one that allowed us to sleep through the night.

"How is Genevieve?" Ms. Beazley enquires politely.

I haven't told her that my wife is in Iceland and may have left me, since nothing is certain in that department and the sharing of this information wouldn't do me any good in my present fix. However, I don't know if she can access the details of the past six months' auto debit withdrawals in our joint chequing account and trace a telltale line to a cash machine sitting in some pharmacy's frosted entrance foyer in Reykjavik. If she can, perhaps she's already determined the answer to the unspoken question concerning the debilitating state of our marriage. I decide to head her off at the pass on this supposition.

"Genevieve is in Iceland tending to her elderly parents. Her father is not well."

I say this with as much brevity as I can summon. I sense that Ms. Beazley is not here to discuss personal matters that don't relate to her responsibilities as my account advisor. I also feel that should I burst into tears and sob into my hanky like a distraught accident survivor, she wouldn't instinctively take it upon herself to come around the desk, one human being to another, and press my tear-streaked face against the coarse, knobby warp of her gray, woolen suit jacket.

"I'm sorry to hear that. Will she be back soon?"

Once again, I am not one hundred percent sure that Genevieve hasn't telephoned telling her the whole sordid tale, confiding that our cash should be frozen in preparation for whatever contingencies may present themselves in the slip-sliding future of a marriage presently adrift and most likely headed for the rocks beyond. I have to presume that Genevieve wouldn't do anything this drastic without talking it over with me first, so I reply innocently, "Hopefully she will be back as soon as she is able."

I now adjust my position in the chair and tilt slightly forward, raising one butt cheek off the chair like a taciturn traveling salesman listing drunkenly on his bar stool readying himself for a long-overdue, all-comforting fart.

"Jodie, I'm thinking of taking out a mortgage on the condo…for investment purposes." I smirk conspiratorially, as if we were two combat-tested pals sharing an obvious truth about the realities of battle. "No point in letting all that equity sit there doing nothing."

I know this is familiar language to her. She must use it every day trying to convince recalcitrant pensioners who are hording gobs of cash in stagnating savings accounts, that there are other "safe" options available.

Jodie reaches for her calculator and pulls it alongside the pad of blank paper sitting to the left of my file folder, readying herself for the numbers.

"How much were you thinking of accessing?"

I lean back in the chair, as if this question has caught me off guard and this whole mortgage scenario were really only at the hypothetical stage in my thoughts so far.

"I don't know. What's available? The place has got to appraise at close to a million dollars in today's market. Maybe half that much?"

She glances down at the file and reviews our combined incomes, which are in excess of $500,000 dollars a year. Our debts, aside from the $300,000 account shortfall, which Jodie doesn't know about and never will, if I can help it, are few and easily manageable. I already know that the problem isn't our ability to service our debt, but whether Jodie Beazley will okay a loan of this size without Genevieve's signature.

She pushes the file away from her and looks up, cracking a reflexive smile that quickly dissolves into a vacant, almost absent, frown.

"It doesn't look like it'll be a problem for us. We need the usual paper-work—appraisal on the condo, two years' tax returns verifying that there are no outstanding income taxes owing, and your and Genevieve's sig-natures." She now plays her trump card, casually watching for a flinch or twinge of remorse, neither of which I volunteer. "If she's not here, since you are preferred bank customers, I can probably arrange to fax her the documents and have her sign them in front of a notary in Iceland."

I lean forward again, like an Olympic runner placing his weight up front, squarely into the starting blocks.

"With Genevieve being so emotionally taken up with her father's health issues at the moment, is there any way to avoid troubling her with the sig-natures? I mean, my income and half ownership in the assets is more than enough security. Maybe I can throw in the recreational property against the loan as well."

She looks at me for a moment, as if sensing a lie. I keep my eyes focused on her, knowing that she's searching them for clues.

"Normally it wouldn't be a problem for people with your incomes and assets, but with the economy running so hot lately, the bank is tightening its lending policies regarding unsecured personal debt. Obviously, I could add another, say, $100,000 to your existing unsecured line of credit. But $500,000 is stretching the envelope beyond my limits or even the branch manager's. Is it urgent that you get this money?"

Here is where I have to back-pedal. I take on the mantle of someone who has just come in on a whim, realizing that he should sit down and figure out where he now stands. Someone who is perhaps caught up in a momentary, financial quandary. A person troubled that his future retire-ment needs may not keep pace with inflation or might possibly, due to unforeseen family issues, be greater in the coming years than he had pre-viously anticipated.

"No, no. Not at all. I've just been thinking about the unused equity in the properties lately and thought I'd have a little chat with you to see what my options might be. That's all."

Jodie Beazley rises from her chair, indicating that all her cards have been put on the table and it's up to me to make the next move.

"If you'd like me to organize an appraiser to come and take a look at the condo and the recreational house on Anderson Lake, just let me know. It won't get done fast, though. The average lead time is a month right now."

I get up and say that she can hold off on the appraiser for the moment. I've been given a bit of stuff to mull over and I'll get back to her. Both of us know that I won't call her or bring this up ever again because there is more to my story than meets the eye. As I exit through the main lobby under the giant pendulum hanging from the vaulted, glass ceiling three stories above, I grapple with how ludicrous this situation really is. Less than an hour ago, I was at a bank down the street that is prepared to offer our consortium upwards of $100,000,000 dollars in project financing, based to some small extent on the fact that I'm the point man, and I can't even get a few hundred grand without my wife's approval. Obviously this is because she is a joint owner of our assets. In the hard light of day, if things went bad it would be me alone, and my income alone, that the bank would attach without a second glance at Genevieve's $75,000 dollar-a-year stipend as a research scientist for the Cancer Agency.

I stampede a flock of warbling pigeons, forcing them off the pavement in alarm. They roll sharply like a squadron of Japanese Zeroes, to avoid the opaque abyss of plate glass windows hedging them in. I watch as they ascend to the tops of the surrounding buildings in a tight military formation. I clomp around the corner of the imposing Hong Kong Shanghai Bank Building and proceed a bit less assertively up the street.

I still have plans B: make the money back on the market and C: borrow it privately from a friend or colleague; and possibly D: fess up and have Genevieve sign the necessary papers. All of these to consider before crunch-time on my account overages. I know, without hesitation, that I could also ask Stump and that he would hand me a cheque, without any questions or explanations required. He would be glad to. But I cannot do that. I cannot include him in any of this. It would make me feel a sense of shame far deeper than the angst I am now wrestling with. My dearest teacher will leave this world without any knowledge or concern for how pitiful my life has become. I owe him that much. Besides, I never really thought I'd get a serious audience from any banker without my wife's signature, so I'm really no further behind the eight ball than I was forty-five minutes ago. However, I bridle at the gall of the likes of Jodie "Fuckin" Beazley. I petulantly toy with the possibility of moving all my business elsewhere, perhaps adding to this indignity a sharp letter to the bank's President citing bureaucratic stonewalling as the reason behind this exodus. Once, of course, I've got nothing further to hide.

When I was a boy, my father always said that telling the truth was one of the most important measures of a man's character. That was only one of the many baffling lies he told me. Saying that *honesty* was an important personal trait would have kept me in far better stead. I have since found that the truth is often not easily recognized. People's version of the truth is sometimes more a circumstance of convenience to further bolster their viewpoint on this or that. This is not unlike the varying testimonies of eyewitnesses, each reporting something entirely of their own creation.

My father built our house. He wasn't a carpenter, but was savvy enough to make a job of anything he took on. In this case, the product of his labor was a sound enough looking structure that to the untrained eye seemed okay. But it wasn't quite right because nothing was square, or "true" as carpenters describe ninety-degree angles. This is what our lives were like inside this house, as well—optically correct, but in every other way askew, or not true. This quest for truth can be vague at times, even undetectable to the naked eye. I don't doubt that more than a few good men or jilted husbands have faced the gallows or slept on the couch based on someone's recollection of the truth as they saw it. Honesty, on the other hand, is a far more dependable compass; because it looks within for the answer, rather than just at the events that frame these often awkward situations.

As I'm walking up Hornby Street, I feel a rising sense of righteous indignation about my situation. No doubt this feeling is no more than a thin mask for my general feelings of self recrimination for allowing these events to displace my once happy home. So what? I stop in front of the office building where Rickie Ricco once rented a lavish penthouse suite. At that time—his umpteenth reincarnation as an investment guru—he was promoting a diamond play in northern Canada that was getting the usual high-flying hype on the street. Each of these deals collided with inevitable disaster and allegations of impropriety. The securities regulators always crying "Foul." but powerless to control them. There are three basic reasons for this: Rickie and his ilk don't scare easily; they don't care about anybody, and, when cornered, will act like treed polecats. When it's all said and done they offer people the one thing that no one can resist—the possibility of something for nothing.

I stand on the street for a minute, wondering whether I want the further aggravation of a confrontation with Rickie "Big Snake" Ricco today or not. I know the chances of ever collecting on this debt are slim at best. Rickie is one of those Gambino family-type Italians who was born in Canada, but acts and looks more Italian than The Godfather. He's stocky with thick-set arms and thighs that make him swagger when he walks, causing his whole body to pivot from side-to-side like an ambling bear. He was also one of the earliest recipients of a hair transplant. This venture left him with large, sparsely-spaced plugs of hair that he dyes jet black, often leaving a charcoal residue, like a radiation burn, on his visible scalp. He wears expensive Italian-tailored suits that always fit a bit too tightly. This corset like constraint leaves the impression that he's always uncomfortable, pulling his arms up and flexing his pectoral muscles like King Kong tethered and anxious. He wears a thick, gold chain around his neck and has a large, zirconium diamond, which he thinks looks real, on his right pinkie finger. If I thought it was real, I'd hire "The Inquisition" to cut his fuckin' finger off. Whenever Rickie is talking to you, he is never standing still, but always looking around, as if whatever you're saying could be incriminating and is perhaps being recorded on a hidden parabolic device by taciturn undercover agents. He makes every conversation sound like a conspiracy, glancing over your shoulder and his own, shrugging off your informal answers as if they were cheap shots. He generally presents the profile of a thug, which isn't surprising because that is what he is. I look up at the building and decide to leave this exhausting audience for another day when I'm more capable of handling a face-to-face confab with the likes of "Big Snake".

CHAPTER SEVEN

....

WHEN I WAS GROWING UP, MY PARENTS OWNED A TOURIST BUSINESS ON Highway 61 in northwestern Ontario, Canada. It sat on the edge of Lake Superior near the Minnesota border of the northern United States. The Canada-US border was heralded as the longest unguarded boundary separating two countries in the world. It is no longer the case, yet another victim of terrorism and mismanaged politics. It was a tourist trap, which, by definition meant that it didn't have or represent anything of real value or substance. It just stood there on the side of an otherwise barren and desolate stretch of two-lane blacktop, like a garish neon highwayman waiting and hoping to lighten the purse of whatever hapless yokel wandered past. It was colder than a polar bear's testicles for a third of the year, bleak and uninteresting for another third of the year, and hot and mosquito-infested for the remaining third…our busiest season. We stayed open only from May until the end of October. The tourist association referred to such enterprises as "seasonal businesses" and fought hard with local and provincial governments for extra considerations with taxes and highway expansion programs, hoping to encourage more people to take that long overdue drive along the north shore of Lake Superior. But in the end, despite these valiant efforts, the results were usually financially dismal for those families clinging, like prairie farmers, to the belief that the coming season would bring a bonanza of good luck and good fortune.

With each new spring, necessity forced my parents to crawl hat in hand before their banker, or any other local Shylock that would bend an ear, trying to beg or borrow enough money to open the doors and stock the shelves with as much junk as they could finagle from their increasingly wary suppliers. As a teenaged boy, I witnessed this annual pilgrimage with dread. Ever since I was old enough to pump gas and make change, I was aware that if those front doors didn't open on the May long weekend and stay open every miserable, soul-sucking day until the drifting snows of October reduced the traffic on Hwy 61 North to a trickle of logging trucks and road maintenance crews, we, as a family, were doomed. I was raised with feelings of uncertainty about tomorrow that have stayed with me to this day.

Nowadays, I do business in the global marketplace no stranger to seven figures—or, in the case of the Cuban deal, "Nine decimal points from nothing." That's what Stump says about the "big ones" to keep everyone's egos in check. Many of my deals occur offshore and require that a subsidiary be established in a country with a reciprocal tax agreement with Canada and, preferably, the United States. At the moment, Canada has tax treaties with three countries: Ireland, Cyprus, and Barbados. Because of proximity and terms of the treaty and, let's face it, climate, Barbados has been my haven of choice for these arrangements. Their treaty allows Canadian-domiciled companies to sell or distribute their goods or services throughout the world at a flat tax rate of two and one half percent, as opposed to the current domestic rate of approximately thirty-five percent. I always contract the on-island management services to Alex Dodge. "Smart Alex" to his friends and business associates.

Most middle-aged ex-pats living in Barbados, including Alex, are golden-handshake retirees from large Canadian, British or u.s. corporations. Most of these companies had been faced with an insurgent uprising at headquarters or were simply under new ownership. The new guys, being savvy about the ways of the corporate world, frequently deemed it prudent and fair to give the old boy being pushed from the oval office a posh and honorable exit package. He was offered the management job in Barbados. This also carried the added bonus of keeping him distant, yet close enough that he could still be of some use as an advisor and as a bridge to the long-standing senior management personnel that had weathered the coup and were staying on. All of this was decidedly preferable to giving him an ignominious boot and having to roll up their sleeves and do public battle with a highly respected but now scorned CEO. This makes guys like Alex a necessary and, at times, expensive requirement. Since there isn't really all that much to do, business-wise, in these subsidiaries, Alex and his cronies have an inordinate amount of time for tennis, golf and Sunday afternoon at the polo grounds, which is probably their due at this stage in their lives after having logged the long hours and put up with the treacherous deceits of a life in upper management. So their new life goes on, the social scene enslaving them to a regimen of recreation, chit-chat, old boys' club story-swapping, and much wine and rum consumption — all of this sometimes too much, resulting in the occasional, serious, head-on collision on the narrow, winding roads that zigzag through the towering cane fields of this tropical paradise.

The one unsettling drawback to this picture-perfect scenario for the outcast executive was the fact that the wives, often of long standing, could all too quickly become disenchanted with the isolated life of the grand lady that the island has to offer. They could grow morose and sullen and suffer spats of depression and anxiety because they were now, in their twilight years, so far removed from their comfort zone of the beloved kids and grandkids that had until so recently filled their lives with a sense of purpose and place. Island life, in all its seeming splendor, held little for them. They were simply along, as was expected, for their husbands' sake. Occasionally, this led to a forty-year union biting the dust because the husband, full of self-congratulatory hubris for having pulled off something as magnificent as this in the home stretch of his diminishing career, would sink his brittle, calcified nails into the nearest date palm and state emphatically that if his shrew of a wife truly insisted on going back to some upscale estuary of Toronto, New York or London she could bloody well do it alone. So at TGIF gatherings at the Canadian Embassy or British Consul General's estate, one would commonly see stiff-legged, freckle-skinned white men, their hairless varicose-veined calves protruding from beneath crisply pressed Bermuda Shorts, suddenly showing concern bordering on contempt for their balding scalps, which they tried to cover up with long flaps of hair lacquered into place like butterflies in a museum display case. These newly risen Casanovas, from time to time, and with varying amounts of discretion, could be seen flitting into or out of nightspots and boisterous local rum bars in the wee hours with cocoa-colored Bajan women of a much younger vintage on their shrunken, tendon-chorded arms.

This was Alex Dodge. Vexed wife, Beatrice, of thirty-seven years now gone and his grown children caught between their feelings of loyalty to a self-martyred and increasingly bitter mother and their love of tropical island visits with their immature, but infinitely less inhibited, father. He was yesterday's man, our Alex Dodge, and, not unlike Faust, had bargained a second chance at life. He knew it for what it was and clasped tightly to the silver chalice held reverentially to his parched rude lips.

The last time I was in Barbados completing the registration of a subsidiary company and installing Alex Dodge as President, we decided to take a couple of the Toronto investment gurus with us out for a day of drinking rum and swapping war stories. The best way that I knew to get someone's spirits lifted and put them at ease while on this sunny isle was to take them out for an afternoon on, *The Buccaneer*. This nautical tourist experience was a part of local legend in Barbados. The boat itself, although equipped with modern diesel engines, was fashioned after the double-masted pirate ships of old. It looked for the world like a demonic galleon to be reckoned with when its sails were up and its skull and cross bones flying. It had room on board for about fifty sun- worshipping revelers. The galley was well stocked with rum and beer. For sixty dollars U.S., a spicy African buffet of jerk chicken and rice was included. The cruise began at Bridgetown harbour and took its merry passengers down the west coast toward Speightstown, approximately an hour's sailing time away. Once there, it moored in a sheltered little cove, allowing passengers to swim and snorkel among the reefs and enjoy the company of thousands of multi-colored marine creatures. Usually none were large enough to devour you, although a big hammerhead shark would occasionally glide past, sending the swimmers onto the decks faster than if Davy Jones had wrung his dinner bell.

I happened to know Roger Reach, the owner of The Buccaneer—a seasoned old salt, who also owned a couple of car dealerships. This kept him busy flogging recycled, right-hand steer Toyotas from Tokyo to the local gentry. Roger, like any red-blooded man, gravitated toward the hands-on management of *The Buccaneer* though. When all was said and done, there was simply far more booty to be had in this line of work than in selling used cars. Now, the subject of booty was an integral part of his pay package for the crew of dauntless mutineers. Of all the beach boys, playboys and cabana rascals that schmoozed their way around the resorts and public watering holes of the Caribbean, the crew of this vessel was, bar none, *numero uno* in the "getting laid" department. Since I had been on The Buccaneer many times during the previous eighteen months, I had gotten to know these ne'er-do-wells and even gone out for drinks with a couple of their ringleaders whenever our paths crossed in Bridgetown.

Sedgwick Braithwhite and Burton Alexander were the main stage actors in the daily melodrama that was played out as the boat drifted along the picturesque shoreline, the passengers generally awe struck by the numerous coves dotted with small boutique resorts and sixteenth-century mansions. These hideaways, once owned by the wealthy, British sugar barons of bygone days, were now owned by dot-com tycoons or emaciated, aging British rock stars with burnt, frizzy hair who could often be glimpsed entering and exiting local rum bars with their young wives fastened jauntily to their leathery elbows.

The shtick on board the boat was undemanding and effective, never varying from one day to the next or from one year to the next. Halfway down the coast, after everyone on board had been ladled a dram of hundred-proof rum followed by another close on its heels, this time hidden in a fruity rum punch concoction that the boys called "panty remover groover, Sedgwick would swiftly emerge from below deck brandishing a wiggling rubber saber, shouting, "Aarrr...aarrr, me hearties." He also wore a pirate's eye patch and bandana knotted at the back of his long, glistening neck and flowing over his shoulder like Errol Flynn in *Captains Courageous*. At this point, Burton, having donned a similar getup, would position himself beside a beautiful, single, young woman passenger, with a suitable female traveling companion, whom he had previously chatted up and made sure finished her two rum drinks. This signaled Sedgwick that these were indeed the day's catch. They would then good-naturedly and with much "aarrr...aarrring," blindfold their prisoner and take her to the starboard poop deck where a plank had been affixed to the gunnels, the idea being that the hapless young woman must atone for the entire entourage's misbehaviors by walking the plank.

By this time, the other passengers were well past feeling any pain and watching these comic proceedings with giddy anticipation. Like all successful, long-running productions, although seemingly skimpy on forethought it was, in fact, quite the opposite. That they always chose to embarrass a pretty, young, single girl appealed to all the other female passengers to no end, and what guy with two eyes and a belly full of Bajan rum didn't want to watch a lovely, bikini-clad damsel squirm helplessly in the hands of two long-limbed, sinewy, muscled, black brigands? After one performance, I happened to be standing at the bar next to Sedgwick and asked how it was going. He looked at me through his ganja-glazed eyes and, parting his full, dark lips in a gold-toothed, shit-eating grin said, "Morsels, mon. I and Burton be two pathetic Bajan lads eatin' the few morsels that drops from de plate of de big boss, mon."

Yeah, really! Most of the men aboard would give serious thought to trading in their sorry-assed lives of daily drudgery for the sun and the sea and the, "morsels."

After the boat returned to its safe harbour and the lads helped the now seriously intoxicated, sun-burned, sleepy passengers off the gangway safely onto terra firma, it was only a matter of minutes before one could spot Sedgwick and Burton beetling down the narrow, corduroy wharf road in their open-topped jeep with their young, jiggling accomplices primed for an evening they would secretly cherish as the harvest moons of their youth waned into the coming decades of responsible suburban life as wives and mothers.

It was on one of these outings, while witnessing these pirates in action, when things went terribly off course. I had arranged an afternoon trip aboard *The Buccaneer* for a couple of institutional finance reps from New York City—two acerbic, young bluebloods with pedigree stamped all over their Ivy League curricula vitae like travel stickers on some '20s-era vaudevillian's tattered suitcase. We had completed the paperwork with our legal beagles in Bridgetown and had the rest of the afternoon free, so I thought it best to keep these two under supervision, as it were, rather than letting them get into any trouble in this foreign environment.

Anyway, one thing led to another and before long we were deep into our rum punches and feeling no pain as the broad prow of our wooden vessel bucked through the azure waters, tacking skillfully toward the all-too-familiar mischief ahead. My colleagues, being younger than I, and out-of-town singles, wasted no time in scouting out their fellow passengers, with an eye to whatever errant possibilities might present themselves. After all, they were far from home surrounded by unimportant strangers from far-off, insignificant places. Aarrr…aarrr.

When we pulled up to moor inside the reef within a short swimming distance of the white sands of Gibbs Beach, Sedgwick approached me with as much brevity as someone like him could possibly muster, and said, "Richard, mon, I be tinkin' you should be watchin' de guy from de Beeg Apple wit jew. He be downin' dose rum punches pretty boldly. If he not be familiar wit de sun, mon, he be having some serious troubles in he head and he stomach."

It was true. One of these guys had gone too heavy with the booze and was now confronting two bikini-clad young nurses from Los Angeles that definitely were advertising their mutual aspirations for a memorable holiday romp. At that point, I wasn't sure if Sedgwick was sounding the alarm bell because of a proprietary interest in the nurses or not. Anyway, unfortunately I chose to ignore this warning signal, to everyone's future peril.

I watched my forthright companion at the timeless nature of such rituals with mixed feelings of amusement and uneasiness because I wasn't absolutely sure if he was the type that would go AWOL after too many drinks and wind up in a punch-up with the bartender or, even worse, with me. As I tried to relax and enjoy the warm sun and tranquil views stretching out across the calm Caribbean Sea into infinity, my fears were temporarily allayed as I saw him heading rather club-footedly toward the forward passageway leading to the heads. As anyone who's been on boats of any size knows, the heads, or bathrooms, are cramped, little, awkward compartments stowed beneath a storage locker or crammed between a bulkhead and a main stay. Wherever nothing else will fit is generally where these facilities are placed.

Fast-forward approximately three quarters of an hour. Sedgwick and Burton have conducted their little two-penny opera to the delight of everyone (including myself) using the gamier of the nurses as their foil, and we were well under sail for home port before it dawned on me that one of the two New Yorkers was nowhere to be seen. Although I didn't particularly like either one of them, I felt an almost fatherly obligation to at least keep them both alive. I moved to the forward deck of the boat with amazing agility and quickness of step for someone who had been imbibing since early afternoon. I met Sedgwick as he was removing his pirate's garb.

"Hey, Seg, have you seen my friend?"

Sedgwick exhibited his usual casual disdain for anything that he suspected might require his immediate attention, thus disturbing the quiet floating atmosphere he chose to inhabit throughout his daily duties. "He be headin' down below when Burton drop de anchor, mon." He smiled, and his beguiling tone now had a hint of sarcasm. "Maybe he be overboard, mon…tragedy."

Well, as a matter of fact, it would be, I was thinking with growing apprehension. "Can you check with Burton and take a look around below? I don't want to trouble you, man, but if he's gone missing, I think we should see if we can locate him, don't you?"

With a quizzical-bordering-on-exasperated huff of air, Sedgwick volunteered, "Ya, mon. I be goin' below and askin' Burty where our wandering young Yankee boy be at." As he was turning to go, he glanced at me with all his Sedgwickness in full display. "Rich, mon. You be chillin'. I and Burton have grown fond bro. No wantin' you to expire wit de heart attack." He smiled widely, his gold-encrusted teeth gleaming like ornamentally capped ivory tusks on a majestic Bengali circus elephant.

What happened next was right out of a British comedy featuring Spike Milligan and John Cleese at their zaniest. It appeared that my young companion had ventured into the head and locked the hatchway door behind him. The jostling of the boat maneuvering to gain purchase at anchor and the subsequent bouncing from people leaping in droves from the upper decks into the warm inviting waters had all been dramatically exaggerated within the cramped quarters of the bathroom and made our friend dizzy. This quickly escalated to what I can only assume to be full-blown sea sickness. In this compromised state and still very drunk, he couldn't unlock the hatchway door. When we set sail, the backwash from the boat's forward motion must have dislodged the sea cock on the toilet's drain pipe, forcing the contents of the sanitary holding tank, under considerable pressure, to back up the pipe and flush through the compartment like some ill-fated tidal wave of shit.

Now panicked, the frightened prisoner tried to reach into the toilet bowl to stop the jammed valve and prevent further waste bilge from flooding the cubicle. Unfortunately, he had somehow gotten his hand stuck in the valve and was now head forward in the bowl, taking every new wave of excrement directly in the face. Traumatized with fear, he began kicking at the door and shrieking, when Sedgwick came upon the scene. Unable to open the latched door and mildly concerned that the man might die, thus interrupting his anticipated trounce with the nurses, Sedgwick most uncharacteristically chose to take extreme action. Freeing the fire axe from its case, he proceeded to chop the door into smithereens with all the gusto of Jack Nicholson.

And it got even bleaker. My young friend—bred with the conviction that no one outside the fifty-two states, especially no one "of colour", can ever do anything properly—began crying and burbling hysterically for "someone to stop this fuckin' nigger before he kills me." Needless to say, using this particular descriptive epithet would demonstrate poor character at best, but using it on a fake pirate ship plying the waters of the Caribbean Sea with a full complement of black people on board would never be in someone's best interests. Upon hearing these disparaging words, Sedgwick perfunctorily ceased his heroic efforts to free said victim, stuck his head through the gaping hole he'd cut in the door, smiled cheerily and said, "Hey, mon, can I be bringin' you another rum punch to wash down dem biscuits an' gravy?"

When we reached our homeport and were safely moored to the dockside, I ventured a peek through the now open hatchway, where the young lion lay amongst the feverishly working rescuers, all consumed by the considerable stench, and awash in the detritus. No one in that small space that day looked very happy. After the final extradition was completed, I must admit to looking on with restrained compassion as my friend was escorted down the gangway in shocked, disoriented silence, suddenly wrenched so far away from his rightful place and his roving band of plucky school fellows. For the moment at least, it looked as if he would never again go bounding into the university common with a white cardigan jauntily knotted about his shoulders trilling like a recent inductee to the Glee Club, "Tennis anyone?"

CHAPTER EIGHT

I STEP THROUGH THE HEAVY GLASS DOOR OF THE SPECIALTY CARS SHOP. My 1957 Ford Edsel is close by, which always makes me feel a bit feverish. It's a classic car, an oppressive reminder to the American corporate mentality of what failure really looks like in all its chromed splendor. Unlike a war-torn jungle rice paddy or faraway desert region replete with snot-nosed hollow-eyed orphans and keening black-shrouded mothers, or wheelchair-bound returning combatants, it is beautiful. However, despite its beauty, its engineering, while unparalleled at the time, failed on a scale unprecedented in American automotive industry history. Why? Bad timing. Although grand, there was no one to stand in line for such a car as my Edsel. Edsel, by the way, was the name of Henry Ford's eldest son, who died in his youth and never got to see what could really happen when America's appetite for Fords reached its full potential.

I am not one of those weekend car enthusiasts who unfolds his lawn chair in a Safeway parking lot or seasonally-vacated ice arena. I do not sit behind my pride and joy, ever watchful for a kid's sticky handprint or some bejeweled lady's pinkie ring causing untold irregularities to the constant and smooth lacquered sheen of the paint. It would be a bold-faced lie to say that I don't think these thoughts, and furl my brow with scornful grimaces when such thoughtless people approach. But alas, I'm not so far removed down the sentimental slick-sided tunnel of nostalgia, at this time anyway. The car is candy-apple red with gold flashing inserted into the side door panels. "Edsel" is emblazoned in an elegantly stylized, handwritten emblem in the center of the continental kit affixed to the rear bumper. The pristine interior leatherette is as shiny as an agate.

There is no one in the reception area when I enter. A small radio in the corner is on, the news announcer somberly droning that, "the hospital's critical care wing has been ordered closed, awaiting further tests confirming that the deadly flesh-eating virus contamination has been successfully eradicated. So far, five people, admitted over the past week for various supposed non- life threatening illnesses, have had their conditions down-graded to critical, but stable condition. The hospital spokesperson expressed guarded confidence regarding their complete recovery" As I wait to get the bill I peek expectantly into the rear garage area, thwarted from entering by the EMPLOYEES ONLY sign tacked above the small, smudged window on the door. I can see the front grill and wide, white sidewall tires on the front left side of the car. I feel like a kid picking up his first two-wheeler. I've been taking the car in for its annual servicing at Specialty Cars for the past five years. They enjoy a top-notch reputation for working on these old standards.

Finally Mike, the owner and head mechanic, emerges from the bathroom wiping his oily, hairy hands dry with a paper towel. He is a workingman and displays all of the telltale evidence of this singular, and for me, consummately reassuring fact. His thick body is as solid and barreled as an oaken cask beneath his faded blue coveralls. The years of accumulated oil residue and workplace grime have made his face, neck, and hands as burnished and shiny as a well-rubbed teak sideboard.

"Hi, Richard. How's things in the money game?"

He tells it like it is, revealing no guile or low-country judgments. Just straight-talk. In my mind, Mike is a good all around guy, even though we wouldn't have more than two words to share over a foaming glass of beer in some neighborhood pub, or anything useful to confide to one another if we were ever left standing beside the open grave of a recently deceased acquaintance. We can both take some small measure of comfort in knowing that deep down we probably like each other and enjoy our business relationship such as it is—even if we never actually consummate a legitimate friendship in any tangible way. I admit to having many of these quasi-relationships with a number of peripheral people in my daily life. Perhaps I am, as Genevieve and Dr. Sitwell have said from time to time, growing increasingly aloof. My daughter Emily is ever-watchful for these telltale signs of suppressed depression. She is mindful and dutiful in the extreme, perhaps making up for her wayward sister's complete disregard for her family's well being. I know people's names and some basic facts about their families and can occasionally even venture a guess as to their superficial likes and dislikes, but other than this, we're as isolated as floating islands in a tidal flood plain.

"If they were any better I'd have to complain about it," I quip, with as much *bon homie* as I can muster, since I know he doesn't seek details. Nor do I want to extend our exchange today beyond the stuff we're here to discuss, namely my car. I've got a pretty tight schedule to keep, and Mike's got other customers to please before he turns around the "*OPEN*" sign on the front door and departs up the Fraser Valley or south into the moist rich topsoil flats of a Richmond suburb to his wife and teenaged children, a cold beer and a good old-fashioned, much- deserved and appreciated home-cooked meal.

After quickly inspecting the work order and paying the hefty but always well-documented bill, I take the keys, walk over to the car, and swing open the solid metal door. Once settled onto the hard leatherette seat, I gently pull the door closed with a reassuring thud that clearly states this car was built at Ford in a bygone time when people still cared. As I nose out onto Burrard Street and head south towards the bridge I feel a rush of adrenaline pump through my veins. I listen studiously to the throaty guttural *chug, chug, chug* of the 390- horse powered v8 engine. The vaporized exhaust reverberates down through the two chrome tailpipes running directly from the manifolds past a matched set of Thrush Glass Pack Mufflers and out along the length of the car, like two ventilation stacks coming directly from Satan's own molten catalytic cracker. The sound says to one and all in no uncertain terms, "I'm not here for anyone's bullshit."

As I merge onto the Burrard Street Bridge, I notice the usual sidelong glances of appreciation for a symbol of what may or may not have been a better place and time. I am not an owner in the egocentric way of this thing that draws so much attention. I am, rather, simply a caretaker, not unlike the warden of a great park that takes his turn at the gate, protecting it and ensuring that something noteworthy from our fading past will remain intact for future eyes to behold.

At the apex of the bridge I glance westward, taking in the gunmetal gray luster of the ocean's undulating surface. The air today is thick with a moist residue that foretells more rain yet to come in this waning afternoon. I turn left onto Broadway, heading toward the optical shop to pick up my new reading glasses. As I drive past the crowded side streets with a forest of trees for names—Elm, Larch, Pine, —my heart suddenly skips a beat and my palms go dead cold and clammy. I could swear I saw a fleeting glimpse of my errant daughter disappearing down an alleyway beside Vancouver General Hospital. I crane my neck back toward the now increasingly distant spot. I can't quite see the alleyway any longer, due to the unrelenting stream of passing vehicles and my forward movement. I jam my foot on the brake, then equally as hard on the gas peddle, desperately searching the busy street for a spot to turn around or park. It's hopeless. There's no place to leave the car within eight blocks of the hospital. In a last-minute exasperated move, I edge it slowly up over the curb and leave it straddling the walkway and the entrance to an old house-turned-state-of-the-art medical specialist's office adjoining the hospital's northerly wing, all a part of the general one-stop health services plan promoted by governments at all levels. People passing on foot or in cars gawk at me as if I'm some lunatic gunman who, having stolen a classic car, is now illegally parking it in full view as he unleashes his righteous demands to cease giving abortions upon an as yet unwary doctor.

I run back down Broadway and cross on a red light, feeling the unimaginable alarm that only a parent can feel when suddenly confronted with the possibility of a face to face meeting with a lost child. My heart is pounding in my chest like a kettledrum. I'm acutely aware of its thump,

thump, thump as I turn up the alleyway, fearing she is long gone, or possibly I'm even more anxious that I will find her kneeling in a back doorway with her miniskirt hoisted high up her bruised and naked thighs as she capriciously sticks a needle into one of her last stalwart veins. What do I want, as her father possibly that she may become my child again. In the end I just want to take her into my arms and hold her and tell her that I'm here and all can still be well. I want to stand alongside her and fight the hordes of demons shrieking in her ears and cradle her shivering body under my coat against the warmth of my chest. I suppose, when all is said and done, and the good counsel of Dr. Sitwell is weighed and measured for its worth, I simply want to be her dad again and take her home.

I stop abruptly beside a large, rusted metal dumpster. She is no longer here, if she ever was. Gone. Lost. Vaporized. Snatched from my ever-hopeful outstretched arms. My breath is wheezing from my aching lungs, as if I've swallowed a whistle or child's nasal-toned kazoo. I gaze upon the insurmountable nothingness, the vacant plain of soiled asphalt, stinking refuse and weathered, crumbling brick —a testament to my failure as a father, a caretaker of despair instead of nurturer of hope. My shoulders sag. I am spent. I turn and slowly retrace my steps back to the car, forlorn, suddenly oblivious to the hustle and bustle around me.

As I approach the car, I see an odd grouping of pedestrians gathered around it. I have to drag myself back from the dazed fog of dejection that has engulfed me. I must stand ready to answer heated questions regarding my thoughtless, even careless, behavior. Owning a fancy car doesn't give me any more right than the next guy to park it askew on someone's front lawn or casually abandon it as I so please. But when I get closer I don't see the disgruntled gynecologist whose office routine I have disrupted or the barrel-chested security guard tapping his heavy stainless-steel flashlight against the flat of his open palm as fair warning that he is no stranger to whatever kind of shit I may be thinking of dishing up.

As I approach, I see instead, a large dog, possibly a Mastiff-Rottweiler-Husky cross, and three men, two of whom are obviously challenged by some unnamed mental affliction, standing by the car. This is not the result of their having suffered a high-speed car crash or some recent industrial accident that a prolonged rehabilitation will help alleviate. I would suspect that it is rather the possible result of an oxygen-rich umbilical cord turned suffocating traitor, cutting off life-sustaining nutrition to their now compromised brains. Maybe the blame lies with an errant doctor and his failure to properly plunge a clogged airway or mucous-plugged nostril soon enough. In the end it could be as innocuous as an infinitesimal chromosome whose ambiguous priming mechanism inexplicably jammed, like a cartridge misfiring in the breach of a gun. Whatever the disheartening cause, the result is standing before me now. One of the trio is huge and oafish; the other is tiny, his somewhat contorted body twisted into a sideways stance, with his feet pointing one way and his upper body another. He holds a soaking handkerchief in his flailing outstretched hand and appears to be attempting to dab an endless stream of spittle foaming from his slackened mouth. The remaining man—a young anemically thin studious-looking fellow with a full beard that attaches seamlessly to his equally tangled head of unkempt hair—is attempting, with obvious difficulty, to place an advertising flyer into the big guy's tightly clenched fists, while at the same time instructing the twisted little geyser of sputum to stand away from the car. He is also trying to disentangle the dog's leash from all of their legs. None of these, including the dog, are cooperating in the least. The smaller out-patient has now taken it upon himself to hug the passenger-side front panel of my car, placing both of his ill-controlled, twitching arms around it, as if it were some gigantic toy he's trying to lift and take home for his further enjoyment.

Needless to say this scene is not the perfect ending to an already troubling moment in my life. I approach with as much casual jocularity in my voice as I can muster. I quickly adopt the guise of an innocent chap who "would love to stay and chat but really must be off to some good works at the local community center. And, yes, isn't it strange that we haven't bumped into each other before at some telethon or the March of Dimes Annual Walk for the Children. We must all do our bit if we have any hope of broadening the public's awareness of such tragic, yet with proper support, manageable maladies."

Instead, I say, "Hi. Nice day" to the man I presume to be in charge, then turn to the little fellow who hasn't let go of my car's fender and add, "Do you want to take my car home?" feigning a goodhearted chortle as I inspect the globules of sputum accumulating on my diamond-hard hood. No sooner are these words out of my mouth than he whirls around and lurches toward me, thrusting both of his spastic, octopus arms up in the air like a crazed maestro about to conduct the Brandenburg Concerto. He then clamps them around my neck before I can lift my hands to defend myself. Through the waterfall of saliva he's trying to say something to me that I can't make out.

For assistance, I turn to the counselor, who is busy patting the dog's head and cooing, "What a good boy, Shrek. What a good boy you are," as the dog sits down beside his leg and begins slapping its tail on the sidewalk. The man gripping my neck has laid his head against my chest affectionately as if we are about to begin some lewd tango dance, and is gurgling more unintelligible endearments at my throat.

The young man trying to manage the duo now turns from me and my immediate dilemma back toward the big fellow assertively grabbing hold of his arms—which this large bruin continues to hold tightly against his chest with the intensity of someone trying to staunch a gaping wound in his thorax and proceeds to pull him toward me, saying over and over to the smaller octopus at my throat, "Jerome, I know it's nice, but remember your rules about *touching*." He then looks at me, speaking with the quiet, off-hand tone of someone who assumes this sort of thing is everyday behaviour, a challenge that we should all embrace this opportunity to be part of the solution of mainstreaming rather than continuing the practice of *exclusion*. "I'm teaching Jerome and Wally to gain further independence through practical work experience."

He turns to big Wally, as if seeking reinforcement for this statement. However, Wally has now started making strange panicked noises that sound like a giant Australian rodent's *Eek- eek-eek* and, in his heightened agitation, has begun to physically bob his massive head back and forth like someone dodging a handful of peas being thrown in his face.

"Wally and Jerome are delivering these flyers to all the businesses along Broadway today. Aren't you?" he continues, seemingly unfazed by Wally's mounting agitation. Turning to me from his cursory and obviously disapproving once-over of the car he adds as an afterthought, "Those old dinosaurs aren't environmentally friendly, you know. They're the worst example of our heedless pillaging of the Earth-Mother-Provider."

Yes, thank you for your opinion. "And maybe we can go and have a cup of Indian Chai while a crack team of eco-terrorists dismantles the car" is what I'd like to say, but don't.

Then the unthinkable happens. Wally breaks free of his caregiver's grasp and attaches himself onto my back like a giant troll. Now, both my arms are pinned tightly to my sides so that my only possible mobility is to winkle my fingers. He towers over me by a good foot and must weigh close to three hundred gelatinous pounds. I am now completely encased in babbling, gurgling humanity. The young man in charge continues to look at my car, as if preparing his next indictment of, my thoughtless kind.

No longer trying to mask my concerns I blurt out, "Can you please do something here, buddy? Are these people dangerous in any way?"

He looks at me with mild academic sincerity and says, "No, don't worry. Jerome is just overly friendly, but Wally has a touch of psycho-pathic behavior associated with his retardation and schizophrenia. Try not to struggle. It will only heighten his agitation and possibly provoke a complete meltdown. But don't worry. Just stay immobile and he'll cool off." And then he says, as if I give a shit, "He got upset with me because I asked him to deliver his pamphlet to the medical research office over there. He's scared of stairs and gets angry whenever anyone tries to make him climb them." He now releases the Mastiff-Rottweiler-Husky from his leash, adding, "They like Shrek. Maybe he will distract them."

As soon as Shrek is freed from his master, he bounds over to us with his tail wagging and panting tongue extended and mounts my leg with a zeal that indicates he, like me, has been denied female companionship for quite some time. I suppose in his doggy mind he thinks this is a game similar to ones they might play back at the sheltered workshop or rehab center. Without pausing, the manic Wally hoists me into the air like a store mannequin. With Jerome still clinging to my chest and Shrek continuing his excited humping motion against my calf, he carries us off the sidewalk into the path of oncoming traffic.

Finally, as if suddenly becoming aware of the potential seriousness of the situation in front of him and maybe even (like me) fearing the worst, the young man jumps into action and signals the speeding cars traveling in both directions to come to a stop. He is hopeful that this will allow us to gain the safety of the sidewalk once again.

"Wally," he now more sternly entreats, "you can't stay on the road. You know the cars are dangerous. Come back onto the sidewalk *now*."

Horns begin to honk and Shrek, having released his grip on my leg, starts barking in excitement as if wanting someone to throw his ball. The loud sounds suddenly unleash some yet unseen dark spirits within Wally's cross-circuiting electrical mainframe. He now starts squeezing me with Herculean strength while continuing to stand frozen in the middle of the road.

I call out, "For chrissake, do something!"

The counselor instantly whips out a Baby Ruth chocolate bar and waves it temptingly in the air above his head. "Wally, look what I have. Chockies!"

Wally suddenly swivels his massive frame, including the elfin Jerome, who continues to hold on as if we're all having great fun on some wild circus ride, and me. As swiftly as Wally began his hostage-taking, he abandons it absently, dropping us back, flatfooted onto the pavement. He lumbers forward like a trained bear who has spied a honey pot swinging from an upper branch. With a deft swipe of his hand, he snatches the chocolate bar and shreds the wrapper, smiling with glee. Like a pilot fish gliding beside a formidable Great White Shark, Shrek follows suit, positioning himself beguilingly next to Wally's tree-trunk leg, eager for the chance to lick the wrapper or snag a vagrant crumb.

I awkwardly manage to maneuver my salivating carbuncle passenger back onto the curb and with newfound determination lift both my hands and break Jerome's finger-lock around the nape of my neck without further incident. I then turn to the counselor, who is slowly shepherding his flock back toward the knapsack full of flyers. I call breathlessly after him in righteous condemnation, "Those two should be properly sedated before you take them out. Maybe you should carry restraints in that bag instead of social manifestos. And get that goddamned dog spayed. He's a menace!"

I have no interest in pressing charges or lingering here to debate our opposite views on social responsibility, so I quickly retrieve my keys and regain control of my car. I back cautiously off the curb and, without further incident, rejoin the flow of traffic. As I drive past the trio, they all turn to watch my car. Shrek is barking his goodbyes. Wally and Jerome offer discombobulated waves, like two Jack-In-The-Boxes whose springs have extended far past their functional capability.

CHAPTER NINE

I STRAIGHTEN MY CLOTHES AND FLATTEN MY TUSSLED HAIR AS I ENTER the small, glaring confines of the optical shop. The tall, young fellow who is apprenticing under the calm, watchful eye of the owner stands and greets me with an exaggerated flamboyance that extends well past mere professional courtesy. This young man possesses an abundance of whatever the opaque quality is that separates the heterosexual male from the homosexual. He may as well be wearing a codpiece or have a feathered boa draped coquettishly around his long slender neck. The owner is an old queen as well. As the young man approaches me, his arms partially scissor open. For an instant I am afraid he's going to embrace me or, at the very least, give me a playful peck on the cheek. But instead, his wide eyes are focused on the front of my shirt. Glancing over my shoulder at the day outside for confirmation, he exclaims in theatrical alarm, "My gawd, you're sopping. Has it started to downpour again?"

I look down at my shirtfront and see that it is indeed wringing wet from the gusher of slime that Jerome spewed onto my person. "Not yet," I volunteer. "I just caught the end of an outburst of sorts." I volunteer no more details.

He ushers me to the swivel chair positioned directly in front of one of the small oval examination mirrors and motions me to be seated. As he turns to retreat, he extracts a couple of facial tissues from a box with two quick flicks of his wrist and, handing them to me adds, "You should really get out of those clothes as soon as possible before you catch your death of cold."

It's nothing that the better part of a martini shaker filled to its brim with a meniscus of vodka and crushed ice won't help, I think to myself, but say nothing to further this exchange.

As I sit waiting for my prescription and looking at my face reflected in the small mirror, my mind reverts to Cuba and what may be waiting to greet me upon my arrival.

The Cuban deal is a conundrum for me. The complexity of a three pronged venture is unsettling. Does the world really need another resort with its bamboo thatch turnstile welcoming and dispatching pale, dimple-thighed patrons from afar, the Cuban workers hearing our veiled criticisms more often each day as they clear tables of dishes or snap crisp, new, linen bed sheets neatly into place?

"Yes, siree, Bob. The beaches are top notch, but the staff training is questionable, and "five star" it ain't!"

Will a bio-research facility turn the island's impoverished people—children included—into test subjects for drugs that may or may not benefit mankind? A clattering dust-belching, remorseless, open-pit mine, whose appetite for raw materials will pockmark the distant tranquil hillsides like cannon shot — is this the best available answer to their poverty?

On the other side of the equation, the global quest for jobs. Jobs that can wash the wanton face of soul-searing poverty from the crumbling back streets of Havana and the country villages near and far.

What to do? I truly don't know. I have sat with these people of the revolution, their small, tattered rooms and tarnished, threadbare furnishings silent witnesses to how long the battle has been fought since the last gunshot's echo. All this spells out one inescapable reality for me—trouble! I've been down these uncharted back roads before—Kazakhstan, Thailand, China Croatia. And now, *bon dias hola* Cuba. Nothing works in this entire, enigmatic place! No one has actually tried to do something in half a century, for fear of getting their noggins blown off. The greater fear is that it won't end up looking like the picture in the glossy marketing magazine, setting ten thousand lights a-flicker as it promised in the engineering manual. Why take the chance? Better to stay put. Whenever a financing project places me in the stark face of despotism—whether from the fanatical right or the somber left—it always reinforces the age-old experience of the failed gods of totalitarianism. If you want to make something tick, tick, tick, you've got to have the dough and the cohones to let it ride once in awhile. And these ham-handed, heavy-fisted guys just don't get it. Increasingly of late, I have moments when I think, to hell with Cuba. I have my own burdens to bear. After all, am I not the husband and father who let treacherous gremlins in the house during my watch?

CHAPTER TEN

I'M BACK AT 777 BEACH VIEW PLACE. HOME. BACK IN THE FOLD. SAFELY closeted in my own reassuring concrete turret, nestled against the abiding, consoling shores of the sea. Although so much of my time is spent out and about, I am, in many ways that I can see growing steadily with each passing year, a homebody. I venture forth each day as a hunter when, in fact, I would prefer to adopt the gatherer's mantle. But today, that's not an option.

I immediately take off my clothes and stand naked in front of the mirror for a moment, mentally cataloguing the further deterioration that is the disheartening evidence of my encroaching age: the softened, drooping pectorals promising the sullen approach of male breast syndrome; slightly slackened biceps; shrunken penis poking its head out of its wrinkled neck, like a shy and taciturn tortoise; and my increasingly hairless legs, looking more like a turkey's with each passing year. I turn on the shower faucets and stand shivering on the soft white bath mat, letting the water warm up before stepping into the wide, glass-fronted cubicle, the charcoal tint dulling the bathroom light's glare. The shower, inviting as a steaming hot-spring cave, promises the comfort and quiet I seek.

Although I am usually in and out of the shower in less than two minutes, today I stand under the hot spray for what seems like an eternity. After this, feeling rejuvenated or at the very least, more comfortable, I dry my hair allowing a scolding smile to cross my lips. I reflect upon the absurd pathos of my afternoon. No doubt, the rambunctious Wally and Jerome are back at the group home, safe and sound and receiving bountiful praise from their caseworkers for a day's work well done. I picture them seated side by side with blunted wooden spoons in hand, their bibs smartly fastened around their rubbery necks, worn with all the pride of regimental ascots on a fusilier's parade uniform. They are dunking their digestive cookies into steamy plastic cups of hot cocoa. With any luck, they are at peace with their world and readying themselves for an evening of pasting colorful stickers onto scrap pages or shaping play dough into Gumby-like characters with stories all their own.

I put on my robe and wander into the living room. I push and hold the starter button on the gas fireplace and hear the reassuring solenoid's click, click, click, signaling the release of a measured spume of gas into the electric ignition's teasing arc. I now watch in timeless fascination as the gas light's bluish flame spreads across the grainy surface of the porcelain logs. It would behoove me to stay right here for the rest of the night, but duty insists that I keep my word , to myself, and attend the open house Narcotics Anonymous Meeting at 6:00 P.M. My conviction is based on the premise that any action produces a like and equal reaction, that if I start a random, seemingly disassociated process leading to my daughter's possible recovery — even if she is unaware of this process — she will be mysteriously drawn to it like a moth to light through the subliminal power inherent in its very existence. Dr. "M" would probably say the obvious— that my priming an imaginary pump and positioning a possible escape hatch in a vacuum oblivious to Tess isn't helping her in the least. I said her name, something that I have rarely been able to do. I think of her as my daughter of many sorrows, or my wayward, tragic child. My folly. My pain. But rarely, of late, as simply my daughter Tess. I guess Dr. Sitwell would conclude that these omissions and empty gestures are all about *me* and my own bugaboos. Maybe all of this is as accurate as a sniper's bullet. Perhaps it does portend to something about myself that I've got to work on? If so, so be it. I will light the lamp tonight and place it in my window facing out to sea and wait to hear the clanging of the bell that summons each of us down to the shore when the shipwrecked are cast before our feet.

Before I get dressed, I want to call Emily, the daughter who is neither a drug addict nor a thorn in the side of anything. On the contrary, she is a dutiful and supportive person in every respect. Paradoxically, that is what makes it so hard for me to talk with her as often as I'd like. She has become a constant stabbing reminder to me of how disappointing her sister really is. Of course, none of this rationale is fair or even remotely close to what most would consider "normal" thinking, but, alas, it is what it is.

Emily has two children upon whom both Genevieve and I dote. They live in the interior of British Columbia, so we get to see them fairly regularly. Not now, of course, since Genevieve lives in Iceland, but I still see them every couple of months and I'm certain that Genevieve speaks with them on the phone every week or so. We both enjoyed watching the kids go through their teething, toddling, tottering stages, the proud grandparents.

I dial expectantly, awaiting either the voice of my daughter or the intermittent speech of one of the two kids fading in and out as they manipulate the telephone receiver to and fro, not yet fully grasping which end should be put to their mouths and which to their ears. Emily answers.

"Hi, sweetie. It's Dad. Just checking in before I go away to see that you guys are all a-okay."

I always try to sound as chipper as possible for these calls and when we get together because I know she worries about her downfallen sister as much, and perhaps more, than my wife and I do. There's really no way of knowing what anyone else's pain or joy really is, since we are captives of our own little bailiwicks. However, I am, to everyone's surprise, including my own, a traditional father in many ways and want to put the best foot forward with my children. I want for them to take some small comfort in knowing that if everything goes for a colossal poop, a safe haven awaits them and theirs, ignoring, of course, dismal fact that my wife has left me and my other child is doing abhorrent things in some unknown place and I may be facing professional sanctions and criminal charges at work. Despite all this, I believe they feel I can be depended upon to "stay the course."

"Hi, Dad. I was just thinking about you. When you're back, can we get together for a family weekend thing?" She doesn't mention my birthday, which is kind of her, since she knows full well it is not something I want to even acknowledge let alone celebrate. This does not mean that she will not willingly conspire with my neighbours or other family friends to create a big splash, but simply means that she will not tease me with details that I may find noisome at the moment.

I love this little chat and am glad that I called. "Sure can, dear. I'm back a week from tomorrow. Let's all get together for a good old time."

This is intended to instill some measure of mock frivolity into both our days, although it falls a bit flatter than I'd like, because almost half of the "all of us" won't be getting together and won't even be extending the courtesy of letting us know exactly why.

"Okay, let me work on it while you're gone," she volunteers obligingly. "Do you want to come here or should we go there?"

I ponder this for a second, running through any possible biases I may have for either. There are none.

"It doesn't matter to me. Whatever suits you guys. You've got the bigger party to organize and move. Figure out if you want a taste of the big city. If not, I can come there and keep it simple."

She thinks about this, weighing the pros and cons before answering. She has always had this quality of truthfulness and openness that I greatly admire and would like to have more of myself.

"Let me talk to Jaco and let you know. He's been working hard lately and may want a bit of the city life to remind him that he's still alive."

Emily and Jack have a solid marriage that's built on mutual consideration and love, evidenced in one small way by her continuing to call him "Jaco" with her voice dropping slightly, as if calling a wayward rascal back from some mischief. She knows and loves and more importantly, accepts his boyish ways as part and parcel of his nature. This nickname is an endearment most married people drop from their vocabulary with time's passing, the routine of our lives insidiously robbing us of most of our youthful spontaneity. Not so with Emily. I know he relishes this because she says it with the same saucy admiration she showed lo those many years ago when she was still his sweetheart and he her knight. Any man throughout history would stand a bit taller having this small, poignant validation of himself from his woman. It warms my heart that I have such a daughter.

The kids are at pre-school, so I don't get a chance to talk with them. My daughter and I go through the usual "What's new?" without mentioning sister or mother and then sign off on a cheery heartfelt note. I believe this is a further testament to her strong character. She never asks any questions about my relationship with her mother or for any knowledge I might have about her sister. These subjects are not broached unless I introduce them first. . No news is just that, no news, so why beat that horse? Besides, she may be in regular contact with her mother. I hope so. She may even talk to her sister occasionally, which I doubt, but I don't ask. We understand each other.

Dr. Martha Sitwell would say that understandings such as this are good and productive, as long as they remain open and transparent. I understand her point because I am sometimes hesitant about such things, uncertain of how close we as humans actually get to anyone, or to anything for that matter. This may be shameful, I know, but still true. I have felt these strong attachments about other family members, both with us and departed, and I must admit to having been drawn up short on occasion by their overall lack of redemptive powers. Take my father's suicide and my older brother Ethan's sudden spiral into lunacy. Ethan is currently whiling away his days under lock and key in a federally administered detention facility for — I shudder to even think it — the criminally insane. Add to this my wife's and daughter's emotional and physical exit. While these stories of abiding grief may serve as painful reminders to us all concerning the hidden gulfs and wide emotional chasms between each of us, both are too painful and too farcical to open for discussion at this time. Let's just say, "let sleeping dogs lie" for now. No harsh judgments or preconceptions about the family unit's overall stability. I think that anyone jigging together a family history for future generations may be well advised to place a footnote here and there to describe a wayward uncle or black-sheep niece. These reminders may be even better served by simply stating that these things happen in all families, and more often than not, in the best of families.

One night in late November the phone awakened us rattling loudly through the stillness of our bedroom. It must have been five or six years ago now. The phone was on Genevieve's side of the bed. I remember this because it seemed to take her an eternity to retrieve it from its cradle. After the sudden jolt of being yanked from a deep and peaceful sleep I was momentarily annoyed at her for taking so long to answer it, my heart and mind already racing through the numbing list of crisis' and accidents that could now be as close to us as the stranger's voice on the other end of the line — a nameless voice that may change our lives forever. Instead it was Emily. She was at a party and Tess was there, she simply said that she thought it would be best if we came and picked up her sister. I recall Genevieve reciting these exact words that, "it would be best" as if it was someone describing directions to a picnic in the park or maybe telling you what cheese would go with a particular vintage of wine. We scrambled into our clothes without combing our hair or fastening all of our various buttons, looking like a woebegone couple emerging from an overturned car or flaming building, the unforeseen emergency stripping us of any sense of vanity or pride. As we drove to the location Emily had given we didn't speak to each other beyond a few mumbled questions or veiled critical comments that came dangerously close to the opening volley of an argument, our frayed nerves lying exposed and raw upon the surface of the darkened night's skin. We were scared and we were both becoming experienced enough in the troubles of parenting a problem-child to know that this kind of fear in a married couple's minds was always hovering close to an angry, regrettable outburst that wouldn't help the situation or the relationships in the least. When we got to the address there were a bunch of kids roaming up and down the street among the glut of parked or idling cars. The popping sound of beer bottles breaking on the pavement empha- sized the tension within us, like the sudden sound of gunfire. The house itself was ablaze with lights and commotion as if this otherwise quiet neighbourhood had suddenly decided that an all-night pizza place or teen dance hall would be a good addition to the block of otherwise lifeless aged houses, a chance to liven things up. Emily and a nice looking young guy who seemed both courteous and genuinely protective of Emily's interests stepped out of the darkness in front of my car so that I came to a stop in the middle of the street. His name was Rick. I have never seen him again, but for some reason can never forget this — strange, when considered beside all of the other names of close colleagues and acquaintances that are now lost to me over the intervening years. They both came around to my side and quickly told me that they had heard about this party and arrived an hour before. When they got through the maze of drunks and loiterers scattered across the lawn and up the stairs they had bad vibes about the scene and were going to leave. It was then that Emily saw her sister seated in the living room. She was flanked by a couple of hard-nosed looking punks that weren't from their school or their immediate circle of friends. Tess was either very drunk or stoned because her head was lolling over against one of these guy's chests. She was definitely not in control of herself or her situation. In the car we decided that Genevieve and Emily and her boyfriend should remain here with the cell phone at the ready in case there was trouble and that I would go in and see if I could find Tess and get her outside as quickly as possible. I also left the car running and told Genevieve to slide over behind the wheel incase anything went wrong placing them in more danger than we were probably already in. I remember looking at them as I exited the car and thinking this, how had it happened that one of my children would place us into a situation like this, with all of the explosive combustion we recognized from news stories about teens running amok bludgeoning neighbours and kindly strangers with the indifference of rodent control personnel stomping on pesky bugs. I walked up the front steps between groupings of indolent young men and their animated girlfriends, flailing their skeletal arms in exaggerated descriptions of barroom confrontations or hip-hop get-togethers. Some of the boys looked at me with passive befuddled expressions pasted on their sullen faces, while others gazed more pointedly with the quirky, edginess of someone that is being pushed beyond their breaking point. I focused my stare straight ahead, without intentionally making direct eye contact with anyone. Once through the door I was confronted with a pulsing mass of people gyrating to and froe like a human wave of heads and torsos and arms gone berserk. The music was loud with the bass drum's rhythms moving up through the floor and continuing up my shins with the intensity of an industrial vibrating sander. It didn't take me long to find Tess. She was where Emily had said, curled up against the chest of someone that quite frankly scared the bejeezus out of me. He was a big mean looking man well into his twenties. He had a bandanna around his head, two large gold earrings and was wearing a thin black mesh muscle shirt that exposed rippling biceps and bulky chiseled shoulder muscles that even in repose were as ripped as someone emerging between the ropes of Wrestle Mania or a Hulk Hogan family reunion television Christmas special. I assessed the best approach was to simply push through the throng and take my daughter into my arms and exit without saying anything to anyone. No explanations or momentary lulls in forward motion, showing this man and his home-boys that there was the slightest hesitation in my resolve. And this is exactly what I did. I picked her up as if she were a feather pillow. I remember that she opened her eyes and looked at me and smiled dumbly like she was glad to see me and unfazed about wherever I was taking her. The guy whose shoulder she was resting on looked up at me for a second with the indifference an assassin might show to his target. His expression said both 'who the fuck are you' and 'it's more trouble to get my butt up off this couch for this sorry piece of ass than it is to snag another one later on tonight.' Anyway, he didn't make a move or protest in any way beyond this infinitesimal acknowledgement, and I exited without incident. We drove home in silence not knowing then, that rather than being one of those pivotal events that many parents and children experience and come to know as a positive turning point in their relationships allowing both to open up and share their feelings, this was simply the first of many such harrowing midnight scenes throughout the next few years that would jolt us like repeated electric shocks, these mournful wounds continuing to lay exposed and raw until this very night.

⋆

I suppose now is as good a time as any to write Genevieve a quick note letting her know my whereabouts for the coming week. Although we don't speak as often as I would like, we both make a point of letting the other know where we are and what we're doing. I sit down at my computer and hastily type my message.

Hello out there. It's me again speaking to you from afar. I just wanted to let you know that I'll be away for the coming week on business. The Cuban deal may be finally reaching the contract stage so I'm going to Havana to set things up. Everything comes to he who waits, as they say. Wish me luck. I hope all is going well there. Give your parents and the rest of the family my best. Take good care of yourself and be strong.

Your loving husband,
Richard

PS *I almost forgot. I'm going to a Narcotics Anonymous Meeting tonight. Hopefully it will tell me something that may help. I'll keep you close.* There. Personal without being needy. Informative, but not cold. I push the "send button". I would have liked to say more about my life and what I am thinking about but don't. I'd rather save these personal things for a warm chat on the phone. I can do this when I'm back from Cuba and hopefully brimming with good news on one front at least.

I slide the heavy, glass clothes closet door open and look around for something suitable to wear to a Narcotics Anonymous meeting. I don't want to appear too "well to do," since I suspect many in attendance will be somewhat down on their luck, having squandered away family fortunes on stimulants and depressants. Yet, I also want to let it be known that I am okay with all of this and pass no harsh judgments, and abide in the knowledge that these kinds of unfortunate debacles visit folks from every walk of life. I choose a pair of tan casual pants, a sky-blue shirt, and sleeveless, dark navy fleece vest. This, with brown socks and Dockers, will betray a hint of athleticism in my life and show an underlying confidence that says I am at the ready for whatever curveballs life may throw my way. Once dressed, I must pop next door to Randy and Clive's to drop off the keys and run through the usual list of what-to-do's and what-not-to-do's before taking off in the wee fragile hours of tomorrow morning.

Having lived in the building for over ten years, I can say with all honesty that Randy and Clive are two of the best neighbors anyone could have. Then, down the hall, on the other side, are Run and Ida Skudmore with their yappy, little terrier Lei Lei. They are relentless ambassadors of gloom, who never let a pin drop or a smudge appear on the hallway or foyer carpets without sounding an alarm bell that the condo council isn't doing its job or complaining that a bewildered fellow tenant is in gross violation of some ambiguous building bylaw. People have actually vacated the premises in exasperation after suffering Run and Ida's systematic badgering and verbal assaults brought on by some alleged, trumped-up misdemeanor. Each floor has only three suites, which is nice for most things, but anonymity is not one of them.

It was actually Genevieve who first met and introduced me to Clive and Randy. On the day we moved in, they presented themselves at our door with a basket containing Clive's own crumble cake, a small quarter-pound package of the darkest and most aromatic African coffee I have ever tasted, a magical bouquet of snap dragons and Irish heather, deftly arranged by Randy; and a small, wicker box lined with excelsior and filled with assorted squat bottles and flat jars of facial creams and abrasive skin cleansers from their sample cases for a line of health products marketed under the Oh So Smooth label. When I arrived, the three were all squeezed together thigh-to-thigh on the one available couch. They each held mismatched mugs of herbal tea and were gabbling away mirthfully like co-conspirators in a farcical Noel Coward play. I suspect the comfortable bond that often exists between homosexual men and beautiful women may be forged from the mutual blast furnace of apprehension as to how the rest of the world will ultimately decide to view them and, perhaps more importantly, use them.

Randy and Clive are senior sponsors in Oh So Smooth, which distributes products touted as being as friendly to the good health and youthful appearance of your skin, as anti-bacterial toothpastes are to the general, all-around mouth and gum hygiene and brightness of your teeth. Oh So Smooth is a network marketing organization. The world of network marketing is a hierarchical structure whose aristocracy is positioned on the "up-line," supposedly as close to the founders as possible, and whose "down-line" is subject to the usual pecking order disdain visited upon the newcomer to the office or the late entrant in the race. Subsequently, a great deal of Randy and Clive's time, both at home and away, is dedicated to the nurturing and what they passionately refer to as "viral marketing" of these products. This, in a nutshell, means the necessity to constantly expand their down-line sponsors like a cancerous mass, in order to retain their hallowed position as senior sponsors. All of this requires them to be continually hosting social get-togethers called "home parties" by the people at Oh So Smooth, in their condo. At these gatherings, they encourage their existing distributors to get off their duffs and become evangelical about making the world's skin as soft as a baby's bottom. They are also the honored poobahs at public gatherings called, Educational Sponsor Seminars, in hotel conference rooms. At these functions they stand in front of a room filled with glassy-eyed converts, and whomever these people have managed to coral into attending with them, and brag about how great their lives are now that they are securely positioned in the Oh So Smooth family. They also hint at the outrageous amounts of money they are making. It's against the laws governing possible pyramid marketing schemes to say any actual numbers, but the epidemic of viral marketing insinuates huge incomes quite effectively through constant whisper campaigns. They always close their presentations with a challenge to these new people. The direct question is posed as to why they have so foolishly chosen ambiguous lives of meaningless drudgery over taking their rightful places making big loot and enjoying the lifestyle and community respect associated with high rollers. They mercilessly berate these misplaced underachievers, bullying them to snap to it and wise up, and see the light before it's too late and some other smart cookie snatches the Oh So Smooth prize.

With all the hoopla aside, Randy and Clive do make inordinate sums of money through their involvement in Oh So Smooth. This, I think, is partially due to the seductive note that this type of anti-aging song sings in the gay community's collective ear. The benefits of the products themselves, aside from the wealth-spawning pyramidal compensation structure and all its siren possibilities, are said to be derived from the wholesome ingredients and manufacturing methods employed by the company. The creams, potions, and balms are made from the purest nuclei of whole grains, germinated in golden sun-spanked fields void of animal offal or other debilitating contaminants claimed to be found in non-organic farming. These "cures" boast such additives as the mucous membrane of a reclusive, Amazonian frog's egg sac, and the stem cell-laden jelly of a newborn lamb's glossy, restorative placenta.

Through my friendship with Randy and Clive, I can more clearly see the gay community and the plight that diseases such as HIV-AIDS have wreaked upon their combined psyche. This alone may be the engine driving their slavish need to defy all probabilities and champion good health and wellness. They are fighters, even though their odds are decidedly negative.

Anyway, the trio welcomed me without reservation into their little tittering cabal,

and we four became fast friends. When it became evident that Clive was HIV-positive, it was Genevieve who took charge of his medication regimen and devoured the most current research circulars and monthlies she could access through her medical affiliations. She then patiently and lovingly explained to both Clive and the distraught Randy what could be expected next. For months they huddled in our living room shoring each other up with hugs, their hands interlaced on each other's laps. Despite all of this stress Randy and Clive have managed, with the sheer grit of vaudeville stumpers, to parlay their use of Oh So Smooth products into one of the most influential, non-pharmaceutical contributors to their apparently valiant resistance against the onslaught of full-blown AIDS. These two guys are marketing gladiators.

And it was they, above all others, who rallied around Genevieve when it became obvious that she was slipping beneath the charcoal gray waters of our "daughter trouble." Like a medical alert response team, they shuffled down the hallway, toting plates of home baking and crock pots full of healing stews or thick, traditional Icelandic seafood bisques. I can say with unabashed sincerity that we have weathered our storms together. No matter what the world has in store for us in the future, we will all look upon these bonds and these shared times with a real and everlasting appreciation.

It is Clive who opens their door. He's thinner than I'd like to see him, but this has happened before with his disease. A slight alteration of his meds and a good old-fashioned blood transfusion, complemented with much ballyhooed generous applications of Oh So Smooth, usually brings him back with a bang within days. He must walk a hard path, but he does so with a heroic and, despite his garrulous ass-kicking personality, understated panache. I secretly suspect he is in fairly regular telephone or email communication with Genevieve regarding his therapy. I also believe they have sworn each other's secrecy on this matter so I won't feel resentful or hurt by their continued dialogue given that I'm somewhat adrift at the moment. I feel no resentment whatsoever and, in fact, take some comfort in the hope that their mutual needs may be helping to reinforce their resolve to carry on.

"Well, look what the cat's dragged in!" Clive calls over his shoulder to Randy, who at this point is out of sight. "Come in, come in, you silly boy. What in hell's name has that butcher done to your hair? How many times have I told you to let me cut it for you," he chides me with a good-natured poke in the ribs, dabbing the side of my head as though visualizing a more suitable cut and color. "Mr. Big Stuff broker here can't abide coming next door for his *eau de toilette*, eh?"

Now, Randy pops out from around the corner wearing an apron over his casual, cream-colored cotton jumpsuit. He is stout in the roly-poly sort of way that British poofters from old BBC comedies were often portrayed. He carries a glass of red wine in one hand and a large stainless-steel mixing spoon in the other.

"Richy." He beams with genuine excitement. "Just the lab rat I've been hoping for to try my *risotto con pesto*."

Genevieve used to crack up hysterically whenever one of us shared a story of "dropping in" to their apartment because no matter what hour of the day or evening, there was always some major cooking fest or social gathering or tiddlywinks tournament taking place that demanded your immediate attention and quite often unfettered assistance. Whenever she interrupted a home party for Oh So Smooth, Randy couldn't help but introduce her as a visiting doctor involved in medical research. He would never claim she was an Oh So Smooth representative, but would let the testimonial-hungry spool of down-line viral thought roll in that direction. Genevieve, although not happy about this, would remain mum, with the mutual understanding that the boys' marketing spiel wouldn't include her or her impressive credentials any further.

Randy and Clive live on some off-the-wall, twenty-four-hour clock that has no set times for breakfasts or dinners or even sleep. They always run with the throttle wide open. Experience has taught me that it is absolutely pointless to even try to beg off lightly from whatever maelstrom is drawing its vortex around your ankles upon entrance to "The Casa," as they both call it. The best that one could hope regarding an early exit was to join in on the sidelines for a bit and slip away when no one was looking.

"And how are my two favorite kooks today?" I ask with a playful glint in my eye because I know how much they treasure the idea of being known as the eccentrics of the building, and rightly so, for they have earned it in spades.

They strike a side-by-side pose, affecting disapproval and say in unison, "Whhelll! And this from the Birthday Boy no less! We all can't come out of the same cookie-cutter mold, darling, so why don't you put that where the monkey hid the peanut."

I don't even bother confronting them regarding any clandestine planning that may be afoot regarding my approaching birthday. It would do no good at best, and at worst, would only further fan their flames of party-arranging resolve. We exchange pats on the back and arm-around-the-waist greetings and shuffle into the living room. There, I run through the basics regarding the household chores. Tasks that they've done a hundred times before. We sit for what I am adamant must be a short moment since I'm running late and want to be on time for the Narcotics Anonymous Meeting at six o'clock. No matter what our conversation, we all share the painful knowledge of life's little quirks. Both our houses have experienced their fair share of pain and sorrow of late. These mutual sorrows escape in our glances and sidelong looks despite the often raucous good-time japes coming out of our mouths. This can make me very sad at times, and I fear that it may have the same effect on them. Although it is comforting to have such intimate bonds with other people it is also an unsettling reminder, like some distant bell calling to each and all, that we are but mortal and our place here on earth is not leased for long. It was the poet Yeats that prophetically mouthed, "Man has created death.." With all of this gloom aside, our little visit goes well.

Finally, after many lingering goodbyes I am back at my condo to pick up a brochure, notepad and pen. As the doors to the elevator close, I feel the usual sense of relief at not having crossed paths with Run or Ida Skudmore, or witnessed the muzzle flash of little Lei Lei's trajectory past the sliding doors, like a flare ominously bursting upon the otherwise stilled horizon.

CHAPTER ELEVEN

FORTUNATELY, THE NARCOTICS ANONYMOUS MEETING IS ONLY A TEN-minute walk. I am looking forward to being out in the evening with the drizzle and nighttime city sounds. Like most of us I suppose, I'm a complicit prisoner of my sentimental thoughts on these nighttime strolls, never fearful of the cloak of darkness but always alert and open to the benevolent ghostly signs invoked by those ever-watchful, beloved departed souls that rise to greet us under night's consoling mask as they try to guide our journey here on earth. They do not live, as we have seen in movies, in abandoned attics with cobwebs draped like curtains over a windowpane, or beneath a gnarled tree whose trunk bears the initials of a tragic youthful unrequited love, but instead live within us and speak to us from within. It is their caring voices that we hear throughout our lives, whispering to us above the confusing chatter and the unsettling din.

*

The building that houses the Narcotics Anonymous gathering is a cramped and faded, two-story stucco walk-up. It is wedged between two new giant towers recently erected during the building boom. The small building's mildew-stained cement speaks of lost opportunities. The ground floor houses a lesbian bookstore and coffee house. Beside these, and nestled further to the rear, is a small shop that sells spiritual paraphernalia, such as crystals and pyramids and possibly Ouija boards. The meeting is on the second floor at the rear of the building. It is down a narrow hallway, where the low ceiling is watermarked from a burst pipe or compromised asphalt roof. I suppose all of this spells affordability of rent for the cash-strapped, recovering addicts who assemble behind these flaking plaster walls in good faith and human harmony, long suffering souls, who with time and a sincere commitment to "the program," have a good shot at the happiness that had previously eluded them.

As I enter the front doorway, going past the lesbian bookstore entrance and the now closed spiritual gadgets shop, and begin climbing the creaky, wooden stairs, the smell of sandalwood incense hangs pungent as mother earth's own sensual body odor in the closeted space. I am a bit nervous, perhaps "uncertain" is a better word to describe my feelings, but as I ascend to the second floor stairwell I pluck up my resolve. I must continually remind myself that all this is ultimately the stuff of being a good father.

The room is surprisingly large, which suggests that although these old buildings look dwarfed from the street beside the new behemoths, they are, in fact, pretty substantial in their own right and for their own day. Several, small clusters of five to seven people are standing or milling about throughout the space. For the moment, no one seems to have seen me or if they have, cares to pay me any heed. Not knowing exactly what to do, I stand by the front table near the door and try to appear completely engrossed in reading the sole piece of paper lying on the desktop. Unfortunately, it has only two words printed on it: WELCOME ALL. I study these words as if their profound meaning is possibly too abstract for me to fully comprehend. As the moments tick by, I begin to feel a little foolish and wonder if I would be conspicuous if I quietly turned around and headed back out the door. I could nod collegially to anyone I passed on the confined stair space, as though I were just popping out to get something of great import from my car, confirming that I would be back in a jiffy, all primed and ready for the weighty matters at hand tonight.

When I look back up, I am, to my relief and possibly mounting dread, face to face with a large, Indian man with tall, white-and-blue eagle feathers sprouting from the back of his head in a festive spray. His long, black braids hang down on his colossal chest, framing an ornamental breastplate of colorful, wooden beads thatched together by an unseen string, no doubt made of moose gut or an elk's lower leg tendon. The rest of his garb is more western, featuring standard boot-cut Levis and a plain, black turtleneck sweater worn under the warrior's accessories. He smiles the laconic, wide-mouthed welcome of someone who has known tremendous sadness but is here, tonight, as an ambassador of good things coming.

"Welcome, my friend," he quietly intones extending his hand, "We have gladness in our hearts that you have come."

I take his broad hand, the fingers of which are as large as a cluster of bananas. I am immediately aware of how little pressure he applies to his grip for such a big fellow. I pump his hand up and down twice, as if sending him some official, coded signal that all is well on the western frontier.

"I am Chief White Eagle Man Buffalo Child," he states and then stands in silence, studying me with an amused twinkle in his deep-set Asiatic eyes. His dark skin stretches smoothly and seamlessly over his high cheekbones and slightly orbital nose.

"Thank you," I say, momentarily unable to unlock my eyes from his. It is as if he has placed me under some kind of shaman's spell, and I may wake up days from now seated naked and shameless as a child on a hillock in Stanley Park with floral paint swatches across my chest and back. I would be unable to explain how I got there or what on earth had happened to my fears. As I continue to stand in silence staring at Chief Whatever-The-Fuck-His-Name-Is, someone else crowds my peripheral vision. I turn my eyes toward this new person. This time, it is a twenty-something woman with a pretty face and forthright manner.

"Hello. My name is Robin. Welcome to our group's NA open-house meeting tonight. I hope you learn something and that we can be of help."

The Chief steps back into the room and is gone as quickly as he appeared.

"My name is Richard Bonhom."

Robin politely interrupts, with the slightest hint of an authoritative edge. "Richard, we have no last names here. For obvious reasons, an important part of our program is protecting anonymity." Now aware that she may be pushing a bit hard for someone on the greeting committee, she retrenches slightly with a smile. "You are simply Richard tonight. Welcome. Please have a seat wherever you like. The meeting will begin in a minute."

I see that rows of folding metal chairs have been placed in the front of the room facing a small lectern with a goose-necked light arching over the top. It casts an austere glow across the face and upper body of the presenter—a man somewhere between forty-five and sixty. From this distance and under this light, he has the semblance of someone fairly young, but looks a little haggard, not so much in his features as the actual mantle and tone of his skin. This is, no doubt, a lingering after-effect of a compromised liver, due to Hepatitis B infection or something equally as destructive, the vagabonds of his squalid past not all that far behind him. He greets us warmly and asks all to rise for a non-denominational moment of silent thankfulness.

I rise with everyone else and once again see the Chief across the room by the far wall, towering over his surroundings like an oak. As I close my eyes and bow my head an involuntary shudder runs through my body. Why is my absent daughter not standing here beside me, helping to guide me along this unknown path? Why must strangers usher me through these sustaining rituals instead of my own flesh and blood? I'm suddenly and inexplicably panic-stricken. I want her here and not out there, wherever *there* may be tonight. Instead of this rising dread, I want her close by where I can see her and feel her presence and know for certain that in this moment she is alright. I am aware that I'm trembling and have the panicked feeling that I may topple forward in the sudden throes of vertigo. My God, I may faint! I open my eyes to locate the back of a chair or something I can hold onto. The queasiness is suffocating and I sit back down with a hard thud, fortunately hitting my chair squarely. At that very moment, everyone else sits down, so I haven't caused a scene. I breathe a deep sigh of relief and feel the claustrophobic giddiness lifting from my head and body. I'm okay again but uneasy, not knowing when the next, more volatile wave might cast me onto the floor, like someone clamped within the tightly knotted fist of an epileptic fit. "Breathe, breathe, breathe," I tell myself. I'm fine again.

The man at the lectern is giving us a basic, boot camp spiel on why we're all here — which we already know in sorrowful abundance. He continues, perhaps more to the point, about what such meetings have been designed to achieve. He has begun with a brief history of his own drug dependency, which started in his mid-twenties and escalated to its zenith when he was caught in a shootout with police in downtown Montreal during a bank heist that went terribly wrong. At that time, it seems he was doing his damnedest to feed a monkey on his back that was gobbling up a thousand smackers a day. Ouch! The story now turns remorseful and introspective as he tearfully begins to detail his time spent behind bars. He sorrowfully catalogues the unsavory things he had to do while inside, in order to keep his gnawing habit alive. It's a pitiful story oft times told. At its conclusion, the people in the room give him a heartfelt, yet respectfully controlled, round of applause, letting him know that we may not completely understand just how fucked up one can allow himself to become, but we hold no judgments and are here for him.

The next person to approach the microphone is Robin, the woman who greeted me when I came in. Her talk is centered on not only her personal struggles with swallowing painkillers and then injecting barbiturates, but also on the common struggle of many of the people in the room tonight and its effects on their families, friends and relationships in general. Recognizing this part of the evening as pointing more in my direction, I sit up a bit straighter and listen for any clue or bit of offhand advice that may help. After twenty or so minutes, I can summarize the upshot as follows: there isn't much anyone can do or say or even think, other than we must somehow wade through this dismal fog of absolute uselessness, trying to remain hopeful that our loved ones will miraculously wake up one day from their selfish stupor and climb onto the recuperative treadmill leading back to us.

I have my pen and paper ready to take some notes, but end up doodling on the corners of the page. The full knowledge uncomfortably creeping over me that there will be no 'quick fix, five key points, whatever you do watch out for these telltale signs' kinds of enlightenment. It's going to be more of the same old, same old, until one way or the other it's finally over. "Keep a stiff upper lip" is tonight's storm-weather beacon. Casting a judgmental glance around me tonight my first and deepest impression is that of systemic failure. Our systems may be outdated and crumbling before our eyes, brick by brick. Now that more and more cracks are appearing, we're scrambling to daub paint on the surface to make it look sound.

Maybe we're afraid to face the fact that the whole thing—our so-called social order—may be coming apart. The cornerstone structures of school, church, government and marriage are falling down. And these people here tonight may well represent those first telltale, cautionary faults spreading out across the surface.

After Robin's talk, we are all invited to have some coffee and chat informally. I place my vacant pad of paper on my chair, all too aware of the absence of anything helpful written on it. I self-consciously wish that I had brought a hat or scarf to conceal this, like a truant child. It is as though it somehow is a reflection of my lack of commitment to my daughter's recovery.

I now move over to the lineup in front of the coffee urn. The man and woman standing directly behind me are rotund people of middle age who look like gnomes from an old world fable. When I glance and smile at them, they take it as a cue to open up. It is as if their voices have been muted for far too long, and if they can't say something, *anything*, they will burst.

In a strong German accent, the man says, "Vot a vonderful place zis iz for dose poor people mit de drugs hapit."

His wife nods approvingly to this statement, her beleaguered frown telling volumes about their story. I shake my head a little too exaggeratedly, perhaps even idiotically, as if the gesture itself is in some alien language whose sympathetic meaning may transcend linguistic differences.

"Wonderful. Wonderful," I say, rocking back and forth slightly on my toes and staring dumbly at the darkened window, as if I am waiting for a sign or good omen of vindication and possibly hope, something miraculous that will ease the tension in the room, for me, at least.

The man now sticks out his little, fat hand. "I am Helmut unt zis iz my vife, Heidi. Ve own Helmut's Sausage Heaven. You may haf zeen our advertising on za teevee, yah?"

It is true. I, like everyone else west of the Rockies, have seen the television ads with the fat little cartoon character in lederhosen who, by the way, looks a hell of a lot like Helmut hailing one and all to "come unt taste my award-winning sausage." This guy's made a bundle stuffing his bratwurst. I must admit, I'm sure I'm not alone in saying that those singsong commercials with the bit about "having a taste of his all meat sausage" have spawned more than one light-hearted sexual jibe around the office. This is especially true when some sweet saucy trainee from the steno pool happens to be within earshot. I can say with confidence that Desiree has been taunted with this shallow, carnal reference by more than one of the brokers on our floor.

Helmut's pleasant, elfin wife shyly proffers her chubby pink hand for a squeeze. She now hums in a kitchen-cozy little purr that makes me feel like being seated at her table eating a giant piece of strudel and washing it down with a scalding cup of creamy, thick, home-made, Swiss hot chocolate.

"Ve are here because of our zon Friedrich. He iz mit de bad mans zootink drugs like crazy people."

She now mimics a person shooting a hypodermic needle into her pudgy, freckled forearm. As if on command, their eyes mist up with emotion, and he takes her hand in his and taps it with bewildered pat, pats. This forlorn gesture signifies more about their family's troubles than any further words can concede. They gaze downward, embarrassed that this one seemingly undemanding sentence uttered countless times over the past years still invokes the same despondent reaction in them.

I look at these two poor souls with the sincerest of empathy. After all, I'm not unlike them in this one all-consuming connection with our wayward children. They have come so far and seen so much turmoil in their years. They have always stood up and done the job required of them, without complaint or reservation. And for all this effort and diligence, they got Friedrich—or maybe on the street he is simply Freddy, or "Big F," or Froggy—who, there is no doubt, repeatedly humiliated them by tipping off his drug-crazed goons about where the safe was hidden in the Helmut's Sausage Heaven Coquitlam location and what time the staff took the cash bag to the late night auto teller, these betrayals forcing his crestfallen parents to change the work schedules for their staff and adjust their patterns for nighttime deposits throughout the stores. I would love to go out on the street and hunt down Freddy or "Big F" or Froggy grabbing him by the scruff of his goddamned jacket and shaking him so violently his teeth rattle. All so that he can have some inkling of knowledge and, even more important, take responsibility for the pain he has visited upon his distraught parents. But I know I can't, and I know it isn't right, and it isn't going to help any of us. But for this split second, it helps me. And Jesus, but that's worth something to me here and now, if not in a soberer moment later on. As we return to our seats I suddenly feel forlorn and abandoned, knowing that my rage at the woebegone Friedrich is really targeted at my estranged beloved daughter.

For the next forty-five minutes or so, the meeting shifts its focus to the guests, the relatives and significant others of the addicts, all of whom carry some of the same scars, plus others reserved for those of us here tonight that were the innocent bystanders. Remembering that we all remained conscious and lucid throughout these monstrous, drug-induced ordeals, our memories clearer and perhaps even more painful than those foggy recollections of the comatose users themselves. I don't get up to speak, but instead sit quietly and listen to the damaged survivors timidly opening their hearts to us.

A woman in her mid-forties now stands self-consciously beside her chair. Turning around bravely to take in the whole room, she laments, in a thin, barely audible voice, how her teenaged son's exit from their loving home for his new life as a crystal meth abuser has broken their spirits and laid waste to their anguished souls. The last time she had seen him was when she posted his bail in the wee hours of the morning after he was apprehended while trying to break into a used furniture store to steal a cheap lamp on display in the window. She shakes her head and shrugs her shoulders in perplexed consternation at this absurdity. Like the rest of us, she seems to be held captive by the unanswerable question of why he would choose something of so little value to steal. Why not a car, or an expensive piece of jewelry, if a possible jail sentence is a part of the equation? Along with her and everyone else here tonight who has been a victim of the addict's mindset, I would guess the answer may be as simple and immediate as the fact that the lamp happened to be in front of him at the very moment he needed some cash, and that this alone was the entire rationale behind the otherwise thoughtless action. Immediate gratification. Supply and demand.

As she sits down, a man stands and tells us of his nephew's disappearance several months before. He asks if there is any group or organization of volunteers that may be able to help locate him. Robin, the acting moderator for this portion of the meeting, gives him a phone number and a glint of hope that someone may know something. And on it goes from one to the other in a seemingly relentless chorus of pain. I want to feel better about coming here tonight, but am not convinced it was the smart thing to do. Rather than acting as a crutch for me to lean on and use to reinforce my determined stance, it has simply reinforced the stark fact that my daughter is out there on her own and will remain in that non-place in our lives until she chooses to come back home or she dies. I guess that's the whole point of these meetings—to let us all know, without any qualms, that we haven't got a damn thing to do with any of it. So we'd better sure as shooting get on with our own lives because two sick people do not a happier family make.

When the meeting finally adjourns at a little past eight o'clock, we all stand and Robin asks us to acknowledge each other. We further share in this acknowledgement that we are all vulnerable to, and powerless before, the vagaries of life's mysterious ways, and that a higher power oversees the whole, sorry picture. I mumble some inanity to the person seated nearest to me, a world-weary looking woman in a wash-worn imitation leopard skin leotard and fake black leather bomber jacket, with ratty looking tufts of synthetic fur pock marking the collar. She has pulled her straw-like, peroxide-fried hair back into a ponytail. The graying roots creep above her pale, scaling scalp, melding unconvincingly with the fading orange tint.

Her cheeks are sunken, her sullen expression pulling her chin back into her long neck. She sports an electric red lipstick. This further dramatizes her sallow skin. Is she a hooker drained of every last vestige of life's precious sustaining juices, now put out to pasture? I do not know, and I do not want to know, nor does she want to tell me anything about any of it — this circumstance that is her life. She half-heartedly thanks me, and our eyes quickly turn away from each other, as if we are both too exhausted to open up to any further intimacy regarding the predictably morose stories that brought us here tonight. For a brief, painful moment, neither of us moves. We stand, mutely staring at nothing in particular. Then, realizing this, and feeling awkward, we simultaneously bolt. It is as if we have suddenly remembered a host of things left unattended somewhere else. We comically bump into each other. We exchange another round of empty pleasantries continuing to keep our eyes fixed elsewhere. It is as if we have both suddenly become acutely aware of time's passing, and are trying to tally up the hours wasted, perhaps suddenly realizing the full weight of knowing that they are never to return. I turn and am almost at the door when The Chief steps into my path of retreat.

"How was the meeting for you?"

I lie and say, "Fine, fine," trying to keep this exchange to a minimum if at all possible since I'd really like nothing better than to be back outside breathing in the cool, moist, night air and trying to clear the last two hours from my thoughts.

"Some of us get together for a coffee and talk after these meetings. It's in a skid row café down on Hastings." He smiles. "Closer to the scene of the crime —reminds us what we have to lose. You're welcome to join us if you'd like."

The idea of traipsing down to the belly of the beast on Vancouver's infamous east side with a ragtag bunch of fringe players is not at the forefront of my "things I wish I could do" list right now. Let me out of here!

"Thanks, Chief White *whatever*, but I'm going out of town very early tomorrow morning, so I've got to get back and finish packing."

He looks at me with a blank expression. I get the uncomfortable feeling that he doesn't believe me. I shouldn't give a shit about this one way or the other, but I do. On the spot, I make a decision to be clear. Isn't this what tonight is supposedly all about? Clean and clear.

"Listen, this evening has taught me some stuff, and I appreciate your invitation, and maybe we can have that cup of coffee and chat some other time, but now I've got to scoot."

As I begin moving around his mountainous frame, he quietly continues. "You taking a plane on your journey?" I confirm this without stopping. I continue to edge toward the doorway. "You take a cab to the airport?"

Now why I would even continue answering these questions I don't really know, but it all seems safe and harmless enough, and if it will help extricate me from this room I'll keep playing along.

"Yes. Five a.m.," I say, rubbing my palms together almost gleefully, as if this early hour holds some possibility or special promise in store for me.

Without pause he confirms to my disbelieving ears, "Sounds good. I'll be there. What's the address?"

I stop now, uncertain of what I've committed myself to. Is he coming over for another long, arduous talk about the perils of drugs at five in the morning, or what? This whole thing is beginning to feel like an episode of *Who Told You?* with me as the guy in the crosshairs. It's not that I don't recognize that the Chief is a man deeply scared by a white culture that snatched him and his kind from loving northern settlements and deposited them into Catholic-run parochial schools, where priests and lay brothers alike meted out their sadistic form of religion to these children's innocent souls. I can well imagine the self-loathing and hatred these long-buried, horrific episodes inflicted onto his psyche. But right now, goddamit, I can't help or even attempt to *feel* any of this. I have my own cross to bear, my own demons to quell. I'm not sick like him or Robin or Friedrich or... Tess! I'm okay, for chrissake. It's my daughter I'm here to help, not myself!

I stop and look at him, a bit dumbfounded I suppose. I try to muster some semblance of authority into my voice. "I'm sorry. Maybe you don't understand. I'm leaving tomorrow morning, bright-eyed and bushy-tailed at 5:00 a.m. in a cab for the airport. Where exactly do you fit into that picture?"

"I'm a cab driver," he says, beaming like a laser right through my astonished gaze. "I'm working tonight and would sure appreciate the opportunity to take you to your flight. It's quiet at that time of the morning anyway, and I'd enjoy the company."

I give him the lamest grin imaginable and say, "Great!"

"How in the name of Jumping H. Christ have I managed this?" I'm thinking as I give him my address, which he doesn't even write down.

"Good. See you tomorrow at 4:45 a.m. I sure appreciate this, mister."

"Richard," I reply.

He repeats "Richard" softly and then turns to hug Helmut and Heidi, whom he seems to know, probably from their presence at other such meetings. No doubt, they're hoping in their stubborn Teutonic way that regular clockwork attendance at these functions will somehow contribute to bringing their apple dumpling son Friedrich to heel. I must admit to realizing that these are no different than my own possibly misplaced ambitions for Tess.

I stumble onto the street and walk with my head down, chastising myself for what I may have inadvertently gotten myself into. What if he doesn't show up and I'm left scrambling for another cab to make my flight? What if he forgets the address and drives around the neighborhood for an extra twenty-five minutes before finding me straddling the curb, waving frantically for him to stop? I hate arriving at airports late, having to bull-moose my way apologetically down lines of exasperated people who show no sympathy and more than a little scorn as I tap the face of my watch smiling and shrugging meekly.

My walk back home is not as I would have hoped. As I open the door of my condo, I hear Lei-Lei snuffling and growling behind the Skudmores' door, her little black nose inserted under the space at the bottom, those highly tuned olfactory glands deftly working to detect a familiar, or possibly menacing scent. I quickly close the door behind me making my way to the bathroom for a much needed pee. I then wash my hands and face trying to regain a degree of refreshment from this evening's disheartening events.

CHAPTER TWELVE

RUN AND IDA SKUDMORE ARE MISPLACED PEOPLE IN OUR BUILDING. THEY are not unlike recent refugees from some far distant tribe, whose culture and general social mores collide head on with those of their newfound home. I say this, not to be catty or unnecessarily hostile, but to state a plain fact of our lives here. They both work at the main branch of Canada Post, often stationed side by side at their wickets. In their daily work they busy themselves selling stamps and directing parcels to faraway places they have no interest in learning more about or will ever venture forth to visit. The truth of the matter is that it takes a certain amount of financial wherewithal to be an owner in this building. This casts an invisible shield that in its own innocuous way may filter people who may not be "right," from entering. This is not a racial or religious or ethnic roadblock. To own at 777 Beach View Place you need money. In most cases, this involves working your way through a multitude of obstacles to acquire enough money to afford the tariff for entry. This life process doesn't necessarily make you a better person than someone who hasn't navigated these same waters, but it often makes you a different person. And this difference may well act like the opposite ends of a magnet, inadvertently helping to attract owners to each other, if for no other reason than they have a shared life experience in one form or other. Birds of a feather, so to speak.

Neither Run nor Ida Skudmore has earned these rights of passage. Run's mother, the late Mrs. Bernt Skudmore, left the place to her son Runyon in her will. Run and Ida are childless and friendless. They enjoy no extracurricular activities like tennis or golf or even the occasional stroll along the seawall taking in a palpable pleasure from the pastoral views of the Pacific waters.

They have each been in their jobs for over twenty years. They met at the post office, she in Lost Items and he in Downtown Deliveries, both working their way up toward the wickets they now inhabit. Ida is also a Shop Steward for their Local, and Run an avid supporter of her selfless duty to their union. Ida has been the guiding force behind member-friendly initiatives relating to the beefed- up "cease delivery" regulations for such things as improperly cleared walkways in winter, unattended dog feces on pathways, and, most recently, the mail carriers' discretionary power to stop delivery if they don't feel hand railings are properly secured on the front steps.

Other than the ceaseless turmoil of labor relations in the post office, the only thing that seems to bring them any sense of human pleasure or mortal compassion is their snarling little Jack Russell Terrier, Lei-Lei. Unlike many inquisitive and companionable dogs of this breed, she has adopted the dour bearing of her owners, feinting behind their legs whenever someone tries to pat her skeletal little head or rocketing forward out of the elevator or down a hallway if some stranger stoops to tickle her under her bristly, pointy chin. Run and Ida and the ferret-like Lei-Lei have but one entertainment and singular purpose here at 777 Beach View Place: to patrol the corridors, entranceways, and grounds on the lookout for anything that could be construed as, or manipulated into being, wrongful or out of place.

Adding to their already abundant unpleasantness is a host of annoying habits that I can only assume have accumulated over their years together as a couple and as disgruntled postal employees. Cloying habits as pronounced and disarming as a nervous facial tick or loud Tourette's outburst. These habits are likely the byproducts of their deliberate and obedient suppression of wistful ideas and possibly even recuperative hopes. For instance, Ida, through years of silent servitude to Run's pent-up rage and nagging criticism, has emotionally distanced herself from all temptation to interact with him. She quite simply ignores his very presence. That is why, prior to actually seeing them face to face at the garbage bins or collecting their mail, one can usually hear Run repeatedly chanting, "Ida, Ida, Ida," as she mutely busies herself sorting their recycling bottles or scanning their letters, seemingly oblivious to his voice. I must admit to feeling my sphincter muscles contract when I run some small errand in the building and suddenly find myself standing behind a closed metal fire door or rounding a blind corner in the hallway to hear this recurrent dirge concerning Ida's mislaid consideration.

And Run is not without his own special, idiosyncratic behavior. He stands too close to you whenever he has something to say. He invades your personal space, forcing listeners to lean backward creating a disquieting feeling of vertigo, as though they may fall over onto their backs like turtles. Not unlike others of Scandinavian or northern coastal heritage, Run Skudmore eats inordinate amounts of raw fish—kippered herring, roll mops, baccalà, sardines, and thin wedges of lox with thick slices of red onion layered on top. Exchanges with him are like having a whispered conversation with a harbour seal or penguin, the rank smell of putrefying fish invading your nostrils and triggering the gag mechanism in your constricting throat. Jean Paul Sartre's definition of hell as being "other people" has never rung so true. These quirks, plus numerous others, accompanied by their incessant, malcontented bitching make the prospect of chance encounters with Run and Ida Skudmore enough to ruin an otherwise pleasant outing.

They are also dyed-in-the-wool working socialists. The buttons affixed to their navy blue uniform cardigans or hat brims tell of gross injustices to farm workers, or of some government's casual contamination of a lost tribe's fresh-water lagoon with their reckless disposal of hot plutonium rods secreted to this Amazonian Eden by rogue nameless atomic energy cleanup contractors. Conspiracies abound. They regularly leave pamphlets shouting their socialist outrage over a litany of wrongs, inevitably pointing to the seemingly obvious fact that the answer to all these ills is readily available. One need only throw ever-increasing amounts of taxpayers' money against the invisible wall of injustice, separating those who truly care from those capital-generating mongrels, like myself, I presume. It's too bad Run and Ida don't manifest some of their social consciousness in a more sensitive manner when dealing with issues closer to home. I guess their brand of social activism is more inclined to human kindness the farther they march from their own front door.

*

In the still of the morning before the city awakens, I sit on my deck, my coffee cup warming my palms against the fresh pre-dawn chill, and gaze forth onto the majesty of sea and sky. An early morning tug boat or transient wind-ripple leave their marks upon the water's changing patterns, their passing mapped onto its surface as if drawn by an unseen hand. Water has memory. At these times, I will quite often allow my mind to catalogue and take stock. I instinctively return, time and time again, to the abiding belief that helps me when society's ineptitude raises its head. These doubts of mine take many forms. They can be hatched from allegations of police brutality, a spineless judiciary, an isolated teen's murderous rampage through a Dairy Queen full of ice cream-licking tots, or a stark revelation that yet another Catholic bishop has fallen to accusations of sexual predation upon his youthful and vulnerable flock. To me, what this all spells is as plain as the nose on your face. *Everyone is busy doing nothing.* This is the fundamental difference between the Skudmores' view of life's possibilities, and my own. They see a solution as close at hand as applying a bandage to a severed limb. In their eyes, it's all as simple as wedging another layer of government between the problem and the citizenry —some *uber* police force dispatched to thwart the greed of globalization. Or perhaps it's something as close to home as creating a condo council for our building that has real teeth when it comes to bylaw infractions, excepting, of course, their own repeated failure to keep the tenacious Lei-Lei on a leash when walking in common areas. Yes, the Skudmores' answer to everything from world economics to labor relations in our postal service comes down to an ever-expanding host of government-administered programs.

I, on the other hand, believe we've already got too many people standing between us and what we actually *think*. This realization crystallized for me while stuck in a traffic jam caused by a pensive suicide jumper. I was trying to navigate my way across the Lion's Gate Bridge, the main thoroughfare connecting the various parts of Vancouver that are separated by fingers of water. It runs through Stanley Park, a beautiful heavily wooded cityscape. It happened during a Friday rush hour in the dead of winter's doldrums. It takes a Vancouverite, or possibly a Dubliner, to fully appreciate the anguish of the drip, drip, dripping of rain that knows no season. I observed the trained SWAT team negotiator's attempts to talk him down. She promised whatever it took — a harmonious reunion with his estranged girlfriend or hypercritical father or wailing mother. If the negotiator could have talked him down his recovery would probably entail being confined to many months or years of psychotherapy, with the likes of Dr. Martha Sitwell, these sessions lubricated with daily, potent, narcotic cocktails.

Like a spectator watching the high wire act at a carnival, I watched the whole sticky business. The cops going in and out, coaxing, cajoling, and promising whatever they promise during such stressful times. Hours later, people became exasperated and began leaving their cars, all chatting like prisoners on a road gang waiting to be moved further up the line. Even the police were glancing at their watches, possibly trying to figure out how in the hell their kids would get back from soccer practice, or what the wife would say to the dinner guests while he was marooned here with Mr. High Step. The general gossip on the road indicated that the man was distraught over losing his job. And that's when it came to me. My epiphany. We have allowed ourselves, cumulatively as well as individually, to hand over our reins to someone else, *anyone else.* We pay them whenever any of the myriad tragedies come knocking. We are convinced that it is prudent and more effective to let others do our bidding. Everyone is an expert, but nobody *knows* anything.

Let's face it, mankind has only had a few fundamentally life-shaping breakthroughs. We've parlayed these into what I believe to be a highly over-rated opinion of ourselves, and our place of importance in the general scheme of things. Merv Hindlich would back me up on this if he were allowed to remain conscious for more than a few minutes of each flat-lining day. What have we accomplished so far? The wheel, a basic spherical shape common to most living beings. It has kept us chugging along since the caveman. Another is the discovery of antibiotics for the control of infection. This is basically vegetable mold. It allows people to fight off deadly infections from bugs as old as time itself. These same chemically enriched bacteria, having lost the battle for a hundred years or so, are now gaining ground on us and are in a good position to ultimately win the war. Also, the Roman Arch in architecture, democracy from the ancient Greeks, Christianity from the Jews over two and a half centuries ago, gunpowder from the pre-historic Chinese, beer from the Mesopotamian Egyptians, and, as of late the miniaturization of phones, radios, watches and cameras from the modern Japanese. This due for the most part to the discovery that sand, one of the world's more basic natural substances, is in fact a good conductor of electricity. We've learned to make things small, tinier than our parents could ever have imagined or, in truth, would have cared. That's about it!

Some of us have children hooked on drugs. I most shamefully do. Self absorbed louts as neighbours, whose delinquent kids threaten our peaceful Sunday mornings with their bass drum booming music. We have an epidemic of spouses and children who have grown emotionally detached. There are fish that are no longer returning to their traditional spawning beds. Our own bodies have grown corpulent and sloth-like. Our dogs won't obey when called. Our dishes don't sparkle. We have come to view our own noses, chests and buttocks as not really right for our needs. And what do we do with all of these concerns? We hand them to people we don't even know. If I were a Dr. Martha Sitwell, or the head of some gothic church, the wise words of counsel I would give to my congregation would be "be careful." Sometimes life is very fragile and our tendency to test its limits and peek into the dark abyss may be foolhardy. Once our balance is interrupted, it's not as easily restored as most would like to believe. In the end, good old self- reliance still accounts for a whole lot. Thus, "everyone is busy doing nothing" is my view of life in the twenty first century. We have everything at our disposal, and nothing is working. The question is, where do we go from here?

The guy on the Stanley Park causeway did jump. Inexplicably he wasn't killed. The impact snapped his neck like a chicken and folded the skin and small bones of his face back like a holdup man removing his stocking mask, but he lived to tell the tale. I saw him on a television news piece six months later, preaching that even though he was now a paraplegic confined to a wheelchair with only limited vision in one of his badly ulcerated eyes, he had found Christ. He was the CEO of his own corporation offering suicide awareness talks at places like Rotary Clubs and churches, that I can only presume potentially suicidal people frequent. Someone once said that religion is for people who are afraid of going to hell, and spirituality is for people who have been there.

CHAPTER THIRTEEN

I DON'T LIKE TRAVEL—AIR TRAVEL IN PARTICULAR. THE WHOLE AIRPORT, airplane, luggage collection thing is unsettling for me. This combined with ticketing, boarding, and exiting leaves me anxious. Sitting in a metal tube full of high-octane gasoline with fire-spewing jet engines whining all around me doesn't help my sense of well being one iota. The aspect of planes themselves that I suppose I like the least — and there are numerous mechanical and theoretical implications included in my list— is the fact that they are too big and heavy to turn in a heartbeat or control in any reasonable fashion when things go amiss. Feathers are light. Clouds are gaseous. Subatomic particles have a molecular structure that's basic enough, and small enough to be absent from Newton's theory on gravitational pull. But airplanes are neither light nor gaseous. They are not immune to suddenly being pulled toward the center of the earth by cosmic forces that can casually override our feeble attempts at controlling external events, our track record here, questionable. They are bulky in the extreme, and can function only if their endless miles of hydraulic tubing are free of punctures or ruptures. Their countless lineal yards of electrical wiring must be devoid of all possible interferences from electromagnetic fields that could cause a momentary voltage arc or finite friction spark. And above all else, these fathomless mechanics and engineering gizmos and gadgets are dependent on *people* to operate them. These systems, and a host of other variables, all have to be in sync if the airplane is to stay aloft. In the end it is the people that cause me the greatest concern.

Whenever I'm standing in an airport boarding area watching the ground crew run through their final pre-flight preparations, I ponder the likelihood of a high-flying osprey or disoriented Canada goose being clutched in the centrifugal talons created by the whirring turbines; or the constant destructive battering of wind resistance and downdraft turbulence and their compromising effects on the rivets holding a wing in place. And then there's the very real possibility of a sudden loss of cabin pressure caused by a suicidal passenger or a dejected flight crew member, the pilot himself, a mere mortal after all, at his wit's end when jilted by a brooding foreign lover in some steamy, exotic stopover—any one of these despondent people could release the emergency lever on an escape hatch, or a loading bay door, causing the plane to spiral helplessly into the sea, where the ever-present circling army of ravenous sharks would claim any battered and badly burned survivors of the initial violent impact. Don't judge me too harshly or slot me into any suspect grouping of emotional cripples or neurotic phobia mongers— I am not any of these. The things I'm talking about are very real and far too common on evening newscasts or popular news magazine covers for my personal liking.

This being said, I still have to pack a few more things for my journey and write a brief salutary note to my older brother Ethan at the hospital for the criminally insane. Ethan is by no stretch of the imagination a well person. The papers at the time of the trial said that he was a cold-blooded killer who calculatedly took a gun and shot another man to death without giving it so much as a second thought. They further somewhat insensitively described how he went home and begged his now ex-wife, Shelley, to stay with him hoping, that they could possibly work things out between them and live happily ever after, ignoring the niggling fact that her lover, who was once his best friend, was lying cold and forlorn on a stainless steel slab in a mortuary as dark as the inside of a cow's stomach. Ethan's only defense in this whole miserable business resides in the undeniable fact that he is mentally ill and that the chances of him returning to a productive place in society are zip—a prognosis almost universally agreed upon by everyone from the judiciary to the parole board to the psychiatric experts.

I try to send him a consoling letter or small box of fudge or shortbreads every month or so, just to let him know that someone out there still cares. It's the least I can do. Everyone else in the family is gone now, and his ex-wife certainly won't send him any care packages, since she is part and parcel of the reason he'll probably spend the rest of his life in such a place. Not that I'm blaming her, since his actions weren't those of a normal thinking person. I'd better write him right now while I'm thinking of it and waiting for the kettle to boil. I'll drop the envelope into the box outside the building before I go to bed in case I have to scramble to find an alternate route to the airport tomorrow.

I go over to my desk and take out the neatly wrapped package of notepaper I use for these missives. They look suspiciously like the parchment a decrepit auntie would use for birthday greetings. I feel that the warm, sentimental qualities of the sepia-toned paper may reach down into his lost mind and pause on a long dormant familial refrain that brings him solace.

Dear Ethan,

I hope this letter finds you as well as can be expected and that you enjoyed the box of Oreos I sent last month. I remember that they were your favorite when we were kids. Do you remember? I was thinking of the times we went fishing after working at Mom and Dad's store and how you would often catch the big one. I don't like traveling any sentimental back roads with Ethan. The sudden rekindling of a bad memory, like our father's suicide, could trigger a catatonic episode lasting for God only knows how long. I try to keep these letters short and to the point, with child-like references to cookies, cakes and any other jolly subject that comes to mind. *I am going on a trip to Cuba tomorrow. Maybe I can bring you back a seashell. You can listen to the sound of the ocean and picture yourself far, far away. Wouldn't that be nice?* I don't know how much of anything Ethan absorbs of life outside his daily routine of brushing his teeth, making up his solitary cot, then waiting for the various clapping bells and arresting buzzers that tell him a mealtime is nigh, or that it's time to go to the exercise yard, where he seems to take some pleasure from pacing back and forth along the perimeter fence like a caged bear. I'm afraid in the end, he often just sits in silent penance, gazing through the steel bars of his cell. Sometimes when I'm actually with him, he seems almost as normal as you or i. At such times we start talking about real stuff. Although, I seldom express my true thoughts and feelings, for that moment we do share some intimate episodes from our childhood, long absented from either of our daily lives now. Then without notice, he'll be gone again, recoiling back into the emotional darkness of his subterranean den. At these times he is lost to all but his own enigmatic notions. *When I'm back home I want to come and see you. I'll bring something good to eat and we can talk and maybe even go for a walk in the exercise yard together. You try and stay as good as you can until then.*

   Your Loving Brother, Richard

I seal the envelope and address it "Ethan Bonhom, Matsqui Penitentiary Hospital, Mission, BC" As I write the postal code, I shudder slightly. In my mind I see the lunatics, and hear their forsaken moans. How has it come to pass that I know details about such a place as the Matsqui Penitentiary Hospital? How is it possible that I am now attending Narcotics Anonymous Meetings? How far off can the time be when I stand up beside my chair and tell one and all that my daughter Tess is nothing more than a common, fucking dope fiend. What happened? I set out with plans that included a wife and a family and, with hard work and persistence, perhaps a career I could really sink my teeth into. Something that would provide for my family and allow me to come home at night tired in the kind of way a farmer is after planting the back forty, or a surgeon is after saving a child's partially severed limb. But this kind of thinking doesn't bode well for me tonight. I dismiss such thoughts with a sigh, getting up to find my keys. I will go down to drop Ethan's letter into the post box beside our front entrance. I will then come back up to a nice warm bath in the Jacuzzi tub. The pulsating jets of water may ease the tension from my muscles, and from my veiled thoughts as well.

*

It wasn't all that long ago that Genevieve and I stood beside each other, watching our daughters walk across the podium to receive their medals for placing in the top five finalists in downhill skiing. This was a first for the Vancouver Ski Club's Girl's Racing Team, two members of one family competing at such a high level. Emily was the better technical skier, always picture perfect in her tiger's crouch, as she slammed down the steepest mountain pitch. The uphill leg bent just so when entering a turn, allowing her weight to be transported smoothly to her downhill ski, never losing forward thrust or control, letting her skis run, the basic laws of physics applied without pause. Textbook skiing, is what her coaches said. But it was Tess that was the champion in the making. She wasn't as strong technically, or as studious in her practices and her analysis of styles. She was quite simply the one that flew closest to the sun. The one, out of all the rest, that pushed past the rigors of style and form and reached out through shear will of spirit to grasp greatness. She wanted to win, this need coming from a place so primal in her being that it could not be duplicated or transferred to anyone else, it wasn't learned. It simply was there. We all saw this natural energy, Emily most. And that was Emily's gift. To know and to hold this knowledge close and to cherish it without ego, because it was a rare thing and, as life would soon prove, a fragile thing as well.

*

My sleep is everything I feared it would be and more. I don't fall into that deep pool of rest, but instead skim across its fitful surface while being pursued by any number of horrors. These take the form of black-caped assassins and wild dogs whose bloodied incisors snap ever closer to my pounding heels. I lift my feet like pistons in my dash for safety. Suddenly, a naked and cavorting Desiree seats herself provocatively on my chest, legs akimbo. Things may be looking up? Then, instead of sliding up toward my expectant lips, she produces a sheaf of papers and accusingly waves them in front of my petrified face as irrefutable evidence of my account irregularities. This final assault jolts me into consciousness as rudely as if being slapped across the face by a leering Gestapo officer. Exhausted, I lie facing the ceiling and wait for the inevitable bing, bing, bing of the clock radio I keep tuned to the classical station. No Wagner this morning, I hope. I am awake until at least 2:00 a.m., my mind racing in and out of every silly rabbit hole a brain can devise at that hour. I think about my ride with Chief Whatever-His-Name-Is, then anguish for a while about my daughter and whether I can handle a lifetime of those meetings. Then if she does decide to straighten out, which I have no way of knowing at this point, what future does life hold for us all. I think about Genevieve and what she is doing and how much I miss her at this moment. Then, heaven forgive me, I think about Desiree again and how she would look suntanned and oiled for water sports. I contemplate whether my grand-kids will be stricken with "the bad gene" and have their own demons to wrestle with later in their lives. And finally, I think about what awaits me on my travels and just how many apparently "handled" things will come undone and require the kind of fixing I'm supposedly good at. I drift off for a couple of hours and once again awaken with a start that I can't trace to anything real or abstract. I'm suddenly conscious but don't know how long I've been lying here thinking these thoughts. Now, I'm stuck between sleep and the transparent veneer of wee-hour consciousness, waiting for the most dismal of all prospects for the sleep-deprived—the alarm.

It's Ravel's Bolero. It could have been much worse. Still feeling exhausted, I climb out of bed, shower and dress, put my toiletries into a shoulder bag and put this and another larger bag by the door. I put the coffee on and stand at the kitchen counter checking my tickets, passport and money. Check. Check. Check. I look out my front window at the twinkling lights of the other towers and out to the darkness of English Bay and the Straits of Georgia that separate the mainland from Vancouver Island. On clear summer days, I can actually see the peaks of Mount Washington on Vancouver Island, approximately seventy miles away. But this morning I see only the occasional red and green running lights from a tugboat or other commercial vessel moving slowly in the pre-dawn ocean chop.

After giving the plants a good drink, I take a small glass of juice to wash down my three daily pills—one for colds, one for prostate protection, —very important for any man my age, —and one for general immune system fortification. There are things going wrong out there—and even more frightening *in here* —that a middle-aged, toxic body of today can't keep a lid on. "The Silent Killers Within" is the title of an article in one of Genevieve's medical periodicals. It isn't some wacky essay written by a crackpot naturopathic practitioner from a mail order university, but an actual research paper from a Harvard, big-brain type. It basically says that real science is becoming concerned about the increasing numbers of autoimmune diseases. *Concerned!* By the time those guys get to the concerned stage of anything, we'll all be dead! Anyway, a good supply of my health food store meds is packed in their original bottles. Hopefully, this will satisfy the prying eyes of the narcs in Miami and the Customs agents in Cuba, both ever vigilant and watchful for illegal substances. There is the growing possibility of being thrown into some rain barrel cold, unlit room in either of these countries, fatigued officers going to work on me with needle-nosed pliers and electric prods, trying to right the wrongs of our fathers.

It's now 4:35 a.m. and I'm all set. I decide to take my stuff down to the lobby and wait exactly fifteen minutes before calling Yellow Cabs and setting Plan B into motion. I extract my key from my door and bend down to pick up my suitcases. I can't believe this! Randy and Clive are shuffling down the hallway toward me wearing their pajamas under bulky trench coats. They are carrying brandy snifters and oversized umbrellas. They smile luminously and shout, "Hola!" before exaggeratedly putting their fingers to their lips and shushing each other with a fit of giggles. Clive is carrying a large, wicker picnic basket on a strap over his shoulder. I don't know whether they're drunk or sober. It's hard to tell with them since they're always hovering on the verge of lunacy. They reside in the world of the paranormal. Randy places his squat hand on my arm conspiratorially and whispers, "We decided that a special guy—Mr. Big Stuff birthday boy himself—needed a special sendoff, so we're your official going-away party!"

Holy Christ! Clive tries to hoist one of my bags to his shoulder, but winces and drops it back onto the carpet. He tries to wedge his foot against the baseboard for better leverage. I take it from him and tell him to go push the button on the elevator. I'll handle the heavy work. Randy takes my briefcase and calls for Clive to hold the elevator door while he stops for a sip of cognac. I can hear Lei-Lei barking from behind Run and Ida's door. No doubt, one or both are jostling to look through their peep hole right now, assessing what possible bylaw infractions are taking place, this sudden early morning awakening leaving their hair standing straight up on their heads like Zulu warriors. I expect a neighbourly letter slid under my door or a coincidental meeting in the hallway or entrance foyer when I return, their accusations casting a large measure of blame for such an outrage, not on me, but rather those gay men down the hall.

Downstairs, Clive sets his cognac glass onto a windowsill and squats down to open the lid of the picnic basket. He carefully extracts a small serving plate piled high with pastries and a thermos with plastic cups inverted on its top.

"Brecky time, Mr. Big Stuff," he announces. "Just like Mom said, it's the single most important meal of the day." He pours a small amount of coffee into a cup and hands it to me. "I don't suppose you'd like a little peck of cognac in that to start your engine?"

I decline. He now stands with the pastry plate in hand. "Then for goodness sakes, have an apple cheese blintz. They're still warm from the oven."

I take one, knowing that Randy's pastry was made from scratch and will melt in my mouth. The apples are organic and the cheese was churned by hand from Jersey cows in Provence. As I stand sipping and munching, I cast my eyes at my new extended family—two old queens acting like maiden aunts sending me off to boarding school. I can't help thinking that we must look like an unusual collective.

At exactly 4:45 a.m. a taxi pulls up in front of the building and blinks its lights at us. Chief White Eagle Man Buffalo Child unfolds his large frame from behind the steering wheel and pops the trunk. Having stowed our drink cups hastily in the picnic basket, Randy, Clive, and I come bustling through the heavy, glass door like a herd of fumbling jugglers. As I stand at the rear of the car sorting my bags for the Chief to put in the trunk, I notice the heads of two people already seated in the backseat. They appear to be older women. The Chief greets us with a certain formality, as if every minor social exchange carries the responsibility of ceremony.

"It is good that we have come together this morning and that The Great Spirit is guiding us on our various journeys."

Randy and Clive stare in astonished and delighted silence at the mountain man standing before them. He may as well have just stepped from a spaceship and told them that there's good water and friendly folks on his planet. Knowing them, I wait for their gushing salutations as they fall all over themselves in an effort to be noticed. Randy makes the first move, sneaking his hand into the picnic basket hanging from Clive's arm and extracting the plate of pastries.

"Apple cheese blintz, Mr. Noble Indian Brother?"

The Chief regards the two men standing in front of him in pajamas and trench coats as if they were the regulars in his daily workplace. Taking a blintz he says, "Thank you, my friends. I am Chief White Eagle Man Buffalo Child." As if reading the puzzled looks on both Clive and Randy's faces as they try to digest all of this information and remember it long enough to spew it back out, he adds, "My friends call me Bird."

A palpable sigh of relief escapes both men's mouths as Clive chimes, "Thank you, Bird. Lord knows, with anyone your size I'm surprised it's not Big Bird."

The Chief now grabs my bags, places them in the wide trunk of the older model Chevy with the ease of someone lifting a bag of cotton and closes the trunk softly. "You can see that I have brought others on our journey today. It is my mother and her sister. Because of my path into drugs, they have adopted the form of spirit guides for me and show up from time to time to accompany me on my way. I hope this is okay with you, Richard."

I open my door and look into the backseat. Two older, native ladies of considerable bulk are staring back at me. One is wearing a kerchief on her head, and the other, like The Chief, has a cluster of feathers attached to a bun at the base of her skull. Both are grinning like Cheshire cats, displaying various gaps where teeth once stood. The one closest to me has a collection of vagrant, bristly hairs sprouting from her chin, and the other has deep, weathered lines chiseled into her cheeks, that remind me of the bark on an ancient, long standing cedar.

As I turn to bid goodbye to Randy and Clive, I hear The Chief inviting them to join us on our pilgrimage to the airport. This will be free of any charges of course. To my mounting consternation they accept the invitation without hesitation. They both sputter apologies for their state of dress as they station themselves beside opposite rear doors. The old gals heft their hulking bottoms toward the middle of the seat to make room. I climb into the front and glance back with a forced smile frozen on my face. Before The Chief has even left the parking area Clive has offered the women apple cheese blintzes and coffee. I know that Randy is critically observing the hairs on the face of the woman seated directly by his side, wishing for the life of him that he could dab a blob of Oh So Smooth's new Hair Away Body Cream onto that chin.

Chief Bird now introduces the ladies to us. The one with the kerchief and whiskers is his mother, Running Deer, and the other is his Aunt Sadie, who doesn't always choose to use her Indian name while mixing with non-natives. She wants to facilitate assimilation into the white culture, which she has so far found confusing. He says that she is perplexed by the white man's ways but fascinated at the same time. I observe the foursome squeezed as close as sardines in a can. They look like a sepia-toned photo of early explorers with their robust, native concubines huddled in a birch bark bivouac waiting patiently for the winter rains to subside.

My phone chimes loudly in the confined space. I fumble for it with a start. I don't know who could be calling me at this hour but suspect it must be Frankie Butts with annoying last-minute queries. When I answer, the frail voice on the other end of the line makes my heart stop momentarily, and my mouth turns bone dry.

"Daddy, it's me…"

For a second, I don't know what to say.

"Sweetheart," I whisper hoarsely, as though I've just been awakened from a deep sleep. Then a prolonged silence that seems to go on too long for anything good to come of it. I fear my daughter, who is out there somewhere but at least partially connected by this phone signal, may be gone.

"I'm getting clean."

She falls silent again. I think that I can hear her crying and I want to tell The Chief to stop this bloody car right now because I have to go to her this very instant. She needs her father. I will not let the words "get clean" coming from my little girl's mouth paralyze me, as such words can. I can still picture a happy home with laughter aplenty. I know I shouldn't say the words I am about to say, because they might terminate the call. But I say them anyway. "Where are you?"

The phone sounds as if it has gone dead. My words somehow construed as judgment, as though I had asked, "What shame have you done?" have increased the distance between us. The air in the car is suddenly so thick I can hardly breath.

"Listen, Daddy, I've got to go. Don't worry, I'll find you when the time's right.— I love you."

And she's gone. I stare at the phone, as if waiting for it to reactivate and for her to say we must have inadvertently been disconnected and why don't we meet for a coffee. But none of this will happen this morning. I snap the phone closed, turn toward The Chief and whisper, "That was my daughter."

Randy reaches from the backseat and squeezes my shoulder. I turn to look at Randy, then Clive. They have watched both girls finish high school and have attended all the important functions associated with their teen-aged lives. Clive's expression, trapped between bewilderment and hope, says more than a dictionary of words. I visualize myself as the critically ill father in some old Hollywood tear-jerker, starring Pat O/Brien and Yvonne De Carlo. I'm lying in a dimly lit hospital room, refusing my pain medication until my wayward daughter, who has been summoned by the parish priest, comes to my bedside and whispers tearfully, "I'll be alright now, Daddy. Don't worry, you can go now." I raise my finger, feebly signaling to the emotionally distraught doctor and nurse looking on that they can commence the lethal morphine drip, for my patriarchal responsibilities here on earth are finally met.

Before I can turn back to face the front of the car, Running Deer removes a medicine bag from around her neck and places the small, animal-hide pouch over my head. It is suspended there, like a sleeping bat, by a leather thong. I accept this gift as if it has been given and received countless times before.

"What is your daughter's name?" The Chief asks.

Dumbfounded, I turn to him. "It's Tess." I repeat the name with more conviction. "Tess."

I suddenly realize that I haven't said her name in a long time, as though the name itself is somehow responsible for her troubles. The Chief contin-ues wheeling the big car through the rain-slick streets effortlessly as if he were herding a team of oxen from one pasture to the next. "You must say her name for the spirit guides to locate her. She must have a name or they cannot separate her from the many others whose souls must wander in the darkness searching for the right path to take."

Aunt Sadie now says something in her Haida language that sounds like "Muk cluk mu gluk klu." The Chief turns to me and says, "My Aunt has given your daughter a spirit name to protect her. She is Shadow Rain Woman because she walks in the shadows with the rain."

I stare straight ahead at the yawning empty roadway. The two elder women in the back begin a low moaning chant that rises and falls in sonorous tones like wild animals communicating in the forest or whales calling out from their ancient, watery depths. The Chief joins in this prayer, his voice coming from a place I may have known once before my birth, while still being cradled in my mother's womb. Leaving one hand on the wheel, he reaches out with the other and takes my hand in his. Without moving my hand away, I sit still and wait. Aunt Sadie reaches over the seat, placing an eagle feather into my right hand, and tells me that if I hold it to my heart it will help me to soar high above my fears and earthly limitations and find my daughter's spirit place. I hold the feather against the medicine bag and press them both to my heart. Their voices rise up with longing to unseen gods that may still be able to coax the buffalo back to the great plains and cleanse the rivers and lakes of our impurities. Clive and Randy now join in the prayer, their displaced voices bouncing across the distant moans like flattened stones over a deep and mysterious pond.

I realize this would all look a tad odd if we were to suddenly pull over to the curb and be greeted by Frankie Butts and the New York Bankers, and maybe even The Inquisition as well. But despite what it may look like, it *feels* like it may be the right thing to be doing at this moment. I press The Chief's hand a little tighter in mine. I gaze out the front window at the lone, shuffling figures. The night people in the darkened alleyways, their shopping carts piled with the cast-offs of other people's lives, their shoulders swollen from layers of clothing, looking like hunchbacked cathedral bell ringers searching for their tower loft of love and acceptance. I turn my head to the striated lights stretching across the side window. I squeeze my eyes shut. I am trying to stay the tears before they become visible to all. One truant droplet slips from my eye down my cheek, coming to rest at the corner of my mouth. I can taste its salty texture. It is my daughter's blood and solitude and pain. I try to hold it on my tongue.

PART TWO: MONEY

*"My heart has searched my whole life long
for something that I cannot name."*

Eugene O'Neill

CHAPTER 14

SIAMESE TWINS ARE ONE OF THE RAREST OF BIRTH ANOMALIES, NUMBER-
ing one in every two hundred thousand babies born. And when one
contemplates how many of these twins actually live, let alone thrive, the
negative odds go through the stratosphere. Now, add to this already tortured scenario the number of these people that become two of the richest
and most fabled financiers in the world and you have Wang and Zang Ton,
(pronounced "tawn," as in wonton.) They grew up, known to associates
and class mates, behind their backs mostly, as "Two Ton." which started
out in their Oxford years as "The-Two-For-One Ton" then "Two-In-One
Ton" eventually abbreviated through the telling to its present simpler
derivative form of Two Ton. They have, more recently become known to
the general traveling public by another signature trademark name, a name
splashed across advertising pamphlets and billboards throughout the
world of leisure travel and recreational property ownership as Tons' Time
Share Vacations.

I have stopped in Toronto for a meeting with the Tons. As of approximately one week ago, Charles Witherspoon informed me that the twenty-
five million dollars of private financing required by the banks, before their
injection of another fifty to one hundred million, was coming from none
other than, The Twins.

Born in China sometime in the mid 1940s, their parents had fled to
the then Portuguese colony of Macao. This was after Mao and his Great
Leap Forward swept into power in 1949. The Twins' father was an itinerant trader, a reviled merchant in an impoverished agrarian society, who I
suppose, could see little future pursuing his bourgeois line of work within
a despotic communist state. Macao, not unlike its bigger and marginally
more respectable kindred colony further up the Sea of China, Hong Kong,
was open for business no matter what the product or service. This was
all presented in a lawless package without the bothersome annoyance of
legal, social or moral responsibility. A good fit.

The senior Ton made his fortune selling intricately carved ivory.
Some exquisite pieces, inscrutably fashioned over an entire lifetime by
the methodical hand of a nameless, pig-tailed enigmatic artisan, were no
thicker or weightier than a hummingbird's tail feather. These curiosities
were sold to wealthy Europeans and Chinese ex-patriots living throughout

the far-flung reaches of the world. It was a world the Ton's forbearers had mapped a full century before Columbus had peeked from behind his mother's skirt. Macao continued to be a place of refuge for the sordid and commercially lucrative. The Tons, now father and son(s), branched out into hotel and gambling casino operations. Later, after their father's death, The Twins entered into hugely profitable general construction projects in the People's Republic of China, as that long slumbering economy grew increasingly restless throughout the 1980s and 90s. This was the self same place that had expelled their father little more than a half century before. It was an irony that didn't escape the Ton brothers' consciousness. Whenever they returned to China to inspect building projects, or conclude negotiations with the less doctrinaire of the post Maoist communist masters, they would often visit the street of shanties in which their father had been born. On such visits, they would bestow welcome gifts of money, precious school supplies and bolts of spun cotton and raw silks, for the mothers and grandmothers to make clothing for their families. These tokens, distributed among the poor of the area, were given in solemn reverence to their father's memory, completing the prophetic ancestral circle, so to speak. Over time, folklore being what it is, these same people grew to view *Ton The Elder* as a modern day saint, a man committed to the common good. A collection was taken up in the neighbourhood and a small bronze plaque was erected with a likeness of the late Ton Senior's face stamped onto its russet surface. A brief catalogue of his now legendary good works were written below. Murmured prayers to his beloved memory flooded the evening skies.

Games of chance are to the Chinese what whiskey is to the Irish. No matter how well educated or technically informed, their history from centuries past dictates that the dowager princess *Lady Luck,* above all else, seals one's fate and determines one's destiny. Joss sticks smolder in pungent homage, welcoming the good blessings of those esteemed departed. Colossal aquariums shine like watery portholes into another rich and luxuriant world. Exotic fish listlessly curve among the brightly coloured coral statuaries like ghostly guides showing the way for good fortune and prosperity to enter. Shrieking Macaws and florescent plumed parrots stand in bamboo cages beside entranceways from balconies and hidden private decks, feathered testaments to the owner's affluence. At tables large and small, centuries old celebrations continue in a seamless unbroken line. Elaborate meals prepared and offered strictly adhering to the traditional courses of rice for wealth, noodles for longevity, meat and sea-foods for health and happiness abounded.

So, the Tons got rich, as only people that are unfettered by regulatory bodies, bureaucratic interference, and income taxes can. There were hefty bribes to be paid, but they were merely considered another cost of doing business and, like any other business expense, were factored into the end price. To the Tons ledgers and financial records were private matters for their eyes only, never to be scrutinized by a tax man or investigated by an outside authority as to their compliance with anyone else's code of conduct.

As children, the Ton boys wandered the cloistered back alleys of Macao, crowded alleyways teaming with hawkers' stalls. Everything in life, and sometimes death, was for sale. The fantastical, the bizarre and the macabre were all here for the taking. Figurines etched painstakingly by ancient and humble human hands from green translucent jade as hard as time. The bones and skeletal shrunken skin of animals, both large and small, ground to fine powder and sold as tonics for life's many irretrievable ills. The rarest of animals for sale, their inflated prices representative of their place on an Endangered Species List. An account compiled in some quieter and cleaner place far away from these dark musty back streets. Herbal remedies tied with hemp twine hung in the sweat stained night breezes beside bamboo cages holding baffled monkeys and tranquil cobras, their majestic fighting resolve diminished to pathetic listlessness in the small confines of these wooden traps. These same snakes waiting for their bellies to be slit open exposing the creamy bile ducts swollen and waiting to be milked and sold as rejuvinating elixirs at seventy-five dollars US a thimble cup. This place was the teenaged Tons' video game store or arcade amusement stop, teaching them to be the hunter not the gatherer, to be the slayer not the slain.

As is oft times the case, over time their ill gotten financial proceeds inevitably found their way into more and more quasi legitimate businesses, and their reputations were expunged like baptismal shrouds with repeated river cleansings. However, their very generous donations to this international university endowment or that medical research project ushered the Born Again Twins into the world of international finance and legitimate enterprise. Their names painstakingly amended until they were synonymous with all that is noble. They were finally renowned not only for good works, but good times for the taking at any one of their twenty-five Tons' Time Share Vacations destinations throughout the world. .And yes, this sanitized, well scrubbed, tri-pedal, two headed financial juggernaut had surfaced in my world as well.

I had first met the Tons five years before when I was helping to finance a mining venture in Canada's North West Territories with a group of Canadians headed by a Chinese exile. My partners and I had gone to Macao to meet with them at that time and give our presentation. I must admit, even after being forewarned about their "difference" to feeling awkward. I felt then, and to some extent still do now, that they might be more trouble than their money was worth. Sometimes money is worth a lot of trouble, but not always. Anyway, that was a while ago and Wang and Zang Ton were now waiting for me in the Board Room of Charles B. Witherspoon who among other things holds a Chair on the Toronto Stock Exchange and is a senior partner in Witherspoon, Owen, Tuttle & Marsh, the brokerage firm that is the main underwriter of the Cuban deal. The mining exploration venture in Canada's north came to naught, but provided me with a chance to go at sundown and watch the vaporous northern lights swan gracefully across the turbulent ionized, sub-polar skies, illuminating for one and all the fact that this is, indeed, a place of beauty and mysterious privilege to be cherished and protected.

Toronto is the place to go in Canada to make things happen. If Canada were a wheel, Toronto would be its hub. Vancouver and Calgary have money, but lack the political connections and the Old Boy Systems to follow through on anything outside of their respective borders and spheres of influence.

The cab ride along Toronto's infamous 401 is not unlike a road race of sorts. It is the gauntlet to be run before being allowed entrance into the domain of big league gamesmanship. I may as well be strapped onto the bitch-seat of a Hell's Angels Harley for an initiation ride. I am pummeled by sudden, stabbing compressions of my spine as the beleaguered late model Chevy bottoms out while rocketing off an exit ramp, or merges with reckless indifference onto the freeway barreling between two over loaded speeding transports. The Pakistani driver is, as always seems to be the case, consumed in an animated conversation on his cell phone, possibly with a distraught parent, unaccustomed to our informal, western ways. Maybe today it's his spouse or his in-laws, his growing responsibility to this extended family taking its toll on his store of energy. I am thinking of The Chief and my ride to the airport in Vancouver this morning. And of Tess's call, and how such things can mean so much, when hope is in short supply. I grapple with these wayward digressions. My thoughts come back to the meeting I am heading toward. The knowledge of how much more bizarre things may become before this day's work is done, sends a low, electric twinge through the pit of my stomach.

The Twins, unlike most normal people, but not unlike most in the world of high finance that they inhabit, are almost impossible to read. Their personalities are very different. Zang, who refers to himself as Number One Son because he was born a nano second ahead of his brother Wang , is always watchful of everything going on within his sightlines. Zang is cunning. His questions, although accompanied by a perpetually sanguine smile, are always pointed and belie an ever-present sense of suspicion not of you alone, but of the world as a whole. It is as if we cumulatively conspired to place him into his unwieldy shell. And no doubt, this is the face the world has presented to one half of conjoined twins, but on the other hand, Wang is a very different person. Where Zang is cunning, Wang is shrewd. He is immensely more human, or at the very least more approachable. His smile seems to be genuinely less guarded, more open and sincere than his brother's. He cordially attempts to be social with anyone sitting or standing close by, often telling an amusing story or recounting a recent event. Unfortunately, these efforts can often fall on deaf or bewildered ears. Unlike his brother, whose elocution is precise despite a strong Chinese accent, Wang was burdened with a cleft palate at birth. Many costly and, I'm sure, painful surgeries have sutured the lesion shut with close to perfect results, leaving only a vague scar and an almost inaudible nasal whoosh when he speaks. This tonal distortion, coupled with a stronger Chinese accent, void of almost every syllabic intonation makes it very difficult to understand much, if anything, of what he is saying. It is a shortcoming, further exacerbated unfortunately, by his being a bit of a chatterbox and social gadfly who rarely shuts up.

Before my previous meeting with The Twins I was forewarned that it might be more comfortable to try to be seated on Zang's side, letting their advisers and black-suited bearers sit by Wang.

Although the brothers can walk quite well, though actually it looks more like a sideways shuffle, not unlike an Orangutan couple out for a stroll, or a team of synchronized gymnasts going through their paces, they are carried in what I can only describe as a sedan chair by two strapping chaps in black suits whenever they have to travel any distance greater than a few hundred steps on foot. This apparatus is very similar to ones that we have seen carrying emperors and empresses in movies. It is comprised of two telescoping aluminum poles. They are about eight feet in length when fully extended. A piece of durable-looking canvas fabric is stretched between these poles. It has three circular holes placed in a loosely shaped isosceles triangle. Two additional strips of cabled material are fastened to either side to be used as handles. It is something for The Twins to hold onto when they are aloft. The Black Suits look for the world like assassins straight out of a James Bond movie, and I suspect they are adept at any number of marshal arts. No doubt, they also pack heat strapped inconspicuously to their calves or against the small of their taut and sinewy backs. With all of this plainly said, I must now differentiate between the private and public personae of The Twins. These are totally at odds with each other. To the public the Tons are, The Time Share Tons or The Kings of Time Share. Most of the brother's wide and luxuriant resort holdings are structured and sold worldwide as Time Shared accommodations. Their pictures are often featured in glossy brochures and in the circulars outlining vacation package purchase options prominently displayed in Travel Agent's information racks. Often, large window displays feature their smiling, round faces. Two young tycoons, who despite their obvious physical disadvantages, can get down and serious about a proper vacation outing. The pictures are heavily doctored, showing only the brother's bodies from above the waist, images not unlike those depicting the youthful octogenarian Mao, swimming in the Yangtzi River. This is to create the image of fun in the sun, without actually showing them doing any thing other than sitting in a deck chair, or astride a surfboard safely harnessed to a floating pontoon raft, or anchored securely at a dockside. This publicity machine has gone so far as to create a mythology attesting to The Twins frequenting these sites, and participating in these water sports, or beach ball tournaments. Some television ads have athletic sun-bronzed actors emerging from the surf, or turning to look and wave at some unseen spectators off camera, implying that they are looking upon the Tons after they have spiked a sure-fire point in volleyball or thrown a low arching gravity defying Frisbee down a secluded date palm dotted beach. The truth of the matter is that Wang and Zang Ton rarely go to any of their resort locations. The brothers harbour no illusions in this regard. The image mongering is the work of others. It's not unlike the old Hollywood machine propelling a Rock Hudson or Montgomery Clift to the center stage as a womanizing hunk, while knowing none of it to be remotely true to their characters.

Another bold-faced lie is that these resorts are user friendly for people with disabilities when in fact, wherever possible, The Twins themselves have nixed socially integrating programs and structural modifications to their properties. To be fair, at first they did try to accommodate this special *inclusive* quality to their operations, but cooled after they perceived that costs were running too high. They are "bottom line" guys. Their previous bout of momentary largesse replaced with the brass tacks assertion that having hordes of people milling about the pool areas, who may in fact have urinary tract or bowel control issues, would not be good for business. When would a vagrant turd, or creeping yellow stain, force the draining of a pool, or bleaching of a hot tub? Downtime was expensive. And what if these same incontinent souls decided that a night of dancing was in order, their cumbersome battery-driven wheel chairs cluttering the disco dance floors, or other equally intrusive, unwieldy apparati blocking entrances and exits. A fire hazard at best. None of these alterations was remotely a cost efficient use of such valuable income generating resort space. So, although they allow the use of their image as people with disabilities in their advertising, they have waged a systematic campaign of non-inclusive policies at the Board Room Table.

Many organizations, specializing in services for the disabled, have received negative feedback from their members, trusting souls who have booked holidays at these paradise locations, only to find an ambivalent and unsympathetic staff. The rooms featuring doorways too narrow to accommodate motorized wheel chairs access. Bathroom commodes situated on elevated ornately tiled pedestals, virtually unattainable to all but the most youthful and athletic. The beaches without excavated pathways for disabled access to the water. The grand design of their discos always framed by opulent entrances, featuring winding staircases that acted as barriers to those that aren't fleet of foot. These criticisms of Tons' Time Share Vacations within the travel community have usually fizzled, the people reporting them having been treated to an all expense paid trip or luxury cruise or Casino Weekend Special replete with complimentary chips, often calculated in the thousands of dollars.

When I exit the private elevator to the penthouse suite of offices, I am greeted by Charles Witherspoon's private secretary, Elise, who is worth every penny of the seventy-five thousand a year she probably earns. She is the personification of poise, a guard at the gate to Witherspoon's inner sanctum sanctorum. She is a shield with as much class and brittle fortitude as a dagger-wielding courtesan to a royal house. Today, Elise is wearing a particularly well-tailored dark skirt accentuating her saddle-hard rump, which I look at for an instant too long, affording her the opportunity to turn and catch me out with a coolish smirk. She holds the door and politely motions for me to pass through and into the Board Room. I feel as if I am being introduced from the audience of *Who Told You*.

The furnishings have just the right measure of discreet presence. The soft burnished autumn-coloured leather testifies to their business like heft, but also indicates an understated elegance. Good taste is whispered, rather than shouted. The floor to ceiling plate glass windows open onto a vista of the city's skyline that is breathtaking, saying loudly and clearly that you have come to the right place with your hard earned millions.

Charles stands and begins walking toward me in his ramrod straight gait, his arm held high and in front of his body, as if pointing out to everyone in the room that a wild boar has just run past the door. He is one of the old boys of Bay Street, with his three-piece pin stripe and old school tie, a colour-coordinated hanky peeking from the double-breasted jacket's pocket. There is another man in his late thirties in the room whom I do not know, but guess to be a senior up-and-comer from the Corporate Brokerage side of the operation. And, of course, Wang and Zang Ton, who remain seated, which I am grateful for, since watching them get to their feet can be a gut-wrenching and awkward spectacle. One is left not knowing whether to offer assistance and risk insulting the disabled person's fiercely won sense of independence, or stand by lamely, waiting for possible calamity. And if a fall does occur, what then? More idle scrutiny or once again risking an unwanted intrusion into unmapped personal space?

The Tons are conjoined at the waist and a little to the front side of their barreled torsos. Both upper bodies, from the lower chest to the tops of their heads, are separate and distinctly owned by each individual brother. It is from the waist down that a certain amount of provisional ambiguity enters. The brother's have only three legs. I'm speculating that a fourth may have existed at one time, due mainly to a rather large, stump-like protrusion from the right hip of Wang. This leg, if it ever was a leg, may have been either surgically removed, for whatever reason, or may never have developed at all and simply been stunted at this point in its early evolution, not unlike a whale's feet or an ape's opposable thumb. Off hand, I don't know which brother controls which of their three legs. For stability, I presume, they always walk with their arms slung around one another's shoulders, like two buddies headed for the showers after a good, hard-fought game of touch football. I have no idea about their manly parts in terms of how many and who owns what, but it has been rumoured, and God only knows on what authority, that they indeed have two functioning sets of male genitalia. Judging from the position of their lower abdomens, I can only assume that they are in close enough proximity to each other to cause a whole set of personal hygiene problems and nocturnal erectile situations, that shall remain unimaginable to the rest of us.

They both smile. At least, Wang smiles widely and mumbles a hearty greeting or anecdote I don't quite catch. I smile equally as broadly, nodding in approval and hoping that it wasn't a question that requires a further verbal response. Zang's lips are parted just far enough to be a sneer and he says,

"Mistah Richawd Bonhom. Long time no see. I trust all is well."

I shake Charles' hand firmly. The course black hairs creeping down around his knuckles and onto the backs of his fingers from under the starched white shirt sleeve are ticklish to the touch, like a newborn porcupine. I bow slightly to The Twins who are seated on the other side of the board table and turn to be introduced to the other man, a Mr. Jonathan Smythe. He is not one of Charles' people, after all, but is, instead, employed by The Twins. This relationship will be made clear to me when, and if, they think that it is necessary information to impart. I glance across the table before sitting, mentally graphing whether it would be wiser to place myself opposite Zang, to dampen the possibility of Wang striking up an informal chat. Generally the elder Zang speaks for them when involved in a business dialogue.

It is Charles Witherspoon that breaks the ice with an informal synopsis outlining the subjects to be covered in today's meeting. He is a take charge kind of guy, and we are in his playpen. I am happy that he has taken this initiative to act as Chairperson. This takes the responsibility from me, and will possibly afford me more latitude in addressing any of The Twins' concerns. I'm certain they have these in abundance.

"There are three main points the Tons would like further explanation on." A last minute drill before the papers are signed in Cuba.

Charles turns to them for affirmation of this, as if it is just something that rolled off his tongue. I know full well they have been huddled in this very office all morning hammering out what exactly is bothering these moneybags, and how it can be smoothed over. The Twins blandly nod like nothing is really on their minds, other than a dim sum luncheon in Toronto's Chinatown. Having strategically placed himself on *their* side of the table Charles resumes addressing me, as if I were the interloper in the hot seat. He is now acting as their tried and true spokesperson, when in fact we all know that he is squarely positioned on *my* side of the negotiation, this being obvious by the unrepentant fact that he is collecting phenomenal fees and percentages numbering in the multi-millions of dollars —all from their money.

"Firstly. What are the assurances that the Executive Team is capable of managing this monster? Are the systems in place to streamline paperwork and financials to keep on top of any leaks in the dam?"

Charles knows full well that this is everyone's concern. Whenever something as diverse and unconnected as a mining, medical and hospitality venture is proposed, systems will always be an issue. He also knows that we have put some of the best people in the world — several of them of his own choosing — in charge. Even more importantly, The Twins know the obvious pitfalls lurking out there for us to tumble into. What Charles is really asking, is whether we can ditch people and cut bait in any of the three sectors at the first whiff of trouble. Remember, although Zang and Wang Ton are Oxford-educated scholars both holding Masters Degrees in Economics and Business Management, they are first and foremost, their father's sons. They were weaned by hireling wet nurses, and no doubt have often watched dad administer severe canings, or crushing reprimands to cowering floor supervisors whose quotas had fallen below expectations. The Twins already know what they will do if things go wonky. They will send in their people to deal with our people. What is really troubling them is their knowledge that their ways, although probably acceptable to Cuba's power elite, who can most certainly always be bribed to look the other way, may not work if their Canadian partners get weak kneed on them. So their first concern isn't Cuba at all, but rather Canada. Are *we* strong enough if hardball rules apply?

My answer has to appear to address the point being verbalized, but more importantly has to address the unspoken matter as well.

"Everyone at this table already knows the endemic problems in the monster that we are creating. And I don't doubt that most of us would walk away from the table without looking back if we also didn't plainly see the huge opportunities that this venture presents, not only for the short term, but for generations yet to come. We are gaining a strategic foothold in an emerging economy that is within spitting distance of the United States and Mexico, with combined populations of close to five hundred million people. Will things go wrong? Most certainly. Have we got the stopgap failsafe measurement systems in place to see the holes and plug them before the boat sinks? I think that there are people in this room that know that better than me. The Tons have financed more of these kind of deals than I have. Are you comfortable with our structures? "

Now I pause for dramatic effect and try to stare into both sets of the Ton brothers' eyes simultaneously,

"Are you comfortable that you can get to your money if all else fails? The answer to that in the First Phase should be *yes,* since the money will be held in a Barbados Bank and invested through a series of draw downs as work progress is verified. Likewise, revenues from operations will be held in US dollar accounts in Barbados prior to a final audit and disbursement to the various partners. Your company has a controlling vote in the Barbados subsidiary, so you have the final word regarding all monies. It is we that are vulnerable to you in the final analysis. Canadian authorities have no jurisdiction over Barbados domiciled companies."

The Twins now look at each other for a second, then both glance down the table toward Jonathon Smythe, who nods his head slightly. He returns his gaze to Charles, as if saying "check"— next item if you please.

Charles continues solemnly as if the weight of these matters is pushing him farther down into his high-backed leather chair.

"Secondly. What political protections are in place regarding our ownership rights to our property on the island, and what measures are in place if we have a dispute with the Cuban government?"

This is really the nub of what is bothering The Twins, as well as the rest of us. What happens if Castro's old gang simply steps up to the plate and say that they want it all. Hasta la vista baby! What court of appeal do we run to? What gunslinger do we dispatch to protect our interests? Whose ear do we bend and whose wrist do we twist? The biggest bad-assed gunslinger in the world is the United States, and they aren't going to come across the gulf with tracers firing from beneath the wings of their radar-defying Stealth Bombers because *we* suddenly find ourselves in trouble. Not only don't they have anything to gain, but they're probably righteously pissed off with us anyway, for being there. They see us as opportunistic carpetbaggers, which we are. They aren't in the deal, and everyone feels better when they are in the room in deals like this, because when everything comes down to dust, they have lots of fire-power and not too many qualms about using it. I look at the tabletop for a moment thinking

carefully of my answer. This isn't the time or place for bullshit. The Twins
and Mr. Jonathan Smythe, whoever the hell he is, can smell it a mile away.
They would also rightly view the attempt at passing it around as an insult
worse than the actual words that it was camouflaged within. There is really
only one answer that is suitable for the occasion. The honest one.

"No guarantees gentlemen. If you're looking for a guarantee, go buy a
toaster. We've got Cuban Law, which is based on the Napoleonic Code,
and many precedents acknowledging the rights of foreign corporations to
do business in the country. But in the end it's a military dictatorship, and
all that we can hope is that the politicians that we've bought, stay bought!"

There is an old saying among salesmen, "Say your piece and shut up.
He who talks first, loses." Let the customer squirm. I button up and wait
out the silence that engulfs the room. Charles wants to say something to
soften my words, but he's too old a hand at this game to interrupt the stillness. He, like me and maybe even The Twins, doesn't know what is on the
other's mind at this moment. It is Wang that speaks. The words, although
breathy, are clear enough to understand.

"What if da gobmit change?"

I look at him without blinking or pausing.

"Then we deal with the new ones. The country is virtually bankrupt.
No matter who is running the show they will need foreign currency to
make things work. If they nationalize again, I think that the Americans
will nuke the island into the gulf waters that surround it."

It is a strong point, for indeed, the US isn't in the mood for another
Bay of Pigs. The plain fact of the matter is that none of us wants to be
entangled in a long, drawn out political upheaval. But in the end, if you
want the prize, you have to be the first to ride through the gates of the for-
bidden city. The Twins stare straight ahead at nothing in particular. None
of this is new to them. They have been places and seen things that would
send Charles and me, and possibly even Mr. Jonathan Smythe, highballing
from the office, shrieking like adolescent schoolgirls after spying the Head
Master rogering Miss Hoople, the gym teacher, across his roll top desk.
After a smidgen longer pause than previously The Twins look down the
table at Jonathan, who blinks twice, then looks back toward Charles for
the conclusive point.

Charles unconsciously extends the middle finger of his left hand. He
bends it back with the index finger of his right hand and, looking directly
at me, blurts,

"The Tons have suggested that they go to Cuba with you for a final site
inspection prior to signing the papers. Is this a problem?"

I am caught off guard. I visibly shudder, as if I had been punched in
the solar plexus and have come up short of breath. This was not discussed

in any previous meetings, and is very much out of sync with how such business is conducted. This type of investor meeting should have taken place much earlier in our dealings and, in fact, did on several previous occasions. The Twins sent their top aids to inspect the properties and sit in on the meetings with government representatives and management partners. If I arrive in Cuba with the Tons, I might as well be stepping from the plane leading a Cyclops on the end of a fucking leash. These people have been in a time warp for the last fifty years. They can barely accept the invention of the transistor radio, let alone a two-headed person. I try to regain my composure, knowing full well that The Tons have seen and noted my initial hesitation. I want to dispel any thoughts that they may be entertaining regarding the cause of that hesitation, this being that I am trying to hide something. I must try to hang it all on protocol.

"I'm quite frankly surprised." I stammer slightly, trying to push my voice back down an octave, closer to its usual pitch. "A late game run like this could be interpreted by our Cuban partners to be a last minute loss of heart, which wouldn't send the right message. They are a proud people and take a lot of slow steps to gain confidence with outsiders."

Christ, I might as well call Chief White Eagle Man Buffalo Child and his family to join us as well. I wonder if Wally and Jerome are up for a little international marketing experience? Maybe it would be good for their tutor to see the end result of pure unfettered socialism along the mean soiled streets of old Havana. By all means bring Clive and Randy along with their plates of blintz's and multi level marketing books and yes, even my daughter Tess can oblige us all with some smack and make a real party of the whole thing. I'm at a loss as to what to say or do, so I do what any normal thinking individual would. Nothing. "Fine, if the Tons want to come to Cuba. Via con dios!"

Everyone smiles weakly before Charles draws this part of the meeting to a close with a final secondary point.

"Of course the Tons will be accompanied by..." here he momentarily stumbles, not knowing what exactly to call the two black suited men that accompany The Twins everywhere. He can't say bearers or handlers or ringmasters or goons. What the fuck do you call these two gazoonies, anyway? It is Zang that now breaks the uncomfortable silence, "Servants," he intones, with all of the casualness reserved for those that have always had people, outside of family members, doing their bidding and tending to their every possible need. It is the kind of word a Queen or a Boy King from Nepal would use freely, but it hangs in the air, separating the rest of us from the *noblesse oblige* like a fine silk curtain of disdain.

So it is settled. The Siamese Twin Ton brothers are accompanying me to meet with our Cuban partners and government liaisons to finalize the deal. I'm sure the presence of "servants" will go over like a big cigar in the Marxist State of Cuba.

I take my leave of Charles Witherspoon's offices proffering excuses for declining a supper invitation at The Twins' hotel suite. I walk the short distance to my hotel, the downtown Hyatt on Richmond Street. After checking in and leaving my overnight valise in the room, I decide to go for a walk along the busy streets of old Yorkville. A chance to clear my head from the day's activities. Dusk's twinkling lights create shimmering hallows in the cooling evening air.

Although Mr. Jonathan Smythe was never properly introduced, in terms of what he exactly does for The Twins, I suspect that he is their marketing consultant for Tons' Time Share Vacations. I have been told that they don't stray too far into a new venture without bringing these sales types into the loop. Mr. Jonathon Smythe was here today to watch and listen. To see if his radar detected any low-flying bandits, any slight change in the direction the winds of recreational commerce were blowing.

CHAPTER FIFTEEN

COMMUTERS HUSTLE AND BUSTLE UP ONE SIDE OF TORONTO'S YORK Street and down the other. Their loving faces are strained from the day's toil, resolutely chiseled into a mask of stoical resolve with the knowledge of the work yet to be done on the home front, before the dishes are cleared and kids are bathed and put to bed.

They are the same people that, when returning from a Tons' Time Share Vacation to exotic locales, are always full of stories of wide cultural chasms magnifying our differences documented with pictures taken beside ancient Chinese tribes people wearing colourful, pointy hats made of bark or thatch. There may be snapshots of the family squatting awkwardly against the flattened mud of the forest floor between bashful pigmies. The visitor's grimaces speaking volumes as they politely share the aboriginals' humble evening meal of blood saturated goat's milk, or bony scorched rodent meat.

I, on the other hand, am always impressed by how alike we all are. Whether dad and mum are returning from a day's numbing labour on a banana plantation in Borneo, or an Inuit couple are mushing their sinewy sled dogs across the last stretch of polar ice, all are basically trying to provide for their families and share a moment to count their blessings and rekindle the cherished embers of parental love.

I once read that Chinese pirates would swoop down on coastal villages, looting, raping and kidnapping the wealthiest people's babies. They would then eat the infants, in the belief that the good fortune that had visited the child's parents would be transferred to them. This is mankind's history. This is ultimately our birthright.

*

I am hungry, but am enjoying the air. It is clearing my head and allowing me to make more sense of this latest wrinkle in the elaborately woven tapestry of the Cuban deal. After all, is it anything more than a complex game of wits? Isn't there always another horse coming around the course? That's the way the game is played. No matter how important a victory seems, it is always in everyone's best interests to live to play another day. Keep getting back on the horse. That's what the Banasi brothers always say, whenever adversity rears up in their path, which it frequently does in the real estate development business. Old Julio just climbs out of his Caddy and stomps right up to the angry crowd of neighbours saying, "What do ja tink you doing? I gotta da right to build da houses por da familias. Then he waves his court ordinance in their faces and stomps back to his car kicking the pavement like an umpire who is being booed for making a bad call in the bottom of the ninth, with two out and the bases loaded. That's the grit I should marshal, although of late, I must admit to feelings that belie other, less righteous postures than the Banasi's would, or even could, possibly imagine. Julio and Tony would shake their heads like threatened water buffalo, waggling their fat fingers in my face like a scolding parent from the brazen back streets of Naples. They would say that it's not my place to take on the weight of other's burdens. Once you get your eye on the ball, you keep it there. You don't take no for an answer. You do whatever it takes, and then you do some more. You fight the bastards! But, alas, I am not a Banasi. Winston Churchill said, "If you find yourself going through hell, then keep going," A rum idea from a plucky chap — keep going! Ha!

Lately, at times like this, I must admit to questioning what I am, what I do, and what I ultimately want for my life. It's clichéd I know, but so be it. These thoughts come to me, as they do most men of my age, I suspect, whenever the full force of my disappointment momentarily seizes me in its bruising grip. And why not? Maybe I should chuck the whole kit and kaboodle and do something else? After all, I'm no slave to what I do. No jackdaw unable to slip its traces and bolt for the open meadow beyond. I am not a thick-necked, hairy-backed Banasi, and that simple goddamned fact must give me options. They would call this weakness and rail against it, their thick muscular arms stabbing at the air in frustration and defiance. My doubts about it all are increasing ten fold at the moment, like red-eyed rabbits in a small hutch.

Despite what our egos tell us in midnight choruses of evangelical esprit de corps, and numerous advertisements for job training on late night cable proclaim, the overall depth and breadth of the employment market is all too limiting for someone of my maturity. If I were ten or fifteen years younger, perhaps it would be a different story. A refresher course offered by, Career College Training Centre in Computer Technology or Seismic Research would put me back on the employment map in the blink of an eye. If one believes their message, there are numerous jobs out there for the taking. The only hurdle between you and a shining new future is a few months of professional training. Radiation Technologist, CAT scan Technician, Physiotherapist. The list seems endless, exciting prospects all. Perhaps the ideal candidate is the disillusioned mid-thirty something that has momentarily stumbled or lost their way while going through a messy divorce or an early bout with a melanoma, or maybe just woke up one day immobilized with fear or ennui and unable to lift one leaden leg over the other to climb out of bed. But would I be comfortable being the oldest guy in my graduating class, or perhaps the entire Career College Training Centre itself? The one that on first blush everyone would look up to for being a scrapper, a never-give-up-do-or-die-mascot? Someone that gets right back up off the mat after taking a good hard shot in the kisser. But with the passage of time would these same classmates turn a more critical eye, wondering, "If I don't play my cards right, someday I could be that poor sap."

Mine is the trap of the successful, middling executive in any job. When you have reached a certain level of performance and income, the lateral variables are thinning substantially. At such times one often thinks of self-employment as the doorway to fulfillment. What can you do that truly reflects your inner passions? The problem here being that at the moment I have none. For instance, I could not open my own model train store, the miniature locomotives dragging their chain of boxcars in an endless circle through tranquil window displays featuring elaborate little balsa wood alpine villages, with snow laden hedgerows fashioned from cotton balls. I could not twist balloons into the swollen, elongated shapes of animals at children's birthday parties, wearing comical, electric suspenders and floppy, over sized shoes. I do not see myself selling hotdogs from a vendor's kiosk on a busy street corner. Practically speaking, I don't know how to do very many things that would be, in the cold light of day, considered useful.

When I was walking to the office the other day I was standing at a red light. As I waited I idly watched a landscape maintenance crew working in one of the raised concrete flowerbeds beside the gleaming brass and glass entrance door of an office tower. It had dipped below zero during the night, turning the rain to a freak dusting of snow. A fine, white, powdery cover was left on the tops of the crocuses and winter pansies. It was one of those spontaneous transitory sights, like one encounters when standing in a shaft of warm morning sunshine, watching a springtime squall across the way form a rainbow. The crew were tilling the fallow winter soil and planting tulip and daffodil bulbs in concentric floral circles. There was one man of approximately my own age, and a young girl in her late teens or early twenties. She was bent double from the waist, with her legs locked in a straight V position, not unlike a young Springbok stooping to drink from a cloudy freshet of water on the equatorial Serengeti. The back waistband of her baggy military-styled camouflage pants was cupped into an arch, allowing passers by to glimpse the pale, white cleavage of her bum. Her plump buttocks were further framed by an ornate tattoo etched onto the small of her back, a picture painted, no doubt, by some fringe-dwelling rascal with multiple piercings and scalloped ink stained arms. Women walking past glanced, sometimes smirked, and turned away. As one would suspect, the men's looks lingered longer. I mused that all in all this didn't look like a bad way to spend one's days. Perhaps I could quite quickly grow accustomed to their seasonal schedule of planting and excavating bulbs and seedlings, my life guided by the earth's timeless rotations. No doubt, they greeted each and every day with a tall Starbucks, kibitzing about last night's escapades, possibly sharing a toke of the pungent marijuana grown throughout the west coast of Canada, a small welcome jolt to help nurture these worker's sluggish early morning minds into the rhythm of the moment. There didn't seem to be any unnecessary risks or pit falls attendant with this line of work—nothing stressful or disarming. The fresh air and exercise would be good for my aging constitution.

If I were to share this thought with anyone, even Genevieve, they would say that I had experienced some sort of mental breakdown or a midlife crisis. My colleagues from work would be angered, calling me a fuckin gardener, which, in their eyes, was on par with an itinerant worker. My lot would be irrevocably cast with that of the Mexican fruit picker or Caribbean cane cutter. An untouchable. When they came upon me kneeling in a flowerbed they would turn their eyes away, fearing that whatever I had gotten was somehow contagious, and that they, too, might awaken one morning and for no apparent reason, suddenly want *out*.

In all likelihood when, for whatever reason, people like me have reached the end of their tether after taking an extended sabbatical exploring India on an elephant's broad and bristly back, or taking a Wine Lovers Walking Tour of Tuscany, we usually end up settling for the more dismal probability of taking a lower form of employment than previously ever dreamt of. It would only be a matter of time before the savings would run precariously low. One morning, we would unexpectedly find ourselves sitting on the patio of our recently listed house, increasingly fearful that if a buyer didn't soon recognize all of the cozy features that drew us to purchasing this very same abode, we might end up one of the shuffling, homeless people we have quizzically watched from our idling cars at busy intersections on our way to or from somewhere. The harsh realization would take hold, as the seasons changed from springtime to the wispy sprigs of autumn, that we might have to start rising before dawn to deliver newspapers door to door. Maybe the Banasis are right. Fighting is the only real truth or option we have left in our post-war, post-modern bag of tricks.

So if I chose to cease working as an international financier earning close to seven figures a year, I suppose, at the very least, I could become a landscaper, or landscaper's helper. Or maybe just drop out and join some fringe religious cult and position myself at transportation terminals, chanting or passing out mimeographed tracts with astral themes that emphasizes the *oneness* of us all.

At the far end of Yorkville, where the African clothing stores, the bohemian bric-a-brac places, and the quaint squat tabled authentically ethnic restaurants give way to the pawn shops and sex stores advertising xxx Rated on their blackened windows, as if they were dismantled and moved here directly from the London Blitz, I see a small cubby hole eatery. The sign above the door is painted on plywood in startling purple letters surrounded by large unidentifiable flowers. It reads, Vlad's Hungarian Delights. It is directly opposite, Blackie's Pawn Shop of Distinction whose sign looks as if it may have been painted by the same person, perhaps a nephew recently arrived from the old country or a vagabond niece flirting with a career in the arts.

I bend slightly to gawk in the window and size up the place. A quick peek at the clientele tells volumes. There are only six or seven small square wooden tables with no one visible at any of them. This could be a warning signal that the food isn't any good or, to give the benefit of the doubt, maybe it's just too early in the evening for Hungarians to eat supper. These European types don't even consider such social graces until nine-ish, then the whole place is probably hopping. I can envision the mustachioed men with their straight black hair plastered back tight and shiny against their scalps like Count Dracula, their heavy-bosomed wives in satiny crepe party dresses, looking like some far away movie star of yesteryear last seen in a grainy, black and white 16mm newsreel attending a Hungarian Movie Festival. The men watching approvingly as the brocade material of these home sewn festive frocks pull tautly across those cherished ample lusty bottoms.

I'm hungry so I pluck up my courage and venture inside. I like Hungarian food and can almost taste a good meaty goulash with thick slabs of heavy rye bread. As I open the door a little bell hanging above it tinkles to let whoever is hidden out back know that a hungry customer has arrived. Once inside I see that the place's quaintness is actually verging on decay. The wooden tables seat two people each. With a bottle of wine and full plates, they would be crowded for space. There are smudged glass ashtrays at several tables. The sour smell of smoke clings to the walls and ceiling and furnishings. I suspect if I were to run my finger over a chair back or across the surface of a table I would feel the oily tar residue on them. But isn't that also typical of such old world haunts? Trench coated men huddle around these tables, smoking and talking in subdued tones about secretive things, things that the police would take a keen interest in noting. The doorway leading to the kitchen is covered with a tattered curtain whose embroidery is thread bare. The golden tassels hanging along its lower edge are frayed. An as yet unseen man in the backroom coughs hoarsely and spits into a sink, running the water for a moment afterward. Then silence again. I stand contemplating whether I should exit before anyone emerges from the back. At this point, my doubts regarding the quality of the food are multiplying appreciably. Before I can turn on my heel and escape the curtain is thrust aside and a heavyset man with unkempt black hair and several days' growth of whiskers on his puffy face steps through. He looks at me without comment. He is wearing a soiled white linen apron and is wiping his hands, of what I can only imagine, on the bottom. His watery eyes and fleshy features attest to someone who was very drunk last night, and quite likely a good many nights before as well. For a split second, I don't quite know what to do, and in that second my fate is sealed. He lifts a thick hairy mitt and, uncoiling a stubby index finger, says gruffly,

"Sit over there." pointing to a seat by the small scallop curtained front window.

I can still leave, I suppose, but may risk being chased out onto the street by this man, wounded by my unintended insult, wielding a chopping cleaver or bayonet sharp meat skewer menacingly above his head. And who knows what other easily angered accomplice from earlier days in The Resistance may be lurking behind a nearby lamppost, a broken soul, listlessly waiting to be snatched from the jaws of indolence and more than eager to assist an old friend whose honour has been unwittingly besmirched. I do as I'm told and sit down, smiling foolishly as if we're hitting it off well so far. He doesn't move toward me but reaches back over his shoulder to separate the curtain again, like a magician readying himself for his grand finale.

"It's early. Ve usually don't see anyone until after nine o'clock. I'm just gettink tings ready. You vant vine?"

I say yes and he is gone. My back is to the entrance, which I am closer to than the curtained doorway to the kitchen, all affording me a good head start if I bolt now. But the bell over the door will alert Vlad and despite his formidable size and the hobbling effects of alcohol and cigarettes, he may still possess the agility of a linebacker having had to run along Budapest's cobbled streets many an evening, anguished minutes ahead of the hee-hawing bray of government agent's sirens. I'll just stay put and take my chances on the food. There is still a fleeting hope that these initial warning flags are simply harbingers of Vlad's Hungarian Delights authenticity, with lots of good things in store for me, although the horking of possibly blood spotted phlegmatic corpuscles into the sink, is not anything to dismiss lightly.

Vlad comes through the curtain carrying a bottle of red wine and two glasses. He also has an unlit cigarette between his lips. He kicks the chair out opposite me with his foot and sits down heavily clapping the two glasses onto the table top just loud enough to make me jump. He fills the two glasses, lights his cigarette with a small, blue, disposable lighter he has palmed in the same hand that held the bottle, and is momentarily wracked with a fit of coughing. He forcefully pounds his chest twice, as if there is an off button hidden under his shirt that will still the cough. It stops, and then he lifts his glass and says, "Salute." Seeing the look of surprise on my face he adds, "No von should eat alone. It's bad for da stomach aches, however the hell you sayink it in dis crazy English place." "Digestion," I say as I lift my glass to his and we both drink a long swallow. He slams his half empty wine glass back down, "Digeteson. Got damned vords." He shakes his massive head letting out a deep, hearty laugh, which triggers another spasm of coughing. I laugh with him, wincing at the rattling sound coming from deep in his over burdened lungs. "So vhat brings you here to my place tonight? You are not ragular customer. Vlad knows his people by name."

I tell him that I am in town on business and that I live in Vancouver. He looks at me without blinking his dark watery eyes, as if every word requires his undivided attention or they will escape to that place that foreign languages spoken too quickly disappear. His hooded eyes are also sad and have a great sense of warmth and instant friendship intermingled in them. He stands suddenly and says, "Hey my friend. Ve vill eat together some goulash eh?" I enthusiastically agree. Vlad refills our two glasses and takes his back toward the kitchen. "Sit tight and enjoy da view. I'll be right back." He laughs at his own joke and disappears behind the curtain as another volley of coughing echoes through the room.

So, here's the other side of the coin regarding money and all that it *is* and *isn't*. Vlad, an old-country guy, has seen societies rise and fall and rise anew. He has traveled far and wide, looking for some peace and quiet where he can hoist his glass and acquaint himself with the local customs. I would hazard that above all else a man whose strong sense of who he is, and what he is, can never be extinguished by any politician's ambiguity or policeman's baton. Like so many others before him arriving in Canada via a refugee camp in some remote Balkan region, he no doubt worked at various menial jobs as he tried to learn the language, which obviously got the better of him. He was diligent and tried not to be judgmental in his efforts to acclimatize himself to our strange ways and hodge-podge customs. Here was a guy that wanted only to be accepted and perhaps raise a kid or two without fear. And he did all of that and much more and now when he should be slowing down and retrenching for this last quarter in the game of life, he has chosen to keep going down field for as long as his ticker holds up and the crust on his lungs remains in its lurking dormant stages. I am glad to be here and glad that I didn't run for cover at the first sign of tubercular perturbation in the otherwise cozy little kitchen.

Vlad is back with large bowls of goulash and slices of rye bread and cheese. He sets the bowls down in front of our places and pours another glass of wine each before sitting. "Bon appetite," he says wiping his bristly face with a casual wave of his hand as he begins spooning the thick stew into his mouth with the gusto of a peasant having recently returned from the fields. The wine is beginning to work its course through my vascular system, my face slightly flushed with the warm glow of dilating arteries and pixelating blood vessels. I feel the comforting warmth spreading through my body "How did you end up here?" I ask. He snorts as if sounding a trumpet to sharpen my attention, "This is a story my friend, such a story of many layers, like za cake for za vedding, you know vhat I'm sayink. One on za top of da odder." He gestures with his hands folding one on top of the other and repeating this movement to verify that it is not a question that can be answered easily. For the next forty minutes or so he tells me his tale of anguished flight, societal betrayal, romantic inspiration, and down-to-earth slogging, all conspiring in one form or other to bring him here to this table tonight.

During this time Vlad's wife, Maria and their youngest daughter, Petra come in to help complete the preparations for tonight's fare. Maria is plump, but not soft, rather more Rubinesque, her rounded haunches and sloping shoulders testifying to her body's strength and stamina. She wears a peasant's blouse. The daughter is slim with the olive skin of a more Mediterranean bloodline. There is a moment in the evolution of living things when the bloom is ripe in its youthful perfection and no amount of plastic surgeries or prosthetic implants can ever recreate that moment again. This is Petra's moment. A charm bracelet on her ankle clinks musically as she walks briskly to and fro, stirring this and straightening that, and moving one thing over there, then bringing another back to here. Everything about Vlad's Hungarian Delights plainly states that there is no rhyme nor reason to how things get done. One might as well ask why an expert fisherman casts his line over there, rather than back this way. Through the sheer repetition a system has evolved and it miraculously flows like water along a familiar creek bed, always determining its most efficient route along the contours of the ground lying beneath its speckled surface. Vlad and Maria and their gamesome daughter, Petra, are here before me tonight as a single unit, a family through and through. They freely offer a place where the rest of us can all come and congregate and feel, for a precious moment, that we somehow belong. Vlad's story, if placed beside so many other immigrant tales that have landed on our shores, is one of abiding faith. It is, none the less, one of survival, overcoming significant obstacles. Maybe the rest of us have strayed too far from the fold and can no longer see the honesty of things without interpreters like Dr. Martha Sitwell whispering these timeless human laws of survival into our ears as we strain to see and hear our life song. I look to my own family.

To what went wrong. Can it be random selection that cast us apart from the fold, without any fault or blame?

Vlad and I are halfway through the second bottle of wine when the place starts filling up with the regular customers. He invites me into the back, propping me up on a stool while he cooks and sings and coughs and smokes to his heart's content. He is enjoying every last moment. His wife Maria and daughter work the tables. They hug and pat and kibitz with each other and with the customers. When they come back into the kitchen with dirty dishes or another order, they chastise and lovingly scold Vlad for his smoking and drinking. He pretends to ignore these endearments and they pretend not to notice how much their affections touch him.

By eleven, I am more than a little drunk and am helping to serve tables. I have my jacket off and an apron wrapped around my waist like someone who has recently stepped from a Renoir restaurant poster of Paris in a past century. The music starts. Although the people are not all from Hungary, there are enough to make the evening bounce along like a scene from some cellar in old Budapest. After the final call and with much coaxing, even I take my turn on the dance floor. We all join in pushing several tables aside. I find myself locking arms with two large hairy men and commencing a slow and deliberate dance that tells of peasant pride and forbearance from centuries long past. By the time Vlad and Maria bundle me into my coat and usher me out of the door with warm hugs and slightly over zealous goodbyes, I am content and feeling the world's soothing touch upon my person.

Walking back to the hotel through the late evening traffic of a Yorkville night, I think about my trading account and what I have to do to make this right. Our corporate policy, of which I was one of the authors, states that no licensed representative shall conduct any margin trading in excess of fifty percent loan to market value for a duration longer than forty-eight hours without giving written notice to their immediate supervisor or the office's Due Diligence and Lawful Practices Officer. I have not only failed to do either of these, having carried a margin deficit of ninety percent of loan against current market value, but have also allowed it to lapse from one month into almost two months.

I cross Bloor Street against a red light. Pulling my collar up around my neck, I bend my back slightly as I sprint to gain the sidewalk. I know that whatever I decide to do had better get done soon or there will most assuredly be unwanted music to hear.

Back at the hotel, I fall into bed and immediately drift into a deep, yet not untroubled, sleep. Tomorrow is going to be another day and I have to be sharp as a tack to complete my objectives, with the recently added burden of ushering Zang and Wang Ton around Cuba. I must rise with my game face in place and my hand steady on the tiller keeping this boat on course and facing into the freshening wind.

PART 3: WRATH

"And I am dumb to tell the hanging man
How of my clay is made the hangman's lime,"

The force that through the green fuse drives the flower

Dylan Thomas

CHAPTER SIXTEEN

IT IS MARCH 15, THE IDES OF MARCH. I FOLD MY NEWSPAPER ACROSS MY lap as we await clearance for take-off in the idling airplane. I have been reading an interesting editorial about, "the alarming rise in firemen taking a full year's absence for stress counseling after attending a fire, one of the distraught firefighters being quoted as saying, "It was terrible. And hot too…something that no one should have to experience." The editorialist asks the leering question as to where all of this may be leading.

The Air Canada Flight from Toronto is direct to Cuba arriving in Havana at noon. I have spoken only a few words to The Twins on the airplane. It is their custom to arrive at airports late and board, unlike other people needing assistance, at the very end of loading, rather than prior to the general boarding call. They are always seated in the first row of Business Class for easier access to bathrooms and personal assistance. I suppose they had found from experience that if they were seated first it created problems when all of the remaining people had to file past them to gain their seats. Gasps and astonished stares were nothing new to Zang and Wang Ton. However, these were often followed by general confusion and disruption of an otherwise uneventful boarding experience. In the end, the airlines were supportive of this arrangement. It was for this very reason I boarded earlier, choosing an Economy Class Seat to the rear, so that the distance between us would prevent the endless stream of repetitive questions I already knew that I would be answering when we were back on the ground in Havana. The Tons were not unlike a team of prosecutors. They rephrased the same relentless questions as if trying to expose the flaw in the story or the deceit in the witness's intentions. "Whah abou the govemint? Is it okay?". Then reframing their question, or accusation. "Who awe the govemint contact an whah is their stake in evwee ting?" And on and on and on. I suppose they simply needed reassurance like any other investor. But I knew that they would repeat themselves when we were on the ground so I was content to simply walk up to the forward section of the aircraft when we were well under way. I would wander up and say a cordial hello to the boys later as we drew nearer to Havana.

When I had gone forward, The Twins were busy fielding salutations and questions like two goodwill ambassadors. The stewardesses and the passengers seated directly around them had equivalent amounts of trouble understanding Wang's rapid-fire quips. They were all eventually resigned to awkwardly baring their teeth and smiling like a school of tiger sharks circling two mewling panda cubs. They alternately held up pillows or blankets or glasses of freshly squeezed orange juice, hoping against diminishing hope that this was related to whatever he was making a stammering reference to.

The Tons were no strangers to these odd behaviours coming from the general public. They had been privy to them since early childhood. Their university years at Oxford had been especially difficult. Away from home for the first time, the boys were desperately wanting to make a good impression with their fellow classmates. They also briefly tried to fit in to the social activities on campus, the school, itself, a British institution heaped with tradition. To the brothers, it was nothing less than a living testament to the scholarship and leadership grooming of western civilization. Their father would have been proud. The voices of leaders and thinkers he had admired, from centuries past, echoed down the hallways. Unfortunately, and tragically, their efforts at anything outside of strict academics, bore less than brilliant results. Hope had been kindled by their Residence Don, a senior graduate student who tradition dictated should be a good chap and do his bit to help integrate the Freshies into the Oxford experience. He had bartered for a possible seat for the Twins in the six man rowing sculls. However this bid fell mutely silent when it was found that their stumpy missing fourth leg, although short and seemingly of no consequence, was still a fraction of an inch too long to allow their behinds to squeeze between the boat's aerodynamic, Finnish spruce gunwales. Volleyball was another slim hopeful. However once again The Twins' compromised capacity to turn and run like panthers in anticipation of a rocketing forward volley rendered the task too daunting. In the end this made them look foolish and helpless, rather than like the plucky fellows that they so wished to be. So, with all avenues for a normal social experience dashed, their's became a school life limited to study hall and quiet evenings chatting with classmates. Their weekends mostly spent reading musty leather bound poetic tomes by Chaucer and Eliot, or invoking the compelling histories of other crestfallen battlers toward whom they felt a flickering kinship. T. E. Lawrence and Bonaparte were both favourites. Their stoical loneliness throughout these formative years proved a breeding ground for their later lives, while the apple-cheeked lads their own age capered and wenched their wanton ways through the dimly lit, heavy-beamed pubs of the English countryside.

*

We architects of the Middle World are keen believers in personal striving and
industriousness. One way we tried to instill this ethos in our daughters was through our *family nights out*. One of these —perhaps the most memorable —was our decision to become members of Miguel's House of Latin Dance. Every Tuesday and Thursday, for almost a year without fail, we packed our shiny, black, patent leather pumps and ruffled shirts into a gym bag and drove downtown to take dance classes. We learned to rumba, tango, fox trot, samba, and jive our ways across any surface slippery enough to defy gravity and friction. This was probably the last really good belly-laughing time we had as a family. Precious moments that we all shared before Tess began leaving us. Miguel's House of Latin Dance was owned by George and Lila Culchinski. In their time, they had been quite something in the world of ballroom dancing. Old black and white photos of them in their various outfits flitting around a festively decorated ballroom or standing together smiling widely at the end of a particularly enthralling trophy winning number, were plastered everywhere, as if to say, "If you really want something, all you have to do is work hard and see where it may take you. Just look at us!."

George was short and tubby, his once stocky muscular build giving way to middle aged puffiness. There had simply been just too many fast food suppers, the monotony of long evenings ushering club-footed suburbanites through their steps robbing him of his once champion's edge.

"Work with me people. Work with me. I can't do this alone," he repeated as he glided haltingly around the room, having to witness the absurd spectacle disapprovingly in the floor-to-ceiling mirrors that covered the far wall.

He consistently chose to dress in his costumes from their heyday on the polished floors. Unfortunately these outfits no longer fit like a glove. The high-wasted black toreador pants with matching cummerbun now constricted like a tourniquet between rolls of midriff bulges, allowing the seat to sag conspicuously. This presented an unbecoming picture of fallen athleticism for the spectators lining the studio walls, trying to focus on his rhythmic technique. The girls and I were in stitches as we watched George, a full foot shorter than Genevieve, bound around the floor with her in his arms, dipping and swirling like a ninja. And I was not immune to such antics, the vivacious Lila being a strapping Ukrainian girl with great galloping thighs, and squared shoulders. She literally threw me around like a rag doll as I tried desperately to follow her spirited commands to lead.

"Move as one darling…As one…Like the wind and the leaves…You are the man…Act like it"

When we tried to compete in the Mixed Doubles, Genevieve with George and I with Lila, it was a scene worthy of a Marx Brothers Classic,

George and Lila steering us like runaway boxcars through our routines. The most enlightening part of remembering these days, the last of the good times in retrospect, was that Genevieve and I knew how hideous we looked and we didn't care. We knew we were the fodder for many jokes from our fellow dancers and suspected that we were also the subject of our instructors' private critiques on what in life had failed them so badly, placing them into this darkened alleyway, far from stardom, so late in their slumping careers. We did this gladly, because it gave us as a family, as a tribe, a sense of belonging to each other. At the time, I thought that, although this exercise was entertaining, it was not delivering the intended results regarding our girl's individual growth. I now know only too well that it was giving us bonus after bonus. We, or possibly only I, just didn't see it for what it was.

I did many other things, both business and personal, related to this quest for excellence in goal setting. I believe that I have developed some skill sets over the years that may well help in the transitioning of The Twins while on this trip. Some of these traits are quite simply a part of my basic nature, while others have been groomed through various courses and management training seminars I have attended. These seminars are advertised regularly in business weeklies and on late night television cable stations, usually parading true life testimonials from people, not unlike myself, that have attended and found a whole new meridian of measurement that extends the boundaries of selling life insurance or building your home-based consulting business. These generally follow the same format with the presenter walking you through their "systems." There is always a *key* to unlocking whatever door is keeping you from succeeding beyond your wildest dreams. "Stay on track" is repeatedly the ticket. With this done, it will provide the results that you are looking for. And it has. At least for the duration of the time that I "lived the system," as it were. Taking a moment at the dawn of each new day to run through my mantra of goals, truths, consequences, actions, then chronicling my results at the end of each day in a diary that became my Bible for living. Anyway, these seminars provided me with some basic tools and fundamental reference points, that although I often shelve for appreciable periods of time, I do not entirely forget. I can bring them down from the shelf, when needed. I have a feeling that the next couple of days with Zang and Wang Ton will provide ample opportunities for me to take them down and dust them off.

*

The final leg of the flight into Havana is always spellbinding for me. The small windows of the plane barely afford enough space to view the aqua marine colours of the reefs and shoals acting as barricades to the eternal movement of the Atlantic's waters. The lush, green, tropical vegetation sways to and fro apathetically in the warm Caribbean breezes below. These images look so peaceful and uninhibited when viewed this way, so far removed from the turbulence these barriers to wind and surf create for those things living in and amongst them.

After landing and taxiing to the terminal entrance, I wait at the bottom of the stairs for The Black Suits to assist The Twins in their convoluted exit from the aircraft. It is decided by the aircrew that the most efficient method of evacuating the pair is to remove the stairs and replace them with a hydraulic hoist used for lifting cargo into the lower hold. This way the Tons can be helped onto the ramp and carried ceremoniously over to the terminal's main doorway like visiting Lamas, then mechanically lowered onto the ground. I watch as the Cuban ground crew prepares to launch this maneuver. Keep in mind that these people are not adept at improvisation of any kind due in no small measure to their half century of inertia under a totalitarian regime that wasn't above lopping off the odd peon's head for insubordination or perceived ineptitude. Then magnify this almost insurmountable obstacle with the introduction of supervision from the Canadian aircrew who speak French fluently, but little or no Spanish and you've pretty much created the perfect storm in terms of inefficiency meeting indecisiveness and uncertainty. There is also the sudden and somewhat alarming appearance of very black clouds across the sky to the west creating sharply gusting winds. These wind thrusts are already creating uncomfortably strong pockets of ground turbulence, taking the form of whirling dervishes that skip and dance across the tarmac. I move to a less conspicuous vantage point beside a cabana wall about halfway between the aircraft and the terminus entrance. From here, I can plainly see The Black Suits ushering the reluctant and petrified Twins out of the airplane's doorway and onto the mobile ramp. The surface area of the device measures about ten feet long by six feet across. It is approximately twenty feet in height. Although sturdy-enough-looking a contraption, it poses the risk of being unwieldy when employed for tasks that it was not designed to carry out. The main body is supported by four fairly large balloon tires attached to a lower fuselage. The hoisting mechanism features two scissoring hydraulic arms attached to the sides. It is the formidable height and open-ended nature of the vehicle that frightens The Twins. If the carrier were to lurch or execute any sudden unexpected turns, they could quite possibly be thrown off balance and topple heads over three heels onto the hard and unforgiving pavement below. No doubt, they have also observed that the Cuban ground crew, their chaperones until their fifteen toes touch safely onto terra firma, are not the sorts of subordinates

137

that The Twins would employ, let alone entrust, with such delicate work concerning their personal safety.

Once The Twins are securely placed in the middle of the elevated ramp and attached to the tubular aluminum side bars with what appear to be looped lengths of bungee cords, the bewildered driver hits the gas a little on the heavy side. This, combined with his sudden execution of a jack rabbit turn, throws The Black Suits and the Tons violently across the width of the ramp surface, causing them all to collide with each other. They are then repelled with equal force, by the now contracting bungees, to extreme opposite ends of the apparatus. The pandemonium that follows is probably not far from the chaos experienced on the bridge of a supertanker, just before it hits an island. A dust devil of significant magnitude now descends onto the entire carrier, forcing everyone above and below to squeeze their eyes shut tight and hope that they aren't lifted off the machine entirely. The Ton brothers have released their hold on the support bars and are clinging to each other in terror, shouting oaths or incoherent instructions in Cantonese to The Black Suits. The driver, now completely disoriented by the wind and commotion, steps on the clutch and the gas pedal in rapid succession causing the vehicle to lunge forward and jerk to a halt, then lunge forward again, in staccato like bursts not unlike someone learning to drive a car with a standard transmission. The added catapult leverage of the vehicle and lack of counter ballasting weight, further magnifies these already frantic bucking gyrations. It is too much to watch. The rest of the carrier spastically wrenches forward creating the effects felt on the upper decks of a whaler navigating the treacherous waters of the Bering Straits. I turn briefly to survey the immediate area for some assistance. There appears to be no one among the legions of uniformed attendants prepared to venture forward to assist the careening vessel. I do notice that the main windows of the terminal building are jammed with people gawking in disbelief and awe at the convulsing spectacle approaching them now. At this point, I fear the worst is in store. If the driver doesn't regain control of his vehicle, he can quite conceivably drive it right into the front of the building. This will not bode well for either the Tons or The Black Suits, as their upper perch is seven feet taller than the doorway. The ceiling of the terminal structure is made of reinforced concrete. Thankfully all of this speculation proves unwarranted. Just before the whole shittery collides with the super structure of the airport terminal, it suddenly comes to an abrupt stop. It sits there for a long drawn out moment of silence, the driver's face frozen in fear. The people looking from the window stare with wide-eyed disbelief at what they have just witnessed. The Twins are clutching the arms of The Black Suits without looking toward the ground, their eyes fixed on two spots, either on the chests of their servants or on the darkening horizon beyond. This, by all accounts, has not been the introduction to Cuban life that any of us has anticipated.

The carriage mechanism is finally deployed and a phalanx of dubious airport officials are dispatched to assist the badly shaken Twins. I follow up the rear of this assemblage, waiting for the opportunity to help in any way that presents itself. I do not know how much information has been forwarded to the Cuban officials about the Tons' visit, so I don't want to interfere with any protocols the government may have arranged. I also know from experience in Cuba, that any and all contacts and subsequent VIP arrangements can simply have vanished into thin air, the right hand not knowing or caring what the left hand is doing. Several hesitant, uniformed people now successfully help the brothers from the litter. Although their efforts to assist seem genuine, their puzzlement at not knowing where or how to actually touch The Twins leaves them in a mystified kind of limbo. They stand frozen, with their arms and hands outstretched in the air as if they were about to start a welcoming dance of sorts.

Both Zang and Wang are in a state. Their bodies are neither pliable nor flexible. The violent thrashing about that they have been subjected to has left them badly bruised. The effects of the sudden wind gusts have further exacerbated this situation by pushing their coal-black hair straight up into the air, like two thick wire brushes. As they stand stock still on the ground after exiting the planks of the ramp, they look like two comical puppets. I place my hand on Wang's arm near the shoulder "Wang, what can I do? How can I help?" Wang turns toward me with a blank stare. He places his hand urgently on my wrist and whispers hoarsely,

"Hep us get out of here. Don't let these peopo near us anymo. Pweese."

I now turn to Zang. He is gesturing for an official, who has cordially wrapped his arm around Zang's shoulder, to release him immediately. His eyes are searching the crowd for The Black Suits. They have been pushed aside by the throng of officialdom, and are waiting on the periphery for some indication of what to do next. Zang now turns to me with his eyes hardened into two black pellets and hisses, "Servants" both as a command and a final plea for help. I lift my hand and gesture for The Black Suits to move in and take their places by The Twins' sides. They both effortlessly squeeze forward, immediately parting the milling throng like two graceful forces of nature. They embody everything that the physical world has denied their bosses. As the Tons begin moving toward the custom's desk I hear murmured exclamations of "Chihuahua" and "Caramba." One older woman crosses herself and whispers, "Madre Dios" as the entourage moves past. By the time our procession reaches the desk, which is only thirty feet from the door, all the minor customs agents have been displaced with some serious ranking hombres. These people are not about to further exacerbate the proceedings with any long drawn out questions or inquiries. Passports are requested and stamped without inspection. They are handed back to The Black Suits with a crisp bow. The snap of boot heels "Bon dias senior...s. Please enjoy your visit to Habana." Someone else, unseen by any of us, has hailed a taxi van and positioned it alongside the exit. Walking is now kept to a minimum. All of our luggage has been spirited from the aircraft and is now being loaded into the back doors of the van. We emerge into the glaring sunlight.

A wall of moist heat descends onto us. The ominous cloudbank that is now hanging on the eastern fringe of the island has brought this intense humidity with it. I glance at these billowing cumulus clouds. A storm is brewing. I only hope that it will wait until our site visits are over before it breaks. The van roars into motion and speeds smoothly past the line of waiting cabs without further incident. Maybe everything that can go wrong has already gone wrong in one terrible, bungling episode, and the rest of the trip will be like clockwork. We will soon see.

The road going into Havana is in good condition. This maintenance of main thoroughfares is more evident in third world countries, an arrogant effort on the part of the governing junta to put on their best face for the casual visitor. It is, as always, the poor people toiling in the tobacco and cane fields and squatting in their ramshackle doorways along the decaying back streets of Havana that pay the painful cost of backing the wrong horse, laying claim to The Soviet Union as opposed to the United States, as their best bet for a better life. Ideology over substance, the power of the gun over the will of the people.

I glance at the Tons as we drive through the derelict neighbourhoods bordering the city limits. I see the dilapidated squatters' shacks. In one a refrigerator tilts precariously in the yard. In another, a dust-covered television set is wedged atop a broken fence. The dismantled half chassis of old Buicks and Caddies lie rusting in the sun. Skinny dogs scrounge a meager bone or hidden insect in the dust, the bitches teats continuously distended from whelping litter after litter. The Twin's stare vacuously, as if they are searching for something across a flat body of water that holds nothing on its opaque surface but the occasional vagrant seabird. It is as if these birds, and these brothers, have no purpose other than the fact that they exist and are there.

CHAPTER SEVENTEEN

THE HOTEL NATIONALE SITS IN OLD HAVANA WITH ITS GRAND ENTRANCE sadly facing the once majestic and now tattered streets and city squares of its colonial past, its back portico abutting the cobbled seawall promenade that holds back the relentless Atlantic surf. Everything that one sees is haunted by the past and the optimism that these elusive times had once promised but not delivered. Now, these decaying monuments must stand and watch and wait for their time once again. They have been silent sentinels before and mutely watched as Spanish conquistadors plundered the gold from the hillsides. A century later corrupt politicians forged partnerships with gringo hoodlums. And now, social reformers languish in ideological denial. Above all else I wish that Genevieve were here with me right now, and not these billionaire misfits and their goons.

The van pulls up outside the hotel's heavy mahogany front doors and stops. I'm immediately aware of the stillness around this area, unusual for this time of day. This is one of the city's landmarks. It is always bustling with people coming and going on business of many kinds. Hotel maids and porters and desk clerks stand in a huddle inside the front lobby, looking out and talking with each other. The airport officials or cab drivers have communicated that an oddity is arriving and they should brace themselves. The island's isolation from advertising has denied most any foreknowledge of the Twins or of Tons' Time Share Vacations. I leap out first and pull the sliding door open to the rear seats. The Black Suits are in the back seat and come forward to position themselves beside the van, waiting for instructions from The Twins. The driver has already opened the back doors and is taking the luggage out. He looks toward the hotel employees in the lobby and shrugs. The Tons emerge from their seat like a large spider trying to climb down a metal drain-pipe that is too shiny and slippery to hold onto. Momentarily stuck, it begins waving its front legs in the air, trying to decide if it will spin a web. The Black Suits know what is needed. One of them darts over to the front door, where a small wooden box is resting. The hotel porters use this to stand on when they are loading or unloading packages from the roof racks of the buses. The Black Suits install the box beneath the side step of the van. This works well for the Tons, allowing them to gain better purchase for their final descent onto the ground. Once the security of flat land has been achieved, the brothers show a sense of relief. They waste no time in commencing their sideways shuffle into the hotel lobby. As I follow, I hear a loud crash coming from the front driveway, where two cabs have collided. No doubt their drivers were momentarily distracted. Muffled gasps and prayers beseeching an unseen god's intervention, can be heard rushing throughout the cathedral like spaces of this grand entrance way. It is what I expected would happen. As my colleagues register at the front desk, the clatter of silver platters falling onto the tile floors can be heard resonating throughout the lobby and attached dining area. I suppose the brothers think that these commotions are a common occurrence. Sloppy workers abound. They find them, wherever they go. I think back to their passive looks when driving into the city, the detachment they exhibit in their daily interactions. I feel a twinge of guilt for my feelings of resentment to their ambivalence to the humanity around them. They have walked a much different path than the rest of us. It has left its mark upon them in more ways than any of us can possibly imagine.

The hotel manager is at the front desk to meet and greet what he believes to be an international celebrity. In Cuba the message transmitted to him via an official with the Ministry of Tourism, is that people of immense importance will be checking into the hotel this afternoon. Some very highly placed government officials would take it as a personal favour if he would extend the courtesy of welcoming them personally and see that they are made to feel at home. However, there was no mention of who these persons were, or what exactly had been the catalyst rocketing them to such VIP prominence. I know these things because I spoke with the doorman before entering behind the Tons. He tipped me off as to why the staff were all on their toes. They were all expecting J Lo or Julio Iglesias, or someone of equal stature. This miscommunication further magnified their disbelief at who and what they were actually greeting.

Thus, the manager now stands rigidly behind the long mahogany desk. He has a pen poised in his left hand, which hovers nervously above the Hotel Registry. He has a shit-eating smile frozen onto his ashen face as if he has just been caught on *Who Told You* giving a blowjob to a dwarf. He now stammers in broken English,

"We have received a wary importanto message from the Minister of Business Development in Coobah. He weeshes to say that he will be here shortly for a brief meeting to welcome jew to de island and make a small presentation directly from el Presidente. He now clicks his heels and stands straighter, only resisting the pregnant urge to salute us by the smallest of margins. It doesn't take a person trained in the arts of torture or covert espionage to determine the extent of this man's discomfort. It is more than evident by the volume of perspiration that is dripping from his forehead. It runs in rivulets down his neck, soaking his shirt collar, and spreading like a growing stain down the center of his uniform's jacket. The hotel manager didn't have the foggiest idea of why he had been commanded to greet this apparition. He is scared stiff that this person with two heads may be some highly placed government mutant. God have mercy, a closely guarded secret from a medical experiment gone wrong. Without the slightest provocation this *thing* could have the manager forcibly paraded from his office in disgrace, buttressed with innuendos suggesting colossal political wrongdoing. Such persons were tortured with impunity, never to be seen by their family or heard from again.

Hearing about this previously unannounced meeting with a big wig doesn't overly surprise me. It's the Cuban way. Although introduced to us as a respectful gesture from the government, it is more than likely either a bid on the part of the Minister to get some additional browny points from the boss or a more intimate opportunity for the Minister to further feel out the possibility of getting a private kickback from us. A way of showing our gratitude for his unwavering support of our projects.

The Black Suits sign in for the brothers and take their room keys without speaking a word as is their custom. I suspect that they have had their tongues surgically removed when first employed by The Twins. This would prevent them from falling victim to a weak moment, blurting out some intimacy about what made the brothers Ton, tick. The hotel manager dabs with a trembling hand at the beads of sweat plopping off his chin. He turns the registry book around, vacantly studying the names written across the bottom line. No doubt, he is contemplating what his chances might be for a clandestine departure under cloak of darkness, like thousands before him, waiting for a running tide to help propel his open wooden boat toward Miami. Upon arrival the vessel's rotted stays, splayed open to the ocean's swells, might possibly trigger a sympathetic welling of generosity of spirit from the American people, the nation watching the boat's fretful beaching on CNN's evening telecast. *Madre Dios,* how quickly one's fortunes can turn.

*

My room is facing west. From my window I look over a small tropical courtyard garden with tall, stately palms and broad-leafed banana fronds. These are planted among mold-encrusted coral stones. It is all enclosed by a crumbling, fieldstone fence. Beyond the fence is the main thoroughfare of cobblestone running along the sea wall. To the south of my window's tranquil view a lone lighthouse stands one hundred feet tall on a small promontory jutting out from the ancient wall. I can see some locals walking along this jetty with their fishing poles and bait pails. Despite the fact that the area has been heavily developed for over three centuries, the warm waters of the gulf current meeting the shallows of the island must still be productive spawning and feeding beds for a wide variety of sea life. I can only imagine the variety of people, not unlike the fish stocks they seek, that have visited these bountiful waters over the generations. Spanish captains have stood upon these rocks, looking out at their galleons resting at anchor in the sparkling azure waters. Indentured Indians and black slaves have taken their turns trying to provide food for their young families, possibly making a little extra money selling their excess catches to the gentry of the day. Wealthy American tourists came for generations at the bidding of one dictator or another, taking their pleasure from the sea like itinerant Hemingways and from the casinos and brothels, for a price. I now look past the shoreline to the horizon beyond at the unseen riches and promise of the United States. These waters and this land have stood with their people and given generously for centuries. Despite these simple expectations those that have come here have not seen fit to grant any wishes or bestow any favours. This hard greed is now part of the inner heritage the island has assumed.

I look up from the sea to the sky and watch the darkening clouds high above move slowly toward me. I have lived by the water for most of my life and know by the murky depth of the shingle green ocean sheen, that the sea is telling one and all to be watchful today. I remember sitting on a rock overlooking Lake Superior when I was a young man contemplating my father's death and feeling some of the things I am feeling right now. Maybe it isn't anything to do with history or human failure at all, but more a function of the haunting quality of water that stirs these emotions within.

I've got to wash up and change into something more junket functional. The next five hours or so will be exhausting. We will go across the island and high into the surrounding mountains to the geological camp for the proposed mine, then back down to the far coast to view the resort site.

When I turn on the water taps, I am greeted by the loud gushing sounds and musky smell of compressed air being released into my sink. Silence follows. I instinctively turn the taps on and off a couple of times, as someone does with anything that isn't working. I am fully aware that it will do no good but do it anyway not unlike talking louder to a blind person. I look at the toilet for a moment. It has water in the bowl. I may be able to dampen a face cloth in the tank behind so that I can at least wipe my face and hands. I lift the porcelain top from the tank and peer inside. I see a murky-looking, sludge-encrusted interior with rusted tubing and bulb stem. The usual ball has been replaced with a piece of Styrofoam that is equally slippery looking. I decide that having a clean face isn't worth the additional risk of catching typhoid fever. I replace the tank top and settle for scrubbing my face and hands with a dry cloth.

In the hallway, I meet a Cuban woman in a chambermaid's uniform and tell her that there is no water in my room. She listens politely and smiles. She shrugs her shoulders and says, "Maybe no supposed to work. Maybe is best?"

I don't understand how no water can be better for anyone. She is folding and refolding a towel on her trolley and adds solicitously without guile, "Maybe Cuba is best kept small secret eh. No big Miami place. No water means not too many people. Just nice, si?" She finishes folding the towel. I watch as she walks down the hallway toward my room. She turns and smiles again. "Hasta la vista," she says and puts her key into my door.

She may have a point. Look at Mexico's border towns. Is this truly the only path to progress we have to offer?

*

I meet the Tons in the lobby. They seem to be more at ease, having settled down considerably from their morning. They are outfitted in casual wear. This consists of khaki shorts that extend past their three knees, an open toed type of heavy walking sandal and two slightly different plaid short-sleeved shirts. The style is a madras pattern popular in the mid 1960s and obviously making a come back with the sporty set. Both Zang and Wang are also wearing peaked baseball caps with logos from the worlds of golf and skiing. They each have sunglasses on. They are looking every inch the outdoor enthusiasts that the billboards for Tons' Time Share Vacations herald. If it weren't for the fact that they have three legs and are stuck together at the hip, they would look like any other tourists venturing out for a day's sight seeing. The servants remain dressed in their black suits. They are now wearing mirrored sunglasses, looking like secret service agents. They stand resolutely to the side with their hands folded in front of their bodies.

We have barely had time to exchange salutations when a motorcade of three black Cadillacs dating from the latter 1950s storm up to the front door of the hotel. Their tires screech. The Cuban flags mounted on each of the car's front fenders flap to the point of shredding. It is military in style. Everything here is ceremonial. I have to suppress a latent urge to salute. Soldiers are seated beside the drivers. They are dressed in combat-ready camouflage gear. They leap from the cars before they have come to a complete stop. In one fluid motion, an arsenal of semi-automatic pistols and standard issue .45 automatics are drawn and held barrel up and ready to discharge. The soldiers on either side of the front door position themselves in a gauntlet.

We cannot see the men seated in the back of the Caddies. All of the cars have darkly smoked windows, preventing nosy bystanders or gun-toting assassins from seeing inside. Security is tight. Why not? The CIA has been trying to kill Castro for half a century. A fourth car, not a Cadillac but rather a black Chevy sedan circa 1965 now pulls up in front of the lead Cadillac. Several army personnel quickly exit carrying Uzi Sten guns with long oversized clips extending in shallow arcs from their oiled metal firing actions. These four additional men now move to stand directly beside the line of cars. The right rear doors open in one rehearsed synchronized motion. Now three dignitaries dressed in soft white linen shirts and loose fitting cotton trousers step from the cars and stand for a moment, as if waiting for music or some other fanfare worthy of their combined offices. After this brief pause they all march briskly toward the hotel's doorway. The Uzi toting officers fall in quickly behind them. The remaining guards scramble and re-group around the marching men, as if they are demonstrating a highly complex maneuver on the parade ground. They now come forward at a breathless pace, looking for all the world like a menacing, armoured wall.

The Tons, The Black Suits, and I all stand looking increasingly like the quarry at a weekend foxhunt. The hotel manager bursts past us without saying a word, the back of his suit now sopping wet with perspiration, his hand extended in greeting. The armed men dismissively ignore this, pushing him aside as they make their way toward us. I have a sudden impulse to dive behind a sofa or fall back, letting The Twins take the first rain of bullets squarely in their distended chest cavities. However, instead of this, I smile widely, looking past the stone-faced soldiers, trying to make eye contact with the leading dignitary. At approximately three paces from my leaden feet, the juggernaut comes to an abrupt halt. The two front-positioned guards step back and to the side, exposing a broadly beaming gentleman in a wide brimmed panama hat. He extends both arms in front of him and leaps forward, embracing me like a long lost brother returning from years of dedicated service to his country. He kisses me brusquely on both cheeks, his midday stubble rubbing against my face like sandpaper, and stands back announcing jubilantly, "Hola Senior Richard. What a sincere pleasure eet is to have jue back with us once again." He now leaps forward a second time, embracing me even more enthusiastically. This done he turns his gaze to the Tons. He is suddenly mystified as to what to do. Should he simply continue this cordial greeting or do something else? A hug would be difficult at best, not knowing whether he is to latch onto one of the brothers at a time, or try to wrap his arms around both. The Tons also appear momentarily uncomfortable at the thought of being tussled so. Since they are not that stable on their feet, such a jostling may send them all sprawling onto the tiled floor, knocking their noggins against the hard porcelain surface like coconuts. The dignitary, always the politician, simply by-passes these intimate formalities and smiles warmly shouting jubilantly . "Hola amigos! Buenos dias each and all." He now turns back to me showing increasing concern. Will the gaping differences in our physical bodies extend to unforeseen problems with linguistics as well? I may be a useful interpreter for him to use during our meeting. "Come, please, we will have a welcoming drink and talk briefly about some business matters." He now raises his arm and snaps his fingers. The hotel manager, as if suddenly hearing a starter's pistol, sprints past us from the back of the pack. He animatedly shouts for bellhops and chambermaids to immediately follow him. They all barrel toward the rear of the cathedral-like foyer with the urgency of people fearing that they all may soon be shot. The dignitary now takes my elbow in his soft, pudgy hand and indicates for us to all follow the manager. We appear to be headed for a meeting room off this main entrance area.

We quickly fall into lockstep, making our way to a set of large, carved mahogany doors opening into a spacious banquet room with high walls and ornately etched plaster ceilings. A mammoth mural covering one entire wall is visible through the open doors. It depicts the peasants' revolt against the usurious landlords. The worker's faces turned heavenward in anguish, their wide eyes shining with hope. I turn around to see if the Tons have managed to keep up. Although the actual walk was relatively short, it was at a fast enough pace to have left them well behind. Wang and Zang are doing their best and making good progress. They are moving at a much quicker gait than they are normally comfortable with. Two of the armed guards have remained behind to accompany them. They seem undeterred by this obvious departure from their regular duties and stare ahead directly past the rest of us to some imaginary place on the far wall. When they have joined us, we all turn once again and step through the heavy doors and into the room.

Preparations are being made for a large reception of some sort in the room. The now completely flustered hotel manager barks orders to all of the maids and service workers. They instantly drop whatever they are doing and commence herding toward the rear exit. They shuffle with all of the precision of people responding to a fire alarm. Several of the bellhops swiftly move a small, rectangular table into the center of the room. They then surround it with chairs. They also place a pitcher of water, glasses, and two bottles of wine on the table. They look from the befuddled hotel manager to the dignitaries for further instructions. One of the lesser dignitaries steps forward. He signals them to depart with a casual wave of his gloved hand. He positions himself behind the head honcho and begins matter-of-factly removing the soft doe skin leather glove from his left hand. We all momentarily watch silently as he tugs each smoothly- fitted chamois finger like the Count of Monte Cristo preparing for a duel.

I recognize some of these men standing beside us in the room. Their leader is the one that gave me the big hugs. He is the Minister of Business Development, whom I have spoken with several times before. I am hopelessly outnumbered and can feel a rising sense of panic regarding how I am going to handle the basic introductions, let alone stick handle my way through these meetings. Before I have time to break out in a sweat rivaling that of the hotel manager, who has conveniently disappeared under a nearby banquet serving trolley or has thrown a white table cloth over his head and is now lying somewhere on the floor like a pile of soiled laundry, another lesser dignitary presents himself before me taking the leading role in orchestrating whatever social niceties need to be dealt with.

"Bon dias Senior Bonhom. I am Miguel Octavio Stella. I am at your service." He bows deferentially as if readying himself to kiss my hand. "I am an attaché to Senior Conceptione," he says, turning to the lead dignitary who is standing, poised like a performer waiting for his introduction to finish before bounding onto the stage with a hilarious joke or breaking into a medley of old Spanish favourites. "We are here to welcome you." he continues, turning to the Tons and The Black Suits, smiling warmly, yet vacantly, "and your associates on this historic occasion." He stops abruptly without completing his thought, as if becoming aware that his official duties are nearing an end. He seems acutely aware of not encroaching on the next dignitary's spiel. He glances toward the Minister, looking for a subtle cue. He is like a dog waiting for a whistle that is unheard by all but his own kind. The Minister simply stares back toward him without perceptively raising an eyebrow or even flinching a facial muscle. The attaché steps back into the line, having recognized his command.

Minister Conceptione now steps forward with a jovial flap of his arm, as if all of this protocol is not important to him. He would like to be seen as a much more humble character, although the rigid adherence to these disciplines by his staff attests to something other than this casual informality.

"Please Reechard. Come let's drink. You all must be thirsty after your long flight from Toronto. I have been there many time on bees-ness and know how slowly time teeks past when sitting on an airplane..." He smiles at what he is about to say. "Even an Air Canada airplane." We both chortle at his small joke, perhaps a little too long, each giving it more attention than it deserves. I turn to include the Tons in our discourse. We all shuffle toward the table holding the wine. He motions to no one in particular, affecting a casual air. It is not sincere, but is a pretty damn good impersonation of affability nonetheless. But then again, this ability to instantly assume a part with seeming effortlessness is probably the ticket to having a long distinguished career in government service. All of this and a retirement package that includes three squares a day and a dacha by the sea instead of a bullet in the nape of the neck.

The Minister is a stocky man with smooth, olive-coloured skin that is almost effeminate in its luster and softness. His hair is receding into a widow's peak with flecks of gray at the temples that look artificial, as if painted on. His eyes are dark and buoyant capturing the light from the room and transmitting it back toward whomever he is looking at. His stare is direct and forceful, like a beam trained on you in a tunnel or other darkened space. It is unsettling and affords no place in which to hide. This quality is what is disarming about the Minister, leaving one with the apprehensive suspicion that the veneer of cordial jocularity can be displaced at a moment's notice. It is the same look that the captain of a firing squad might have just before he lowers his arm as a signal to commence shooting.

No one ever comes directly to the point in Cuba. It is a process of elimination. Both the host and the guests have their roles to play, and it is considered very bad form and appalling manners to try and circumvent this vignette by rushing the situation. This is especially true if your reason for this is related to saving time. Time, for these people, is not something to be doled out sparingly, as if it is in short supply. It is, instead, a concept, to be cultivated and nurtured with due care for the process. Time in Cuba is patient like a garden. It is as gentle as making love on an early spring-time morning.

The Tons are not patient men. They are men that take considerable pride in working long, punishing hours. They cherish the results over the process. However, they are, above all else, students of culture. They understand the necessity of being respectful toward others when doing business in foreign places. They take such measures seriously. This includes dinners with business colleagues and their families, and occasional weekend cruises with joint venture partners or influential political supporters aboard one of their luxury liners. The Twins have even been known to watch Macy's Christmas Parade toot and whistle its way down Broadway Avenue in New York, if one of their corporations is hosting a float, though they never appear too happy if a camera catches them sitting like two distraught Eskimos looking out over the frozen tundra for something to eat. They look out of place, with their bodies wrapped in layered bolts of woolen material, their two oafish, furry hats pulled down over their ears like musk oxen resolutely facing into a winter storm. But they oblige, when duty calls.

We all gather around the table that has been hastily set for us as two waiters scurry in with plates of steamed shrimp, bowls of mashed avocado dip and roughly broken hunks of crumbling corn bread hot from the oven. Senior Stella motions for the waiters to pour glasses of wine for everyone. When we have all had sufficient time to scoop some of the lemony avocado dip onto pieces of corn bread and eat a shrimp or two, the Minister clears his throat and turns to me, and then, as if revising his agenda on the fly, turns directly facing the Tons. "First, let me offer our humble apologies to these honoured guests regarding the unfortunate incident at the airport upon jor arrival this morning, most regrettable El Presidente heemself, when told of this I was shocked and ordered a full investigation into who was respon-seeble." His piercing eyes moisten for a moment's pause, as if they are a theatrical prop used when dramatic effect is called for, then turn toward me instantly transforming into thin splinters of refracted light as sharp as shards of broken glass. His mouth widens in a self-congratulatory smile, like a cat that knows he has the mouse. The cat knowing how far it can let the trembling mouse go without risk of loss. "Reechard. Reechard. What a pleasure to be here weeth jue today. We have great thee-ings to discuss and even greater accomplishments to mutually work toward." He now lifts his glass and turns to his minions, who quickly take a glass from the table and smile hesitantly. It is as if they are momentarily uncertain whether he wants them to exhibit a boisterous, companionable good will to the guests or adopt a more serious expression, as if they are witnessing a momentous historical occasion that they will proudly tell their grandchildren of one day. He frowns slightly, growing aware of their indecisiveness and annoyed that he must deal with this as well as be the host of other official daily functions that he is called upon to perform. Little did they know the full weight of his office. They are also aware of his thoughts and look on obliquely. Each man is probably wishing to Christ he'd never risen to his current position, momentarily preferring to be more anonymously hidden in a back office or even out in a tobacco field many hundreds of miles from here. He then turns back to the Tons and me, "Congratulations amigos. On behalf of the government of Coobah,.and jes, the people of our small yet happy leetle country, we pledge only one thing to jue, our trust and our friendship." He throws back the wine as if it were French cognac. He wipes his mouth with the back of his hand and holds his glass aloft for someone, anyone, to pour an instant refill. The waiters have wisely absented themselves, thus leaving only Senior Stella and his beleaguered colleagues and the guards to perform this task. The soldiers, being fighting men, would rather stand in front of a firing squad than stoop to domestic servitude. Both of the sub-dignitaries now look almost apoplectically at one another, suddenly confused at not knowing exactly who should do what, even further unsettled by the possibility that whatever either one does will be grossly incompetent. This realization ushers in the further nightmare that the hapless offender may well be on his way to the bowels of a tin mine buried deep in the frozen boreal forests of Siberia. Sensing that all of this is leading to one of these junior officials having a heart attack on the spot, I step forward, grab a bottle of wine, and pour Minister Conceptione a healthy portion. He is initially startled by my actions and seems at a loss

as to what to do. Should he chastise his subordinates for their lackadaisi-
cal manners, or simply accept this act as a further testament to our good
friendship, a friendship, in no small measure, having blossomed under his
astute supervision? Fortunately for the men standing directly behind him,
he chooses the latter, and grasping another bottle of wine, moves forward
amongst us pouring our glasses full to almost overflowing. We all chuckle
amiably at nothing in particular, as we have often seen gangsters doing
in movies when Big Al shows some form of genuine human compassion,
which is usually followed by a mass execution or the bludgeoning of one
of the guests with a baseball bat. "Lee-sten my friends, please take this
opportunity to eat and drink to jor heart's content. We will meet again
later tonight and have supper. Then, God willing, tomorrow morning we
will sign all of the documents and exchange the payment amount. Now,
I must be off to another meeting." He furrows his brow and rolls his eyes
up at the ceiling, indicating how bloody tough his job truly is. He smashes
back the full glass of wine in one monstrous gulp and, dropping the glass
onto the table with a heavy smack, shouts, "Aribba Muchachos!" The other
men hastily swallow their wine and turn in unison toward the exit. They
are instantly surrounded by their armed military cortège. The officials all
march out of the door, as if they are prisoners heading out to the execution
yard rather than high government officials going forth to perform their
next important duty.

I have to smile at this performance and how the Tons must perceive
the complete lack of sincerity behind each of his strong pronouncements.
Neither he, nor the government of "Coobah" are our friends for life or even
our conditional supporters. They are, in fact, simply corrupt representatives of a poor nation trying to complete a deal that will bring upwards
of $100,000,000 dollars into their cash-strapped economy, much of this
money and its residual spin-off income going directly into the pockets of
these same men and many others down the line. This trail will go all the
way to the lone night watchman that lets a few amigos slip past the gate in
the dead of night to relieve the company of an extension hose, expensive
tire jack, or a coveted box of welding rods.

The Twins have been quiet throughout this entire greeting experience,
which is not uncommon for them at such public times. They are not shy,
but rather like to stay in the background hoping to catch a whiff of something gone slightly off, maybe not yet bad or even foul, but just different
from what they were previously told. They are smart like a fox is smart
and because of this they know, like the fox, that the farmer will have taken
some precautions and set some traps on the path toward the henhouse.
Knowing all of this will not deter them from their course, but merely alert
them to the inherent dangers involved in being a fox and not a hen. With
this said, I can't read any signs or thoughts when looking into either Wang

or Zang's face. I can only assume that one way or the other they will let me know in due course whatever information they feel needs to be shared.

*

A nine-passenger van has been arranged by the Cuban government for our stay and is waiting out front for us. I assume the driver has been told what to expect. He is standing at attention beside the vehicle, trying to act as casual as possible. As we approach, he slides the side door open and watches The Black Suits assist The Twins getting into their seat. All goes without incident and we are soon edging our way through the congested streets. The driver relentlessly honks his horn in a steady cacophony. He tries to get the milling people to move aside far enough so that we may pass. I have brought a map to guide us into the surrounding hills. Since these streets have, for the most part, been laid out over a hundred years ago, they are not suited to car travel. Paving has taken place on a random basis. The roadways are too narrow to ever qualify as modern thorough-fares. The buildings stand flush against the streets. There are no sidewalks. Fetid, open gutters run down along the building's foundations. There is simply no room for the throngs of people and vehicles. The sounds of the city and smell of diesel fuel mixed with the pungent presence of humanity trapped in the hot humid air all conspire to numb your senses. This is the reality for most of the world. There is also a powerful energy of spirit wandering through the musical rhythms of their daily lives here. This life force is evident everywhere. It is from inside these people so it cannot be removed by political proclamation or by military force. It is like Vlad and Maria's life force, bigger than a mere Bartoke tune and more imposing than a tank commander's gun.

The old city squares and communal wells soon give way to the sub-urban squalor of shanties, and low concrete warehouses. These are either dormant factories or some other failed economic initiative of the defunct soviet tutors. Our driver speaks English fairly well and also speaks Russian, French, and Italian. This is not uncommon to find among service workers here. He had been trained as an engineer in Moscow, but could not raise a family on the twenty-five dollars a week plus accommodations and food stamps that such a job paid. He chose to drive a taxi instead and make fifty dollars (US) a day. This also removed the risk of being imprisoned for making any engineering boo boos while constructing a road or designing a bridge. I have shown him the map and he actually knows the general area that we are going into, since he did some initial fieldwork on a neigh-bouring site as a student. It was in his final year of engineering.

The ambient noise of the engine and the wind coming through the open windows because the air conditioning isn't working has muted most conversation coming from the Tons and made for a pleasant drive. However, as we slow to begin our ascent into the mountains, the road has narrowed to little more than a goat path. It leaves the opportunity open for the Tons to voice whatever concerns have been silently accumulating momentum in their heads since their arrival. I am looking out at the vegetation when Zang clears his throat to speak. "Rishawd. My broser an I were wondering wha awternative measures awe awailable fo processing raw materials in Cubaw?" I turn to face them. They are looking unusually chipper, like two private school kids going on a field trip. All they need is butterfly nets and beaker jars and two Star Wars Lunch boxes sitting beside them on the seat.

"The mining consortium is planning another milling operation for Santa Cruz, which is the little town we just passed a while back. This, coupled with the existing government-run mill should be more than ample to meet their production quotas for the first ten years or so. After that, it's do whatever we have to do."

The Twins already know this answer. Lord knows unforeseen things do come up however. Being caught with your pants down in places like this is always bad business. The proposed mine site has accommodated geological crews and exploratory blasting, trenching and drilling operations for the past seven years. There are building structures in place and roadways graded throughout an area of approximately fifty acres in size. The main technical players are a consortium of Canadian and Dutch -African mining companies and the Cuban government's geo-technical arm, Minerale de Cuba. The area has been mined since the early seventeen hundreds by the Spanish and Portuguese, distant kings looking for gold and silver as part of their general plan to plunder South America and the Caribbean of anything of value. Companies today often use the abandoned digs from these early mine sites as proving grounds for their current exploration programs. The theory behind this is that since these early explorers lacked any sophisticated equipment for digging, other than the local Indians they enslaved in the name of Jesus Christ and Queen Isabella, they pursued only the richest veins of ore. This high grading technique was efficient and still holds geological merit today because where there is a proven concentrated mass of precious metals there is a good chance of finding volume, as well.

I notice the wind gusting through the tops of the palm and tamarind trees with increasing force as we emerge into the site clearing. The sky doesn't look good.

The van stops beside a dusty Atco trailer that is the main geological office. I instruct the driver to shut off the engine. I review the basic chronological history of how the site has been developed and why this is the obvious choice for the main mining operation. The proposed exploitation method is an open pit strip mine. This is due to the relatively moderate grades of ore and the lack of depth of mineralization. The general feeling is that an open pit is the most cost efficient way to extract the minerals from the ground. Obviously, there are serious environmental issues that have to be addressed by both the Cuban government and several non-affiliated international environmental groups that act as watch-dogs throughout the region. The government has little patience or tolerance for dissenting voices regarding many of these issues, and I suspect side agreements are being made with respect to how much reclamation and restoration work will be required to satisfy these issues. The government is desperate for someone to come and do something to generate jobs and cash flow into their bankrupt coffers.

As I retrace the story of the project to the Tons, a man emerges from the geological trailer, followed by two Cuban workers, and looks us over for a moment to ascertain whether we are banditos or some other form of nuisance. He now recognizes me and approaches my side of the van. He is the head geologist on the project. His name is Don Chipman. He is a Canadian in his early thirties and looks for all the world like a young Castro, with a full, bushy, black beard and olive green army fatigues. I roll the side window down. "Senior Donald. Hasta la veigo, amigo?" "Bueno Senior Bonhom. "We shake hands and he bends to survey the other passengers. From his vantage point, The Twins are just two Asian gentlemen sitting side by side in a van. The Black Suits are nothing more than two black suits. I introduce the Tons, and Don nods to them dispensing with any handshakes due to the awkwardness of opening doors. I tell Don a bit about why we are here and how these people just wanted to come up and see the site with their own eyes. Don asks if we would like to take a walking tour of the site so that he can explain the different work programs and their relevance to why this site was chosen over several others. The brothers decline with wide smiles and head shakes, saying that it isn't necessary. They have been well informed of these details. They simply wanted to put a face on all of this data. We all chat about a few isolated bits of very recent information, the most encouraging being a just completed geo magnetic survey of the areas surrounding the actual property and their findings of heavy possible extensions of mineralization. This is good news here in Cuba, where the government can acquire these other attached lands without too much red tape. This differs from other jurisdictions where such news would mean serious negotiations with our neighbours who would all suspect that our riches extended onto their properties, and a king's ransom would be their price.

As we talk, I notice the workers milling around the grounds, digging holes or filling holes in. Some are carrying lengths of pipe over there, while others are busy bringing them back over here. They move slowly in the humid heat, their very movements a testament to the servitude of their existences. They don't ask questions or pledge allegiances through the singing of a company song or mutter condemnations at their fates. They are beyond all of these, simply doing whatever they are told with the suppressed hope that it may lead to something better for themselves and their children.

When Don is finished and another invitation to come in and have coffee and look at the maps is graciously declined, I end the conversation with a hearty handshake and fond farewells to Don and his two wide-eyed helpers. They are trying their best to peek into the van and see who the visitors are, and more importantly, what we may have brought with us that would be of any use to them. They have slowly migrated around the van to the driver's side as Don and the Tons and I talk. I hear a muffled conversation in Spanish going on between them and the driver. When we are finished we turn around and head out of the road leading back down the mountain. All in all, that went as well as could be expected. The Twins seem satisfied with what they have seen. As simple as it may seem, this quick pit stop may have been all that was necessary to expunge any nagging doubts that they may have had in regard to the actual presence of a legitimate mining project. I understand this thinking. I am also a big fan of going to the place and seeing things with my own eyes.

CHAPTER EIGHTEEN

VERADARO IS A LUSH AND TROPICAL PARADISE OF SUN AND SURF AND swaying palm fronds. It says to everyone that emerges from their bus that the next two weeks are going to be sheer heaven at a bargain basement price. These resort developments spring up much the same everywhere around the globe. They can be along a lonely beach or across the top of a jagged mountain or down the fringe of a scrub desert mesa. Suddenly, the once distant beach becomes a vibrant town. A morose mountaintop becomes a snowy chalet village. A drought stricken desert becomes a lush oasis of golf or a favouite cartoon character's water slide theme park. Fred Flintstoneville or The Littlest Mermaid Water World. Initially, they look out of place and forlorn, out there by themselves. This is the case in Cuba. At this early stage in development, there are several resorts forming these clusters of modernity along the miles of pristine, desolate beaches of Veradaro. Between these lay the odd fisherman's hut or squatter's shacks dotting the seemingly endless barren grasses and white sands of a storybook island. We nose our van off the main road onto a patch of sand and grass that looks as if it has been used for parking by others coming along this way and stopping to rest or perhaps walk out onto the sand. We sit and look at the open beauty. The wind has continued to grow, and although the sky is not completely clouded over, the sea has picked up the mood of turbulence in the atmosphere. It is beginning to roll with increasing strength as the waves crash upon the sand. The trees are bending slightly to the wind, and the sound that is coming from the surf and wind is loud enough that we must shout to be heard. We have left the van and are standing, looking out at the magnificent spectacle before us.

The Twins are having a tough time walking in the soft sand. They seem to be thrilled by the vastness of the scene and have momentarily put aside their inclination to remain on the fringes. They stand with me about half way out onto the beach. They are both holding onto their caps in the stiff breeze, and Zang is shouting,

"Where is da main hotel going to be?"

I have to place my face close to his ear so that my words are not swept away above the thunderous sound of the flowing tides.

"Over there by the point." I gesture in the general direction of the spit of land forming a peninsula about a hundred yards from where we are standing. To my surprise, Zang turns to his brother and mumbles something. He then turns back to me and says that they would like to go closer. They now motion to The Black Suits to bring their sedan chair from the back of the van. When The Black Suits return, the device is placed on the sand like a blanket. The brothers step onto it and position their three feet into each of the holes. The Black Suits then slowly lift the contrivance so that the brother's legs are extending through the holes. Once it is high enough to reach their thighs, the brothers take hold of the handles. The servants squat on either end with the poles on their shoulders and hoist the whole shebang into the air. We then start across the beach and onto the sand spit. It is heavy slogging through the soft sand for The Black Suits, but they remain stoical, looking neither left nor right. They remain focused on their destination, like two Eskimo hunters carrying their litter of seal meat across an undulating ice flow. The wind is blowing with such force now that we all have to hold onto our hats and glasses. I am surprised that the brothers are doing this and am also a bit concerned. As we near the beach, each new wave is exceeding the previous one, exploding onto the sand in all their hellish fury. It is both thrilling and disconcerting. At the brother's bidding, we continue venturing farther out into the storm. I would have never dreamt of doing this if I were by myself, let alone accompanying The Twins. Once we are about half way out on the sand spit, the brothers signal for The Black Suits to put them down. As they are lowered onto the sand, they are holding each other's shoulders for support. They step away from the carrier and stare out at the frenzy as if transfixed by the power and freedom of the wind and sea. I am standing behind them watching, uncertain as to what they want me to do, if anything. Wang now turns to The Black Suits and shouts an instruction in Cantonese. Both servants turn and run past me back toward the van. Zang motions for me to join them. The sandspit that we are standing on is approximately forty feet across and extends about two hundred yards into the ocean. It acts as a natural sea wall breaking the force of the waves. One side is being pummeled ferociously, while the other is relatively calm. This wave action has sculpted the edge of the side that we are standing closest to into a steep bank of sand falling about seven feet into the water. The other, gentler side is smooth and quite flat. Zang takes hold of my arm and pulls me close to his face so that I can hear.

"We want to take piture of this scene fo our photo abum."

I nod my understanding and supposed approval. I don't think that either of the brothers has ever had to seek approval from anyone since the death of their revered father. It is simply one of those gestures that you do that signifies nothing, as when I once nodded at a mentally ill person screaming some incoherent message to me on the street as I stood counting the seconds waiting for the light to change.

The Black Suits return at a breathless clip. They traverse the sand like Roman Legionaires on drill or Ninja warriors attacking. They carry a digital stills camera and a larger video recorder. Zang indicates that he would like pictures taken of him and his brother with both cameras and signals for The Black Suits and I to go back up onto the beach and start photographing the whole pulsating scene.

It is now a full-fledged gale. Walking is increasingly difficult. Each of us has to bend almost double into the wind to make any forward progress. I am concerned that the lighter and less agile Tons may topple over.

The Black Suits and I are now a good fifty feet from The Twins. We have a magnificent viewpoint of the entire length of the beach. The rollers are crashing onto the shore and the tall palm trees bordering the sand are bending, almost touching the water. The van driver comes across the sand now, shouting that he is afraid that a hurricane is coming. He warns that we should get back to the city before the roads are washed out. I agree, telling him that this won't take us long. We will soon head back to the city. This all may prove to be good in the broader scheme of things because it will give us a bit of extra time to get ready for our meetings with Minister Conceptione and the legion of other Cuban dignitaries that will show up, invited or otherwise, for a free drink and a look see at the newly arrived meal ticket. I now turn back to watch the brothers. They are enjoying what I can only imagine to be one of their few moments of absolute ecstasy and freedom from their physical bonds and limitations. I stand, watching approvingly, like an older uncle along to keep things in check. The Black Suits continue photographing the brothers. It is then that the unthinkable happens. Suddenly, the sand under the Tons' feet is sucked away by the increased yet unseen vacuum of the undertow. A giant wave rises from the primordial depths to at least twice the height of any other we have seen coming onto the beach today. It hovers like a skulking sea monster for a fleeting second above their heads. They turn as one and begin their fruitless, crab-like ascent up the steep bank of collapsing sand. It is as if I am watching this through the viewfinder of their video camera and I can push the pause button and defy the laws of gravity and time for an instant. Everything stops. I can clearly see the brothers' faces, their eyes wide and filled with terror as they cling to each other in a final embrace. In that instant perhaps they know that their fates are sealed and their time allocated on earth has passed. The wave now crashes down, engulfing them in the white broiling surf. There are no moans or cries for help. There are no quotable last words to take away or share with the world at large. All are lost to the mounting wail of wind and thunderous clap of water. They are gone.

I turn to The Black Suits who stand frozen with the cameras still outstretched in their hands. The moment drags on, as if they are waiting for

The Twins to re-surface, laughing and beckoning for them to keep the cameras rolling as if this were some advertising prank for a Tons' Time Share Vacations promotion. Something completely out of character, but alright, nonetheless. I can't see anything in the water other than the next wave pounding up further onto the embankment. There should be something left, some sign of life, a hand flailing from the trough behind an incoming wave, a shoe being spit up onto the sand like an undigested bone, or a hat floating on the surface of the water like a testament to the fact that the brothers Ton were here and that their existence has been marked upon this place. But there is nothing.

For the next two hours, we run along the sand as close as we can come to the rising water's lapping tongue, but none of us sees any sign of the brothers. The Black Suits turn to me in bewilderment. It is as if they are now a matched brace of homeless guard dogs that need to find another master. I sit down on the sand and stare in disbelief at what I have just seen. I am momentarily incapable of grasping or, perhaps, accepting what has just happened before my eyes. It is as if I were an unwilling witness to an assassination and am now frozen in the muzzle flash, uncertain of what to do next. But there is no clap of igniting gunpowder or the sound of sirens growing louder in my ears. There are no messages of alarm confirming the inevitable facts. There is only the intensity of the natural elements guided by nothing more than the earth's rotations. The Twins, the Brothers Ton, Two Ton, the masters and founders of Tons' Time Share Vacations are no more, having disappeared back into the sea as if this watery grave was a fitting place for them to end.

PART FOUR: SALVATION

"Home is the sailor, home from the sea, And the hunter home from the hill."

Epitaph on the gravestone of Robert Louis Stevenson

CHAPTER NINETEEN

AS I EXIT THE AIRPORT TERMINAL'S UPPER DECK IN VANCOUVER, I SEE Bird standing beside his cab about ten cars back in the lineup of taxis waiting for the next flight disgorge. He waves me over and nods to several of the other East Indian and Somali drivers ahead of him. They respond with nods or waves of the hand, indicating that they have registered the signal and everything on their end is okay. I guess queue jumping is one of the biggest no-no's in their line of work, and one has to be extra vigilant about giving the heads-up when they are there to retrieve a relative or friend. Courtesy between tribes and all.

Chief White Eagle Man Buffalo Child is dressed in his customary warrior gear. As I walk toward him, the sunlight filters through the plume of eagle feathers sticking up from the back of his large head, making his silhouette look even more imposing. His long shadow looks like an ostrich wearing a tiara on its head. A small group of newly arrived Japanese exchange students are huddled around their gigantic metal suitcases waiting for their host families to pick them up. Their black, sparkling eyes are transfixed by the mythic spectacle of Bird. Their western odyssey has begun.

I am glad to see Bird here. Even though he asked me for my itinerary before we parted company five days ago, I still wasn't sure that he would follow through with his stated intentions of meeting me. I now know that he measures everything that he says for its accuracy and its veracity, and unlike the casual word-bound culture that surrounds him, he means what he says

We shake hands and before I can withdraw my arm he has taken me into a full bear hug that, although brief, is warm and heartfelt. He grabs my suitcase and valise before I can protest. Moving swiftly around to the trunk of the car, he says,

"So Rich, how was your trip? Did you do what you meant to?"

I stop beside the passenger-side door and wait for him to deposit the bags before I get into the car.

"It's a long story. Let's just say that I accomplished some things that I intended to and not others."

He comes around to his door. We both get in and fasten our seat belts. "Was it the important things that got done or the other ones?"

I think back to everything that has happened over this past week and shrug.

"The jury's still out on some things and has come in thumbs down on some others."

Bird looks at me, smiling, as he pulls out of the line and begins driving down the exit ramp.

"I guess it's all good when you stop and think about it. I mean, it's all supposed to teach us something about ourselves that we didn't know before. So the elders say anyway." He looks at me and winks, "They never make it simple, those damn elders, do they?"

I look out of the front window at the road ahead as the airport traffic merges into the travel lanes heading toward the city.

The Black Suits and I had stayed at the beach for the afternoon, tracking the surf for any sign of The Twins, without success. I had sent the taxi driver back to town to notify the police or whatever other government authorities needed to be told of this unfortunate tragic turn of events, while we continued running up and down the sand. By that time, I, at least, had given up any hope of finding the Tons alive, but wished that we might recover their body or even some articles of their clothing, some form of confirmation that they had actually been there and now were really and truly gone. The Black Suits said nothing. They showed no emotions, other than a determined unity whose seemingly ambiguous purpose did not waiver. The storm had continued to grow. Although there was no rain while we remained at the scene, the ferocity of the elements increased in every other respect. I suppose that the under currents created in the exploding surf had snatched up their limp form and pulled it out to sea in minutes.

When our driver returned with several officials from both the police department and the army, they repeated our activities of the past two hours. They scoured the beach and, cupping their hands over their eyes, squinted aimlessly out at the white-capped water. Finally it was concluded that the touristas were indeed no more and that no foul play of any kind had occurred. The head honcho at the scene was a Colonel Ortega. He summed it all up as an unfortunate and unavoidable combination of circumstances leading up to a calamity of unfathomable proportions. They would write their reports and make the necessary arrangements, which would be minimal without any body to prepare for travel, and not detain us any further.

I returned to the hotel in the cab alone. The Black Suits had silently gotten into Colonel Ortega's Hummer and left the scene without so much as a backward glance. I went to the remaining meetings with the government officials, all of whom had been made aware of the accident. They solemnly said that everything would have to be put on hold until we had an opportunity to revise our financing plans. They were basically there to sign reams of contracts that were devoid of any ultimate meaning or relevance now that this would not culminate in the deposit of a twenty-five million US dollar cheque into the Cuban subsidiary's bank account in Barbados. Without this payday, these meetings took on all of the enthusiasm of witnessing a balloon fizzle away its air and collapse limp as a used condom on the Mediterranean tile floor. What can one say or do when somber death marches into the room and throttles the very life force out of all hope and anticipation, leaving the stark and naked truth in its wake?

As I was leaving Havana the next day, I saw The Black Suits walking brusquely behind Colonel Ortega and a military entourage. They were heading across the tarmac to a waiting private government plane. I then saw none other than Minister Conceptione's head pop out of the open doorway of the plane and bawl some undecipherable instructions to a man waiting on the ground. These orders sent him running toward the airport terminal as if he were trying to qualify for a place on the Cuban Olympic track team. If any of them saw me, they didn't register any recognition. It was as if yesterday and all the other days before it had now evaporated. This moment, and possibly tomorrow, were the only reality of anyone's existence. Surprisingly, as I watched them board their plane, I didn't speculate or question what might or might not be taking place. Like them, I suppose, I had adopted a fresh face and new perspective on everything. I didn't care to be a party to their plans. I simply wanted to board my flight and watch the island disappear beneath the airplane's wings. I guess I also hoped that some of the things that would come after us would bring a measure of well deserved comfort to the people on the streets and in the bistros and rum bars. They had waited so long and so patiently for anyone to bring them hope.

"I saw your daughter, Tess, yesterday." Bird says these words without emphasis. It is not a proclamation, yet they hit me with all of the force of a punch. He now looks over at me. "She has begun her healing quest. My mother and Aunt Sadie have prepared strong medicine bags to help her spirit find its right path."

I am dumb-struck, like an ox at slaughter. I hadn't heard anything more from Tess, so assumed that she was still waiting to make a final decision.

"Where is she?" I ask, trying to suppress any hint of confrontation in my voice. It would be a lie to say that I am not disappointed that this virtual stranger to our five years from hell has seen and spoken with the daughter that I cannot even *find*.

"Do not worry Rich, she is doing as well as can be expected. She needs space for herself right now. It wouldn't be good for her or for you to see each other until she says so. It is early in her journey, and any outside distractions could set her back or make her lose her footing." He turns toward me, and his voice softens, as if sensing my rising agitation. "She has lost control of so much it is good to let her hold onto the little bit that she feels she can still manage. She said that she will phone you soon and you can both take it from there. This path that she must walk is treacherous and narrow in many places."

I bite my lip so that I don't yell out, "Who the fuck do you think you are talking to?" As if I don't know the fucking path is narrow and easily lost. Where does he think that Genevieve and I and Emily have been for the past five years, at the fucking movies? She may god damn well be Shadow Rain Woman to aunt fucking Sadie, but she's my child and our baby and someone's sister, and that must mean something, for Christ's sake. But I already know that it doesn't. I also know that my anger is a part of my path and that it must not cross her way today. She already knows about other people's rage, and that there are other's judgments to face. For today, at least, she must only own that which is hers, and leave aside that which is ours.

I look out of the window at the familiar scene passing by: the old, baronial British mansions with their stone fences and iron gates that dot the landscape along Granville Street, now interspersed with the boxed super houses of the rich Chinese immigrants. Their big square exteriors like fortresses. No room left for the flowerbeds and rolling lawns that had once filled these newly cemented spaces.

"Is she sick? HIV sick, I mean."

Bird keeps his eyes on the road as he thinks about his answer before speaking.

"I don't know that. It is for her to know such things and for her to share them with us when the time is right." He now looks at me. "Although these things are important to us, they are also not urgent as well. She is not coming back the way that she left. Whether it is HIV or any number of other mental and physical scars, there are some things other than Aids that may never heal. We must accept the package at our door as it is, not as we would wish it to be."

We are now crossing Broadway Avenue at Granville, heading toward the Granville Street Bridge. I look down Broadway toward the Vancouver General Hospital and think of five short days ago when I had left my car on someone's front lawn and had run down a blind alley all because I thought that I had seen Tess. Now we knew where she was and that she was, at least for today, alive and safe. That is something. Bird was right in saying that this journey had to be one step at a time and one day at a time and one wish at a time, without any preconceptions. We had no right to pile our predetermined outcomes on Tess.

We pull up in front of my apartment building. I reach into my pocket and take out some bills. The meter says twenty-eight dollars. I extend thirty-five. He takes them in his huge hand and smiles.

"I can give you something worth more than thirty-five bucks, but you have to promise to take it with you upstairs." I agree. He looks into my face with the same calm quality I felt emanating from him that night at the NA Meeting. "Rich, let her find her spirit self and learn to live with it better than she has lived with her physical self as your daughter and someone's kid sister and someone else's this or that. She is Shadow Rain Woman, and if she doesn't grow to understand who that person is, she will not complete her journey toward the light and love we all have for her. Your daughter Tess is gone, and it is hard for this new person to let her go and hard for you and your wife to see her disappear as well but it is necessary if this new person is going to survive and be."

We get out of the car, retrieve my bag from the trunk, and shake hands at the door. I watch as Bird drives away and raise my hand in a dismal, little wave that feels all too much like a punctuation mark at the end of a sentence completing a letter of goodbye. It is the clinical notation a doctor may make in a patient's file regarding a serious, life-altering illness. I think that I should call Genevieve and let her know that Tess, or Shadow Rain Woman, is safe for the moment. I don't want to say too much or get her hopes up too high just yet, but I feel that I should tell her something. After all, she is waiting far from here, and this distance must play havoc with her nerves. Wherever possible, I will do my bit, to ease these tensions. However, I am also increasingly aware that I am being pulled in two directions, or if I throw Ethan into the mix, three directions and that these sometimes opposing tensions are not doing me or these others any good if they weaken my energies. I have to consciously find a way to keep them within my control without becoming too controlling in the process. Not an easy tight-rope to walk, but one that I must accomplish for a while longer. At least until either Tess or Genevieve, or both, are strong enough in their respective recoveries to take the reins into their own hands and lead the way forward. I will leave Ethan out of this picture of recovery since his looks more and more dismal with each passing year, the spiral downward absorbed at best by increasing doses of medication, and at worst by the onslaught of old-age and the sputtering life- force that it brings. Once past a certain point in the future, none of us will really care that much who is saner or more balanced than the other, all being increasingly pre-occupied with the immediate tasks of dressing and bathing and watching what we eat and drink, to be too critically judgmental of the broader spectrum of the lives of others.

It is now mid afternoon on Friday. I will take my luggage upstairs, shower, change my clothes, and then walk down to the office to review the week's trading slips. I will have to assess what is urgent, where damage control is required, and what can wait until Monday. I also should phone Charles Witherspoon in Toronto and get a pulse on what he's thinking about the Cuban fiasco. I called him from Havana before I left to drop the bomb regarding the inopportune drowning of the Ton brothers. He, as one would expect, was shocked beyond comprehension. He stammered that in all of his years in business with all of the fumbling eventualities this was something completely and uncomprehendingly new. He furthered that even a great Russian chess master surveying the board twelve moves in advance of play could never have even dreamt of such a thing as this. I think it would be safe to say that Charles was upset. He needed some time to digest everything. I may be a touch sensitive about the entire episode, in that The Twins did expire on my watch, but I felt that there was an ever so veiled hint of blame in Charles' tone, the dangling question being whether I should have plunged headlong into the raging surf like a loin- clothed Japanese pearl diver to save the deal. I guess that sort of hardball focus comes with the territory when you're in Charles Witherspoon's league. And no small wonder I suppose. When it's all added up the lost commissions and Finder's Fees and Administrative Fees and Signing Adjustment Allocation and Lending Bonus all lumped on top of the healthy percentage Marsh, Tuttle, Witherspoon & Gillespie would take on the currency exchange would probably round out to between eight and ten million us, a million of this bounty coming my way. And add to this a sizeable allocation of stock options. Anyway, it's no use crying over spilt milk. Life's too short and this ain't no dress rehearsal, so let's all just roll up our sleeves and play us some bitchin' ball, eh.

*

My apartment looks better than I had left it. This is no surprise because I suspect that Clive and Randy give it a deep cleaning prior to my return from these business trips, vacuuming and dusting and probably even polishing the stemware and any other hard surface to a jewel like lustre. I leave the bags on the bedroom floor for unpacking later tonight. I decide to skip the shower and change of clothes. I'd like to get down to the office to hear whatever other bad news stories there are to tell before the staff leaves for the weekend. I seem to be on a roll since assisting in the deaths of two billionaires and feel capable of handling just about anything else that comes down the old pipe. As I'm leaving, I see the phone light blinking and decide to retrieve my messages in case one is from Tess. There is no message from Tess, but rather there are messages from Emily saying that they will be coming to Vancouver next week, and from our Condominium Council President asking for confirmation that I carry extended theft and vandalism insurance on the Edsel. Run and Ida Skudmore's doing no doubt. There is a reminder that I have a dental appointment on Monday and a short terse message from Run Skudmore saying that he and Ida have to talk with me ASAP. Everything with Run and Ida, no matter how seemingly trivial, is of utmost importance. It wouldn't be unlike them to be giving me a heads-up about the car insurance thing, as if they were confidants of mine rather than the back-stabbers that have instigated the Condo Council's concerns about the car and its possible additional liability factor for all residents of 777 Beach View Place. Lastly, a call from my brother, Ethan, asking rather apprehensively if I am coming out to see him tomorrow as planned. I'll call him later and confirm that I am coming. I know how much these visits mean to him. I can tell by the slight quavering in his voice that he is getting anxious and needs to talk to someone that he feels won't judge him too harshly. I erase the messages and head out the door. I'll see Clive and Randy later tonight.

*

On my way back from Cuba, I stopped in Thunder Bay, which is something I have done for the past fifteen years or so whenever convenient, to visit the cemetery and tend my parents' graves. I suppose this is representative of a life cycle of sorts. The salmon returning to their spawning beds, the bees to their hive, the ghosts of the past to their final places of rest. No matter how many millions of grains of sand one turns over in their life, the answer to each of those lives often lies beneath the one left unturned. It is a riddle wrapped within an enigma. I am still captive in my little metaphoric sandbox, sifting through the fine grains seeking answers.

Northern Ontario stretches for thousands of miles, like a jagged robe thrown down by some fabled Ojibwa God. This coverlet is a protector for all that lies beneath. The stone is hardened by untold millennia and fired by volcanic episodes whose record is etched into fissures of granite and quartz. These faults striate up through the earth's plates to the surface, like jewel- encrusted serpents of ancient legends told in tongues long silenced. Wolf lichen hangs gray and limp as witch's hair from the stunted branches of the scrub spruce and tall, spindly jack pines dotting the landscape like snap shots from a Tom Thomson painting. Winter- kill has taken its toll on everything that grows in the north, including the people. Many years ago, I went out to the bay where my father died and sat on a large rock by the shore. It is the same rock upon which my father placed his clothes, neatly folded, a pocket watch and a letter to me. I suppose that he placed these items there just before he entered the lake and swam way out beyond the point of hope or rescue. I went back there to bury ghosts that had walked the hallways of memory, lo these many years ago. They are not ghosts of the storybook kind, shrieking goblins with bloodied hands and tortured groans that stand within my bedchamber of an evening. It's not like they have plagued my daily life, ushering an oppressive uncertainty to my door. They've just been there, quietly and patiently waiting. I feel that they may be waiting for me to do or say something that will put them to rest.

On this trip, I was thinking about making some important life changes, as well. These may have to do with my employment and even with where I am living. I am not yet sure. I am not what anyone would say is an overly sentimental person, but that does not mean that I do not know my own heart and its attachments to the places and people from whence I came. Family history, no matter how unsettling it may be at times, is still something to take ownership of and, with time, to accept. It is all, for each of us, a continuous cycle, like the perpetual abundance of the earth itself, its growth and fallow seasons often as predictable as a clock and at other times as disturbing as a serpent's apparition, casting its coiled tail to and fro, striking whomever stands in its wake. "Do not ask for whom the bell tolls." I guess is the message here for all of us to pay attention to.

It was late September, almost twenty years ago now that my father stood on the very spot I have often stood upon and made his final arrangements for life here on earth. My mother had predeceased him from a melanoma that had stubbornly resisted treatment and suddenly exploded throughout her body like a quilt of mold on a ripening piece of fruit. She had gone from looking and feeling fine, even joking about how all of her sun tanning had finally caught up to her, to spiraling into chronic pain. It was only two short months later that she was in palliative care. It was so fast that neither Ethan nor I had time to adjust before we were actually summoned to her bedside for the final, fateful vigil. Our father had taken it very hard having depended on our mother more than anyone ,other than she, could possibly ever have guessed. She was the one constant on his orbiting emotional and financial compass, and her untimely departure left him vulnerable to all of the forces that could be brought to bear. The next few years of loneliness were the most severe and debilitating for him. As I stood on that shore, I was profoundly aware of his desperation and how feeble his efforts must have become to avert this unwelcome destiny.

On my last visit to this bay, I climbed down from the rock that he stood upon and moved closer to the water's edge so that I could retrace his steps. I wanted to feel his presence throughout my being, each step resonating like an electric shock or thunder clap, startling me into the moment. My earlier thoughts that this might be a vain exercise were pushed aside. I felt a force moving through my body. It drove a chill down my spine and I shuddered involuntarily. The lake was calm that day, as it may have been on his day. The sunlight dappling on the surface like countless little fires awakened from their sleep. There was an osprey overhead. A sign? It rose on a wind current and dropped off into its tunnel describing a gentle arc as it watched for a fish rising to the surface far below. The shoreline in this place is mostly rock. Stones worn smooth by the water and sand, packed hard by the wind and waves. This surface is uncomfortable on your bare feet forcing you to walk hesitantly like a long legged bird. Is this the last ungainly stride my father took as he entered the cold water? Did this discomfort prod him to change his mind. Was he already oblivious to us? The thought of him being cold and uncomfortable strikes me again and again in the center of my chest. I wanted him to feel the warmth of the sun and maybe see the osprey circling. This thought gives me some comfort and hopefully gave him some as well.

I continue these rituals because they often make me feel better, not only about myself, but about everything that's happened since those times. I don't even know why I should care, since everyone, except Ethan, is long gone now, and he's hovering very close to the edge of oblivion as well. Despite this, I continue to keep these few remaining rituals alive for whatever reasons. My father is technically not buried here in the cemetery I go to visit. His body was never recovered. His absent bones are still being washed smooth by the cold, clear waters of Lake Superior.

I had almost cancelled this Thunder Bay duty with everything that happened in Cuba. But in the end, I chose to stay my course and see these things through. My father often said that in a storm the passengers turned to the captain, not to the wind. So, you see that leadership was instilled in me from a very young age although my teachers were often ultimately proven to not be up to the tasks that they championed.

When in Thunder Bay, I methodically follow a routine of sorts. I drive directly to the nearest mall, where I purchase a plastic shovel and pail, then pick up a couple of bags of planting soil and a variety of flower seeds. I then go to the cemetery plots and spend a few hours scraping and hoeing and mulching and sprinkling the seeds. I wind up with a nicely cleaned and tended area fronting the old family tombstone. I will often sit and contemplate life in the present and in the past for another hour or two. With this done I pick up all of the gear and deposit it into the closest garbage container, bid my adieus to my mother and father and jump back into the rental car that will carry me to the airport and back into the present day. And this is pretty well exactly what I did do that day. I stooped to dig the dry clods of earth around the base of the stone, using the edge of the plastic shovel to scrape the moss and lichens from its granite and marble surfaces. I realized that my feelings, instead of being pensive, as they well could have been, were increasingly calm and buoyed by a sense of anticipation that seemed strangely misplaced in the reality of my current situation. This being said, an abiding thrill at being alive and being able to do something uncommon and even uncalled for like this was like a spark that ran through my body and into my hands. I knelt before the harrowed area beside the marble obelisk and dug into the parched soil with my bare hands, trying to loosen the chunks of hardened clay as much as possible so that they could better accept the small packets of wild flower seeds and poppies. I sprinkled the seeds with care, as if I were placing a dampened cloth to my ailing mother's cracked lips, or washing the water mottled stain of suicide's lonely despair from my father's vacant eyes. As I tamped the ground back into place I thought of my people and their people before them. I looked from this place where I knelt and I knew hope and love once again. We all have our chance for happiness. Some fail and some pull through and I feel gratitude for this gift of another chance and this opportunity to take my shot. I looked around the cemetery at the stone angels bearing mute witness to the stilled choir of souls residing beneath them. And I knew something other than sorrow or loneliness. They were all here with me, as if they had never left. They were mine.

CHAPTER TWENTY

DESIREE IS STANDING BESIDE HER DESK AS I ROUND THE CORNER HEADING to my office. She is on the phone with her back turned to me. She turns her upper body from the waist and faces me. Her perky breasts are thinly cloaked under a cream-coloured, silk blouse. She knows their allure well enough. She winks as I walk past and covers the mouthpiece on the phone with her hand, miming that she needs to talk with me about something. I nod to acknowledge that I understand. I signal back that I will be in my office anytime she's ready. My breathing constricts slightly as I consider what her message may contain. I may be looking for a meaning deeper and perhaps darker than is necessary. I am off balance and I know it, which makes me even more pensive.

*

I sit down at my desk and survey the piles of paper neatly placed across its surface. There are three newspapers all folded open to head lines shouting, "Time Share Tons Killed In Freak Storm" and "Rogue Wave Claims Billionaire Founders of Tons' Time Share Dynasty" and "Time Share Twins Taken In Torrential Tides." There are trading slips to let me know what's been bought or sold and by whom. There are phone messages from the main receptionist stacked in the double digits. I will also have many more saved on my direct line. There are faxes, letters, trading bulletins, and memos from the admin department. No doubt, these are what Desiree wants to peruse with me. I decide that the phone messages are my first priority, followed by whatever Miss D. decides should go to the top of the pile. I'll leave the emails and other general correspondence for Monday. I listen to the phone messages, making notations on a legal pad. Some are lengthy, others short. Most are boring. I try to capture the gist of what's being said. For the most part they are the usual things, nothing of any startling consequence, other than the three messages from Frankie Butts, each one sounding more urgent than the previous. There is a rather long message from Julio Banasi. It would appear that the Port Moody project is continuing to hit roadblocks and may be relegated to a holding position for the next few months. This is related to the inconclusive geotech soils reports that have now led the municipality's engineering and planning people to dig in their heels, requesting further soils testing. All of this could start to become very expensive, with the continued looming possibility of inconclusive results. There is also further community resistance to higher-density housing. He says that signs are already springing up shouting, *Not In My Neighbourhood* and *Let's Keep Our Schools*. The politicians that had previously supported the whole concept of increased densities, are now probably weighing the impact of this sudden groundswell of support against their chances for re-election and opting for a stay-the-course approach to development. They are quickly losing words like "eye sore" which they had used to describe the neighbourhood, replacing them with other descriptive words like, "mature" and "comfortable." There's nothing new here, but coupled with the stability issues of the hillside, they may be the beginnings of a tsunami of rebellion to the over all acceptability of the project. The Banasis may be being forced into a cut and dried fight or flight scenario that is unnerving to the guys writing the cheques. No one can see the bottom of the well, and a bottomless downside is of legitimate concern to all, including me. Julio sounds a bit down in the mouth about this latest juncture. I am already mentally pushing the whole Port Moody proposition to the periphery of my daily thinking. It still has a chance, and with the Banasis pushing the cart it may even stand a better than average chance. But there's no denying that the first alarm bell has rung. The age-old sign-post reading *caveat emptor* is not one to casually ignore.

I also see a call from Charles Witherspoon that came in this morning. I momentarily juggle all these messages in my mind and quickly decide to deal with Frankie first, simply because it won't take long. I have no intention of being drawn into a systematic blow by blow on what happened in Cuba, since Frankie isn't the guy to make any of it go away. He's only the hand wringer that wants to whine about it all in an effort to make everyone understand what an absolutely awful affect this is having on his life. Charles, on the other hand, is the guy that can help make this thing right if, in fact, that is what I'm interested in doing. My feelings about the Cuban deal have dulled appreciably. I haven't had the time to determine whether this is related to seeing the Tons die before my very eyes or whether it is something inherently smelly with the whole damn thing. I'll hear what Charles has to say and give it all some thought through the weekend.

I put my headset on and push the autodial for Frankie's number. He picks up on the first ring. This is a bad sign. He's been hovering over his phone watching the call display.

"Frankie..Richard..What's up?"

"Richard, what in the hell happened? Have you seen the newspapers? They had pictures of the accident site on CNN last night for God sakes. I got a call from the guys at Global yesterday saying that the deals been put on what could be permanent hold. I thought it was a done deal. What went wrong?"

Frankie is spooked, the panicked sound in his voice betraying every emotion and accusatory feeling that he has in his entire body. In one fell swoop, he has become everybody's fretting grandmother or nervous spinster aunt, a festering boil of condemnation. There is an old saying that successes have many fathers, while failures are always orphans. This is Frankie's code.

"Listen Frankie, I only just got back and I've got other calls to make, so all I can tell you at this point is that the deal has been put on hold pending any number of things which we are presently investigating." This guy's hysterics aren't part of my plan at the moment, either. "And you should know something as well as any of us pal, a deal's NEVER over until it's over, so don't gnash your fuckin' teeth about things not working out as you had planned. You aren't the only one upset here,l Frankie. Some of the rest of us have a stake in this too, or have you forgotten that already?" He is now conciliatory, ducking back, trying to regain any turf he may have lost through his self-serving bitching. This also pisses me off, because I don't like people that wimp out at the first sign of resistance.

"Hey, Richard. No, I haven't forgotten anything, man. It's just that I mean people getting killed It's, it's like something out of a movie. I mean how the hell do two billionaires drown anyway? It's mind boggling."

I don't want to get into this side of things right now, or possibly ever, with him. "Yeah,well billionaires drown pretty much like the rest of us. They swallow too much water. I guess you had to be there. Anyway, I'm going to be talking to Charles Witherspoon sometime early next week and we'll get their read on things and go from there. Listen, I've got to go to another line here. We'll talk next week."

I hang up the phone. I now place a quick call to Matsqui Federal Penitentiary and let them know that I will be coming out at regular visiting hours tomorrow to see my brother. Due to the additional duty arrangements required for a visit to this mostly locked-down wing of the institution, they appreciate getting prior notice of a visit. I comply, hoping that it will help to foster a more positive environment for daily staff inter-actions with my brother. Once this is done I locate Charles Witherspoon's private office number on my speed dial pad and push the send button. I take a deep breath, waiting for the call to connect. After the fourth ring, he answers,

"Charles Witherspoon here. Who is calling please?" I already *know* that if it's a man's voice and it's answering his personal private line that it's going to be him. He also has Call Alert on his phone pad. He would never pick up without checking to see who is on the line. These yester-year salutations are part and parcel of his old boy's school corporate culture, where form was as important as substance.

"Hello Charles, it's Richard Bonhom calling. I'm returning your call from this morning. Have I reached you at a convenient time?" Charles' old world ways makes me act more formally with our interactions.

"Yes, Richard. It's fine. I hope that your return from Cuba was more pleasant than your stay there. I'm sitting here looking at a Globe and Mail piece that very cautiously alludes to possible wrongdoing in the Tons' deaths. I guess a whiff of possible intrigue will sell more news papers."

I give him a brief rundown of how the Cuban authorities conducted their part of the post -accident wrap up.

"It sounds like they did whatever had to be done in such a situation Richard."

Charles is already pretty much focused on today and possibly tomorrow, with yesterday and the emotional claptrap of yesterday's newspaper headlines fading from his focus. He knows that there was no collusion to do the Tons in, because he is a rational man and can easily see that no one, especially me, had anything to gain from their untimely deaths. Some radical environmental group or anti free enterprise faction, could have decided to take extreme measures, but this was highly unlikely. Anyway, from Charles' perspective, the Tons' deaths are really only a part of the subtext of the saga's main story now. The money, as always, in his view, is the main story.

"I was calling to bring you up to speed on two matters. The first is the process of extracting the Tons from the legal side of things. This will require a Trustee from their Corporate Department, which by the way, won't happen over night I can assure you." I'm sure he's scoring a bulls-eye here. The paper-work spreads across three countries, with an equal number of legal precedents. "The second matter is Witherspoon, Owen Tuttle & Marsh's continued commitment to see this project through to a successful conclusion. I thought that you should know that whatever the guys over at Global or your people are thinking or saying, we are fully committed and will revive our end of things, however we manage it, and hopefully will remain as the *go to* guys on the private capital side."

I confirm that this is my understanding, as well. We agree to talk early next week, hanging up the phones with a cordial exchange of more personal pleasantries about weekend activities. His Sunday was spent at the polo grounds. He and a couple of old school chums he affectionately calls Spikey and Quaff own a considerable stake in several ponies. This extended fare thee well is Charles Witherspoon's way of saying he holds no ill will toward me for helping to kill off two of his biggest private capital bankers. Someday, we may even share a drink and a sly rueful aside about how fantastical and chock-a-block full of textbook dark comic pathos this whole business truly is.

Charles is concerned that the deck will be reshuffled, now that the Tons are off the play roster, and that with the deal near completion, someone else will step up to the plate with the twenty-five million smackers in their hot little hands. Someone else may take all of those luscious fees with them in the handshake. The cold reality, when viewed in the harsh light of recent events, is that they may well have something to fear here. The deal's profile has surfaced on more than one firm's commercial lender's radar screens, and there will be more than a few calls lighting up the switchboards here and in New York and even in Havana, vying for a place at the table. The places at these high-stakes tables are not that easily won, and when all of the back slapping and hip hip hurrahing is pushed aside, Charles Witherspoon and his cronies can unleash a rear guard attack to protect their turf that would make Genghis Khan drool with envy. At the end of the day, men don't get to the penthouse suite looking over the city's twinkling lights and receive deprecating nods from the Bay Street Boys and the Wall Street Club without mucking it out in the trenches like Irish navvies mining coal, whenever active duty calls.

I honestly don't know what I am thinking concerning my future here. I may possibly know only too well, but don't want to acknowledge it because these thoughts will turn over the old apple cart at a time in my life when I don't want or need the added weight of these additional burdensome life changes. Then again, maybe it's just the right time, as Charles Witherspoon believes, to knuckle down to some good, old-fashioned ass kicking to get this whole Cuban thing back on track.

*

Desiree peeks her dark curls around the half open door and coos, "Are we open for business or are we licking our wounds?"

I really don't feel like going over the stacks of corporate jingo laying in a deadening pile in front of me, but am taken aback at how much I want to be near her and savour the pungent aroma of her Voodoo. This is the name of her perfume. She confided this to me once when I commented on how much I liked its subtle bouquet. I beckon her forward, placing the correspondence on top of the stabbing newspaper banners. I pull these memos toward me as if they are a succulent meal I have been waiting to share.

"So what's been happening on the company front? Anyone fired, quit, married, or murdered?" As soon as this last word escapes my mouth, I regret it. I know that the rumour mills about what happened in Cuba have probably already spun out of control and dubbed The Twins' deaths as *suspicious* at the very least, with many of my long-standing partners readying the machinery, both business and personal, to create an impenetrable distance between themselves and me. As Desiree enters, she purposefully turns, closing the door. Great confidences are going to be shared that best remain ours alone to keep. She is wearing a tight-fitting, short, black skirt that pulls across her thighs provocatively. She walks over to the desk and stops, looking down at the memos, as if trying to gauge the most productive way to present an overview of their contents.

"No to all of the above. Merv Hindlich is back. Heavily sedated. He looks like something out of a zombie movie. The admin people have started a pool on how long he'll hang in. I put five bucks on the July long weekend. I figured the additional pressure of family visits and talk of grand new beginnings and how important family is will push him over the top again." She adjusts her stance and takes a breath, as if this gesture punctuates what is coming next. "It's mostly been Dullsville here other than what we hear about you of course." She smirks, her dimpled cheeks reddening slightly as if we are devilish co-conspirators. "So, are you going to tell me absolutely everything, or am I going to be forced to jump to my own, possibly erroneous, conclusions?"

I know that she is the conduit in the office gossip mill for information about all of the senior partners. This is because she handles most of our transaction slips. I also feel that she is somewhat more protective of me than of the others, due to this *thing* of mutual attraction that seems to have evolved over the past six months or so. Knowing all of this, I still am not going to take Desiree into my inner confidence. It is quite simply a bad business decision that would lead to all sorts of complications if, for whatever reason down the road, I have to be the one to fire her. It is true that I have mentally conjured on more than one occasion about throwing her across my desk and wallowing in her like some moon struck shepherd from her ancestral Mediterranean village. It is also true that I will do my level best not to. Doing this would foster a host of issues that I'd rather leave for the next guy to collide with. I also resist any physical contact because I still love Genevieve and, although we've been apart for over half a year, I am reluctant to drive any further wedge between us until I know for certain that there's no hope of a reconciliation. Anyway, we'll cross that bridge when we come to it. For now, it's good enough just to be here with Desiree and gambol about in these small innocent deceits.

"So, I guess the stories are flying fast and loose around these corridors." The fact that she is the office gossip is a sword that cuts both ways. It also extends whatever scuttlebutt making the workplace rounds available to me on demand.

"Well it is running the complete gamut. The senior partners are calling it an accident, long standing admin people are saying that it may have been a suicide, and the junior admin girls on the next floor are saying that it's a vicious murder and that you are the prime suspect."

She still hasn't sat down. I am reluctant to offer her a chair because I don't want to belabour the details of my Cuban misadventure any more than I have to at this time. I also don't want to appear to be distant, or a poor host, since Desiree and I are "friendly," and for some reason I don't want to cut that cord. Perhaps the burning bridges theory. If all is lost, one last tumble in the hay before falling on my sword may be in order.

"Let's just say that the smart money is backing the accident scenario and leave it at that for today. Don't chew your well-manicured cuticles to a stub thinking about it, though. I'll tell you the whole sorry business over coffee next week." This should put a stop to any further questions while leaving the door ajar for more detailed insider type info. Hopefully, by following this path, I have not hurt her feelings through any hint of exclusion.

I now turn my attention, with as much feigned earnestness as I can muster, to the stacks of memos and trading slips. I suddenly recognize that they have a newly minted value as a buffer between Desiree's curiosity and my reluctance to share intimacies. She takes this cue in stride and moves around the desk to my side, seeming to have a genuine interest in alerting me to any possible obstacles on the often bumpy paper trail of which she is the gate keeper. She bends now with her right breast touching my shoulder, our flesh separated only by two thin skeins of fabric. Desiree's long nimble fingers deftly riffle through the piles of paper. She makes quick judgments concerning what is wheat and what is chaff. I close my eyes, trying to resist the muscle contraction restricting my throat and tightening through my upper chest. I languish beneath the all too appealing veil of Voodoo.

CHAPTER TWENTY-ONE

I FEEL THAT IT IS TIME FOR A CLEAN-UP, IF NOT A COMPLETE OVERTHROW of all known order, then certainly a tidying of sorts. A chance to make reparations where necessary, cultivate healthier life choices where possible, and make clean cuts where inevitable. Strangely enough, I'm beginning to feel better about it all, as if the past week's tribulations may conspire to some ultimate triumph of a kind not totally clear to me at this point. After completing the review of administrative stuff with Desiree, we exchange warm wishes for a good, fun-filled weekend. I get the distinct impression that if I were to suggest she come over to my place for a drink, followed by a dip in the large Jacuzzi tub with moi, both of us as naked as jay birds, she would say a heartfelt *yes* before the last words of my invitation had parted my saucy lips. But I don't. Buck up. Soldier on. I leave the office alone, bidding casual farewells to the skeleton staff of office workers still completing last minute paper work before calling it a day.

As I am standing in front of the elevators, I hear a muffled cough coming from behind. I stand for a moment collecting myself for what I may see. J.J. Stump's office door is ajar. I slowly walk away from the elevators, stopping at the doorway to peer inside. I do not want to disturb him in his time of grave troubles. I see the man, my friend and teacher, standing behind his desk. He is stooped over a small cardboard box that he has put onto the desktop. He is slowly placing items from his cabinet drawers into the box. These are objects of a personal nature. I continue standing, silently watching him without being noticed. He has grown so thin and frail since I last saw him at his house. It was only a few short weeks ago, but the deterioration of his body is significant. We talk on the phone almost daily, but he never lets these conversations digress into anything concerning his health or his feelings about his disease. He is an old school gentleman, a quiet reserved trooper. I clear my throat to alert him of my presence. He looks up toward me almost without recognition for a moment, then smiles softly and waves an arm encouraging me to enter.

"Mr. Bonhom. Good to see you. And how's the main man?" He chuckles with that deep warm sound that laughs at the world and at its misfortunes, while telling one and all that life is still good and worthwhile. "You standing there long? I wouldn't want to think that I'm so pathetic that people recoil from the very sight of me."

"Never my friend. Never. You're a lion, JJ."

"When lions get old and sick they starve, or are killed by their younger siblings." He now sits down in his chair. The dark suit jacket he is wearing bunches up around his scrawny neck and diminished shoulders like a sack. It is as if the disease has worn a trench through the center of the man, leaving only the voice and the indomitable spirit of him in tact. "Tell me something Richard, over the past months when you have so kindly taken the time to visit with me at my home or at that super sanitized hospital, I have sensed that something may be wrong in your world. I don't mean to pry, you know that's not my way, but since time is growing to be an ever more precious commodity, maybe you should just say what you have to say, get it off your chest, if you want."

I do not want to tell this man that I have grown so fond of, and that is going to be leaving us behind so soon, that I am a disappointment on so many fronts. I do not want his last thoughts of me to be vexing in any way. I want him to see me strong and fit, ready to embrace the life that is now being denied him.

"Just the usual Stump, you know, the family saga. Nothing that I can't handle."

He looks down and sputters a guttural cough that is almost a gag. He lifts a white tissue to his mouth and wipes away a pale smear of blood. It is almost pink in colour. He seems uncertain of where to put this, but settles for his jacket pocket. He looks up.

"So you say." He knows a lie. "I'm going to miss you Richard. And our little chats over the years. You know that you're really something. You're the genuine article. Don't let anyone or anything tell you different. And don't take any of their shit, either. You have my permission to tell them to stick it, if it feels right to you."

I smile at him, the last person in my cheering section.

"If I am what you say, it's because I've had a good teacher, someone to show me the way. Someone to admire." I choke on this last word, but dig deep down to maintain my composure.

He continues looking at me, his eyes watery, but fixed and determined. "Thank you, that means a lot. It says something about us both, I suppose." He has folded his hands in front of him resting them on the desk. He looks at them for a moment as if weighing his thoughts and words carefully. "I'd ask one favour of you."

I wait, letting the silence speak louder than any answer I can say. It is showing him my respect, not interrupting or diluting his time, or his words. He clears his throat

"Don't look for all the pieces to always fit. I mean in the big puzzle of this life. Because they won't. Just accept that and make due with the occasional imperfections, even if they appear to be large at the time.

They're still only part of the bigger picture. When you remember me, try to remember how the obstacles ultimately helped me. For instance, it's ironic, but the thing that kept me isolated for so many years, the system not wanting me or my kind, in the end was the very thing that saved me, made me stronger, more independent." He chuckles. "That is, if you care to remember me at all."

I remain silent for a moment, staring at him without expression, then smile slowly, "I'll try to fit you in."

The afternoon light is coming through the office window with increasing warmth. It settles on Stump's form for an instant, like a protective blanket. He now stands once again.

"My granddaughter is downstairs waiting. She is my chauffeur for today. One of the small bonuses of being ill, getting to spend more time with loved ones." I volunteer to carry his box of memorabilia down to the lobby. We chat some more about life and what his final plans are for his last days with his family. When we are in the building foyer waiting for his granddaughter to bring the car to the front door we take our final moment to say our goodbyes. He says that he is going over to stay at his sister's place. She is a nurse and has requested that he let her help him on this final leg of his mortal journey. We shake hands. Stump is not one for embraces or maudlin scenes. He is dignified in his approach to such things as this. I touch his shoulder, and he places his gaunt hand upon my elbow. He pats my arm and squeezes it softly, but it is an unmistakable punctuation. It is Jackson Jefferson Stump's candid way of saying

that he knows and that he cares, too. This is the last time that I will see him. When his granddaughter pulls the car up in front, I help him to the curb and place the box into the back seat. His final words to me are, "Remember to fly straight now, Richard. Be self-reliant. That's the key. Don't let those headwinds or those bastards steer you off course." I assure him that I will not, and we part company. I stand on the sidewalk, watching the taillights disappear into the afternoon traffic. I continue looking in this direction after they have gone, I am looking at nothing in particular. Just at lives lived. As I am standing there, I know something as strongly as I have known anything. I want the things that I do to represent the man that he sees in me. And I also know that this man, that he so clearly sees, does not bend to adversity, or cower in the face of truth. To some extent, it is a fabled person, a Lincoln or Gandhi, or such. Maybe not a man like me at all, at least in anyone else's eyes.

*

I walk up Howe Street with a newly found sense of purpose. There isn't anyone on the sidewalk, which is strange for this time of day. Maybe the Friday afternoon exodus from these glass towers adding substance to Vancouver's reputation as a laid back environment has already begun. The weekend summer season getting off to an early start. I am grateful for having had this last opportunity to be with JJ., my resolve to make things right further bolstered. I will face life head-on for now and see where this lands me.

Then it happens. The unexpected, one of those uncanny things that sometimes presents itself to us like a sacrificial lamb or omen of good things ahead, but as often as not is just another fathomless coincidence in our lives. Coming out of an office tower not more than fifty feet in front of me steps none other than Rickie Ricco. I know it's him by his round-shouldered skulk. He glances up the street and then back down toward me, like some wild thing exiting a protective grove of shade trees in the forest, cautious, momentarily stopping to survey the surroundings for any possible threat, or unexpected easy opportunity to take a meal. He sees me. I know this by the way his frame bridles, an infinitesimal reflexive stiffening of his spine. It is as if his whole body is saying fuck at the very sight of me. Like any predator, he is instantly aware that this almost insignificant lapse may have been detected, such detection placing him on the defensive, rather than on the firmer, controlling ground he prefers. He now pulls himself back up to his most formidable bruin-like stance and, lighting a cigarette, smiles thinly as I approach. He gruffly chirps,

"Well, look what I found. This must be my lucky day. Richie, how's it going?"

I move up close to him as Run Skudmore does when he is going to start one of his scheming diatribes. He relaxes his shoulders, adopting a slightly less rigorous physical attitude. Rickie probably fosters a high degree of emotional indifference to these otherwise strained meetings with old investors or rebuffed creditors. It is Rickie's life, taking advantage of people's basic reluctance to make a stand and call him on his sordid record. Introspection is as foreign to him as baking his own bread or volunteering in an after school program teaching the neighbourhood tots how to build model airplanes. He looks me in the eye, as if to say, Don't even bring up the fuckin' hundred g's, because you and I both know that it's a non issue."

I punch him squarely in the mouth. The blow sends the glowing cigarette down his throat. A piece of the lit ash sticks to my knuckles, burning my flesh. Rickie's head is jerked back, his whole body rolling behind it toward the smooth granite wall of the building. I move forward and punch him again. This time I miss my mark by an inch, my blow glancing off his chunky neck. The punch's force is dispersed into his chamois jacket, which is now bunched up on his shoulder. He is choking and clutches both hands up to his throat, like a bewildered President Kennedy when struck by the sniper's first mushroom-tipped, fragmenting bullet. I can see the blood congealing in his mouth. He spits and gasps, his astonished look hovering between surprise and righteous indignation.

"What the fuck is wrong with you, for fuck sakes? Are you nuts?"

I then grab him in a headlock with one arm around his non-existent neck and awkwardly begin trying to drag him back around the corner of the building and into an alleyway where I have every intention of beating the living piss out of him. I punch him on the top of the head a couple of times. My hand is suddenly throbbing. It may be badly hurt, even broken. I am running on pure adrenaline and ignore the pain. I grab at his isolated tufts of transplanted hair. I am pulling with all my might, trying to dislodge the coal-black plugs, but the calcified scar tissue holds. He has regained his composure now and is wrestling with me, trying to free himself from my headlock. He tries to punch me. Asshole. I have tucked my head down into my shoulder cavity, like some palooka readying himself for a possible offensive thrubbing, his wind-milling blows bounce off my hunched back and barreled arms without measurable damage. His weight and burly stance have arrested any forward movement toward the alley. We are now locked in a jostling match of sorts, thrashing back and forth on the side-walk, like two drunks trying to help each other up the steps.

He finally breaks free from my grip, pulling back trying to assess the situation and figure out what's the best thing for him to do, stand and fight or turn and run for his pathetic life? I lunge forward and propel my right leg into an arching, roundhouse kick that catches him on the left thigh. He almost topples over and winces with pain as he grabs the spot that my shoe has indented in the fleshy part of his upper leg. For an instant he looks like he is going to start to cry. He now beseeches me,

"For Christ sakes Rich..."

Before he can finish I wind up another slingshot karate kick aimed at his other thigh or big fat ass, but miss by a good measure and spin out of control across the sidewalk, falling down on my back against the curb. For a split second I can trace the imbecilic movement of thought flicker-ing across Rickie's eyes, telling him to pounce and mete out some serious fuckin' retribution, but instead, he brushes back his delinquent thatch of inky doll's hair and looks around, checking to see if anyone he knows is witnessing this absurd spectacle. The chicken shit is embarrassed. This realization alone is worth the hundred grand to me right now. I quickly exploit this lull in retaliatory aggression and scramble to my feet. I stand my ground, straightening my rumpled suit. I am now consciously favour-ing my swollen hand, a blister already forming where Rickie's cigarette flame has seared me. I look over at him and say,

Fuck you Rickie. And fuck the horse that you rode in on! And as far as 'how's it going?' not very fuckin 'good for you today, buddy."

I now turn, attempting to bolster whatever remnant of dignity I can muster. I strive to walk, sporting a victorious stride. However, I twisted my knee with that last kick and am limping quite badly. My neck is also in spasms from the sudden jolt it took when Rickie freed himself from my grip in his cowardly bid to buy himself some precious maneuvering time. He remains standing on the sidewalk with a sluggish expression frozen onto his moronic face. I limp past a woman that has been approaching from down the block. She must have seen a part of our fray at least. She moves over to the farthest side of the sidewalk, giving me as wide a berth as she can. I see her side long glance of apprehension. She is uncertain whether I'm a crazy person randomly attacking people I encounter on the street, or an unsuspecting, hapless victim. My natural impulse is to pacify her with reassurances that it's all okay, but I don't, choosing instead to walk on with my eyes focused straight ahead. I am fully aware that by saying nothing I am actually saying "Fuck you lady and fuck everyone else today, too." For the moment this is fine by me. Although I'm in more pain than I want to acknowledge, I must admit to feeling light headed about the whole business. I feel like someone must feel after hurtling himself off a trestle spanning a remote forest canyon on the end of a bungee cord. I smile thinly to no one, or maybe to JJ. The clean-up has begun.

My account overage is going to be dealt with swiftly. I made a decision about this when I was kneeling by my parents' graveside in Thunder Bay. I didn't even know how firmly I was committed to this then, or precisely how it was going to be accomplished, but I did know that the time for vacillating about it was coming to an end. Now, I realize what course of action I am going to take. First, I am going to call Genevieve on the weekend and explain my situation, leaving it up to her to volunteer the idea of a mortgage on our mutually held properties. If she does not come forth with this suggestion without equivocation or hesitation of any kind, I am going to call a meeting of our company's senior partners, of which I am one. I will state the situation and my position regarding possible remedial action. This is not the first time such a turn of events has occurred. Only last year, another senior broker of long standing was found to be fudging his trading account balances. He did not come forward and, upon being discovered in a random audit by our administrative personnel, immediately went straight into an embarrassing tailspin of denial. He brazenly threatened to expose corporate wrong doing on a grand scale. There wasn't any. He raved that he would have the lot of us suspended or possibly even brought up on serious Regulation Sanctions. This is actually when our partner's struck a Due Diligence and Proper Practices Committee to tighten up our own internal reporting policies. I was the chairperson. Anyway, I really don't give a shit what anyone thinks or says or even does with all of this information. All I know is that putting the record straight is the right thing for me to do and will make me feel a whole hell of a lot better about things. At best, the company will front me the money to cover these irregularities, with the stern admonishment that these monies will be paid back from commissions or a quick injection of outside cash on my part. At worst, and this is highly unlikely, they will ask for my voluntary resignation, suspend my trading license, pay the overages from their corporate slush fund, and proceed to sue me for the outstanding balance. This is an unlikely scenario for several salient reasons, all of them predicated on the Company's best interests instead of on the pursuit of truth and honesty. First, they always have their large, blood-shot eyes fixed on the income column, the bread and butter. I am still considered a good catch, a big hitter who brings sizable payloads into the office. Second, they don't want the attention such a public garroting would entail, perhaps even resulting in a Securities Commission audit of the entire company. This also would be made public, with the press feasting on innuendos and insinuations of wide-spread corporate high jinks and possible collusion to defraud clients. This type of news spreads like ink stains on the fine white linen of a reputation. Third, they have to pay out the loot to cover the overages in either case, so why further jeopardize their chances of getting paid back by alienating me? Better for them to appear to have some familial concern for my welfare. This kindness may keep me beholden and in the camp. The thinking here being that it is always better to have a loose cannon standing in the tent pissing out, than standing outside pissing in.

I feel good about myself and my situation for the first time in a long time. My knee may be throbbing, and my back and shoulder may be on the verge of going into a painful contraction, but for the moment I don't care. All of this superfluous shit will soon to be out of my hands. Once this is done, let the chips fall where they may. I look at the bruises and crusted blood smear where the cigarette burned my knuckle. I feel good about all of this, too. It's like a badge of honour rather than the remnants of a misguided, churlish escapade. As I limp across Burrard Street, I catch a fleeting glimpse of myself in a store window. I look like a disheveled Don Quixote returning from some innocuous joust. I think of my grandfather and of Stump, and of what they have said to me about accountability. Today I stood up to be counted! In a small and disconcerting way, I balanced a ledger.

*

It is ten minutes to six when I get back to 777 Beach View Place. Just as the elevator doors are droning open, Lei Lei starts yapping and rocketing back and forth across the widening gap. She is sticking her muzzle in and out of the space, as if gauging her chances for an attack. I would love to scissor the doors closed on her scrawny neck and smack her little, prickly chops with the back of my hand as her distraught owners look on helplessly from the other side. I settle for a penetrating focused glare that says, "You could be next you anemic little pest ." This instinctively sends her scuttling.

As I step into the hallway, I am confronted with the disheartening specter of Run and Ida. Lei Lei is now cradled in Ida's arms. Her torpedo shaped body, as hard as flint, is trembling and her little beady black eyes framing her cone-shaped, rodent-like muzzle stare accusingly at me from their deep sockets. All three are vigilant plotters waiting to apprise me of whatever intrigue has been spawned in my absence. Run glances at Ida, possibly for some form of subliminal assurance that their timing is right and their cause is just. She does not acknowledge this, nuzzling her stark, pallid face affectionately against the dog's heaving rib cage and cooing,

"Shhhh...Shhhh...you bad little babykins."

Run moves into my immediate space, lifting his herring-crusted jowls toward my compressing nostrils.

"Richard. There's something that I think you should know before you talk to anyone else." He now jerks his head back toward the hallway leading to Randy and Clive's door.

I sigh audibly. I have told both Run and Ida that I consider Randy and Clive to be friends, and that I am not the least interested in joining one of their conspiracies to rout them from the building. Before I can confirm this Ida moves in closer. I see Lei Lei tense her already rigid body as if, her confidence newly restored, she is sizing up her chances at taking a nip at my forearm from the reassuring security of Ida's protective hold. Run anticipates my reaction and continues anyway,

"While you were away, we think that you should know that *the girls*," he jerks his head again indicating the neighbour's door, "had quite a little party...at your place." He now looks toward Ida for confirmation of this seemingly appalling fact. She squiggles in even closer, pursing her dry lips as if the indignation of it all is too much for her to shoulder. They both stand stock-still, waiting for my reaction. Lei Lei has also stopped trembling and stares pointedly at me. For a brief moment, I almost burst out in a fit of laughter, suddenly seeing a kind of familial resemblance of sorts in their faces, their anger and dumb instinct betraying every mean spirited thought and punitive action with equal tenacity. I now start moving toward my door,

"Listen. Randy and Clive have the keys to my place whenever I'm away. If they, for whatever reason, decide to have someone over, that's okay by me." I stop now and acknowledge them with a thin, conclusive smile. I want to end this exchange before they begin traipsing along the hallway, readying themselves for another volley. I want to keep this as short as humanly possible. "Thank you for watching the place. I hope that it didn't put you out too much."

I turn to insert my key into the door lock, when Run deftly moves around my shoulder. He is now positioned directly in the narrow space between me and the door. Ida follows more cautiously. I think that Lei Lei's attitude indicates a heightened awareness once again as well, but to what? A possible confrontation? In my mind's eye I see a fleeting image of Run, suddenly grabbing me by the lapels and slamming me repeatedly against the hard wooden surface of the oak door. I am increasingly uncomfortable once again, the growing silence suddenly shouting that it's high time I start taking things around here a fuck of a lot more seriously or it may be me that's heading out of the front door.

"Richard, they're using their bloody apartment for …public meetings for Christ sakes. It's against our bylaws to allow any commercial activities on the premises. Next, they'll be installing a goddamned cash register by their front door. We'll all be awake day and night listening to the ching-chinging as they tally up their sales."

Run has brought this up before, both with me and at Condominium Council Meetings. He is right in this regard. In the past, the building's occupants, myself included, have taken a dim view of anyone conducting business in their suites. But when all was said and done it was the tenant's utter resentment for Run and Ida that swayed the consensus away from this obvious infraction on the parts of Randy and Clive. The beleaguered Skudmores' stark indictments came to no avail. An informal note was slipped under Randy and Clive's door by the then Council President, Jolene Formosa, gently telling the boys to cool it. It was later disclosed by Run and Ida that Jolene herself was a recent inductee into Oh So Smooth, their paranoid, conspiratorial thinking once and for all confirmed. Poor, dear Jolene had great potential to make a name for herself in the Oh So Smooth organization before she was unexpectedly and sadly stricken with a debilitating stroke and forced to move from the building into long term care.

I straighten my body to its full alpha male height, thinking that the shorter and more rotund Run, will take this as an animal act of aggression and move himself out of my immediate forward path. He appears to sense this and shuffles back a mere foot or so before leaning forward, as if to reclaim this marginally forfeited space.

"You know what can happen if someone is injured in the common areas?" —He waits, knowing full well that I haven't a ready answer. "If their claim states that they were working at the time here at the invitation of their bosses whose offices are proven to be located in the building, our insurance policies will be deemed null and void. They won't cover a workplace wrongful injury suit. Our joint tenant liability could escalate into the millions."

I know that this insurance angle is a sure fire card in Run and Ida's closely concealed hand. It is a card that they palm whenever they think it convenient. I now know the reason the new Council President has left a message on my phone's answering machine regarding my extended liability insurance on the Edsel. It is because the Skudmores have been informally approaching council members and baiting them concerning this additional unforeseen financial risk —an expensive collector's vehicle sitting there like a Judas Goat, the car's very presence on the property possibly attracting cat burglars and second story men. They would make their case that these additional, costly break-ins could adversely affect our already escalating insurance premiums.

Lei Lei, like me, has grown bored with these proceedings and is now lolling across Ida's shrunken wrist, her bullet-shaped snout aimed listlessly toward the floor.

"Listen, Run. I appreciate that things aren't perfect, and if we all work together, we can improve them some, I'm sure. But I've just gotten back from a business trip," and here I inexplicably raise my voice a forced octave higher, causing it to break with emotion, leaving them momentarily stunned. "I was just in a fist fight on the street, for Christ's sake." I hold up my burned and bloodied hand in their faces as proof "So now isn't the best time for me." The fact that they haven't even taken stock of my dishev-eled appearance or battle-scarred hand, offering some small amount of concern for my well being, is a further, irritating reminder to me of the Skudmore's self-centred perspective. I push the key into the lock and turn the door handle, authoritatively signaling an end to this exchange. Once through the door, I turn and look at them with a stony expression before closing it matter-of-factly behind me. In the narrowing crack, all I can see are Run and Ida and Lei Lei's beseeching faces wistfully looking into my entrance hall in befuddled amazement. They stand stock-still and wait, all faintly holding onto the diminishing hope of being invited in for a cup of cocoa and some good old-fashioned lynch mob revivalist rhetoric. The door closes with a concluding thud.

Finally standing alone in front of my bay window, I look out over the steely waters of English Bay. I try to regain my equilibrium. My hand has swelled slightly. I can move all of my fingers, so, other than a sprain and the purplish nub from the cigarette burn it appears to be fine. The violent twisting of my body in the scuffle and whiplash snap of my knee from my Bruce Lee kicks have left me feeling aches and pains here and there but hopefully, for the most part, they are nothing that a good, hot Jacuzzi tub can't fix.

The sky is burdened with its unyielding cape of springtime gloom. The sky and water all lack definition from each other, hanging in their gray cloak, these seasonal rains capturing our city and holding it at ransom from the absented sun. I think of Zang and Wang Ton. I remember the frightened determination that was in their eyes as they made their last, heroic pitch up the crumbling sand bank. I can still see the vacant resolve of their final embrace. I have seen this look before. It was in the eyes of likewise doomed people or things. A dog laying panting on the roadside after being struck by a passing car, unaware that it is death that is stalking before his glazed eyes. A vaquero's horse in Argentina with a broken foreleg who stood patiently, almost valiantly, as its owner readied his rifle to put him down. I saw this same look in Genevieve's eyes more than once during our anguished nights, wondering where our daughter may be, and strangely, or not so strangely, in Emily's eyes when the full impact of the reality that she may be losing her only sister forever, settled upon her.

I go over to the island bar and, taking a glass from the rack, pour myself a good stiff shot of Grey Goose Vodka. I remember, not so very many years ago, when drinking was fun. "I have always liked to take a drink," my mother used to say by way of innocent exclamation, bewildered at my father's sullen, sporadic, solitary binges. Now, I too feel a sneaking isolation from those halcyon days when Genevieve and I would tie one on and have a jolly good time doing so. We had more friends, or better friends, or maybe just plain friends, of which my life seems to be increasingly bereft. It may just be a phase in our lives, this sudden friendlessness, brought on by the distraction over our daughter Tess. I somehow suspect not. Perhaps I am wrong and it will pass, with comforting old ways creeping obligingly back into our ken. But for now, at times at least, I suspect that alcohol's prowling effect on me, not unlike my father, is slipping farther away from jubilance. Sometimes it is now ushering in a solemn pique, at other times hinting at a less than attractive belligerence. Maybe this life on my own isn't working out well for me on any level.

As I hold my glass beneath the ice dispenser on the fridge door I see the message light blinking on my phone. I take a long drink of Vodka and sit down on the couch, placing my glass on a coffee table coaster that has a picture of some ancient Mayan ruin embossed on its enameled wooden finish. I do not remember how we acquired these coasters, but do know that while in Mexico we did not purchase them ourselves from some market gardener's stall or merchant's street corner day table. They were a gift, but from whom I cannot say. My life is increasingly cluttered with these small reminders of places and people and times, that although eerily familiar, I can no longer name. I push the button on the phone and retrieve my glass for another sip. The cold vodka feels good on my throat. I can already trace its narcotic journey through my constricting capillaries and blood vessels causing a slight numbness in my head. I am anxious for the message to be from Tess. At the same time, I am also apprehensive about hearing her voice. What is this strange thing? A father grown frightened of his own child. But it is not Tess's detached and quavering voice I hear, it is Genevieve's calm and steady tone, instead.

I listen to it, then save it and replay it. I am consciously attempting to make sure that I don't miss anything, either said or implied.

"Hi Honey, it's me, remember? Your estranged wife or ex-wifey or what-ever they would label me in the tabloids these days. Anyway, I just wanted to touch base and say hello and tell you some things, but I don't want to leave them in a phone message because that would be too tacky, and I know how you analyze the poop out of everything, so I'm not about to let myself get drawn into that web, so I guess I'll ask that you give me a call back. Oh, I forgot that you may still be in Cuba until tomorrow. Anyway, I'm planning on coming to Vancouver in two weeks and I'd like to spend some time with you, a lot of time actually, if that's okay I mean, and maybe try to make up for causing so much pain and trouble on top of the other troubles you have. So, I guess I'm saying that I'm sorry and I don't know where that leaves us, .if there even is an us left. Let's talk. I love you. You know that, don't you? That never stopped. Bye."

I sit back on the couch and continue staring out of the window. The sun has now set and the view of the Pacific has been replaced with my own solitary reflection. Seated in my living room now, the subdued light-ing casts an image of warmth and safety around me. I see myself as not completely unlike a Van Gogh self-portrait, perhaps one of those painted in his more strangled period. I am alone and, although frazzled in appear-ance am also comforted to some extent by the knowledge that i, unlike dear Vincent, am loved. I want to phone Genevieve, but realize that with the time difference it is late in Iceland. I don't want to wake her or her aged parents. I am suddenly acutely aware of how little I know of her past six months. Although I'm with her in spirit and trying to be sensitive to her needs through this difficult time and fully knowing just how debilitating having a heroin addict as a child can be, I also am almost reluctant to pry. This may possibly be a by-product of my rising concern that Genevieve's problems will not end with Tess. Tess's problems may continue in their tragic descent, engulfing our lives as a couple. It also could be my own guilt for failing to provide whatever it is that she is presently missing. I am bone weary and spiritually bereft and do not think that I can take another punch just now. Yet, as I sit and sip my drink and let the quiet of the evening invade my senses, I am also conscious of a growing sense of relief that is not quite gladness, but is very definitely heading in that direction. Whether this is simply another way that exhaustion manifests itself within us, as a transient kind of giddiness, or whether this feeling of wellness is the proverbial tip of the iceberg or ultimate moment of truth after experiencing a maelstrom of distorted realities, I do not know, I only know that the feeling within me is quite possibly the nucleus of an abiding peace. At this stage I'll sit tight and gratefully take whatever comes my way.

My mind momentarily wanders back to the news story a few days ago on CNN and that Mexican village with those poor people fighting for what — their families, their honour, a sense of hope in the mire of hopelessness that is their burden and their infinite destiny? There has been scant news over the past few days of their siege upon the little adobe schoolhouse, perhaps it was felt by the broadcasters that the viewing public's appetite for a peasant revolt has waned in favour of a natural disaster like a hurricane or mud slide or maybe something with more zing like a movie star studded wedding gone amiss with bride and groom throwing insults and accusations around like stinging confetti through their spokespeople. What is truth and what is a lie? Why would these Mexican farmers take their own people's children into harm's way? When I first listened to this story I felt deep in my gut that something was not right in its telling. But why would a government elected and sworn to uphold a constitution protecting the rights of such people become so estranged from their duties and the job at hand? What has happened throughout this world that allows us, the spectators and in the end the beneficiaries of these dark deeds to stand down from our vigil and abandon our posts in these times of need? I have done this to one extent or other in my own family, yet I do not completely comprehend why. I suppose I looked the other way and when I turned back, the page had turned and although the faces were familiar, they were no longer completely recognizable. I want these people in Mexico to capture some form of success, to steal their precious moment on the world stage and bring this just prize, however small or fleeting, back home for those kids to have and to hold — but can they, or is it all a demoralizing harbinger of something bigger and more ominous. In the end I do not know whether the problems of this world are out there, or whether they are in here.

I sit on the couch for over an hour before I get up and pour myself another vodka. I am feeling the full soothing weight of drink now. I consciously straighten my posture and glance at my reflection in the window to confirm that I am not looking any more the worse for wear. I'm feeling a little more optimistic after listening to Genevieve's message and decide that this is a good time to pop over to say hello to Randy and Clive and let them know that I am back and their services were much appreciated in my absence. I won't mention my encounter with Run and Ida and Lei Lei, not wanting to stir the pot of simmering hostilities. I have a quick shower and change my clothes. I pull on a pair of faded blue jeans and a black v-necked sweater. I put on my brown Dockers without socks.

I can hear the melodious strains of what I presume to be Hawaiian music. It is, in fact, Polynesian. Who would know? The boys are in their usual festive mood, having researched and organized a retrospective evening entitled, A Celebration of French Polynesia. They have prepared exotic foods and drinks reminiscent of this bygone colonial period. They are also having a special midnight showing of the old Steve McQueen and Dustin Hoffman Oscar classic, *Papillon*. Guests have been encouraged to wear authentic attire of the period, which explains both Clive and Randy being dressed in colourful mumus with laurels braided into their thinning hair. After ten years of living beside these two, it doesn't even phase me. They could have answered the door stark naked or dressed like The Village People or camel herders from some Arab Emirate, and I would have accepted it as par for the course.

There are twenty or so people here. I notice an unusually high number are Indians. I see Aunt Sadie seated in the corner, talking animatedly with a wafer-thin slip of a gay man with close-cropped hair and several piercings in each ear. He also has a metal spike running through his lower lip. She sees me and waves her free hand, the other one cupping a mini-quiche. Randy hands me a drink. It is a rum concoction served in a hollowed-out coconut shell. They both tell me that, "Bitch One and Bitch Two and their little dog Toto down the hall are on the warpath again," and that I look like hell.

Clive looks like hell, too, but I say nothing. They conclude that I had better go to bed and sleep in tomorrow. I tell them that I am very tired from my trip. I don't mention Cuba beyond this. I tell them what Bird had said about Tess. I know how much they are affected by her problems. After all, they are her doting uncles. I also mention that Genevieve may be coming back in the next couple of weeks and that I am sure that she would want to see them. They are thrilled. I know they will be planning a supper menu featuring Icelandic reindeer roast or apple-glazed caribou steaks or some such northern fare. As I edge my way toward the door, letting Randy get back to his fledgling reps, the down-line inductees, a young man approaches me and asks,

"How's the glasses?" I look at him for a moment, not fully understanding where this question is coming from or leading to. "Your new eye glasses. I sold them to you."

He now sticks out his hand.

"Bruce," he says.

As I take his hand in mine, he gives it a playful little squeeze. He then drops his hand and arm back down to his side as if they have suddenly grown too heavy. He turns to a burly, chrome-domed man, clad from head to toe in black leather. This outfit includes a pair of skintight chaps. He isn't wearing a shirt under his leather vest. Although there is no hair on his head or face, his back and shoulders are covered in a layer of dark, wooly tufts, a good opportunity to put Oh So Smooth's Hair Away to the test. Bruce continues.

"This is my fiancé, George." He turns back to me. "I'm sorry, I've forgotten your name. Names aren't my strong suit, but I never forget a face. That's why I recognized you instantly, even without your glasses on." I shake George's hand. He presses harder than necessary, as if taking the opportunity to make a point.

"Richard Bonhom," I say.

Bruce now puts his right hand up to his mouth and, extending his index finger, starts tapping on his chin as if a thought charged with insight or candor has just entered his head.

"I wouldn't have taken you for an Oh So Smooth type. Isn't it fascinating how broad the appeal is for the products?" He now turns again to George, as if he expects some back-up for his next comment. "George and I are in Alfie and Wanda's organization. We're just new, but so excited about what we've seen so far." He now reaches back over his shoulder and taps a stocky man in his mid-thirties on the shoulder. The man immediately whirls around, automatically extending his hand, as if it were on a hydraulic system triggered by Bruce's touch. He smiles broadly and chirps in a thick Australian accent.

"Alfie. Alfie Knowles. Whose down-line are you in mate? I'm George and Bruce's up-line sponsor. We just met last week when my wife Wand-er was gettin' er new glasses adjusted."

Bruce now jumps in.

"The boss at work doesn't like me talking about Oh So Smooth with our optical customers, but I don't know if I can contain myself, I'm so thrilled with literally everything, and everyone. Wanda and Alfie have been god sends" Leaning in conspiratorially he whispers, "They've pulled some strings and gotten George and me our Starter's Package Kit, including four cases of each product all within a week of our signing on."

Alfie smiles proudly. It is these kinds of comments that further bolster his confidence, underpinning the belief that joining Oh So Smooth is shaping up to be a life-affirming experience.

Wanda snuggles in between Alfie and Bruce, holding her hand out to me. She snaps her cherry red gum into a small bubble, breaking it with her teeth, which she momentarily bares. She is like a cat hissing at some unseen but detected rodent hidden in the wall,

"Hi, I'm Wanda Alfie's better half." She ever so slightly pulls on Alfie's elbow, signaling that his presence is required elsewhere, the salesperson's instinct to move along and mingle kicking in. They depart, possibly recalling, like Pavlov's dogs, the sage advice from one of Oh So Smooth's Sponsor Training Tapes. The message pointing out that every social inter- action is nothing more or less than an opportunity to work the room. This tells one and all that, although they are closeted here tonight dressed like Arab sheiks, it is all about *business* and French Polynesia aside, with the hard costs of baby sitters and gas accounted for, there had better be some pretty hefty boxes of Oh So Smooth changing hands, and god damned fasto.

I decline an invitation to eat. Randy puts together a small plate of sticky rice wrapped in a leaf of some kind, some pork ribs drenched with a sweet pineapple sauce, and some other green thing that looks like steamed kale or bok choy. I take this without protest, even though I'm not feeling hungry. We are all emotionally frayed, and the combined gestures of giving and receiving suddenly mean a lot to us. Once in the hallway, I sneak a peek at the Skudmore's closed door. I suppress the urge to stick my tongue out. I know that all three may be cloistered behind the peep hole like undercover officers, my presence duly noted.

*

It is nine o'clock Saturday morning. This is late by several hours for me to awaken. I am refreshed and, if not enthusiastic, I am at peace with my life and want to get on with it and stick handle my way through whatever is waiting out there for me. My aches and pains from battle have subsided appreciably. I'm confident that Rickie Ricco's abrasions, both emotional and physical, will take a longer time to heal. I have already decided to take the Edsel out to the prison hospital to see Ethan today. Sometimes, if I talk nicely to the guards and convince Ethan that it's a good idea, they will shackle him in leg irons and arm restraints and let him come out into the secured prison parking area to see the car. This seems to register some degree of enjoyment on his often comatose emotional scale. Anyway, it's always worth a shot. I also think that the guards themselves like to see the old classic automobile. This appreciation may in some small way filter back through, affecting the way they treat him during night rounds or shower breaks or meal times. Those isolated moments when the echoes of metal doors crashing shut or patient's bloodcurdling screams in the dark- ness may unnerve him.

The Head of Psychiatry for the institution is one of the clinical experts called by Ethan's lawyer as a friendly witness for the defense. He is Dr. Emile Nutt. I have spoken with Dr. Nutt on several occasions in the hospi- tal about my brother's condition and how things are generally going. Like everyone else, I suspect, I have got to bite the insides of my cheeks until it almost forces me to cry out, trying to suppress a fit of laughter whenever I am in his presence and forced to ask,

"And what is your prognosis Dr. Nutt? Is there anything else we can do, Dr. Nutt? What about a different regimen of anti-psychotic medications, Dr. Nutt?"

During the trial, I more than once caught the judge studying his hands, as if some important and captivating message was written in hieroglyphic code along his fingers as the prosecutor mercilessly railed,

"And is that your best clinical observation, Dr. Nutt? If you had a crystal ball what would you estimate the defendant's chances of recidivism to be, Dr. Nutt? In laymen's terms, please, Dr. Nutt." On and on it went.

Ethan is a high-risk paranoid schizophrenic with psychotic delusions that can trigger violent outbursts. On the other hand, he is one of the gentlest people I know. Both caring and compassionate to a fault. The sad irony is that when he killed his wife's lover, he wasn't having any out-of-body, wild-eyed delusional experience. She *was* cheating on him, and her lover was his best friend. They were planning on running away without telling him. I'm not saying that Ethan isn't sick. Maybe even as squirrelly as they come. I'm just stating for the record, as it were, that everything he suspected was, in fact, true. Where does paranoia go in the face of blatant, vile lies? This is the tragic —one could say almost comic, in a dark medieval sort of way — little twist of the knife. Ethan's ex-wife, Shelley, actually called me in hysterics after the police had gone to their apartment and taken my brother into custody. She told me that she was going to see if she could launch a civil suit against *me,* of all people. This was precipitated because I was the only surviving member of Ethan's family. She claimed that I was partially to blame for not alerting her of my brother's possible violence. They were going to use our father's suicide as evidence of instability in the family. Bad genetics breeding sociopathic tendencies, I presume. Anyway, the whole sorry mess was beginning to look like the makings of a three ring circus. This was sad in itself, since there was a dead man with a family of his own to consider. When it's all said and done, the additional stress and publicity surrounding a vexatious suit such as this didn't exactly do me or Ethan, in his more lucid moments, any bloody good. Basically, I began to see Shelley in a whole new light. I unabashedly started to detest her with a vengeance that probably rivaled Ethan's enduring love for her. Another odd twist of events he being a sociopathic personality that wouldn't hurt a hair on her head, harbouring the insane person's abstract and fixated blinding love; and me, by all accounts a regular fellow, holding a seething dislike for her that at a moment's notice could well have exploded into a violent and most assuredly regrettable act of aggression. All of this was coupled with one more dismal, yet unalterable, fact, something to further undermine the gravity of Ethan's clinical diagnosis. It is something that would drive a wedge between us that could never be displaced with trust ever again. I feel sickened to say the words. It is actually me that doesn't want him out. He is too fragile now to survive with us, the normal ones. I am afraid that we do not treat those with mental afflictions all that well. We have not moved very far from those dark days of Charles Dickens' work house mentality. So, this is the final irony of my take on this tragic farce. I supported the notion of Ethan remaining in confinement, possibly for the rest of his natural life, because I thought that he needed protection from us as a society. Conversely, the courts wanted him inside because they felt that he was a threat to Shelley. Alas, what a debacle. I love Ethan very much and have been a vigilant resource for him, and with god's help will continue to be until the day that one of us dies. In a lifetime of habitual negotiation and compromise, the one constant in my being is that I will never leave Ethan alone to rot away in that place. He literally has no one else. I owe him that much as his brother.

*

I pull out of the parking garage beneath my building and move slowly down the street to the traffic lights. The car feels good and solid, its barely muffled engine sounds establishing a low, audible growl that ricochets off the parked cars and fences along the roadside. The sun has come out this morning. We coastal dwellers seize upon the moment to enjoy its healing rays, we don't make plans around the fact that it may, or may not, stay burning in the sky. We simply take it as it comes. The drive out on the Fraser Valley Highway will be a good chance to blow some of the winter's carbon from the cylinders. This will also help to further clear my head of its cobwebs from the past week.

Soon, I'm suspended high in the air, crossing the Port Mann Bridge spanning the turbid, snow-fed waters of the mighty Fraser River, a great Canadian water course that runs from the mountains westward to the Pacific. I hit the loud pedal, opening up the four barrels on the carburetor. This lifts the front of the car in a shallow arc. The machine is not unlike a stallion now, a brute making ready to mount an imaginary mare. I run up the long hill leading from the bridge exit watching the speedometer climb steadily past the green numbers 70 80 90 96. The road in front of me is wide and empty. I press my foot down harder 99 100. I hold the gas peddle against the thick red carpet.

CHAPTER TWENTY-TWO

I MAKE THE DRIVE IN JUST UNDER ONE HOUR. THIS IS A PERSONAL BEST for me in the Edsel. I don't like to push the car too hard. I felt that today was an exception, it being springtime and my first visit to Ethan in just over a month. I usually try to get out this way every two or three weeks, but the Cuba trip threw a wrench into things. This may extend throughout the rest of my life, as well. I will wait and see.

Whenever I pull into a parking lot with the Edsel, I always check things out. A thorough inspection of the surroundings is in order before selecting a parking spot. The space must be as far removed from any other cars as possible. Today, I find my spot against the perimeter fence beside a metal barrier post. This post will prevent anyone from parking directly beside me. I take a moment and note with pad and pencil the makes, license numbers and body paint colours of the cars nearest to me. If I come back and find my headlights broken, or front grill mangled, because some distraught visitor is lost in their tearful goodbyes to their crazed husband or pathological son, I have some hard evidence to track them down and demand compensation.

Walking through the imposing high metal doors of a federal prison is like going to the very gates of hell and knocking repeatedly, hoping that Satan will hear and let you enter. Everything is monitored by batteries of unseen eyes, either electronic or human, and the feeling instilled in every-one, no matter how case hardened, is one of an empty nagging dread. It is as if we have all failed in our duties and are now condemned to being perpetual victims of these people caged within.

"Snap!" That is the sound my brother said he heard when he was interviewed by police. It was inside his brain. His story was video taped and recorded, word for paralyzing word. Ethan's attorney agreed to let the prosecution use the tape as evidence against Ethan. He thought that it would help in his plea. I have watched the police tapes taken during these initial interrogation sessions. The police call them interviews. Watching them, it doesn't feel like this. No matter how many times that I sit through them, I am always brought up short by one undeniable question. Why didn't he shoot her and then himself, like so many others we have seen or read about over the years? When the jig is up, it's up. What possible joy could he have thought would be waiting for him the next day or month or year or decade? This fact proves to me how desperate and condemning his mental illness truly is. He still clung to the farcical possibility that there was still a chance for happiness. I suspect that he still does.

The tape begins with Ethan sitting in a small room. There is a single table and two plain metal chairs. The camera is mounted in the corner of the ceiling away from his line of vision. He is speaking in the present tense, as if he is back in that apartment. It is as if he is witnessing it all happening again in real time. Once this interview was over, he never quite came back to us. He remained distant, out there in no-man's land, without a clear definition of what was here and now and real, and what was past and possibly imagined. I can see that tape in my mind as if I am viewing it. Ethan says, "*That was then. This is now*" Those were the words my brother's wife aped to him that night. They came directly from the mouth of her then lover, now dead from a bullet to the frontal lobe. Ethan then said that she abruptly stood and languidly lifted her black shoulder bag in a move-ment that was both too grand and almost theatrical for either his or my liking, although, knowing her as I do, I'd have to concede that the whole movement could have been "*achingly beautiful*" his words, not mine. "*The clock read 12:05 in the morning or in daytime. I have momentarily lost my bearings. I pop another pill. It must be that time.*" The way he said each sentence, so ultra-hyper-present-tense that his voice was irritatingly, if not outright starkly disturbing. But what is even more unsettling is that it is bordering on poetic. A trait which Ethan had never exhibited before that night. He was speaking out-of-body, like a man suddenly possessed by some monster of blank-verse.

"*My upper body is soaked with sweat yet cold as seaweed. I am unsure of what it is out there just beyond my thoughts. I will change, I shout trying to strangle my airway so as to smother the anger and make the sound more as a whisper so that I won't frighten her away. In my mind's eye I can see Warren's face, lifeless and pallid, with darkening clots of blood matting in his thick black hair.*" This segment was obviously terribly incriminating, a con-fession. He then becomes alternately hysterical and seemingly calculating. "*I see a movement across the room and turn my head too late. I slump to the floor exhausted but instantly rise. I am agitated and look around the room. The red light is blinking on the phone message machine. I push the button. 'Snooky's dead... You starved my cat,' a woman sobs in a tinny nasal tone. That crazy woman again. Wrong number. Wrongo! Stop calling me! I shout, bending over the blink, blink, blinking red light the rush of air from deep in my lungs forcing me off balance.*"

Ethan then begins a frantic search up and down the hallway, banging on the neighbour's doors. Then he goes into this whole frightening dia-tribe about cat food. At the time, I didn't know what it meant. In the trial, it came out that the old lady down the hall had left the cat food for Ethan to feed her cat Snooky while she was away visiting her sister in Montreal. He had forgotten and the cat had died. Starved. There was an audible gasp in the courtroom at this news. There hadn't been any sounds coming from the gallery when evidence relating to Ethan or his wife's dead lover was introduced.

"*There are cans of Miss Whiskers cat food on the hall table. A note is scotch taped to one of the cans. A woman's writing, but not Shelley's. No languid tails arching softly into thin air. "I read the note. 'Feed my pussy' Mon., Tues., Wed., Thurs., printed in black marker across the top of each can. I count the cans. Fourteen. I press my fingers to my temples. Something is wrong. I know it, but I can't quite see a clear picture of what it is. I accidentally knock the cans of cat food off the table onto the floor. They crash loudly, with one tin landing on its side and rolling slowly across the hardwood toward the living room. It stops just before touching the black travel bag bunched down under the round, sloping arm of the couch. I stand and watch it. What is it that I am trying to remember?*" At this point in the tape he starts to cry. Not necessarily because he is a devout animal lover, but more because he is really quite a gentle hearted soul and he doesn't like to hurt anybody. When he gets a grip on himself, he begins again with a strangely detached resolve that truly sounds crazed.

"*Motion is everywhere, but I can't move my head to look. I wipe the perspiration from my eyes. Now I see the gun lying on the arm of the couch by Shelley's black bag. One neighbour. Two neighbour. Three neighbour. I pound on their doors. I just want to chat like we all did with Shelley on the stoop or by the mailboxes before this thing, this goddamn thing. No one answers. I'm giddy as I come back through the hallway, unable to catch my breath. My pants are falling down. Nobody home. Homer. Homo. Home is the hunter home from the hill. What a pity. Not even the old lady down the hall with the cat. She always calls us the nice young couple. What a crying shame. I know they'd all be glad to see me.*" This section of the tape, as pathetic as it is, always drew a reluctant smirk from the jurors and courtroom gallery. I guess that we all can imagine the ludicrous, comic picture of a naked mad man coming to our door in the middle of the night. The smiles fade quickly as he begins his final lonely baffled entreaty.

"*I look at my reflection in the mirror beside the bedroom door. The door is ajar, the hall light filtering into the darkened room. I hear a broken voice coming through the darkness. It's Shelley's . She is telling me, or the person in the mirror that is or isn't me, that everything will be okay if I can just stop and think and allow the silence and stillness to bring me comfort. I fumble in my breast pocket for another pill. Crunch, crunch, crunch. Doctors full of shit, shit, shit. Right now there is something that I have to do, but what? I have lint in my mouth from the pocket that holds my pills and I spit it off my tongue and look at the walls now crawling with blue and red and amber*" *bugs that flit across the furniture like fireflies. They dart above the fire arcing coldly throughout the room. They are everywhere, these damn bugs, even on my hands and clothes. They are coming through the window up the outside walls from the cars on the street below. There are more voices than before and there are cars everywhere with blinking lights. Now I see Shelley standing beside her black shoulder bag. Is she coming back to me from far away? I hold my arms out for her, but am lost and don't know what to say. Her mouth contorts into a moan,' What have you done?' I look down and see the Smith & Wesson .357 hanging limply in both her pale hands. I hear others shouting and I turn my head, catching a fleeting glimpse of Shelley and me momentarily trapped in the mirror like two disheveled wedding dancers."* Ethan now registers the exact time which alerts us all that, despite his creeping insanity, he is conscious of time's passing.

"The clock reads 12:07. And now I hear the boom, boom, booming on the front door as it explodes into splinters. I lean my head so slowly and gently, gently against the mirror that shatters into jagged, bloodied shards. These glass prisms throw splashes of light upon my face and chest and legs as they fall around my feet. I am naked. I open my throat emitting a hoarse guttural wail. A final hallway salutation to the neighbours.

"THAT WAS THEN AND THIS IS NOW!"

The video tape ends. It's not like a television program or a movie concluding. It just stops in a brief flicker of snow. The audio portion continues as their chairs scrape on the linoleum floor. I always wondered what the police officers did after participating in something like this. Did they share any bond with the accused, having both been through a sobering experience, or did the cop hate his fucking guts through and through and want to pull his service revolver and shoot him in the same, cold-blooded assassin's manner that Ethan had killed Warren.

What can one say about the experience of sitting through a murder trial as the only remaining family member of the accused? To the outsider, dispassionately watching something like this, Ethan's act would be all that much more egregious. I mean his open admittance of the crime, a murder most foul, coupled with his lawyer's trickery in trying to hide behind the seemingly convenient legal technicality of mental illness. And I, seated each day across from the victim's family, some of whom I knew quite well, now shunned by all, as if I were a leper at their back door. Perhaps they saw me equally as culpable as Ethan in all of this, as if I had counseled their dead son and absented brother to take his dick out of his pants and stick it repeatedly into my brother's wife's pussy. Didn't anyone know that infidelity is the leading cause of homicides in the world? That it was the final act pushing already emotionally fragile people over the top. I'm certainly not defending Ethan's actions. I'm just stating the cold hard facts of life here.

The question on everyone's mind was, was Ethan crazy? And even of more consequence, was he still too crazy to be cognizant of his actions and conscious of the importance of these proceedings. I, for one, didn't know the answer. At times, when I was speaking to Ethan it was as if he was okay upstairs. We chatted, never animatedly, but within the range of normalcy, given the circumstances. And then at other times, he would simply slip away. I would see it happening as clearly as if he had gotten up and left the room. The doctor said that when this happened, he was trying to cope with the realization of the situation and his part in the colossal events that had led to Shelly no longer being his friend. The loss of her deeply-needed and coveted intimacy had pushed him down further into his delusional hole, further even than the act of violence itself. He felt abandoned on a basic level so fundamental to his humanity that we, those of us in our right minds, could not fully comprehend. Hal Holsom, Ethan's lawyer, had to convince at least one of the twelve people seated on the jury that this could happen, and did in fact happen to Ethan. With this established the only verdict that they could deliver was, Guilty of Manslaughter By Reason of Insanity.

Once you're right inside such proceedings, it's surprising how clinical your own thinking becomes. I guess it's partly a reflex action, a defensive shield that comes down allowing you to hear things and see medical evidence and crime scene pictures that would otherwise make you swoon or send you running to the washroom. Anyway, you sit every day listening, even taking notes, thinking that this will all somehow help the loved one now sitting forlornly in the Defendant's Box.

I still don't think that Shelly did the right thing when she removed herself from Ethan's side entirely. I realize that she was going through her own private hell but she had also been the chief cook controlling the heat in the kitchen. I understand when things aren't working out in a marriage. I've got first hand information on that score, but not when someone makes a bad situation even worse by introducing an often hapless third party to the scene. Not that I believe this to be the case here. After all, the deceased was Ethan's best friend and confident. He heard of Ethan's growing suspicions concerning his wife's fidelity first hand. Unthinkable, yes, unforgivable, probably, but grounds for a murder? Yet who really knows where the button is in each of us, the awful thing that rockets us to another dimension at warp speed, never allowing us to ever return to what we once knew and loved?

Believe it or not, there is a faintly positive consequence of going through something like this. I don't judge others too harshly on anecdotal first impressions any more, which, I, like most of us, once did without equivocation. When confronted by an obese person, a disheveled appearance, inappropriate body language, poor grammar, a lazy eye, or an implied discourtesy, I try to remain open minded, taking each at their face value. A kind of Dr. Seuss perspective, a person's a person, no matter how small. I do this with full knowledge of what harsh judgments others must be thinking and sharing about me and mine.

"Sick. Depraved. Mutated genetics. Sociopathic throwbacks. Bad seeds the lot of them."

In desperation, (when are defense attorneys called at any other time?) I had phoned Hal Holsom from my office at four in the morning. This was after Shelley had called me at home and told me that Ethan had murdered Warren and was in police custody and that she was thinking of suing me. She then hung up the phone. She hadn't volunteered any more details and to this day has never spoken to me again. It was as if she wiped the slate clean with these words erasing any further responsibility or obligation to be there for any of us, or any of it. I had to go down to the office because I didn't have Hal's unlisted home number with me. Why would I ever need to call a client that I had no deep personal friendship with from anywhere other than the office, unless of course it was to tell him that the police had just taken my only brother into custody for murdering his best friend? Although Hal and I were not friends, we liked each other. We had the occasional cup of coffee together to exchange documents or a cheque. Hal Holsom was a busy guy. His picture was in the papers more than once when he was defending a high profile case. He was good at what he did and was considered a good advocate by both the crown prosecutor's office and the judiciary on the bench. I was grateful to him for taking Ethan's case, which he certainly didn't need.

Dr. Nutt's testimony was damning. This was good for our side. It cast extreme doubts on Ethan's mental state. He was a friendly witness for the defense. How could Ethan have gone to bed one night a troubled but by all accounts normal, person and awoken in the morning a stark raving lunatic? The psychiatrist described this as rare, but not unknown in the annals of his profession. The jurors and everyone else silently thinking that it was at best a dubious profession. Ethan's illness fell loosely into the category of amnesiacs or shell-shocked war casualties, unfortunates who see something or hear something or even simply *think* something and in that instant lose everything. Their lives disappear into a closeted part of their sub conscious brain. We have seen these people on news reports or television specials, walking the halls of isolated institutions in a comatose stupor, their footsteps echoing through the empty void. At such times loving parents or spouses follow behind clutching old family photo albums or hand drawn Father's Day Cards from the kids, the entire family now like zombies, more dead than alive.

It seemed ass backwards to me. The Prosecution argued that Ethan was basically of sound mind and perfectly fit to face the music, while the Defense fought tooth and nail to get him thrown into the darkest psychiatric hospital in the land. The legal problem that had led to Hal taking this rear guard approach to the defense was straight forward. The Crown had taken the unusual step of charging Ethan with First Degree Murder rather than the lesser offences of either Second Degree Murder or Manslaughter or even Aggravated Assault Causing Death. I was told that under the circumstances a Manslaughter By Reason of Insanity plea was our best all around bet to save Ethan from a possible sentence of twenty-five years with no possibility for parole. The First Degree charge was infinitely harder for the Crown to prove, but, if successful, it left little or no options on appeal. The truth of it was that Hal was not confident. At least if Ethan was found guilty on the Manslaughter charge, he had some chance, however slim, of seeing the outside sometime before the final sunset of his now seemingly doomed life.

CHAPTER TWENTY-THREE

WE ARE NOT RESTRICTED TO TALKING OVER A TELEPHONE SEPARATED BY a bullet proof glass window as we often see on television, instead, Ethan and I meet in a small room with a single table in the center and two chairs, one on either side. The door is locked from the outside. An armed guard is positioned at the door with a clear view of the entire room. The window has a heavy screen of wire mesh criss-crossing through it. We are not allowed to touch each other at any time and if the guard witnesses any attempt at physical contact, he or she can terminate the visiting session and recommend disciplinary action be taken. This usually means the suspension of any further visits for a specified period of time. I have spoken to Ethan about these rules on many occasions. Despite these warnings at different times, he will become increasingly agitated and will express a need to hold onto me. I tell him that this is not possible. I console him saying that he will be all right if he just stands or sits still for a moment. Hopefully, this will allow him to get a grip on his emotions. These episodes break my heart. I see the agony that he is going through and want to take him in my arms and hold onto him as tightly as I can. But I can't, and both of us have to accept this reality and try to move forward.

I am always escorted into the visiting room after Ethan has been brought in. I cannot leave until he has been escorted out by a guard. When I enter the room today, the first thing that I notice is that Ethan has shaved his head completely bald. I also see the remnants of deep gashes across his forearms. They are already scabbed. This tells me that they are not new. I do not know whether these wounds were self-inflicted or the result of an altercation with another inmate or, God forbid, one or more of the guards. I will call Dr. Nutt later and ask about the exact nature of these cuts. The dismal reality of all this is that it really doesn't probably matter. Whatever their cause, they are just another discouraging part of my brother's daily existence here. None of it is going away any time soon.

Ethan is glad to see me. He has difficulty adjusting to this excited state. He wrings his hands, which is a common repetitive behaviour among those with similar mental illnesses. His hollowed eyes stare distraughtly down at the tabletop. He only occasionally gains sufficient confidence or courage to look directly up into my face.

"Hi Ethan. How are you doing, buddy?"

He continues looking down, occasionally glancing up at the window in the door to see if the guard is looking, hoping to sneak a fast touch of my hand. He sees the guard's head through the glass and adopts a slight edge in his voice,

"Hi little brother. Long time no see. I thought maybe you'd gone away and weren't going to come and see me anymore. The bad seed, and all that. You know."

It hurts me to hear him say this. I know how much troubling thought and anguish has gone on inside of his head before the words escape his lips.

"Hey, buddy. You know that I would never go away and leave you here without a visit now and again. You're my brother, Ethan. You know that and that I care about you."

He rocks back and forth in his chair like a jockey riding a winning mount.

"Ya, you're my brother and you're my friend and you're my buddy, too, eh, Richy Rich?"

He has a certain degree of anger or accusatory intonation in his voice today which is not uncommon. This is sometimes due to the nature of his mental illness. It may also be triggered by the effects of the potent anti-psychotic meds they administer to him throughout the day.

"I brought the Edsel out today. It's running really good."

Ethan smiles and looks me dead in the eye.

"That has to be some bitchin' piece of car, Rich. I'd love to drive that baby sometime."

I look at him and grin widely, holding this position until it hurts my facial muscles.

"You and me both, bro. I'd love to see you driving that car. We could pack up our bags and go clear across the country." Ethan now turns his gaze back to his fidgeting hands once again.

"No Rich. No more road trips for me, man. Too hot to handle. Too big a risk, man. Too much too much" he searches for the words that his medications or years of confinement have hidden from him, "too much love too much love for one man to handle. Too much love can be a bad thing, little brother."

"Not all the time Ethan. Sometimes it's only what it is just love. Nothing else attached. No expectations. No disappointments."

I am looking directly into his eyes, trying to see if any of this will register or whether we are merely playing a game of semantics, one thrust, one parry. He makes eye contact ever so briefly, then shifts his gaze toward the tabletop. His hands are folded, with his fingers momentarily stilled. He holds them as if he is in prayer. He really never comes back to me fully from this moment on. I stay for another half hour or so, but the contact has been broken. Our words are more forced now and their meanings less sincere. I have left a box of candies with the guards. I tell Ethan what is inside them. When the visit is over and the guard comes to take Ethan away, he starts to cry. He repeats the same thing to me that he has said on many other such visits. He shouts these words before he shuffles out of the door.

"Please come back, little brother. I need to talk with you about things."

I always assure him that I will not leave him and not to worry. I know that despite these words of encouragement the empty void in his soul will continue to engulf him. The realization of this momentarily robs me of any hope, as well. This all hatches feelings of deep remorse inside me, the weight of the world once again seemingly squarely set upon my shoulders. I feel an almost giddy, claustrophobic urge to get out of this place as fast as I possibly can. Suddenly, I want to walk through those heavy metal doors and keep walking, never to look back or whisper Ethan's name again. I feel terrible about this, knowing the other truth that accompanies it also, that at times, I wish he would have turned that god-damned gun on himself. It would have left a messy scene, but perhaps in a strange way, a cleaner slate. Something that, with time, I could have cleared up in my own mind, at least, and then moved on. But this, this is a life sentence for us both. I hate these thoughts and will honour my pledge. I will be back here soon and add some small measure of hope to his otherwise dreary days.

Gaining the highway again, I am driving fast. I am running away from Ethan and his disarming pathology for a minute or two. He is the Fool in a Shakespearian Tragedy, often speaking the most insightful truths to the King. Saying things that no one else dares, "Sometimes too much love can be a bad thing."

*

The drive back to Vancouver in the Edsel quells my agitated state somewhat, allowing me to try and see the realities of my life and those of my family with a little more balanced perspective. I roll the window down and crank the radio up, listening to a golden oldies station. They start their weekend countdown by playing the Marvin Gay classic, "I Heard It Through The Grape Vine." I must admit to allowing a drib or drab of sentimentality to sneak under the doormat and grab the old heartstrings of late. Who knows what triggers the seemingly random synapses and electrical arching that sparks this thought or that impulse in anyone's noggin. All of the experts at the Matsqui Penitentiary Maximum Security Psychiatric Hospital probably think they have a pretty good handle on it, but I'm no longer too sure about accepting at face value what any experts tell me is true.

"I heard it through the grape-vine
Not much longer would you be mine
Oh I heard it through the grape-vine
I'm just about to lose my mind."

The song cheers me up and makes me want to get out of the car and dance like Mr. Bojangles along the side of the highway. For the rest of the way into downtown,the oldies keep coming. Bette Midler, "The Rose."

"Some say love it is a river
that drowns the tender reed
Some say love it is a razor
That leaves your soul to bleed"

Then Ray Charles, "Hit The Road Jack" with the Raylettes chiding rhythmically,
"That's right,
Hit the road Jack and don't you come back no more no more no more no more,
Hit the road Jack and don't you come back no more."

As I glide through the west end of the city, Dion comes on the radio growling out one of the best, "The Wanderer."

"Oh well I'm the type of guy who will never settle down
Where pretty girls are, you know that I'm around
I kiss 'em and I leave 'em cause to me they're all the same
I hug 'em and I squeeze 'em, they don't even know my name
They call me the wanderer-yeah-the wanderer
I roam around around around around"

The first thing that I do when I'm back at 777 Beach View Place is check the message machine. The blinking red light is like a homing beacon, taunting me to be brave and keep faith. Hope is always out there waiting for us to find its beam. I'm right, for it is Tess's disconnected voice I hear on the machine. My heart starts pounding in my chest and my hands are instantly cold and clammy. Every word hits my ears like a note from a cello concerto, alone, distinct and melancholic.
"Hi Dad, it's Tess. Just wanted to let you know where I am so that you and Mom know what's happening. I guess that you guys already know that this is going to be a long ordeal with no short cuts in sight for any of us. I'm sorry. .Some get the cake, others get the dirty dishes. Scrub scrub. .Ha

ha. Anyway, I'm out in New Westminster at the Villa Rosa Rehabilitation Retreat. It's in some grand old Catholic mausoleum that was once a nun's residence they say. Ha ha. Get thee to a nunnery. Anyway, the people here call it The House That Abstinence Built, which is kind of a joke on the nuns' celibacy and the junkie's withdrawal I guess. Ha ha. One of the first things that they teach us here is to leave our cynicism at the front door, so I've got to embrace it all as one big helpful package or I won't get anywhere with it. Sooo, here goes. I guess you've got to be here to feel the love, in a manner of speaking. I don't know whether you want to see me or you think that it's too much for you right now, but if you're up to it, so am I. Visiting hours are on Sundays starting at 2 PM. Don't call. I can't take calls, anyway, only make them. No trust for the untrustworthy I guess. Just show up if you want and check in at the front desk. They'll let me know that you're here. Love you Daddy. Oh, and please tell mum about all of this, since I don't have access to long distance lines either and I'm presuming that she's still in Iceland with grandma and grandpa. Bye."

*

I arrive at the Villa Rosa Rehabilitation Retreat at 1:45 PM on Sunday afternoon. Once again, I am in the Edsel thinking that it may get a rise out of Tess. When she was a teenager, she loved going for rides in it with her giggling friends. We would wheel around the Stanley Park Drive with the radio blaring. The girls would sing along to "Grease" or whatever other top fifty hit was playing. Perhaps I should start thinking of the Edsel as a therapeutic tool for rehab work. I angle into the winding tree-lined driveway. I immediately feel better about leaving the car parked here, rather than out at the pen. The people here are, at best, only marginally more prepared to deal with life on the outside. With this said, the general ambience of the grounds are more refreshing. The building's stately old stone cornices and Tudor gables give it a comfortable sense of pastoral *noblesse oblige* that is lacking in the lackluster watch towers and harsh buzzers and clanging heavy metal doors that greet the visitor in Ethan's somewhat less hospitable quarters. I find a parking spot that, in my moderately anal opinion, is pure unadulterated perfection. There are two spots marked on the driveway, with thick, yellow lines. They are set apart from the other cars. They sit under a large, stately oak tree, whose branches extend in either direction for at least fifty feet. There are several benches placed under and around the general circumference of the shaded area that the tree provides. All in all, a nice place to sit with the recovering addict, trying to capture how marvelous this all is, and how glad we all are that these simple pleasures are once again on the rehabilitating person's viewing screen. I park the car, without noting any license plate numbers or particulars of nearby vehicles.

I have angle parked the car so that it is hogging both of the two spaces in this alcove. It is a trick all owners of special automobiles learn as a matter of course.

The building is probably from the early 1900s and has all of the pomp and circumstance that the church of the day would have deemed appropriate. Something well fortified to lull the masses into some form of idolatry or submission to a higher earthly power. All of this fosters unrequited obedience to whatever the dogma of the time dictated. Give us your hard earned money. We don't have regular jobs, either. The various owners over the decades have removed all but a few of the religious icons and statuettes depicting the Blessed Virgin Mary contemplating any number of long-suffering human foibles. One or two of these figures still remain, depicting Mother Mary in repose overlooking a resplendent flower garden or meditative lily pond symbolically devoid of anything tainted by man's treacherous hand.

The rolling, treed grounds enclose fifteen acres of prime residential land that I'm sure more than one recently recovering coke snorting real estate developer salivated over as they slowly weaned themselves from the daily cleansing rituals of *parking cynicism at the door* and returned to the destructive habits of thought that landed them here once or twice before. There are a few small, familial clusters of three or four people walking the grounds in animated conversations about all of the time lost and what boundless possibilities lie just on the other side of these tall pruned hedges. I look at these folks for a moment, thinking back to my old friends Heidi and Helmut and wondering if they have made further contact with their oblique son Friedrich. I hope so, for all of their sakes. If Big Freddy can peel away the misery-inducing layers of self-loathing it may not seem all that improbable or far fetched to place himself firmly into the forefront of the sausage business. It is not too late to enjoy the financial rewards and public appreciation that such endeavors hold for the taking.

I climb the wide, stone steps slowly, suddenly frozen with apprehension for what's to come. I have so many questions for my daughter, but must let her lead the conversation. In previous sessions with Dr. "м," it was made abundantly clear to all that the recovering addict must be allowed to provide whatever subliminal or clearly marked directions may be required to keep this on a manageable course. A path that she or he can navigate without running aground on the shoal of a perceived criticism or the rocky bluff of a momentary sense of despair over the time lost. There was no place in recovery for the pointless reticulation of past damages done. Yet, I cannot let this precious time be spent in idle chat about the weather or what's been happening in my business for the past five years —five long years that she's been incapacitated with a needle protruding from her scaled forearms or puckered midriff. But I have to tread carefully and let this young woman that I love so much and that is as fragile and precious as a Ming vase take control of our time together and guide it wherever she feels that it should go. As I reach the top step and stand looking back over the calming greenery before me, I take a few good gulps of air, bracing myself for this long anticipated moment of reconciliation.

I introduce myself at the front desk and am told by a pleasant, white haired woman possibly entering her mid sixties that Tess is expecting me and has left word for me to go and seat myself on one of the benches in the yard. She will find me momentarily. I thank this woman a little more profusely than is necessary. I am probably trying to say to her that none of this is my doing or my fault. I was a damn good father and provider, but my daughter fell in with a bad crowd or experienced a severe emotional downturn at puberty or just darn well ran away from us without provocation, leaving her mother and me, truly two of the nicest people you would ever want to meet, bewildered and shattered, like two tattered piñatas hanging from a low slung limb. What the hell, who cares? I'm sure that this kindly-looking, snow-capped soul has witnessed and heard things that would make the most case hardened person stop and stare. Perhaps she is here as a volunteer doing penance for her own wayward child, maybe one that didn't make the final cut, but instead passed away in some fetid gutter. Or it could well be remotely possible that she, herself, although hard to believe, may have been a down and outer, prostituting her once lithe body for the price of a fix. With this well behind her she is here now to help make amends and keep on track.

Once outside again, I feel stronger, more able bodied a man than moments before when trying to make pointless explanations to a stranger. If I am going to be any bloody good at this, I'm going to have to throttle these urges to...what? To apologize. I look over the grounds again as I descend the steps trying to pick out the perfect spot for my meeting with my daughter. It's not unlike a film cinematographer or art director casing the place for just the right location and lighting in which to shoot the emotionally gripping and sure to be Kleenex-soaking final fade out. The two estranged protagonists meeting. Their glistening eyes telling that come hell or high water, things are going to be a lot better from here on in. I see just such a spot down beneath the oak tree in clear view of the Edsel.

The sky is a hazy blue, without the threat of rain for the short term. I decide to scoot down and lower the hardtop of the car into its seat in the trunk thus setting the stage with a smidgen of nostalgia. I know Tess loved to ride in the car when the top was down. The mechanics of this model, although state of the art in 1957, leave a bit of hand-work, not unlike removing a soft convertible top of the day. I snap the necessary buckles into place and check the trunk to see that no foreign objects are there to impede the action of the hard top's slide into its resting place. All is okay, so I start the engine and push the button, activating the loud, groaning electric motor hidden under the rear seat. Several people stop to look at me, no doubt marveling at the old car's beauty, maybe reflecting on a time in their own pasts when they rode in a similar car or saw one on a smart-looking billboard of the day. With the hood safely down, I give myself a quick look in the rear view mirror to see that my hair is combed and that I'm looking as chipper as any dad would want to appear for his daughter's home coming.

There is no sign of Tess. I go over and sit on the wooden bench under the tree. I try to look as calm as possible. I am now feeling immune to any of life's set backs, my feet of clay now firmly planted against lapses in emotional atmospheric pressure. I feel very good, indeed, almost like I once did, before my world was rocked by these larger, unwieldy forces. As I bask in this feeling of well being, I look up and see her standing on the tall stone steps watching me. I am relieved because a small part of me was afraid that I wouldn't recognize her. My own daughter grown so distant a stranger that we could pass each other on a busy street and I would not even know it. But this is not so. I realize now that Tess and I have always been too close for that. Too near to ever not feel the other's presence in a crowded room, or on a lonely pathway. It was Genevieve who was the outsider, not Tess or I. It was Genevieve who couldn't accept when these seemingly improbable monsters landed squarely at our feet. I'm not being critical here, or casting about for a convenient place to lay blame. There is no blame and there is no fault. There are just the people and the events. All I'm trying to say, is that Genevieve absented herself long before she went to Iceland, and in the end it may be her that has the longest journey back. I do not know nor do I have the energy stores to speculate on these feelings at the moment. They are simply there, waiting.

Tess is thinner than she was the last time I saw her two years ago, almost waif like. This is so different from the athleticism that she exuded in her boisterous early teens. I sit stock-still. I am afraid to move for fear that she will disappear into thin air again. I am seized with a controlling fear that I will be awakened with a sudden start, all of this lost to me once more. She is wearing jeans and a knitted, pale blue sweater with a high rolled collar. She has white runners on her feet. She stuffs her hands down into her pant's pockets as she hesitantly descends the steps. She looks around the grounds as she slowly moves toward me, as if checking to see who else may be here positioned in some remote corner of the yard for a better surveillance. It is a habit learned on the streets, where a keen sense of your surroundings can make the difference between getting high or curling in a fetal position on some damp and cold bathroom floor. Or at other times even between life and death.

She has seen me. I know this for she turns directly toward me now and skips a little two-step jig shrugging her shoulders at me as if suddenly aware of a creeping shyness between us. I remember her doing this when she was a little girl, turning unexpectedly and finding me coming across the schoolyard to fetch her home. I stand up and smile proudly as I watch the features of her pale and drawn face come into focus. I see that she is smiling and wiping away her tears. Her hair is short and gelled in front. I can see her eyes. They are blue and clear. I hold out my arms and open my hands and bite down on my lower lip trying to stop it from quaking. She quickens her gait and extends her arms up above her head, like a victorious long distance runner crossing the finish line well ahead of the field.

EPILOGUE

IDA SKUDMORE PRESSES HER LIPS TIGHTLY TO MY PARTIALLY OPEN mouth, her tongue slithering hesitantly forward feeling like the cold dry skin of a snake against my palate. She has one arm around my neck, pulling my head forward toward her. The other free hand moves slowly across my chest and ominously down my torso to my belt buckle. I gaze on in horror as she draws her head back for a languid moment and whispers seductively in a throaty voice not unlike that of a bejeweled and sequined Marilyn Munroe,

"Happy birthday to you Mr. Big Stuff"

The rest of the room erupts in a loud boisterous chorus, cheering and weeping openly with pure unadulterated joy, their eyes moist with emotion. Their bodies crush in ever closer to me, wanting to touch me and hold onto me as if I am something so precious the very thought of me being taken from them would forever shatter their world and disrupt any possibility for lasting peace of mind and happiness. They are all here, Randy and Clive, The Inquisition, Sadie and Running Deer, The Chief and Frankie Butts, their arms slung loosely and comfortably over each other's shoulders. And there's Desiree and Genevieve standing side by side unassuming in their single-minded purpose in wishing me the very best. Can that be the Black Suits wedged over in the corner against the window sill, their smiling faces a testament to brotherly love. So can the Tons be here as well back from the dead? Where's J.J. Stump, he must be here, strong and well. There's Tess and Emily with her brood. I must go over and hold them close and tell them how much I love them and need them. I think that I see old Merv Hindlich, fully clothed and functional. And look, it's Wally and Jerome and even the lop eared Shrek smacking his bushy tail against the hardwood floor and panting jubilantly. But my legs will not move. I struggle to make them work, applying all of my mental strength to the task of telling one leg to lift and swing forward and the other to follow. I lunge like a robotic monster into the crowd, watching as their faces turn from joy to perplexity then evaporating into masks of sheer pain and frantic dismay. They are all suddenly frightened of me. They move away as one, not unlike a wave after it has crashed head-long against the immovable surface a cliff face or rocky promontory.

In that instant I realize that I may lose them all and the realization stops me cold. It sends a shiver through me with such force that I am fully aware I may shatter into a million little pieces. I waken with a start. I sit for the longest time, breathing and waiting, breathing and waiting, each breath slow and deliberate. Each methodically supplanting a needed cache of energy throughout the cells of my body and brain, like a transfusion which I can draw upon at will.

I am now fully awake and watching the morning light creep slowly across the window and into my empty bedroom.

It is my birthday today. I am uncharacteristically accepting of this. If I am not whimsically joyous, I am at least no longer dreading the thought that there could well be a gathering of sorts, even an exchanging of gifts, a bit of bubbly. Oh what the hell a bloody party, maybe even, God forbid, a previously all too disquieting surprise party.

As I sit and stare at what is now my life I also know that I am ready to go forward. I feel that I can more openly greet whatever life has planned for me and, more importantly, can welcome those people closest to me back into my life allowing them to simply be. No strings. No expectations beyond those ones mutually shared and collaboratively nurtured.

I see something shiny on the pillow beside me. It is a silver embossed card with a chocolate heart affixed to it by a curling piece of scotch tape. I realize that Randy and Clive must have left it there yesterday while I was out with Tess. I didn't notice it resting here when I came home in the darkness. The chocolate heart has melted slightly, leaving a dark stain on the clean, white surface of the card. I touch the place where the softening heart has left a smudge and bring my finger up to my lips to taste the bitter sweet flavour.

The card reads,

"Happy Birthday Mr. Big Stuff,"

and it is signed

"Love, The Gang."

CPSIA information can be obtained at www.ICGtesting.com
Printed in the USA
LVOW041951240912

300113LV00002B/7/P